DAMSEL TO THE RESCUE

Brides By Chance
Regency Adventures
Book Six

Elizabeth Bailey

SAPERE
BOOKS

Also in the Brides By Chance Series
In Honour Bound
A Chance Gone By
Knight for a Lady
A Winter's Madcap Escapade
Marriage for Music
Widow in Mistletoe

DAMSEL TO THE RESCUE

Published by Sapere Books.

20 Windermere Drive, Leeds, England, LS17 7UZ,
United Kingdom

saperebooks.com

ISBN: 978-1-80055-173-2

CHAPTER ONE

Summer 1805

A hazy sun threw ripples of shadow through the coach window. Watching the play of shapes across the empty forward seat with an idle gaze, Miss Burloyne lent but half an ear to the droning buzz of her great-aunt's rambling enumeration of the treats in store. Combined with the rhythmic motion of the vehicle, it made her sleepy.

Besides, she had heard it all already. After four years of failure, she had no expectation that a summer in Weymouth would prove any more fruitful in producing a prospective husband than had the metropolis. Not that Delia for a moment believed in Mama's spurious reason for persuading her to accompany Lady Matterson on her annual excursion to the seaside.

"In a smaller milieu, dearest, you may attract better notice. It will do you the world of good too. You are looking decidedly peaky."

That at least was true. Delia felt decidedly peaky. Or piqued might better fit the bill. What would you? When one's younger sister's first season disgorged a plethora of eligibles ready to lay their hearts at her feet, just as Delia had foreseen, she might be pardoned a trifle of pique.

"The sea-bathing will do you good. Dear Aunt Gertrude swears by it, you must know, and you may benefit in addition to doing us all the greatest favour by lending her your company."

Delia was not deceived. Favour? When it served to confirm her relegation to the status of old maid? Henceforth, a round of duty visits would become her life. If it was not a widowed great-aunt, it would be the wife of one of her brothers needing a drudge to help them through a crisis. Or her sister Sophia, once she'd decided which of the rich handkerchiefs to pick up and began popping babies like a manic rabbit. In which regard, Delia had to admit to a preference for Weymouth to being obliged to drool over Jocasta's infant had she been free to accept the invitation to spend the summer with her friend at Tazewell Manor again — where she must also observe the wedded bliss of the Hetheringtons. She wished Edith, Lady Hetherington well, but it would be too galling. Weymouth was indeed a better prospect, as Mama had insisted.

"Just think how entertained you must be, dearest, what with the balls, the library and the theatre, as well as the bathing and excursions. Why, you will be gay to dissipation!"

"I thought I was supposed to be recuperating."

Mama had ignored the dry note. "And so you will be. Aunt Gertrude will be glad of the company of a lively young woman in place of her friend."

Said friend being too ill to go to Weymouth this year, which was why Lady Matterson had demanded her niece's presence. Lady Burloyne had promptly shuffled off the burden onto the shoulders of her unmarriageable elder daughter.

Delia sighed a little, recalling Edith's joking assertion last year that her prince would come upon her unexpectedly. *No sign of him yet, Edith.* And she dared say he would remain firmly entrenched in the fairy tale. Princesses did not come with sandy hair and freckles.

Even as the thought passed through her mind, a sound that had been vaguely intrusive grew louder. Galloping hooves?

Her aunt ceased speaking and looked round at her in mute question. Delia shifted towards the door and leaned her head out of the open window, craning her neck to see behind the coach.

"It's a rider. No, more than one."

They were coming up fast. Lady Matterson began to fidget. "Heavens! I do hope it is not footpads!"

Delia brought her head in, though she remained perched forward on the seat. "Surely not? We're only a few miles out of Dorchester."

"Well, one of my friends was held up along this stretch of forest last year."

"Not in broad daylight, Aunt, surely?"

"Well, no, but still."

The thunder was coming closer. Delia's pulse quickened, but she maintained her calm. "Perhaps they only mean to pass."

The words were barely out of her mouth when an explosion shattered on the air.

A yell of fright from the one of the servants on the box was followed immediately by a rattling bump and the coach swerved horribly, throwing Delia off the seat. She landed in a heap in the narrow space between the seats as the coach plunged from side to side and the whinnying of terrified horses mingled with the galloping hooves. A muffled shout came from without.

"Hold, there! Hold!"

Delia grabbed the edge of the seat to steady herself and the rocking world came at last to stillness. For an instant she sat mumchance, getting her breath, but remembrance hit. Aunt Gertrude!

She looked up to find the old lady miraculously still in her place, both hands grasping the leather loop near the door. She caught Delia's eye and released a hand to put a finger to her lips. Delia nodded.

The silence was broken by rough voices speaking to the coachman or groom.

"Hoy, you! Get down off the box!"

"Leave 'em, Sam! He's off in the woods."

The other's grunt was barely audible. "Stow it! They might 'a seen summat."

What in the world? Then were they not footpads? A whisper reached Delia's ears.

"I am going to investigate."

Alarmed, Delia started up, keeping her tone low. "Aunt, are you mad?"

The elder lady's fingers came to her shoulder. Her grip was surprisingly strong. "Stay where you are, Delia. They must not see you."

"But, Aunt, you can't go out there!"

"Have no fear. I am armed." Before Delia's astonished eyes, Lady Matterson produced a pistol from the pocket set into the seat's padded armrest.

"Good heavens, Aunt Gertrude!"

"Hush! Did you take me for a ninny? I never travel without protection, my dear."

Appalled to see the old lady reach towards the door handle, Delia pushed forward and seized the wrist of her pistol hand. "I can't let you go out there!"

"Pish and tush! In my day, we had backbone. I am not in the least afraid of a couple of ruffians." Then, before Delia could act, she thrust the door open and leaned out, speaking in an imperious tone. "Ho, there! Vowles? Scoley? One of you come and let down these steps so I may descend."

The rough voices that had continued to murmur abruptly ceased. No answer came from either groom or coachman.

Delia's heart was racing. "Aunt, for heaven's sake!"

Lady Matterson turned her head. "Be silent! If anything untoward happens, escape into the forest, Delia."

"What? But —"

"A young girl is too much at risk. At all costs, stay safe!"

About to embark on vehement argument, Delia was forestalled by the shadow of a man looming up outside. Instinctively, she shrank down, although her great-aunt's form in the doorway likely blocked her from view. Lady Matterson's suddenly haughty tones assailed her ears.

"Who are you, my man? What do you want?"

For answer the fellow let out a rasping laugh. "Yer money or yer life, is it? Come on out of that, you old trot, and we'll see."

"If you will be good enough to let down the steps, I may do so."

"Ooh, lah-di-dah! As yer please, missus."

A creak and thump indicated the ruffian was complying with Lady Matterson's demand. Delia was tempted to seize her aunt's clothing to try to hold her from getting down. But she descended with dignity intact, somehow managing to keep her pistol hand hidden beneath her voluminous petticoats of sprigged lawn. The ruffian shifted out of sight as her aunt moved towards the front of the coach and out of Delia's view.

"Now then, what is the meaning of this outrage?"

A different voice took this up. "Ain't meaning no harm to you, leddy."

"Then why are you holding my servants at gunpoint?"

"We was arsting them if they seen a feller on horseback is all."

The deeper tones of the first man cut in. "Stow it, I said!"

An altercation seemed to go on between the two, but in lowered tones so that Delia could not make out the words. She heard her aunt again.

"Vowles? Scoley? Are you hurt?"

"No, my lady. Only the horses are resty."

"In that case, we must resume our journey as quickly as possible."

Delia was just beginning to entertain the hope the situation was coming under control when the worst happened.

"You there! Put away your firearm or I will shoot you down!"

Her aunt's threat produced a deathly silence. *Oh, no! Why, Aunt?*

"Sam, what do I do?"

The other man did not answer. A quick footstep sounded and then a dull thud. Delia heard a croaking cry in her aunt's voice, shouted protests from several throats and the unmistakeable thump of a body hitting the ground.

"What you go and do that fer?"

"Stubble it!"

Alarm racing through her veins, Delia crept forward and dared to peep out of the doorway. Lady Matterson lay in a heap, one of the ruffians leaning over her, while the other still held a pistol levelled at the groom Scoley, who stood aghast, his frantic eyes on his mistress's prone body. Delia could not see the coachman, who must still be on the box controlling his team.

Everything in Delia screamed to go to the rescue, but her aunt's parting words rankled. It would not help matters if she was also rendered unconscious — or worse. A vision of hideous violation sprang into her head. Was that what Aunt Gertrude meant?

Reluctant, but mindful of her instructions, Delia inched back out of sight and turned as quietly as she could. The argument without between the two ruffians had now reached near violent proportions and the coach shifted forward and back slightly. The horses were indeed restive.

Under cover of the noise, Delia stealthily opened the offside door, wincing as the latch clicked. Already on the floor, she was able to slide her legs down until her toes reached the ground. Her petticoats rode up, exposing a good deal of stockinged leg, but that could not be helped. Pushing up, she held the door slightly open and slid carefully through the narrow gap, slipping it to behind her. The latch clicked again and she went still, holding her breath with her fingers on the handle and listening hard.

The men's argumentative voices had been joined by a low-toned conversation between Vowles and Scoley. Delia recognised their voices, but she could not hear what was said.

Heart in mouth, hoping her escape would be concealed by the bulk of the coach and the horses, Delia trod softly across the narrow piece of road and onto the verge, slipping at once between two trees, and hiding behind the largest.

She dared to turn and look back. Nothing had changed. She could see the coachman's back as he leaned to talk to Scoley, and dropping to her haunches to peer beneath the coach, she was able to catch a glimpse of the edge of her aunt's petticoats and a pair of boots marching up and down while another pair stood firm. She could make out the voices now.

"Let's get out of it, Sam," pleaded one.

"Not before I check if he's hiding in this here rattler."

Fright claimed Delia. If the ruffian meant to look inside the coach, he might see her through the window. She must get further into the trees. Turning, she penetrated deeper into the forest, slipping from tree to tree until she was sure she was far enough away to be safe from discovery.

When she turned again, peeping from behind a concealing trunk, she saw the ruffian had got into the coach and seemed to be employed in hunting behind the squabs. Was he looking for a strongbox? Fury swamped her. Not content with knocking poor Aunt Gertrude out of her senses, he must needs rob her as well. For two pins, she would go back and harangue the man for his cruelty.

Except that she would put herself in danger, and then she would not be able to help her great-aunt once the men rode away again. If they rode away. Surely they must, once they found nothing.

Lady Matterson's jewellery was safely disposed around the person of her elderly maid. Miss Pegler had gone on ahead to Weymouth in the luggage coach, accompanied by Delia's Sally. There were no concealed valuables in this coach, thank heavens. If only her aunt was merely stunned and not seriously injured, there was hope they might get out of this horror intact.

Then she heard a slight sound behind her and her breath caught.

Before she could turn, a hand came about her mouth, an arm snaked around her waist, and she found herself pulled back tight against a solid body.

CHAPTER TWO

Unable to scream, Delia gave a muffled whimper. A male voice murmured in her ear.

"Don't screech! I mean you no harm, but you must be quiet!"

She managed to turn her head and found a strong jaw and unshaven cheek close to hers. Her heart was leaping like a landed fish, but the voice soothed.

"If I take my hand away, will you promise not to scream?"

Delia managed to nod and gasped for breath as the hand came away. She was still clamped hard against the man's chest. "Let me go!"

"Yes, but don't go haring off, will you? They're still arguing."

"I'm not going anywhere. Let me go!"

Indignant now, she sank against the tree as she was released, getting her breath. Then she turned on the man, ready with a mouthful of invective.

The words died on her lips. She'd been accosted by a god!

The fleeting thought passed through her mind as she drank in the sculptured features, beautifully moulded yet taut and tanned, with long-lashed azure eyes just now trained upon the road where the sound of voices barely penetrated Delia's startled absorption.

The stranger was dressed for riding, booted and spurred, his dark-coloured frock-coat open over a loose shirt, with no waistcoat, and a spotted handkerchief knotted about his neck in place of a cravat. Strands of long, coffee-brown hair, escaping from a queue at the back and from under an old-fashioned three-cornered hat, hugged his lean cheeks and strong jaw. A stubble of beard only added to his air of contained energy.

Delia found her tongue, keeping to a whisper. "Are you a highwayman?"

The startling eyes came back to her and Delia thought a ripple of amusement crossed his face. "Something of the sort."

Remembrance flitted through her brain. "No, you're not! You're the one they're after, aren't you? They kept saying *he*."

The blue gaze continued to regard her. "Astute of you."

A flush of warmth rose up inside Delia and she hurried into speech again. "They hurt my aunt."

"Yes, I saw."

"She's unconscious." Her pulse began to speed up again as the memories flooded back. "She would go out there. She threatened them with her pistol. She told me to escape if anything bad happened. I wouldn't have left her — I wanted to go out to her — but…"

Her voice died as he put a finger to her lips. "Quiet!"

Delia was pushed back against the tree and the stranger crowded into her, his body shielding hers. The close contact was stifling, warm and alarmingly pleasurable. Delia's pulse shot into high gear and her heart thumped painfully in her breast, heat flooding through her veins.

She could barely think. But a corner of her mind noted his attention was concentrated on whatever was going forward in the road. A murmur reached her.

"One of them is casting around this side of the coach. Keep still!"

As if she could move if she wanted to! Her eyes were level with the hollow of his throat, her breath stirring the blue-spotted kerchief. An aroma of maleness assailed her nostrils and the heat within intensified. Delia lost all control of her thoughts and her limbs felt as if they were melting.

Forever passed.

Release came abruptly as he stepped back. Delia nearly fell and had to grab at the tree behind. Her gaze rose to her captor's face and found him frowning.

"To the devil with those fools! I'll have to draw them away."

Delia's mind shot to attention. "How?"

His eyes came back to her. "Stay hid here until they ride off."

"But what are you —?"

"And stay quiet!"

With which, he was off, slipping through the trees with such stealth and swiftness that Delia half wondered if she'd imagined him.

His slim figure disappeared and re-appeared a couple of times. And then he was gone. However much Delia strained to get a sight of him, she found no sign of his ever having been there. A sneaking sense of loss invaded her bosom, but she brushed it off.

Ridiculous. But the brief instant of shared intimacy lingered in her deeps despite every precept of common sense.

With a sigh, Delia turned back towards the road and peeped to see what was happening.

Nothing appeared to have changed. The voices were still rough with argument. She could see Vowles on the box, his hands loose on the reins. The horses appeared to have calmed down. For the first time, she noticed two other mounts, cropping at the grass on the other side, a little way behind the coach. These must belong to the ruffians.

A whinny drew her attention, coming from somewhere away from the coach. She saw the two horses lift their heads and prick their ears.

All at once it dawned on her that the voices had ceased. In the silence, she heard the clop of hooves along with a crackling of twigs. Delia's pulse quickened and she trained her gaze along the road behind the coach, alert now.

Realisation hit just as a rider burst out of the woods onto the road, heading back in the direction of Dorchester.

"It's him!"

"Get to horse!"

Delia's stranger put his mount at the gallop, the queue of his long hair bouncing on his shoulders as his horse thundered away down the road.

The two ruffians scrambled into sight behind the coach, yelling as they ran for their horses. Mounting up with less dignity than haste, the two riders started after him, imprecations and curses rolling off their tongues.

Delia's heart was in her mouth. All she could think of was the hideous notion that her stranger might be captured. Without knowing who he was or why they pursued him, she prayed desperately that he would manage to outrun them. Or outwit them somehow as he had before.

He'd called them fools. Then he must know how he could evade them, must he not? *Oh, let him stay safe!*

The riders were out of sight by the time she recalled the coach and her injured great-aunt. Conscience swept her. She slipped out from behind her concealing tree and began to pick her way towards the road.

She could see Vowles still on the box, but there was no sign of Scoley, though she could hear grunting as if some effort were undertaken. Was he helping Aunt Gertrude?

Her attention half on where she put her feet and half on the coach, she saw movement through the window and glimpsed

Lady Matterson's sprigged gown. The coach door slammed. Running footsteps were accompanied by a frantic shout.

"She's in! Get us out of here, Vowles!"

Scoley! The groom was climbing up to the box. Hadn't he seen Delia was not in the coach? She began to hurry, calling out a warning.

"Hi, wait!"

The coach was already in motion, the horses' hooves loud enough to cover her voice. She raised it, breaking into a trot.

"Wait! Vowles, wait!"

The coach accelerated. They could not hear her! Delia reached the road and ran after the vehicle, yelling at the top of her voice.

"Wait for me! Don't leave me here! Scoley! Vowles! Stop! Oh, dear God, stop!"

Horror overwhelmed her as Delia's cries vanished into the air, drowned out by the thundering rattle of wheels and hooves as the coach outstripped her without mercy. Blown, Delia staggered to a halt, knees sagging, her hands going to her thighs as she watched her last hope disappear around a bend.

For a moment she was preoccupied with getting her breath, random thoughts pestering her mind. They were gone. She was alone in the forest. Why hadn't they heard her? Oh, help, what should she do?

As her breathing slowed, so did her panic. Granted, she was alone, but she need only follow the road. The day was warm and bright; she need not fear to become cold or damp. They were bound to realise sooner or later, and then they would come back for her.

But that might be hours, protested a small voice in her head. Common sense said otherwise. Weymouth was less than nine miles distant. An hour's drive. Perhaps a little more. Would they stop before? Unlikely. If they supposed her to be in the coach, they must be intent upon getting to Weymouth where Aunt Gertrude could be properly looked after. She couldn't be dead. Scoley must have carried her into the coach. They would not have hurried so if she'd been dead, would they?

As the questions mounted, Delia found she'd begun walking. At least she need not fear those ruffians. The stranger would have led them quite away. He'd done it to give Delia and her people a chance to make their escape. If he only knew she'd managed instead to get herself left behind!

Not that it would make any difference. He was obviously a fugitive. But from whom, or from what? Intrigued she might be, but she would never know now. Best forget him. Or remember him only as a phantom, a tiny spark of adventure in her otherwise humdrum life. A chuckle escaped her. Had her prince come after all? If so, he'd made but a fleeting appearance. She would cherish his memory nevertheless.

Her feet, encased in light shoes not meant for hard walking, began to protest. Delia ignored them. Also the beginnings of thirst. But within a very short time, it seemed, she found it hard to think of anything but aching feet, tired legs and a dry mouth. Not to mention the awakening of hunger.

How long had she been walking? Her spirits drooped as she realised it could not be more than a quarter of an hour or so. The sun was still high in the sky and any hope of the coach having already reached Weymouth was vain.

She'd seen no one on the road. It was eerily silent. Too much so, because now she could hear the soughing of wind in the trees, a scurrying of something in the undergrowth, and the distant clopping of hooves.

Hooves? Oh, no! The clopping became a chorus. Many hooves there were. And coming fast. Oh, not again!

Delia stopped dead, turning in the road. She could see a couple of hundred yards back the way she had walked, and her eyes anxiously sought the source of the sound beyond the curving highway.

Before she could well take them in, a coterie of horsemen swept around the bend, travelling fast, one ahead of the rest.

Delia did not wait to find out if these were the same villains who had knocked her aunt senseless. Lifting her skirts, she fled into the trees, uncaring where she went as long as she was well off the road before they reached her.

Brambles caught at her petticoats, slowing her progress. She wrenched free and ran on, stumbling against bushes and trees that scratched at her arms and face. Behind, she could hear the galloping hooves coming nearer.

The crashing of branches threw her pulses into disarray and she glanced behind. The lead horseman had turned into the forest! He'd slowed of necessity, but was he following her?

Delia ran as for her life, crushing twigs and fallen leaves. A broken branch lying on the ground ahead loomed. She picked up her skirts, heedless of showing her legs, and leapt over it, praying the rider would not follow. She saw a gap leading into what looked like a copse and made for it, hoping it would provide a hiding place.

As she reached it, the hoofbeats ceased. Turning, she looked for the horse and rider and could not see them. Where had he gone?

At a distance, she could hear the clip-clop of more horses, together with a good deal of thrashing. But the near one had vanished. A sudden impossible hope leapt into Delia's bosom. Could it be? If it was the stranger, he'd hidden himself as well as he had before, even on horseback.

She slid between the trees she'd noted and found she was indeed in a small space, enclosed within a clump of leafy vegetation. Her heart was chittering like a mouse in a cheese, half fearful, half in undisguised anticipation. She peeped out of the makeshift entrance, but could see no one. She heard voices. Rough voices they were too. A sliver of recognition filtered into Delia's mind and her veins froze.

Those same men! She was sure of it. Then her stranger prince was indeed here. Had he seen her? Did he know she'd been left behind? She'd left the road so swiftly, it was all too possible he'd not been following her. Perhaps he had merely sought to conceal himself.

"Come away from there! You'll be seen."

Delia's heart leapt. She swung about and found the stranger had entered the little enclosure. She gasped out the first thought in her head. "You did see me!"

He took her arm and drew her right into the small space, pulling her down to the ground. "Sit! And stay quiet!"

Delia obeyed without even thinking about it, her whole mind concentrated on his presence, her bosom alive with elation, her eyes devouring him as he settled by her side. She dropped into a whisper. "Where is your horse?"

"Safely hidden. Hush!"

She didn't want to hush. She wanted to gabble incoherently. To tell him how happy she was to see him, to know that he'd spotted her and come after her. She could not doubt he meant to help her, even if he was paying her scant attention at this moment.

He was sitting cross-legged, elbows on his knees, his chin in his hand, his eyes searching beyond the close bank of brush and trees in which they sat concealed. Delia found herself listening with him, her gaze hunting as his did, trying to see through the intervening leaves.

Voices sounded without and now she could indeed catch glimpses of figures scouting around the environs.

The stranger dropped his hands and sat up, craning his neck. One hand seized Delia's wrist and she looked round. She received a warning look as his grip tightened and his free finger went to his lips. Delia nodded and he let her go.

As well he'd warned her, for the rough voice she remembered abruptly rose in anger.

"Ain't no use squeaking, Barney. If we loses 'im we don't get no blunt."

The other voice protested. "'E's too leery, Sam. Led us a merry dance again, and we ain't had nothing to eat in hours. I'm for the boozing ken."

A thump and a yell. Did it signify a blow? Straining to see, Delia caught a glimpse of motion.

"What yer do that for?"

"Hold yer whining. When we got him, his nibs'll pay 'andsome."

"Aye, and we sleeps in Rumbo fer kidnapping."

"Nah, we doesn't. Remember, he ain't shown hisself. No one don't know he's in the country even, that's what his nibs said."

"Well, I don't like it."

"Yer don't have ter like it. We just does it. He can't double us forever. We'll get 'im."

Footsteps stamped through the undergrowth, making no attempt to be quiet as the stranger had done. The voices retreated, fading away.

The implications lingered in Delia's head and she looked round at the stranger's still intent features. A riffle disturbed her pulses. Questions tumbled in her mind.

Why were they seeking to kidnap him? Who wanted him captured? Where had he come from if no one knew he was in England? Though someone did. The villain who had sent those men after him. Then how did he know? Heavens, but into what bumble-broth had she intruded? It felt unreal, like a dream or an adventurous tale borrowed from the circulating library.

A hysterical chuckle escaped her. The stranger looked round, a quick frown admonishing the sound. Contrite, Delia threw a hand to her mouth. But she could not keep from whispering around it.

"I just had the maddest thought."

One eyebrow shot up over the blue gaze. "And?"

Delia dropped her hand, smiling. "I feel like I've strayed into the pages of a gothic novel."

A grin dispelled his stern look. "You may be pardoned for thinking so."

Mesmerised all over again by his presence, Delia could not take her eyes from his face. She tried for a neutral tone. "Have they gone, do you think?"

"What do you think?"

She sighed at the sceptical note. "I suppose it was too much to hope for. What now?"

The disconcerting gaze scanned her, dropping from her face to her clothing, to her feet and back again. "You're hardly dressed for it, but I'll have to take you up on Tiger."

"Your horse? But you can't take me all the way to Weymouth!"

"Is that where you were headed? It's a pity you missed the coach."

Lurking distress she'd thought she had suppressed threw Delia into irritation. "Thanks to your friends!"

"They're no friends of mine. Come on." He leapt lithely to his feet, holding his hand down to her.

Delia allowed him to help her up, but entered a caveat nonetheless. "But where will you take me?"

"Not to Weymouth, that's certain."

Apprehension swept through Delia. "But you must! I can't just go off on your horse. How will they find me?"

"We'll deal with that later. There's no time now. And keep quiet!" Seizing her hand, he led her through a gap and began to thread a path in and out of the trees.

Delia dropped to an agitated whisper. "I can't be quiet! We must settle this. If you can't take me to Weymouth —"

"How far do you think we'd get along the road with those two still scouting the area?"

"Those men? But you can't take me with you!"

"I don't have a choice. I can't leave you here alone, can I?"

The thought of him leaving her was anathema, but Delia was even less happy at the notion of him riding off with her to heaven knew where. She fell back on the only thing that came into her head. "I don't even know your name!"

He did not break stride. "Nor I yours. You can call me Giff."

"Just Giff? Is it really your name?"

"Good question. It'll do for now."

Oh, this was too much! Delia pulled back, wrenching her fingers from out of his hold and bringing them both to a halt. She addressed him in a furious whisper. "Listen, Giff — or whoever you really are — this simply won't do! I'm going no further until you tell me what you intend."

Giff's brows were climbing his forehead. He gave a grunt. "There's more to you than meets the eye. What's your name?"

"Delia." She snapped it out. She was not going to give him more than he'd given her.

His gaze swept her again, in an appraising look. "Nice. It sounds like a flower of some kind. Suits you." Then he reached for her hand and moved on. "I'll see you safely where you need to go, but for now we've got to get away from here. You can fuss later."

Silenced, Delia followed in his wake, her mind humming with Giff's pleasing allusion to a flower. She felt both flattered and doubtful. She would not even toy with the foolish notion he might admire her. No man had before. Certainly none as breathlessly attractive as Giff.

Warmth slid through her veins as she remembered her hand was locked in his grip. Then a whiffle and a snort alerted her to the presence of a horse. Rounding a tree, they came bang upon a huge chestnut. Tiger? He was not even tethered. Giff must have a strong connection to the animal.

He was taking the reins. "Up you get, Delia. Can you put your foot in the stirrup?"

Not without displaying far too much leg. It struck her then and she felt a flush mounting. "You saw me getting out of the coach!"

His lips twitched. "If you mean, have I seen it all before, the answer is yes. It's only a pair of legs, when all is said."

Heat flared in her cheeks and Delia could not speak. A devil inside her she had not known existed took possession. She moved to the horse and, without looking at Giff, grabbed hold of the saddle above and set one foot in the stirrup. It felt alien without a riding boot, but she had no time to indulge this thought.

Before she could gather her wits, two strong hands seized her by the waist.

"Jump!"

She thrust up from the ground and Giff threw her into the saddle. Delia seized the pommel and held on, trying to get her balance.

Next moment, Giff landed behind her. His arms came about her and he shifted the reins into his right hand.

"Get your knee around the pommel. I'll hold you on, never fear."

Delia felt the powerful arm that held her pinned against his solid strength. Her breath caught, but she struggled to shift her right leg and hook it about the pommel, showing stockinged flesh as she did so. Once settled, she covered her bared leg, thanking fashion for the volume of her muslin petticoats.

Giff's impatient voice came, close to her ear. "Ready?"

"No!"

"What's the matter?"

"I'm horribly uncomfortable!"

"I'm sorry for that, but it can't be helped."

The horse began to move and Delia found herself seething. It was all very well in a novel, but this was becoming more and more ridiculous. She had been stranded, and now to all intents and purposes, she was being abducted with no means of getting to her destination. When her people came back for her, she'd be long gone. And to crown all, she'd never been so uncomfortable in her life.

It was not merely the pommel that dug into her flesh, or the bouncing on the saddle she was unable to control. It was the perfectly unbearable sensations engendered by the proximity of the body behind and the arms encircling her as Giff held the reins.

If this was adventure, it was decidedly less romantic than the novels she'd read had led Delia to believe. Real life, with its attendant physical actualities, bore little resemblance to the fairy tale. And now she was perspiring, she was thirsty and the recurrence of hunger pangs stirred in her stomach. What was worse, the prince was turning out to be all too apt to want everything his own way.

Delia could not help a sneaking wish she was still in the coach, with no prospect before her but the drudgery she'd been outlining before all this began.

CHAPTER THREE

Giff cursed inwardly as he manoeuvred Tiger through the undergrowth, the stallion's unshod hooves making little sound. The last thing he needed at this juncture was the burden of a petticoat. But what could he do? He could scarcely leave the girl to be found by his cousin's incompetent tools.

It didn't take a genius to guess what had happened. He'd seen the wench sneaking out of the coach, but the male servants clearly knew nothing of her absence. They'd no doubt collected the old lady and got themselves out of there in a hurry. And who could blame them? The girl had delayed getting herself back to the coach and that was that.

A good thing he'd not left the road before he saw her. He'd meant to keep Tiger at the gallop long enough to tire out the mounts chasing him. Then he'd have left the road and vanished into the trees with ample time to escape. Now their horses would've had enough rest and they'd be after him again if they caught a sight of him. Even Tiger couldn't outrun them with the added weight atop.

Nothing for it. They must not be seen. Only he'd got to get back to the road and head west. He gave a whistle and Tiger's ears pricked. The girl Delia winced and he grinned.

"Was that in your ear?"

"Yes! And ouch!"

"Beg pardon. I'm just warning Tiger I'm going to weave faster."

She half turned to look at him, her brows knitting. "He understands that?"

"We have a number of signals. Tiger is a very intelligent horse."

"He must be."

The dry note made him laugh. She had an amusing way with her, this flower girl. A bit small and dumpy, but the sprinkling of freckles across her nose and cheeks gave her face character. He liked that. Too many females he'd known seemed to wish to look like alabaster statues. Impossible in the sun. He concentrated on guiding Tiger through the trees, his ears tuned to the slightest sound of pursuit. Had those fellows gone to ground? The man Barney had been anxious for food.

"If we're lucky," he said aloud, "they've gone off to find sustenance."

Delia looked round again, anxiety in her eyes. "Not Sam. He was determined to find you."

He eyed her with renewed interest. "You listened well."

"I did and I've got a lot of questions."

His mind closed. He was not going to embroil her in his tangled affairs if he could help it. "Not now."

The frown descended and the freckles shifted as she wrinkled her nose. "Why not now? I can't hear them, can you?"

"No, but I've got to stay alert. I don't need you distracting me with badgering questions."

He felt her stiffen and turn her head pointedly to look forward again. Giff had an impulse to retract, but he was not going to give in to it. The less she knew the better. They were in enough trouble as it was.

Even as the thought passed through his mind, his ears caught the betraying sound of a creaking branch. He looked in that direction and the familiar surge rose up in his blood.

"Hell and the devil!"

His pursuers were only yards away, half concealed in a thicket. Not such fools as he had thought. They were mounted and Giff saw a gleam of metal in the leader's hand.

"He's got a pistol! Now we're for it! Hold tight!"

Urging Tiger to quicken his pace, he took a swerving path between two trees, aiming to present a moving target. He heard a frightened gasp from Delia, but there was no time to reassure her. Besides, the danger was acute. He had no notion if he could get them out of this.

Obedient to his will, Tiger tore through the trees. Giff ducked down, the girl going down with him willy-nilly.

"Stay low, Delia!"

He could hear the riders start up behind. The reckless exultance for the chase he knew too well threatened to take over. He struggled to suppress it. It was not only his own life at stake now. But he could try one throw at least. He whistled the signal to give Tiger his head and the horse took control, weaving as he'd learned to do in years gone by in the Indian forests.

Leaning over Delia to protect her as best he could, Giff took the reins in his left hand and reached the right to the holster on his saddlebag. The strap lifted and he grasped the butt of his pistol. It was primed and ready.

"Dear heaven, you're going to shoot?"

"If I can get a clear shot." He'd not reckoned on Delia noticing his actions. An observant wench. Too damned observant at this moment, if truth be told. He'd answered without thinking.

"Shall I take the reins?"

Surprised, he risked a glance. Delia's face was turned to his, despite her crouched position. He could not withhold a grin. "Plucky wench, aren't you?"

"No! I just don't want to fall off if you're busy shooting that thing."

He laughed. "Tiger knows what to do. Hold onto his mane."

He saw her fingers weave into the long dark hair and clutch tight. Satisfied, he risked rising in the saddle to look back.

He knew they were still on his heels, for they'd abandoned the attempt to stay quiet the minute he spurred his horse. The crashing and bumping followed as they tried to keep up, emulating his weaving progress. With luck, the fellow Sam wouldn't attempt a shot under these conditions.

"Don't screech now! I'm going to fire."

Twisting around, he levelled the pistol, aiming above the heads of the riders. He wanted no corpses on his hands. The explosion elicited a muffled whimper from Delia. At least she'd managed not to scream. He nudged her with his arm.

"Good girl!"

A mutter reached him. "I feel perfectly filleted."

"You did well. Don't fail now!"

He looked back. One of the mounts behind reared, whinnying, and both came to a halt.

"That'll hold them for a while."

He slid the now useless gun back into its holster and gave another whistle as he seized back control of the reins. Delia was still crouched over the pommel.

"You can sit up now."

She let go of Tiger's mane and pushed up, her breathing ragged. No time to let her recover.

"Hold the pommel! We've got to flee!"

With which, he touched his spurs to Tiger's flanks and the horse shot forward. Giff glanced up at the sky. The sun was dropping and he turned to follow its pointer, heading west.

The trees were growing a little more sparse. They ought to hit the road in a moment. As well, for the pursuit was up again, the riders behind gaining on them.

The ribbon of the road came into sight and Giff made for it. He hoped they would expect him to ride along it, but his only thought was to take the road briefly and head into the trees on the other side. It was their only chance with the flower girl up before him.

Just as Tiger thrust out of the trees and into the road, a shot rang out.

Fire thudded into Giff's thigh. The impact threw his whole body forward and he cannoned into Delia, who grunted.

"Hell and damnation, I'm hit!"

Without pause for thought, he kept Tiger's path straight and the horse pounded into the trees on the far side of the road.

The wound made itself felt. Giff paid it scant attention, intent upon the game. He had to lose them now or hell would take him. And the girl with him.

She was leaning to the left, looking down. "You're bleeding."

"A flesh wound. Can't attend to it now. No time."

Was it merely a flesh wound? If he had a bullet in him, he was for it. Change of plan. Once he'd outfoxed these blighted hunters, he'd have to head for Stepleton. No possible way he could take the flower girl to Weymouth. Not yet awhile. Nothing for it. She'd have to come with him.

Thunder and the devil! His mind was slowing. Losing too much blood. He fought off the dizziness, forcing his concentration to the task of foxing his pursuers. He listened out for the sound of their horses, but his ears felt as if they were filled with cotton. He nudged the girl nestling between his arms.

"Can you hear them?"

"Not any longer."

He breathed out relief. "Then I think we've lost them."

"Not for long." Delia was leaning a little to the side, studying the ground. "You're leaving a trail of blood."

"The devil and the deuce!"

He pulled Tiger up and slumped a little in the saddle. His mind was none too clear, but one thing emerged intact.

"You'd best get down. Hide yourself. I'll lead them away from you before they can get to me."

He caught sight of her swinging hand. A stinging blow landed on his cheek. He flinched back, hissing in a breath, and stared at her.

"What in hell?"

"Wake up!" She both sounded and looked fierce. "I'm not leaving you to get captured, so just stop that nonsense right now!"

Giff blinked into eyes suddenly bright with colour instead of the nondescript grey he'd seen before. "Delia…"

She held up a warning finger. "Don't say a word!"

To his astonishment, she then turned from him and tugged at the voluminous covering of petticoats. Giff recognised Indian muslin in passing but a protest rose up. "What the deuce are you about?"

"I'm going to bind your wound."

She did not look round, intent on her task. Giff saw a flash of stocking as she grasped the edges of an undergarment, as full in material as the gown she wore. A fretful murmur reached him.

"I wish I had my scissors."

Then an edge of cotton cloth was in her teeth. He watched with a glow of admiration as she ripped a tear in the fabric with her teeth and then proceeded to lengthen it. With some violence, she tore off a wide strip.

"I need a pad." Frowning with concentration, she looked round at him. "Give me your neckerchief, Giff."

He let go the rein with one hand and brought it up, but Delia was before him. Slipping her improvised bandage over her arm, she had her fingers at his throat, undoing the knot that held his large kerchief in place. It was whipped from about his neck.

Then she was leaning down towards his thigh. All too precariously. Giff reached an arm across her. "You'll fall!"

"Then hold me."

Giff grabbed her round the waist and felt a degree safer himself. He was beginning to feel dizzy again.

"Can you lift your leg at all?"

He slipped his heel from the stirrup and tried. To his annoyance, the wretched leg felt like lead. But with the toe of his boot on the stirrup, he was able to shift his thigh a trifle. "Just, but not much."

"That will work. It only needs to be slight so I can get the bandage underneath."

"You'd do better doing it from the ground."

She sat up abruptly, giving him another glare. "And how will I mount up again, pray? It's no use saying you'll help me because it's obvious you can't. Besides, if you fall off, we'll really be in trouble."

As if they weren't in trouble enough! He forced a reluctant grin. "I'm in your hands."

Delia smiled at him and Giff's mind went blank.

"Hold me tight."

An easy order to obey. Tiger was standing quietly, so he was able to use both hands. He tugged her close, dug his right leg into the stirrup for a purchase and set his teeth.

"Ready?"

He nodded, and watched Delia make a pad of his kerchief. Then she leaned down and he could only feel what she was doing, intent on keeping her on the horse. Her leg around the pommel helped, but she was bent almost double as she laid her pad to the wound, causing a sharp pain.

Giff tightened his jaw and closed his eyes, feeling Delia's fingers as she began to wind the torn cloth around his thigh. He had to grit his teeth each time she made him shift the leg so she could slide the cloth underneath. The tightening band was both agony and relief.

At last he heard Delia's muffled voice. "Pull me up, Giff!"

He helped her into a sitting posture, his attention on his aching leg.

"It's not ideal — but it will have to do. At least it's stopped — the bleeding."

"It hurts like hell!"

"Well, I'm sorry — but I had to tie it — as tight as I could."

Delia's breathless panting and her red face tugged Giff's attention back. "Speaking of blood, yours has gone to your head. And your hair's come undone."

The grey eyes regarded him with a steely stare. "And you're surprised?"

He grinned and put up a hand to straighten her bonnet for her. "Good thing this is tied on." A wave of faintness swept over him and his hand dropped.

"Are you all right?"

"A bit dizzy. Give me the reins."

"No! I'll take the reins. You hold onto me."

Irritation rose up. "Listen, you troublesome wench —"

But Delia was not paying attention. She had the reins in her hands and Tiger was already in motion. "Hold onto me, Giff!"

Curse the wench! But he did as she bid him, reaching his arms about her and holding her to him. "Head west."

"How do I know which is west?"

"Follow the sun." He felt her raise her head.

"I see it. Come up!"

Tiger turned and took his orders from Delia's instruction. Aware the stallion only obeyed because his master was atop, Giff allowed himself the indulgence of letting the girl take charge. She was capable enough, he had to give her that.

Delia felt as if every nerve in her body was afire. She'd never been so scared or so elated. She'd never felt so *alive*.

Weymouth had vanished from her horizons. The only future was the immediate need to get Giff to safety. For no consideration in the world would she leave him now. Why those men were after him she had no notion, and cared less. If they got him, he was doomed. And wounded as he was, they would surely get him if she did not play her part well.

Grateful for a mount as intuitive as Tiger, she urged him from a walk to a trot, despite the acute discomfort. The leg over the pommel had gone numb, which was probably a mercy. As long as she wasn't obliged to dismount. It would likely collapse under her. Giff was leaning heavily against her back and she was already saddle sore. And, to crown all, she felt damp with sweat in too many places. Moreover, she stank. Likely they both did.

None of it mattered. A part of her mind was still in a state of disbelief. Such things didn't happen to Delia Burloyne. Even if she came awake and found it all a dream, at this present there was nothing more important than keeping her prince safe.

A gleam of water ahead drew her attention.

"Giff, there's a stream or brook coming up."

She felt him raise himself a little. He sounded groggy. "How wide?"

"I can't tell yet."

She nudged Tiger with her left foot and clicked her tongue. He speeded up, seeming to know exactly how to course a path through the trees without danger to his passengers. Delia kept her gaze trained on the water, which looked to be more of a river than a stream. Abruptly, as they left the shelter of the trees, the environment became less alien. Delia pulled up.

"It must be a tributary of the Frome. We can't be all that far from Dorchester."

Giff seemed to rouse himself, releasing his hold on Delia and sitting up straighter. "We must cross. Follow upstream. There's bound to be a bridge or a shallow place for Tiger to pick his way over."

Delia turned the horse's head in the right direction. He understood at once and proceeded along the bank, which at least bore fewer obstacles than had the dense forest.

"Wait! Pull up!"

Instant fright gripped Delia as she tugged on the reins. "What is it? Do you hear them?"

His voice came faintly. "Flask — in the saddlebag — brandy…"

Help! Was he going to fall off? Alarmed, Delia dropped low over Tiger's withers and dove a hand into the bag at his side, scrabbling for the feel of something hard. She found it. Cool to the touch and shaped right.

Dragging it out, she found herself in possession of a flat silver flask. "Here, take it!"

"Open it!"

Slipping the reins over her arm, she unscrewed the lid and handed it across. Giff took it, raised the open neck to his mouth and drank. Delia watched in fascination as his throat shifted as he swallowed. It had the oddest effect, as if the blood sang in her veins.

He lowered the flask, shook his head and handed it back with a grin. "That's better. I'll do now."

In proof of which, he sat up straighter as Delia screwed the top back on. She was about to slip it back into the saddlebag when she changed her mind. Reaching to Giff's coat, she found one of his pockets and slipped it in, aware of his eyes following her movements.

The blue gaze met hers and his mouth twitched. "Canny wench, aren't you?"

Delia had to laugh. "It's just you might need it if you feel faint again."

He nodded. "My thanks. Onward!"

She settled the reins and set Tiger in motion again. "Do you think they've given up?"

"What, abandoned the chase? Not for long, if they have. The wretches have been after me for days. I've managed to avoid them for the most part. Sheer bad luck they caught up with me today."

"Why are they chasing you?"

"Set on by my cousin. At least, I'm pretty sure that's it. I can't see who else would hire ruffians to get me out of the way."

A riffle of fear swept through Delia. "But they won't kill you! I thought they just meant to capture you."

"And then kill me." His matter-of-fact tone chilled Delia. "Silly to go leaving the evidence about. My cousin wouldn't want the justices on his tail."

Horrified, and not a little indignant, Delia found herself unconsciously urging Tiger to go faster. "But why does he want you dead?"

"I'm in the way. According to my great-uncle, Piers claimed I was already dead."

"Who is your great-uncle?"

"You'll find out. That's where we're headed."

"Where?"

"Stepleton. He has the rectory living." Giff broke off. "There's a bridge!"

Delia followed his pointing finger. "I see it! Come up!"

The stallion lengthened his stride to a canter. Delia pulled him up as they reached the bridge, regarding it with disfavour. "It looks rickety to me."

"Give me the reins!"

She relinquished them with alacrity, having no desire to attempt to negotiate the narrow wooden slats leading across, along with the aged and broken railing. Just as Giff guided Tiger's steps onto the precarious structure, a familiar sound reached Delia's ears.

Hoofbeats. More than one set. And crackling twigs along with the swish of shifting leaves.

"Oh, dear heaven, I think they're coming!"

"Damn them to hell!"

Delia's heart leapt into her mouth as the horse took the bridge at a pace that threatened to upturn the lot of them into the river below. The clatter of Tiger's hooves on the wooden surface sent her senses flying into apprehension.

"They'll hear that for sure!" Forgetting to be afraid of the crossing, she trained her eyes on the thickets behind and caught movement in the trees. "I can see them! Giff, hurry, for heaven's sake!"

The horse's hooves hit terra firma again and Tiger shot into the forest, going straight through a gap in the trees. Delia looked back, trying to see if their pursuers were on the trail and saw instead the worn path winding away behind them. Oh, help! If those ruffians were able to cross the bridge, they could follow just as easily.

Impatience claimed her as Tiger's pace slowed. "He's tiring!"

She saw Giff glance up through the canopy of leaves. Was he finding the sun to guide them west again? "Not far now."

"How do you know?"

"Should hit a lane at any moment."

"But what if they get across the bridge?"

"We must hope they're too faint-hearted to attempt it."

Delia was not convinced. "They've shown nerve enough so far."

"But not common sense. With luck, one of them at least will fall in."

At which instant, Delia heard a loud cry and a splash. Elation soared and she laughed out. "They have fallen in!" She was craning to try and see behind Giff and caught an amused look.

"It's to be hoped they never find out how pleased you are about it."

"Pleased? I hope the wretch has broken his leg. But I'm sorry for the horse." Giff's laughter echoed in the trees and Delia gave him a buffet on the arm. "Hush, for heaven's sake! They'll hear you."

His brows flew up. "If I ever met such a bossy chit!"

"If it comes to that, I've never met such an autocratic fellow!" She regarded him a moment, a little concerned to see strain in his face. "Do you need another swig of brandy?"

He shook his head briefly, his gaze concentrated on path ahead.

Delia studied his face without meaning to, forgetful of everything save his danger. A pang smote her. He mustn't die!

"Why is your cousin trying to make away with you? What did you mean when you said you were in the way?"

But she'd lost Giff's attention. His brows had drawn together and he turned his head to look back. A fretful mutter escaped him. "What, are they bloodhounds?" His glance swept Delia's face. "I don't think you've got your wish."

Her pulse shot in high gear. "They're still coming? Oh, no!"

"Not fast, though. We still have a chance. Hold on now!"

His piercing whistle made Delia catch at her ear, but she was obliged to grab the horse's mane again and hang on for dear life as Tiger lengthened his stride to a canter. Hoarse shouts sounded in the rear, but they rapidly diminished as the distance grew between them and the fleeing stallion.

In seconds, the path opened into a lane. The horse swerved into it and then he was galloping hell for leather. Giff bent low, forcing Delia to do the same.

The country began to change around them, the woodlands giving way to pasture fields bounded by hedges, with the welcome sight of cottages nestling in the midst and a church spire some way ahead.

Tiger dropped to a canter, and Delia was able to push up from her crouch as Giff lifted away. She was obliged to catch her breath before she could attempt to speak, and was thankful as the horse slowed to a trot, evidently also in some distress.

"Is the church where your uncle lives?"

Giff did not respond and Delia looked quickly round. He was pale, his jaw tight and the strain was evident.

"Is it hurting?"

He nodded. His jaw unclenched. "Nearly there."

A man with a bundle of sticks on his shoulders came into sight, and then another carrying a couple of full sacks. Looking about, Delia realised they were entering a village. Relief swept over her.

"Stepleton, didn't you say?"

Giff merely nodded again and urgency crept over her. He was nearly spent. What was more, so was Tiger. Steam was rising from the horse's flanks and his breath was coming in heavy snorts.

She nearly cried with relief when they turned a corner and the lane opened out into a green, surrounded by a number of dwellings. There was no one about beyond a couple of boys working the pump in the middle of a small square. The church lay directly to the right and Giff urged Tiger into a pathway running behind.

"We're going in by the cemetery?"

"Don't want the villagers gossiping."

For the first time it occurred to Delia they must present a sight to elicit a good deal of talk. If she looked half as dishevelled as Giff, who knew what anyone might make of their unconventional arrival, with her up before him on the horse?

A break in the cemetery wall came up. Giff turned into it. Was he in the habit of coming in by this route?

"Are you staying here?"

"Where Piers may find me in a heartbeat? I'm not such a fool."

Tiger picked his way along a row of graves to the back of the church and followed a curving path that led around it and across to an enclosure. Delia saw gabled roofs beyond the ivy-covered surrounding wall with a closed gate at the end of the path.

A horrid necessity leapt to mind. "One of us is going to have to dismount. And I think it had better be me."

Giff did not argue. She was convinced he was only able to stay in the saddle by sheer force of will.

It proved as difficult as she'd anticipated. She managed to get her leg out from its position about the pommel, but her gown caught and she heard it rip as she slid to the ground. Giff had done his best to break her descent by holding her, but his strength was gone and Delia very nearly slumped to the ground. She staggered to the gate and grabbed hold of it, stamping her foot to bring life back into it.

By the time she was able to turn, Giff had swung his right leg over and was cursing as his weight came onto the left. He landed heavily, and stood panting, the left foot still in the stirrup.

Delia went quickly to his side and slipped her shoulder under his arm. "Lean on me, Giff."

She took little weight until he tugged his left foot free. He gave a grunt of pain as it came to the ground and he was suddenly heavy, using Delia's support while he hissed his breath. "Damn it to hell!"

Delia braced every muscle. "Let's get you inside."

His arm tightened briefly. "I said you were plucky. Didn't know the half of it."

A glow lit in her breast, but the urgency of the moment would not allow of savouring it. Urging him onward, she unlatched the gate and led through it into a neat patchwork of a vegetable garden with a clear path to two back doors.

As they limped unsteadily towards the nearest one, it opened and a stout dame in a voluminous apron stepped out and stopped, staring.

Delia had no time for the niceties and called out. "We need help. Where is your master? Please fetch him at once!"

"And then Giff rode hell for leather down the road and we made it at last to your back gate," Delia finished breathlessly, dismayed to feel a trickle of tears down her cheeks.

The Reverend Gaunt, a spare and gentle creature with wispy grey hair, cast her a reassuring glance. "You did well, my child, but rest now and drink your tea."

He was kneeling by Giff's prone and unconscious body, laid on a cot in a servant's room in the back premises of the rectory. The plump woman who'd led them in through the kitchen hovered, ready with a selection of cloths over her arm and bandages in her hand while the rector worked on Giff's wound.

His breeches had been cut away to expose the damage and Delia's improvised and bloodied bandage lay discarded on the floor. The bowl of warm water was red with Giff's blood, but the wound, ugly if clean now, bled only sluggishly. The bullet had cut through the thigh, but was not embedded, the reverend had said.

"For which we must be thankful. But he's lost a deal of blood for all that."

"Yes, he did, because we rode for ages before I had a chance to tie it up."

Which proved the trigger for Delia to begin upon her story. She'd refused to leave Giff, who'd passed out the moment he'd been helped to the bed by a footman who'd been in the kitchen when they got there. But the hurried arrival of the elderly rector, who took immediate charge, sending his servants on flying errands, was reassuring enough that she agreed to vacate her place by Giff's side and allow him to attend to the injury.

The plump woman had given her tea, which Delia sipped in between blurting out the tale of their adventures from where she sat on a stool by the only window in the small room. With the danger passed— if those horrid creatures were not even now hunting through the village — her overwrought nerves were taking hold.

She must not give in to them. Until she knew Giff was truly safe, she could not afford to crumple. Sniffing, she wiped the wet from her cheeks and took up her cup again. The china edge clattered against her teeth and she realised she was shaking. Grasping the cup with both hands, she managed to sip the hot, sweet liquid, and found it soothing.

Her eyes strayed to Giff's pale face, remembering the bright of his azure eyes, now distressingly veiled. She wanted him to wake, but yet hoped he would not do so until his uncle had finished with the wound. The rector was pouring a powder over the pink flesh. Basilicum? Delia felt relieved when no trace of pink was visible. It had made her decidedly squeamish as she had not been when she'd bandaged it herself. The urgency of the moment had allowed no such missishness. But now, with Giff so unnaturally pale and silent, it was perfectly horrid to be obliged to see what had affected him so badly.

She watched the rector lift Giff's leg at the knee.

"Hold the leg steady, Aggy, while I apply a bandage."

Instinct urged Delia to leap up to perform this office, but she was afraid to try and stand. Her legs felt as if her bones had melted and every muscle was stiff and sore.

While the cook held the leg in position, the reverend folded a pristine cloth into a pad and laid it over the wound. His bandaging was a good deal more efficient than Delia's had been. But then he was not trying to do it while hanging upside-down on Tiger's back, which was a trifle consoling.

She kept her eyes on Giff's face, willing him to wake. She wanted to pledge herself to his aid, though she had no notion what she could do. But the very thought of this hateful cousin of his hiring men to kill him made her insides curl into knots. Why? Why did the wretch want him dead? Dared she ask the Reverend Gaunt?

Was he even safe here? Giff had said he would not stay at his uncle's for his cousin might find him there. If those men followed their trail to this place, would the man Piers not find it out?

She must at least warn the rector, though she dared not speak out before the cook. Of course the woman had heard all her story already. But how much did she know? Surely this great-uncle of Giff's must know the whole. He had certainly known Giff on the instant. Giffard, he'd called him. At least she now knew his name. Giffard Gaunt, was it? His uncle knew that and more. But would he tell her? How much could she discover before she must leave Giff to return to her own life?

Remembrance brought her up short. Until this moment, she'd completely forgotten her predicament. By now Vowles and Scoley must have discovered her absence. Would they have set out in search of her at once? She could not believe otherwise. And what of poor Aunt Gertrude? Had she regained consciousness before reaching Weymouth? Assuming they'd continued on that far, which Delia dared not doubt.

The whole affair seemed a world away, like something from another life. Reality was in this little back room with her rescuer prince out cold on the sofa, his life at constant risk. How was she ever to settle back to normality after this?

As if he read her thought, the Reverend Gaunt rose from his knees and surveyed Delia, a little smile creasing his wrinkled features. "Well now, my dear child, I think we must see to your needs."

Delia tried to smile. "I don't know how, sir. But the tea is very welcome."

"We will feed you too, I think. Are you not hungry?"

In all the flurry and excitement, Delia had forgotten the natural demands of her body. But the mention of food gave instant vent to a niggle in her stomach, and a far more urgent need.

"Yes, indeed I am. And I would be grateful for a chance to — er — to —"

"To freshen up?" The reverend cast her an understanding look and turned to his cook. "Aggy, take Miss — gracious me, I have been remiss! What is your name, my dear?"

"Delia, sir. Delia Burloyne."

"Thank you. Take Miss Burloyne to one of the spare bedchambers and provide her with hot water." His gaze ran down Delia's person as she stood up in preparation. "And I think perhaps we might find you something a little more presentable to wear. I am sure there is a suitable gown or two amongst my late wife's effects, or my daughter may have left a couple here."

About to thank him, Delia abruptly realised she could not possibly accept. "It is generous of you, sir, but it will not do."

His brows rose. "Are you too proud to take charity, my child?"

"Heavens, it is not that! Don't you see? How could I satisfactorily explain a change of raiment? Indeed, it is impossible, for I dare not mention Giff. As it is, I will have to fabricate some tale to account for my condition. And I ought to be found where I was left."

Consternation entered the elderly features. "I had not thought, but you are right, of course." He hesitated, frowning, and threw a glance at his nephew on the bed.

Delia fretted inwardly, unable to think what she should do now the question of her own affairs had arisen. At last the rector gave a decisive nod.

"I will think on it, child. Go with Aggy and you may at least clean away the dirt of the roads."

Feeling altogether disturbed, and not a little scared, Delia followed the woman Aggy into the passage.

CHAPTER FOUR

Seated next to the Reverend Gaunt in his phaeton, with a groom up behind, Delia struggled to re-orient herself to the present. It was hard, when her mind kept straying to her last image of Giff, still in the cot where he'd been laid, still pallid in sleep, but a deal more comfortably bestowed.

While she was busy taking care of her body's needs, washing away the dirt from her face and hands and partaking of a bowl of sustaining broth with bread and cheese in the kitchen, the reverend and his footman had stripped Giff and put him into a nightshirt.

Upon enquiry, she learned he'd woken briefly, only long enough to drink down the draught which sent him into a more natural sleep.

"Have no fear, child. I will take every care of him. You may trust Aggy and Wilfred to deputise in my absence."

Delia could not be satisfied. "What if those men come looking for him?"

"In my house? I hardly think so."

"And that horrid cousin of his? Piers?"

"Ah, yes, my other great-nephew. He may come, of course, but he will not find Giffard, be sure. There is a stout lock on that door, if need be. But he would not have the temerity to demand to search my house. That would be to show his hand, you know."

This was the first intimation Delia had from Giff's uncle that he was conversant with all the circumstances. A stir of determination burgeoned. She would have the story from him before he deposited her at Weymouth.

He had disclosed his plan upon coming into the kitchen where Delia was polishing off the last of a plate of tartlets stout Aggy had pressed upon her, along with a flagon of lemonade.

"I have thought it all out, my dear child. You were hiding from those ruffians, which fits with your story. You missed the coach and began walking, but they returned and you ran away into the forest and became lost. Perhaps they were scouting around and you were obliged to run and hide, which will satisfactorily account for your torn gown, will it not?"

"Indeed, and it is quite true for I snagged it several times before Giff found me." Doubt smote her. "Though whether anyone will believe it became so torn…"

"I suspect your people will be so relieved to find you safe, they will not look too closely."

Delia breathed again. "Yes, and I imagine they will be more worried for Aunt Gertrude."

The rector smiled but made no direct response to this. "In any event, once you were satisfied the men had gone, you found your way to the road again where I happened to be passing —"

"— and I attracted your attention and asked for help. Yes, that is excellent, sir." A caveat entered her mind. "But how shall we explain my having washed and eaten?"

"There is no difficulty there, my child. You were so distraught, we stopped at an inn that you might rest and do just as you have done here. Will that serve, do you think?"

Relief swept through Delia. "You are very kind, sir. I am sorry to put you to so much trouble."

The elderly features crumpled into warmth. "On the contrary, Delia — if I may? It is the least I can do, and I fear it will hardly suffice to repay my indebtedness to you. Without your valorous endeavours, my dear child, I shudder to think what would have become of my poor nephew."

Gratified, if a trifle overwhelmed, Delia argued no further. In her view, she was quite as indebted to Giff, who need not have taken her up, and to whom she was sure she'd been more of a hindrance than a help. If he had not been obliged to take care of her, he would not have been shot. With his skills, and Tiger's too, he would have escaped detection. And that was another creature she'd needlessly worried over. The horse had not been forgotten. He'd been groomed and fed by the servant Chaffe, now on his perch behind the phaeton, and was safely hidden in the Reverend Gaunt's stables.

Delia found it odd to retrace the lane she'd fled along with Giff, and could not see the entrance to the path where they'd made the turn. The lane ran for some miles before ending at a crossroads which permitted the rector to take another he said would lead to the Dorchester to Weymouth road.

It occurred to Delia that time was passing, and she'd not yet begun upon her investigations. She glanced at the groom up behind and lowered her voice. "How freely may I speak before your man there, sir?"

The Reverend Gaunt looked round, regarding her with a slight frown. "He is discretion itself, are you not, Chaffe?"

"Beg pardon, Reverend?"

"You'll not chatter about anything Miss Burloyne says, I trust."

A grunt came from behind. "Ain't heard nothing to chatter about, Reverend."

The rector laughed. "As I thought. You may speak as you wish, my child. What is on your mind?"

Despite this permission, Delia kept her tone low. "You evidently know what is going on, sir. Pray tell me, why is this Piers trying to — to dispose of Giff?"

"If he is trying so to do."

She gazed at his profile. "You don't believe it?"

A flickering glance came her way. "There is no proof, but the suspicion cannot but obtrude. To my knowledge, there is none other who might benefit from Giffard's demise."

"How would he benefit? What has Giff done to him?"

The rector gave her a sidelong look. "How much did Giffard tell you?"

"Nothing at all. He would not answer my questions. I learned only what he inadvertently let fall. That these men wish to capture him so they might kill him in secret. And that his cousin Piers hired them to do so. Which I believe, for I heard them talking of someone who would pay them for capturing him. Oh, and they said no one knew Giff was in the country. Only that can't be so, if this horrid Piers knows it. And you too."

"That, my dear child, is precisely the problem. Believing his cousin to be dead, my great-nephew took over Giffard's property and has been lobbying for the title."

Delia stared. "Title? What title?"

"Giffard, if he can prove he is indeed Giffard Gaunt, is rightfully the Earl of Baunton."

The blood was dancing in Delia's veins as she digested this. An earl? Her fugitive prince was really an earl. Heavens above, and she'd taken him at first for a highwayman!

An anomaly surfaced. "But you recognise him, sir, do you not?"

The rector laughed out. "Hardly, my dear Delia. He was but three years old when his mother took him out of England."

"Out of England? To where, sir?"

"India. I had heard nothing of Giffard beyond his sojourn in that continent, until he visited me a matter of three weeks past, or thereabouts. I've lost track, I fear."

"But you believe him?" Anxiety sat in the pit of Delia's stomach as she waited for his reply. There was no doubt in her mind that Giff spoke the truth, though she had no means of knowing anything about him. Yet she trusted her instinct. As ridiculous as it was, as devoid of any sort of sense, she felt she *knew*.

His uncle spoke at last. "I had my doubts."

"But no longer? Because he's being pursued?"

"My dear child, I wish I might satisfy you, but I cannot. If this wickedness indeed emanates from Piers, one is tempted to think it proof of Giffard's identity. But the melancholy truth is that the mere possibility he is the rightful Earl of Baunton might be sufficient to turn a determined man from the path of right."

Delia could not be satisfied. "Yes, but could it not be he is afraid Giff has proof? Or that he knows somehow Giff is the rightful earl?"

"Anything is possible. But if Giffard has proof, he has only to produce it. I gave him the direction of the family lawyer, but he is convinced the fellow will be in Piers's pocket and refuses to consult him."

"Is there no one who can speak for him? None who can verify his identity?" Delia began to feel desperate. It was monstrous that Giff should return from abroad to take up his inheritance and find it occupied.

The Reverend Gaunt's silence was answer enough. There was no one. Then how was Giff to do? Half unknowing, she spoke her thoughts aloud.

"It's no good him skulking and hiding. Those men are bound to get him sooner or later, and as he said, none will be the wiser. He ought to be out in public. Declare himself, even. Then, if anything happened to him, the authorities must take notice." Conviction seized her, together with remembrance, and she turned to the rector. "Don't you see, sir? He said something of the sort to me. Piers would not wish to have the justices suspect him of wrongdoing, which is why he has hired these men to hunt Giff down. But if he made his claim public, Piers could not touch him without suspicion falling upon him."

She was gratified to receive a beaming look from her companion.

"My dear Delia, that is ingenious! Whether Giffard will agree is another matter. But it must serve him better at least to appear in public places and to make acquaintance with the gentry hereabouts."

A trickle of hope seeped into Delia's breast. "If it makes him safe, it must be worth it, even if he does not manage to prove who he is." Doubt smote her and she could not keep silent. "But how would he support the life of a gentleman? Has he any money?"

A laugh escaped the reverend. "As I understand it, he does not want for means. He has not told me how, but I gather he has come with a respectable fortune."

"Then he must stop playing at hide and seek and enter society. Pray tell him I said so." Remembrance caused a tremor at her lip and a pricking in her eyes. "Tell him … tell him the flower girl insists upon it."

She heard a murmur from the rector, possibly of assent. However, she was quite unable to speak for several minutes, concentrating on the necessity to keep her countenance.

She turned her hazy gaze onto the road and her surroundings came into focus. Heavens, were they on the Weymouth road already? Surely she recognised the pattern of the woodlands either side. They must be close to where the adventure had started.

Within minutes, her vague notion was confirmed when she caught sight of a redcoat in the periphery of her vision. Instinct cut in.

"Oh, stop, sir!"

As the phaeton slowed, she gazed this way and that, finding several flashes of red among the trees. Her mind leapt, her heart suddenly racing.

"Militia! Good heavens, do you suppose they are searching for me?"

The rector brought his pair to a standstill and looked both right and left, peering into the trees. "If they are indeed militia, it seems a safe assumption. Your people must have alerted them."

Delia's pulse was behaving in a most uncomfortable fashion, but she could not rest without knowing for sure.

One of the red-coated individuals shifted within full sight. Delia trumpeted her hands at her lips and called out. "Hi, you there! Hello!"

The militiaman turned. Delia waved, calling out again. He lifted a hand and came hurrying through the trees towards the phaeton.

"This is dreadful! Aunt Gertrude must be frantic, if indeed she is well enough to have sent for them."

"It is comforting to know you were sought with such assiduity, my dear child."

By this time, the militiaman was coming up to the carriage. He touched a hand to his cap. "Miss?"

Delia wasted no time. "You are looking for someone, aren't you?"

A wary expression came into the man's eyes. "Miss?"

Impatience gripped Delia. "I think you are looking for me. I am Miss Burloyne and I was left behind when my aunt's coach went off after being waylaid."

His eyes widening, the militiaman stared. "You're the lady as got left?"

"Yes, I tell you. Who is in charge here?"

"That would be the captain, miss."

"Well, fetch him, if you please!"

Effecting another salute, the fellow hurried off, crossing the road in front of the carriage. He vanished into the trees and Delia turned to the rector, struck by a horrid thought.

"What a beastly mischance, sir! How in the world are we to explain you are only now taking me to Weymouth?"

He transferred the reins to his right hand and reached out to pat her knee. "No difficulty, my dear. I was travelling in the other direction when I came upon you, and proceeded to an inn I know. There is the Black Cat a little way beyond the turn which will admirably serve our purpose."

A man older than the first, wearing the braided red coat of an officer, came hurrying out of the forest. He greeted the occupants of the phaeton with a salute and addressed himself to Delia.

"Miss Burloyne?"

The presence of Captain Rhoades riding beside the phaeton prevented Delia from further questions concerning Giff. Besides, she was too much occupied in answering the captain's queries to have leisure for anything except the urgent necessity to keep any mention of her real rescuer out of her story.

"You say there were only two men?"

"Yes, and one is called Sam and the other Barney. Sam is the leader, I think. He is a big fellow, and has a rough way with him."

"Are you sure, ma'am?"

Delia's pulse quickened. "What do you mean? Of course I'm sure. I heard them talking and they were close by."

The captain gave her a frowning look as he sat his horse. "As I understand it, ma'am, there was another. The groom — Scoley, is it? — spoke of a rider who came out of the trees. The two men who had waylaid her ladyship's coach went after him. Which, I gather, gave them an opportunity to escape."

Her mouth dry, heart hammering, Delia willed her mind to rapid thought. She improvised, hesitating over her response. "Yes … I saw him too. I think — I believe those men were … were looking for him." Inspiration came. "Yes, they were, for I recall they spoke of *he* evading them. They were angry. Might he have been a member of their gang, do you think?"

Light came into the captain's face as he turned to her again. "Ah. Tipped them the double, I dare say."

Delia's pulses were in disarray, but puzzlement overtook her. "I beg your pardon?"

The captain cleared his throat. "Double crossed them. Made off with the takings, or some such thing."

She seized on this convenient excuse. "Yes, that must be it. They were wild with him, I know that much. It was that made me so fearful."

"I don't wonder, ma'am."

"Yes, I was terribly afraid of what they might do if they caught me," pursued Delia, hoping to distract his mind from the third man by enlarging on this theme. "Ruffians, both of them. And that Sam was the worst. He's a big man, unshaven,

56

and the way he thrashed about the bushes with a stick quite terrified me. And he had a pistol!"

She stopped, fearing she'd gone too far. Why in the world had she to mention pistols? But the captain merely nodded.

"So I understand, ma'am. The coachman told me the whole affair began with a pistol shot. Were both men armed?"

"I don't know, Captain." Her veins ran with relief. "I heard that shot too, you know. That's how I knew they were armed."

He inclined his head and she hoped his questions would cease. With gratitude, she heard the Reverend Gaunt take a hand.

"Might it not be better to postpone your questions, sir? I feel it is of more importance to get Miss Burloyne to Weymouth as swiftly as we may."

With which, he exhorted his pair to a trot. They had been held to a walk to facilitate the captain speaking to Delia. He made no objection to the change, but signalled to his four men riding behind and put his own mount to the same pace.

Delia spoke low-voiced to the rector. "Thank you, sir. He was flustering me horribly."

"You did very well, child." A reassuring smile reached her. "Stick to your two ruffians and you will be fine. You had no further sight of the third man beyond seeing him ride out of the forest, is that not so?"

A trifle overwrought, Delia giggled. "It had better be so. And thank you also for insisting on taking me back yourself."

"I hardly think the captain could have got you back otherwise. Unless he proposed to mount you before him."

"I had not thought of that. I dare say he meant to mount me and lead the horse. Two of his men could very well have ridden together, I suppose."

"Most unsatisfactory. The phaeton is by far more comfortable for you, I don't doubt."

"Indeed it is, and I'm glad of the chance to say this much." She drew an unsteady breath and dropped her voice to a near whisper. "Keep him safe, sir! Don't let him run his head into danger."

"I doubt I could stop him, my dear child. He is nothing if not headstrong."

"That is just what worries me!"

She cast a glance at the captain, fearful of being overheard. But he was riding at a little distance now and she breathed more easily, despite the constriction in her bosom.

Becoming aware presently of an increasing presence in the environment of dwellings and passers-by, a creeping sensation of loss began to invade her. The adventure was coming to its close and the author of it lay helpless in the rectory in Stepleton, and the despicable truth was Delia might never see him again.

Urgency threw her into hasty speech, of necessity in another frantic whisper. "I won't get the chance to speak of this again, sir. Pray tell him… Tell Giff…" *Oh, say it, Delia!* To the devil with caution! "Tell him I will never forget. He brought excitement into a very dull life." She saw the rector's brows lift and hurried on. "I know it was hideously dangerous and I would not willingly go through it again. You will think it odd of me, sir, but I would not have missed it for the world."

A dry laugh came and the Reverend Gaunt set one hand on hers where she gripped them in her lap and pressed them. "What it is to be young! But I do trust you will not again be obliged suffer such excitement on my nephew's behalf."

Delia's spirits drooped. "Highly unlikely, since he won't again cross my path."

The rector said nothing to this. Delia wondered briefly if he noticed her distress and did her best to suppress it. She must appear relieved and happy to be back among her people, if she was not to invite comment and question. Aunt Gertrude was all too shrewd.

As it chanced, her great-aunt proved to be a good deal debilitated by the knock on the head she'd received and was far from her usual self. She greeted Delia with tearfulness and a convulsive hug, although she did not attempt to rise from the chaise longue where she was lying.

"My poor, dear child, thank heavens you are safe! How in the world would I have explained myself to your mama, if I had lost you forever?"

"But here I am, Aunt, if a little the worse for wear. And thanks to the Reverend Gaunt here, who kindly took me up."

She was happy to see how Aunt Gertrude, clasping the rector's hand between both her own, took her story without a blink, giving him effusive thanks and shedding tears again.

The reverend managed to turn her attention with an ease Delia could only admire. "But what of you, dear lady? Miss Burloyne told me you had sustained a severe blow."

Lady Matterson waved dismissive hands. "Yes, yes, but that was nothing to the dismay I felt when I heard they had left Delia behind. My fault too! For I told her to escape the carriage. Only neither Vowles nor Scoley knew it. And I did not recover consciousness until they had carried me to my bed and brought a doctor to me." She then begged everyone to be seated and exhorted Delia to ring the bell. "We will have in the Madeira. A little celebration is in order, I think."

There was limited space in the only parlour provided in Lady Matterson's lodging, for which she apologised. "Weymouth is always so crowded, one can scarcely move, and my usual lodgings, which are a deal more commodious, were taken. My fault. I dithered too long when I knew my poor Maria could not join me here. My friend, you must know. We have been spending the summer here together for years."

Looking round, Delia saw nothing amiss with the parlour. It was small but airy, furnished with a couple of armchairs upholstered in chintz to the seats and back in addition to the chaise longue which evidently doubled as a sofa, and a small writing bureau and straight chair set into the window embrasure, which overlooked the Esplanade.

The rector disposed himself in a chair close enough to the chaise longue that he might continue to converse, while the captain perched nearer the door and Delia plonked down on a cushioned stool beside the chaise longue. All were barely settled when her ladyship's gaunt dresser came in.

"Ah, Pegler! Here she is, the resilient creature, safe and sound."

"So I see, my lady." The woman gave Delia a dour smile as she came across the room. She was almost as elderly as her mistress, having been with Lady Matterson from her youth, and was, as Delia knew, more companion to her than maid. There was a hint of apology in her withered features. "I am very glad, miss, and must blame myself for your tardy return."

Delia stared. "How so, Peggy?"

The nursery name, which she and her siblings had ever used, caused a spasm to cross the woman's face, but she was evidently labouring under too much emotion to object. "I'm afraid I gave you little thought at first, what with my mistress as near death as made no odds."

"Pish and tush, woman! Nothing of the sort!"

"You may say so, my lady, but I will not readily forget the turn it gave me when the fellows carried you in. Thank the

Lord I had all in readiness and we were able to put you to bed and I sent young Sally for Doctor Hayter straight."

"Utterly ridiculous! What mattered it when my niece was missing?"

"It was quite a time before I knew, my lady, as I've told you a dozen times." She turned back to Delia. "I confess I dallied too long, even when I found it out, for I knew not what to do for the best. But Doctor Hayter suggested the militia and I sent to them by Scoley."

"We set out at once, ma'am," Captain Rhoades assured her great-aunt, "but it seems we had been forestalled by the rector here."

Delia was once again obliged to repeat the story concocted by the Reverend Gaunt, which provoked so much exclamation and comment that she could not but wonder what would have been said did her aunt and Peggy know the truth. She was relieved when the maid went off to fetch the Madeira, and she was able to turn the subject. "But what of you, Aunt Gertrude? What did the doctor say?"

"Oh, he insists upon my resting for a week, but I shall do no such thing. A day or two will see me right again."

"But does it not pain you?"

The redoubtable dame waved a dismissive hand. "Not now, for Hayter gave me one of his ghastly doses. But it did the trick. I had the devil of a head when I woke, I admit, and I could not remember how I came by it until Scoley told me. And that wretch took my pistol! Now I shall have to procure another."

A burst of laughter from the Reverend Gaunt drowned Delia's half-formed protest. "As resilient as your niece, ma'am, if I may say so. Miss Burloyne told me you threatened the ruffians with a pistol."

A twitch disturbed the corner of Aunt Gertrude's mouth and her eyes twinkled. "A mistake, I admit. But I've never been one to play the helpless female. Pathetic, squeamish things they are now. We were more robust in my day."

"Very true, ma'am. Ladies are indeed more delicate in these times."

But Delia received a comical lift of the eyebrows and a conspiratorial look from the rector as he spoke, which very nearly sent her into an unseemly fit of the giggles. *Delicate? If Aunt only knew!*

"However, I can't think where I shall get a new pistol in Weymouth," she went on, unheeding. "I shall have to send to Manton's. I cannot be without one. A pox on the thieving wretch! I shall give him a piece of my mind when he is caught."

A pox on him indeed! Realisation quenched Delia's urge to laugh. That vile Sam must have made use of Aunt Gertrude's pistol. He can't have had time to reload his own. How horrible that he'd shot Giff with that very weapon! Ironic indeed to find her aunt had inadvertently provided the means for Delia's rescuer to be injured.

The agitation induced by this thought rendered her tongue-tied. If only she might retire. Yet if she did, she would lose contact with the rector, her only connection with Giff.

Lady Matterson turned her attention to Captain Rhoades. "I hope you mean to lay those fellows by the heels, sir?"

The officer cleared his throat. "I trust we may, my lady, though there was no sign of them in the area where we were searching. Miss Burloyne has provided a description, however, and we will do our damn —" He broke off, reddening. "I mean, we will put forth our best endeavours."

"Well, with a whole garrison of soldiers at your disposal, you may do so."

A positive battery of throat clearing followed this. "I regret, my lady, it is not in my power to request assistance from the regular army. And there is only the cavalry now. The bulk of our soldiery is in the Bexhill camp."

Lady Matterson was having none of this. "Even better. Cavalry may cover more ground. It is not as if they have anything better to do until that monster Napoleon attempts to invade, which he won't. The Admiral will keep him out, you'll see."

"I sincerely trust he may, my lady, but whether or not Lord Nelson's fleet is at hand, I regret the cavalry are not mine to command."

"Pish and tush, man! Then I shall send to their commanding officer myself!"

Delia could not but be relieved that Miss Pegler chose this moment to re-enter with a tray, conveniently deflecting Aunt Gertrude's attention as she directed the serving of wine to the company. Lady Matterson was ever precise in the social niceties, and she abandoned the argument in favour of responding to the rector, who seized the chance to change the subject.

"Is His Majesty expected this season, do you know, ma'am?"

"I have not yet had time to ascertain the general opinion, but I confess I am not sanguine. The reports of his health are worrying."

Thankful for the deflection, Delia settled to her wine, her mind drifting away from King George's possible attendance at his favoured watering place and back to a little room in the rectory at Stepleton.

Had Giff yet woken? Would he wonder at her absence when he did? Would he even remember?

A deep voice cut into Giff's dream, dragging him from sleep.

"Wake, sahib! You must wake!"

Giff blinked into the dimly shadowed face leaning over him. Recognition flittered into his fogged brain. "Sattar?"

"It is I, Sahib. I gained entry, but I can remain but a moment. Sahib, I have much to tell you."

Struggling, Giff dragged himself onto his elbow, setting off a shriek of agony in his thigh. He winced and hissed in a breath.

"You are wounded, sahib. One told me this." The well-known tones of Giff's faithful Indian servant deepened to severity. "You cannot be a day without Sattar but you are getting yourself shot. Such a reckless boy you are, sahib. What would Sahib Favell say?"

A flicker of amusement lit Giff's dulled mind as he thought of his stepfather, but he croaked his response. "He would say be damned to the devilish imp! Throw him to the tigers!"

Sattar made no answer, but a glass appeared before Giff's face. "Drink!"

His hand wavered as he tried to take it, but his henchman put the glass to his lips and he sipped the water, realising he was parched. Done, his strength failed and he slid heavily back onto his pillow and closed his eyes.

Sattar grunted. "This uncle drugged you, I think. Listen well then, sahib."

Giff forced his lids apart and reached out. "Proceed. I hear you."

The old man's strong fingers gripped his. "I tracked the man as you bade me, sahib. He met with two others. Rough were they, one evil in the eye."

Vague remembrance surfaced. "Must have been he who shot me."

"I know not, sahib. But what I know is I have seen him here as I came to find you. You told me this was the place if ever I missed you. I found you not at the alehouse where we lodged, so I came here." His tone darkened again. "To find you laid by the heels with bullets in you, careless boy!"

"Never mind that. Besides, I have no bullet in me. It passed through the flesh, my uncle said."

A harsh laugh greeted this. "Always you have the devil on your side, sahib."

Giff was growing more alert, forced to it by the intelligence his servant brought. "You saw the man here? When?"

"As I approached, sahib. He was with another, but him I could not swear to. They were afoot, drinking without the tavern, but I saw a horse tethered. He spoke with that man and others. I fear me he seeks to get news of you."

"He'll get nothing. I came in by the church and was not seen."

"Yes, you have learned well our ways. Nor was I seen, you may be sure. But better it is if I watch and listen. Thus must I go quickly, sahib."

Giff nodded, but when Sattar would have risen, detained him. "Where did you see my cousin meeting with the men?"

"In a beggar's alehouse, sahib. Faugh!"

"In Dorchester?"

"It was so. At once I knew they must be these same rogues who are dogging your steps ever since you so foolishly went to this Village Keep."

"Waldiche Keep, Sattar. Waldiche."

"What difference, sahib? Did not I tell you it was folly to walk into the tiger's den?"

A mulish irritation came into Giff's breast. "It's not his den. It's mine."

"So said Master Favell. Yet this man may hold if he possess."

"I'll oust him, never fear."

Sattar banged his fist on the bed. "You cannot oust if you are dead, sahib! Did not I say you must await me?"

Giff sighed. "It was sheer chance they caught sight of me. And I would have escaped them unmolested, if not for the wench."

The memory of his flower girl leapt into his head. Delia! What had become of her?

As if he heard the thought, Sattar spoke again. "That whom you brought here? The uncle has taken her, one told me."

Giff remembered where she had been headed when the coach was waylaid. "To Weymouth?"

"I know not. What I know is I will have this tale of your tomfoolery from you, but not now. I go, sahib. Pray you, stay safe. I will return after I find where are these men hid when they go to ground. If I can keep them in sight."

With a word of farewell, he was gone, leaving Giff with a tumble of images in his head wherein the girl figured strongly.

He'd thought her a nuisance at first, demanding the ordinary chivalry of any man who knew himself to be at fault in her predicament. He'd approached her when he saw her hiding with the object of ensuring she did not alert his pursuers. A sound would have brought them down on his head again just when he'd managed to evade them.

If that fool Sam had not fired his pistol, Giff would not have stopped and looped back. He'd heard the rumbling of the coach. What the deuce the fellow meant by firing on bystanders was a mystery. According to Delia's account, he supposed his quarry might have taken refuge within the coach.

Madness! And then to strike down an elderly woman and leave her senseless? By God, if they were his tools, they would know his wrath for such bungling!

Yet the fellow Sam had managed to find his mark. Another mistake. It could be no part of Piers's plan for his fellows to make such a stir. And had he not seen he had the girl up before him? What if his bullet had taken her instead?

The thought sent ice slicing through his veins. Bad as it was to have put her through what he had done, at least he was spared that. Though his flower girl had proved more than equal to the challenge. Exulting, he recalled how she'd refused to be set down, instead turning the tables. Binding his wound, by God, and taking the reins! Espousing his cause, turning all her energies to securing him. And never a word of complaint. What a woman!

Sattar had claimed he'd the devil's own luck, and he was right. To have lit upon one such in his circumstances was a miracle. The petticoats he'd known would have swooned or fallen into hysterics. But not his flower girl. She'd shown courage from the start, now he thought about it. Accosted and secured by a strange man in a situation fraught with danger, she'd behaved with remarkable calm. She'd obeyed his commands without question too, no doubt recognising the wisdom of silence. Not a word, not a whimper to give away their position, plucky wench. He owed her his life.

Warmth swept through him. He must find means to thank her. If his uncle was taking her back, he would know where she was to be found. When this cursed wound was enough recovered to enable him to ride again, he would reconnoitre the place and see what was to be done. He must not embroil her further in his chaotic affairs. That was a given. But equally, he was too indebted to allow her to pass out of his life, unrewarded, un-thanked.

Besides, he thought as sleep began creeping over his mind again, she was his flower girl, bonded now by their shared adventure. Not to meet her again was out of the question.

CHAPTER FIVE

"Sit you down, Miss Delia, do, before you fall down, and let me manage all."

Pushed onto the bed by her determined maid, Delia gave in without protest. Truth to tell, she felt as weak as a kitten and tired enough to obey her great-aunt's dictum, once Captain Rhoades had departed, that she remove her soiled clothing and rest until the dinner hour. The wine had made her head woozy, making it hard to say what she wished when she bid the Reverend Gaunt farewell. She'd been obliged to content herself with profuse thanks and a speaking look, which he answered with an understanding smile. Delia hoped he would not forget to give her messages to Giff.

Her eyes pricked as remembrance hit, and she hardly noticed as Sally undid the strings of her bodice and drew the garment down her arms, so that it fell open and slid to her waist.

"Dearie me, Miss Delia, this gown is fair ruined! I'll have a task to make it good, that I will."

"It doesn't matter. I have other gowns."

"That you have, but there's no need to let this one go to waste, if I can mend it. Stand up a moment, dovey, so I can slip it off."

Delia dragged herself up and Sally deftly slid the gown down. It pooled at her feet as she sank back onto the bed, but her maid did not pick it up as expected. Instead, she was staring at the bottom of Delia's under-petticoat, eyes wide as her mouth dropped open.

For an instant, Delia was confused. Then the penny dropped. Heavens, Giff's bandage! She'd forgotten how she'd ripped off strips to bind him.

"Lordy, Miss Delia, what have you been doing?"

Her mind jumped this way and that, seeking an excuse. Any excuse! The maid fixed her with a fulminating eye.

"You never did that running through the forest. That's been torn off proper, that has."

Distracted and trembling, Delia seized on this. "How do you know I was running through the forest?"

"I was listening at the door when you told her ladyship, of course," said Sally, unabashed. "'Sides, we knew you'd been left in the midst of the trees an' all. What else was I to think?"

"I had to hide too. There were brambles and Lord knows what. You can see I'm scratched." Which was true enough, for her bared arms showed several scratches and a few weals too. "I must have done it then."

Delia's fingers quivered as they clutched the petticoats, pulling them away in a bid to conceal the damage.

The maid set her arms akimbo, standing over her in rising wrath as she'd done so often when Delia was a girl. Sally had begun to maid her before she emerged from the schoolroom, and their relationship had the ease of long intimacy.

"That there petticoat never lost its flounce by accident, Miss Delia. If there's one thing I understand, it's clothing, and you won't fool me with such taradiddles. What happened that you needs must go tearing your clothes to pieces?"

Glancing past her at the closed door, Delia put a finger to her quivering lips. "Quiet, Sally, or you'll be heard!"

The accusing eyes did not leave her face, but the maid lowered her voice. "You'll not fool me, Miss Delia, so you'd best come clean."

A huge sigh escaped Delia. "I suppose I will have to take you into my confidence." She leaned forward, reaching up to grip the maid's wrist. "But you must promise me, on your life, Sally, not to divulge a word to anyone. Least of all, her ladyship."

The maid's eyes grew round, shock entering in. "Gracious, miss! As bad as that, is it?"

"Worse, if you must know."

Sally put a hand to her bosom and plonked down on the bed beside her. "You're alarming me horribly, Miss Delia!"

"Well, I shan't tell you then!"

Tiredness was making her irritable, but it was of no use. Sally was nothing if not persistent. She would not rest until she had the whole story.

As if to underline this thought, the maid patted her leg, her manner changing abruptly. "You'll tell me once you're safe in your bed." She got up again. "Let's get you out of them horrid clothes and into a fresh shift."

The transformation did not take long and was peculiarly unwelcome. As the wrecked petticoat was bundled up and shoved to one side, preparatory to being disposed of, Delia felt as if Giff himself was being cut out of her life. Each piece of clothing as it came off seemed to take him farther away from her, as if the very garments in which she'd partaken of his company were a part of him.

In a way they were, she thought drowsily as Sally began to rub a hot damp cloth about her face and limbs, washing away the sweat and the stains. The close contact on Tiger's back, Giff's hands holding her in the saddle as she bent to tie his wound, his arms threaded about her as he took the reins at the bridge. Her gown, her arms, her fingers were infused with his being. And Sally was washing him away.

Common sense reasserted itself. This was nonsense and she knew it. What, was she such a fanciful creature? Had she learned to be romantic in the space of a day?

But she had, a small voice protested. She'd lived a fairy tale, complete with a handsome prince who'd woken her from real life into a living dream. Except that Giff was no prince, and his life was in danger. That cousin of his! A usurper, taking what did not belong to him. And now the true heir had returned, his wickedness evidenced by the hiring of men to be rid of Giff. Despicable.

It occurred to Delia all at once that her aunt might know of the missing lord or of Piers Gaunt. If the seat was in the district, which seemed likely, Piers might have shown his face in Weymouth in past years. Delia determined to ask her, obliquely. It would not do to excite her curiosity. She had best wait for a few days, until she'd met some of the residents. She might pretend to have heard his name mentioned.

Her weaving plans were interrupted. "There, Miss Delia, that'll do. You look a deal more presentable."

Sally set down the towel she'd been using and went to pick up the shift she'd laid ready. "Let's get you into this and then you can slip under the quilt. No need to get between sheets altogether. I can fetch you a cup of hot chocolate, if you like."

A welcome and comforting notion. "That would be wonderful, Sally, thank you."

Delia allowed herself to be ushered onto her bed and sank into the pillows with a sigh. She really was dog tired. The maid tucked the covering about her and went off to procure the promised chocolate. Delia snuggled under the quilt, her thoughts returning to Giff.

How was he faring? Had he yet woken? Unlikely, for his uncle had said the draught should make him sleep for hours.

Long enough to give him relief from the pain of his wound? Delia hoped for it. To think of him hurting and faint as he had been by the time they got to the rectory was anathema. He was much better off asleep in that bed. Except that it left him vulnerable to those dreadful ruffians.

Could they still be searching around Stepleton? Surely they would not dare try to gain entrance to the rectory. The Reverend Gaunt had said this Piers would not come there, for it must condemn him if he gave evidence of knowing Giff was in residence. Even so, it was comforting to know he was secured in a back servant's room. If his cousin did come, he would expect him to be staying openly in his uncle's house, would he not? And he knew Giff was in the area. How did he know, though?

She had so many questions and no means by which to get them answered. So frustrating. She had no hope of getting any answers, if truth be told. No hope of seeing Giff again to ask him.

This thought was so melancholy a knot formed in Delia's bosom and her eyes misted. Oh, help! She must not give in to this. It was nonsensical. Absurd. She'd known him what, an hour or two? But an hour or two filled with incident, protested the ubiquitous voice in her head. Such incident as must form a lasting bond. Or so Delia supposed. Giff might not see it that way. Why should he? He'd felt obliged to take her up and she'd done nothing but get him shot. And with Aunt Gertrude's pistol!

No, if anything, he must be relieved to be rid of her. To Giff she was but a passing stranger, an interlude best forgotten, she had no doubt.

The small voice piped up. *He said you were a plucky wench.*

Well, yes, he did. Several times, as it happened. A couple anyway. Delia was glad to think she'd had sense enough not to worsen his difficulties.

And you bound up his wound and took the reins when he was faint.

Well, of course. Anyone would have done the same. No one could expect her to do less. He was bleeding badly. Even so, those men managed to follow the bloody trail, or how else did they catch up?

Ah, but Giff would not have escaped without your help.

Delia examined this notion in as detached a manner as she could and found it wanting. Giff would not have needed her help if he hadn't had to take her up in the first place, because he would not have been shot. What had the voice to say to that?

No answer came. Of course not, because there was none. She was palpably to blame. She should have stayed in the coach. It was of no use to protest that she might have been caught by those ruffians, because she knew very well they were only after Giff and would have gone on their way when they found he was not hiding inside it. Giff would have escaped them without being wounded and she would never have known of his existence.

This thought so depressed Delia she was inordinately glad to be distracted by the return of her maid, armed with the promised treat.

"Here you are, Miss Delia."

She sat up, taking the cup between her hands. The warmth of it soothed as Sally banked the pillows behind her.

"There, now, is that more comfy?"

Sitting back, Delia sighed, and the uncomfortable knot in her bosom eased a little. She sipped the hot liquid, grateful for its bitter tang and the honeyed sweetness that followed. She took several swallows, feeling the comfort all the way down to her toes.

"Mm, that's good. Thank you, Sally."

The maid nodded, but her expression was grim as she perched on the edge of the bed. "Now then, young madam, what's the tale?"

All Delia's careful arguments vanished, along with restraint as a heartfelt sob escaped. "Oh, Sally…"

"Miss Delia! Ah, don't cry, dovey! What a wretch I am to plague you after such an ordeal."

Delia tried to sniff back the tears, but it was of no use. As fast as she dashed them away, more trickled down her cheeks. The cup was taken out of her hand and set aside. Next moment she was pulled into her maid's arms, just as she had been in years gone by, and Sally was crooning into her ear.

The incongruity of it made her laugh and she recovered swiftly, pulling back and groping under her pillows for the handkerchief that was always there. Sally waited for her to wipe her eyes and blow her nose and then handed her the cup of chocolate again.

"There, finish that up, dovey, and then I'll leave you to rest. You can tell it all later."

But the urge to talk about Giff was too strong. "No, I'll tell you now, only you must promise to keep mum."

The maid bridled. "As if I'd give away one of your secrets, Miss Delia! You know me better than that."

Agitation crept back. "But this isn't my secret, Sally. It's vital you don't speak of it. A man's life is at stake!"

Sally's eyes grew round, half in astonishment, half sparkling in gathering wrath. "A man, Miss Delia? What man is this, if I may ask?"

Delia let out an overwrought breath. "I knew you'd start! For heaven's sake, Sally, if you are going to be difficult, I shan't be able to tell you."

"You'll tell me right now, young madam, or you'll be telling her ladyship."

"Betray me to my aunt? You wouldn't!"

"I'll have to if you won't start talking."

"Ha! So much for all your dovey stuff, you traitress!"

Delia thrust the empty cup at her and threw herself back against the cushions, folding her arms and glaring at the maid, who stared her out in silence. Many an argument had she won thus, but Delia was determined she would not win this one. She knew Sally would never carry out her threat. The maid was far too fond of her to prove disloyal.

Sure enough, in a moment Sally began to fidget and look away. She uttered a mewl of frustration. "Try the patience of a saint, you would, Miss Delia! All right, you have my word. I won't say nothing to no one." She put up a warning finger. "But I'll have the truth now and no nonsense, you hear me?"

Delia smiled at her, leaning in and putting out her hands, which the maid grasped and squeezed. "You're a treasure, Sally. I'll trust you."

"So I should hope, my dovey. Now, then, what's all this about a man?"

Delia drew an unsteady breath. "His name is Giff and he's a fugitive."

Waking all too early again, Delia lay blinking in the dazzle of morning. It was too hot to be enclosed in the stuffy cocoon of the bed-curtains, and she'd left them tied at the posts and kept the shutters open at the windows too.

Another glorious dawn awaited. She wished she might find it in her to rejoice, but her mind obstinately dwelled on a back room in a far rectory. If she'd not been obliged endlessly to repeat the expurgated tale of her so-called adventure, she could have allowed the whole episode to sink into the background. In the few days since Aunt Gertrude had recovered enough to venture forth, it seemed every second person wanted to hear Delia's story.

The tale had spread within hours, bringing Lady Matterson's friends to their parlour to exclaim and bless themselves. Delia could escape from there, but it was impossible to evade the questions once she accompanied her aunt abroad. Scarce a moment in the routine of the day was spent without company. Aunt's cronies even came to breakfast once or twice to partake of the fresh fish procured from the fishing boats down at the market on the beach.

Delia thrust herself out of bed and padded over to the window, from where she had a view of the sea beyond the Esplanade, bounded by a stretch of sand. The dippers were already busy, but it was no use hoping for a bathe this early. Aunt Gertrude would be cross if she went without her. A longing to be out in the fresh air would not be contained. She would dress and accompany Scoley down to the fish market.

Thus determined, she rang the bell for Sally.

Wrapped in a light cloak against a sharp wind, Delia was presently able to enjoy the brisk walk along the Esplanade to the far corner of the beach where the boats came in. To her consternation, a number of gentry were already haggling with the fishermen along with a collection of servants. She didn't feel like doing the pretty this morning.

"I'll wait here, Scoley, while you do the honours."

"As you wish, miss." But the groom frowned. "You'll stay within sight now, miss, will you? I'd not answer for my place with her ladyship if I was to lose you again."

Delia smiled her reassurance. "I won't shift from this spot, never fear."

Though how she could be lost on Weymouth beach with so many persons about, she could not fathom. There were several boats pulled ashore, but a number of larger vessels were tacking back and forth across the bay, one heading for the Isle of Portland, Delia thought as she gazed idly across the waters.

She breathed in the salty tang in the air, the odour of fish melding with that of seaweed. The wind blew her loose hair about her face and she lifted a hand to clear her view, holding the tresses back. Like most females, she'd abandoned the attempt to dress her hair high in the day. The wind defeated all efforts to maintain elaborate styles. It was simpler to leave it loose.

She turned away from the boat where Scoley had joined the throng, not wishing to be recognised, if she could help it. One might suppose her tale had been told enough, but each new arrival at the resort provoked questions, since a discussion of each journey appeared to be de rigueur.

It was infuriating. Every time she told the false story, images of the true version swam through her head. The whole thing had taken on the aspect of a dream. Without the repetition, Delia felt she might have been able to relegate it to just that status. A fairy-tale interlude existing only in her imagination, where it ought to remain. Would remain, if the wretched prince in the case had not been wounded. How was she to help wondering how he was faring? How to forget him, as she must, when his life remained in jeopardy?

She wished there were no single gentlemen in Weymouth. Then she would not have to keep comparing them with Giff when Aunt Gertrude gave her those horrid meaning looks at each introduction. A tiny giggle escaped her. Ironic, when she'd spent four seasons being ignored by every eligible gentleman on the town, that she must now appear of interest to those who could not hold a candle to her secret prince.

The thoughts died as an eerie sensation crept over her. She felt herself to be under scrutiny. A shiver shook her frame and she glanced wildly around.

Apart from the knot of persons surrounding the near fishing boat, there was a man walking his dog, a couple of riders in the distance, and two elderly women slowly traversing the Esplanade above the beach.

Delia could not shake the feeling. She trained her eyes upon the crowd around the boat. There was Scoley, thankfully now in discussion with one of the fish wives. He would not be long. A couple of gentleman, both armed with fish on a string, we moving up the beach. A stout woman was threading fis several people watching her.

Delia eyed each in turn, but could see none staring in direction. Was she mistaken, then?

The sensation persisted. Her eye was drawn to a moving near the shore. One man plied the oars, which splashed at every drip. Another sat in the stern, his gaze on a skiff way out to sea.

Abruptly, Delia sensed eyes boring into the back of he She swung about, her gaze casting this way and that al upper beach and the walk above. Her heart sank. An several ambling males could have been watching her. now.

The elderly gentleman had his attention on his gouty foot, his servant hovering behind. And was that a groom, hobnobbing with a fellow in homespuns? A pair of maids tripped along, casting admiring glances at the groom.

"Are you ready, miss?"

Delia jumped and turned. "Scoley! How — how you startled me!"

"Beg pardon, miss." He held up the fish. "We'd best get back. Mrs Tuckett will be waiting to get these cleaned and cooked."

Feeling filleted herself, Delia began to walk at his side. She felt jumpy and could not refrain from staring at every person they met. Though the odd feeling had vanished when the groom came up.

Had her instincts betrayed her? Perhaps it was this concentration on the adventure that made her stupidly nervous. Why in the world would anyone be watching her? She was being ridiculous.

But the oddity clouded her day.

Her aunt rose late, in a twitty mood, and complaining of her maid's neglect and Delia's excursion both.

"Pegler should have woken me. She will cosset me as if I am not now perfectly well again. It's far too late to take a dip. We will be at the back of the queue. And I wish you won't go traipsing about on the beach alone, Delia."

"I wasn't alone. I went with Scoley."

"There is not the least need for you to go buying fish."

"I didn't. I wanted some fresh air, that's all. The beach was invigorating at that hour."

Lady Matterson was chewing a portion of the freshly grilled fish and made no answer, instead throwing Delia a minatory

frown. Delia could only be glad they had no company to breakfast today.

Her aunt swallowed down her mouthful and pointed her fork at her great-niece. "And another thing. I am not at all happy with you splashing about in the waves the way you do."

Delia set down her fork and sighed. She'd had this battle already. "Aunt, I am not going to suffer myself to be dipped again by one of those dreadful creatures. Once was enough."

"But you may be washed out to sea!"

"I hardly think so. It's shallow where ladies are permitted to swim."

Aunt Gertrude leaned a little across the small table, lowering her voice. "I have not liked to mention it before, but there are unscrupulous gentlemen who think nothing of employing telescopes to catch a glimpse of beauty in the waves. Disgraceful, but what would you? Men are men all over!"

The devil got into Delia. "Perhaps we should welcome it, Aunt? Who knows but what my unclothed charms may attract me a husband at last."

"Delia, you dreadful child!"

But a quivering lip betrayed Aunt Gertrude's amusement, and Delia took instant advantage. "I wish you will come out of the mops, Aunt, and cease scolding. Did you sleep ill?"

For a moment, the issue hung in the balance. A spark in the old lady's eye warned of rising temper, but then she gave a reluctant bark of laughter. "I like your spirit, Delia. Never knew you had it in you." She gave a disgruntled sigh and picked up her coffee cup. "It's my sciatica, child. Giving me gyp. Dare say I've walked too much."

"Then we won't walk today."

"Good heavens, don't be ridiculous, girl! Of course I will walk. One cannot do other in Weymouth. Besides, I'll not have everyone imagining I'm incapacitated again."

Delia mustered patience. "I only meant we need not promenade. We may remain in the Assembly Rooms and I can fetch and carry for you. There's no ball tonight, is there?"

It took a deal of argument, but at length Lady Matterson consented to settle for a quieter day, though Delia was torn. On the one hand, she was relieved to be barred from encountering those prying eyes — if they were real. On the other, curiosity niggled to discover if she really was under observation. And by whom.

She could not avoid the suspicion that the eyes might belong to one of the men employed by Giff's cousin. But she had seen no one resembling the fellows Sam or Barney. And why in the world should they be watching her? Here, of all places, too, where they might be caught by the militia.

Or, no. The soldiery were searching in the forest, if indeed they continued to try to find those men. Several days had elapsed and Captain Rhoades had not returned with any news.

As the day wore on, Delia became convinced she had been mistaken. She was obliged to trip through the streets a couple of times on errands for her aunt, and the odd feeling did not resurface.

The following morning, she accompanied Lady Matterson to the bathing room at an early hour and left her there as she made her way down to the beach reserved for ladies, with Sally in attendance as usual.

"It's no manner of use objecting, Miss Delia," had said this worthy on the first occasion, "for I've my orders from her ladyship."

In the event, it was helpful to leave her towel and wrapper with the maid while she entered the water in her bathing dress, but it was restrictive since she felt she could not dawdle as long as she wished.

Today, however, she determined to take her time. There were several hardy creatures like herself who preferred to take to the waves without the assistance of a dipper. Delia greeted those that came near, but she preferred to take her swim alone.

There was pleasure in lying on her back in the buoyant water, keeping her balance with a little movement of her limbs, and gazing up at the skies.

They were grey today, overcast with the prospect of drizzle. The waves were stronger too, but her shift-like garment spreading about her helped to keep her afloat. One could lie here for hours, bobbing on the water like a cork, alone in a breathless world with nothing but the crying gulls and the swish of the surf on the shore to disturb one's peace.

A sudden shriek of alarm smote her ears. Losing balance, Delia tipped up, swallowed water and came coughing to her feet in the shallows.

She glanced about for the source of the cry and saw the other women hurrying out of the water as best they could for their clinging garments. She threw an arm out towards the nearest one, calling. "What is it? What's to do?"

The woman's attention caught and she half-turned, pointing back to sea.

Delia looked in that direction and her heart stilled.

A rowboat! Two men, plying far too near the shore.

Her mind jumped to the previous day buying fish. Was it the same one? Were these the same men?

"Miss Delia! Miss Delia! Come on out!"

Sally! She sounded panicked.

Hesitating, Delia stared at the nearby rower, trying to judge if the image fit the one from yesterday. He had a sturdy build as far as she could judge. Sam? Could it be? And was the other Barney? Neither man was looking towards her, and their faces were shadowed in the gloom of the day.

"Miss Delia, for pity's sake!"

The boat was making way fast now, moving out to sea. She heard a male voice, loud into the wind. "Ahoy! Get yon boat out of that! This is for ladies only! Get you gone!"

Turning, Delia saw a burly individual shaking his fist and dodging the waves. The guardian of the beach, it would seem.

Sally was still calling and Delia pushed her way through to the shore, a thrum in her veins as the questions continued to plough through her mind.

"Goodness knows what's got into you, Miss Delia! Why didn't you come out at once?"

Delia listened with only half an ear as Sally scolded, rubbing her down with the towel. The wrapper was flung about her still damp limbs.

"Shove your feet into the sandals, dovey, and let's get you back. Her ladyship should never have allowed it. Young ladies these days, I don't know."

Delia could not resist looking back as she was hurried up the beach, Sally's arm protectively about her. The little boat was already at a distance, tacking off towards the mouth of the estuary. The guardian was standing watching it still, arms akimbo.

As they reached the entrance to the bathing room, a huddle of the other swimmers was found to be in the way, exclaiming and complaining of ill-usage.

"If they cannot keep it private, I for one shall not swim again."

"I shall report it to Mr Rodber."

"Yes, indeed. He'll see to it the authorities are alerted."

Delia resisted the urge to say that the guardian would no doubt inform them, instead requesting a passage. "Will you excuse me, if you please?"

The little crowd parted to let her through, and she received one or two minatory looks. What, because she had not rushed out of the water like a demented hen?

Sally hurried her through and up the steps into the bathing room where she lost no time in informing Lady Matterson, who had just come back from her dip, of the shocking event.

Chagrined, Delia heard the exclamations break out around her.

"Gracious heaven!"

"I've never heard of such a thing!"

"Oh, I should have been mortified!"

"Were you not dreadfully afraid, dear Miss Burloyne?"

Delia turned to the speaker, a youthful creature and, like herself, companion to an older relative. "No, I wasn't at all afraid. It was only a couple of men in a rowing boat after all."

She spoke more stoutly than she felt. She had been apprehensive, but only on account of the men possibly having a more sinister purpose than trying to catch a glimpse of scantily clad female forms.

Her rebuttal produced a chorus of protest, but Delia excused herself on the score of needing to go home and change. She found her way to Lady Matterson. "Aunt, are you ready?"

A gimlet eye raked her, but the response was mild enough. "Indeed. I am ready for my breakfast too. By your leave, ladies."

Grateful for her aunt's ready acquiescence, Delia exited the place with her, Sally at their heels. She sighed inwardly, however. Lady Matterson's aspect warned of a coming interrogation. Heaven grant she might think up a convenient excuse for her tardiness in leaving the water.

CHAPTER SIX

The rector's calm served only to increase Giff's impatience.

"I'm grateful, sir, for your concern, but it's time and past I left here."

He was partaking of a hearty breakfast in the kitchen, Aggy having piled his plate with cold beef and a thick wedge from the remains of last night's pigeon pie which she'd heated in the bread oven. His uncle's cook-housekeeper amused Giff with her evident enjoyment of his voracious appetite. The Reverend Gaunt, he'd discovered, regularly incurred her displeasure for his habit of eating sparely.

His great-uncle set down his empty coffee cup. "Time enough to be off when your wound is fully healed."

"It's sufficiently mended, thanks to your ministrations. I hardly feel it."

"You are limping still and you've not yet tried to ride." The rector waved away the coffee pot Aggy was holding poised over his cup, his mild gaze still on Giff. "No more, I thank you, Aggy. Save it for my nephew."

Giff pushed his cup towards the woman, watching the black liquid splash into it. He was fast acquiring a taste for the bitter brew, though truth to tell he preferred the milder flavour of the China tea he'd grown up with in India.

"At least wait for that fellow of yours to return from his mission," pursued the rector. "And I wish you will give some thought to this notion put forward by Delia."

The thought of his flower girl drew a smile from him. He'd relished her messages. Especially the notion of his having brought excitement into her dull life. Excitement! When he'd put her in danger of death? How like Delia to make light of all they'd gone through. He'd laughed over the ridiculous notion she could ever be dull. What, a female of her courage and capabilities?

As for never forgetting, did she suppose he could forget? As if she thought they must never meet again too. What sort of a creature did she think he was? Accept her saving his life and not find means to see her for the purpose of thanking her? And then there was the suggestion to which his uncle was referring.

"There is much to be said for it, Giffard. I am persuaded you would be safer within society rather than out of it."

Giff grunted. "Hide in plain sight?"

"Exactly so, my dear boy. If it is indeed Piers who seeks your death —"

"There can be no doubt of it, sir. Sattar saw him large as life conferring with those incompetent tools of his."

"Yes, so you told me. But we do not know that he plots your death."

Aggy, busy at the range, turned her head at this, tutting furiously. Giff had been chary of speaking freely before her at first, but the rector's confidence in her discretion soon dissipated his doubts. Besides, the woman had been his nurse, along with his great-uncle's man Wilfred, who was both groom and footman. And indeed everything else where a man's hand was needed, as far as Giff could judge.

There were only the two servants, and Aggy swore she had kept the village wench who cleaned for her ignorant of his presence in the back room.

"Well, I don't see how else Piers thinks to be rid of me," he said, returning to the point at issue. "In his place, I would take no chances."

"If that is what you believe, all the more reason to make your appearance in public."

"How? As Giffard Gaunt, pretender to the Earldom of Baunton? That would be to invite speculation and scandal, sir. I've no wish to become an object of interest. Or infamy, as some would no doubt have it."

"Others may accuse Piers instead. The point, my dear boy, is to be visible. Any disappearance would then occasion remark."

"Yes, if everyone knows my state and my purpose here. But you surely cannot wish for our affairs to be made the subject of gossip, sir?"

"They will be in any event, if you succeed."

"If?" Giff eyed him, a forkful of beef poised in the air. "You doubt I can do it?"

The rector sighed. "I'm torn, Giffard, if I am honest. While I am ready to espouse your cause, I cannot but feel for Piers. I could wish Matthew Favell had sent to me as well as to your father. I might have averted this sorry battle between you."

A growling resentment overtook Giff. "You don't believe me, do you?"

A gentle smile came his way. "Oh, yes, I believe you. You have a great look of your poor mother, Giffard."

The pang was immediate and acute. "You knew her well?"

"I baptised her, my dear boy. And watched her grow. I was very fond of Flora. Her conduct was reprehensible, but I could not wholly blame her for running away from Henry." His tone hardened. "Your father was a pompous prig with decided views on women's place, and I have no doubt he made her life a misery. She was a deal better off with Favell, whom she should have married in the first place."

"She told me her father forbade her to think of him."

"Was it so? I admit I was surprised when she married my nephew. I had thought it a case between Matthew and Flora." His gentle smile came. "One sees a great deal more from the pulpit than one's flock supposes."

Giff was tempted to pursue the theme, but his mother's demise, though several years past now, was still too raw for him to hear of her early life with equanimity. Besides, it put him no further forward.

"Well, I'm grateful for your support, sir, but —"

"My support will not help you prove your claim. If you would go and see Hammersley —"

"There's no point, sir. As you said, I have no proof. I must suppose Piers has destroyed the letters from my stepfather. Else he would not have taken my place in all but name."

The rector brought his hand down, slapping the table, his voice turning sharp. "I've told you, your father is to blame. He treated Piers as if he was his own son. Once you were thought to be dead, there was nothing ill in Piers trying for the title. He is next in line."

Bitterness rose up in Giff. "No doubt my father would have been glad of my death."

"You have no reason to say so. Do you suppose Henry took your disappearance tamely? Searches were made. Enquiries pursued. Agents sent hither and yon. He spared no pains. Not to recover Flora, but to find his heir. She had no right to take you with her, and that even I could not forgive."

"Well, I'm glad she did." Defiant, Giff stared his great-uncle out. "If I fail, I have a life in India. I may return there and pursue my stepfather's business interests. Indeed, I am not sure but what I'd prefer it. I am not enamoured of what I've seen of this England of yours."

"Yours too, Giffard. This is your home."

"Never." A stray memory of a mad ride through a forest caused him to amend this. "At least, not yet."

The rector forced his attention back. "But will you remain, Giffard? You are safe here, for a time at least."

Giff took another swallow of his coffee and set down the cup, pushing away his plate and throwing the cook a grin. "To be fattened up by Aggy? You'll have an idle pig on your hands."

Aggy simpered and chuckled, the frills on her mob cap wobbling. "Never fear, young sir. You'll not easily empty my larder."

"Giffard, attend to me, I beg of you! This is serious."

He gave his great-uncle a wry look. "I'm not likely to forget."

"At least promise you will await your man. If he discovers where your pursuers are quartered, as he said he would, you will be better placed to evade them."

So much was true. But nothing had been seen of Sattar for several days and Giff was beginning to be anxious, if he was honest. If those rogues had spotted him, or realised his connection to their quarry...

Shying away from the possible consequences, Giff told himself his elderly Indian henchman was too fly to be taken unawares. None knew better than he how to vanish into his surroundings. He'd taken to wearing European clothes so as to remain inconspicuous, hiding his brown complexion under a battered slouch hat with a broad brim. Sattar would return.

Giff looked back at his great-uncle's anxious features, surprised to find affection within himself as well as gratitude. "Very well, sir. I'll trespass upon your hospitality a little longer, since you insist."

Unless he was driven to go hunting down his henchman instead. Where the deuce was he?

Sattar surprised him late the same evening, sliding into the Reverend Gaunt's study where both men were closeted, engaged in a game of chess. With the windows and doors shuttered against the night, it was secure enough, his great-uncle decided, for Giff to emerge from his hidey-hole and give him the pleasure of his company, as he put it. Giff suspected the rector hoped a glass of brandy and a diverting game would hold him sufficiently entertained not to be fidgeted into leaving.

Concentrated on the board set between the two chairs by the fire, Giff did not hear the door nor notice his servant's presence until a shadow fell across the pool of light falling from the candelabrum on the mantel.

He jerked upright, startling his uncle into turning his head. "Sattar!"

"It is indeed I, sahib," came the deep voice.

Giff glanced towards the closed door. "How the devil did you get in?"

"The woman let me in by the kitchen. She said you were in here."

The Reverend Gaunt found his tongue. "Gracious me, I thought Aggy had gone to bed!"

Sattar had no answer to this. His eyes strayed to Giff's left leg. "Your wound, sahib?"

"Much better, thanks to my uncle."

Sattar turned to the rector and executed a bow, setting his palms together. "My thanks to you, reverend sir."

"None are needed," returned his uncle, smiling.

"This boy needs such a one as you. It is good you have succeeded in holding him in this place. I feared to find him gone, reckless boy as he is."

"That's right. Abuse me to my uncle, old sobersides."

But the rector was laughing. "A worthy guardian, my dear boy. Sattar, is it? You are very welcome here. Will you take a seat? Brandy?"

Sattar pulled up a straight chair, but lifted his hand palm up. "It is not my habit, reverend sir. I drink nothing."

"Nothing but tea." Giff waved his henchman to be seated. "You shall have some after you report." He looked across at his uncle. "We won't raid Aggy's precious store, sir. Sattar will make it himself. He goes nowhere without his own supply and we are well stocked."

His uncle stared. "You brought tea?"

Giff grinned. "A crate of the stuff. My father — or rather, my stepfather, but I've long thought of him as my father — imports the tea from China."

"Good heavens above! Favell made his money in tea?"

"Tea is but a side line. His main interest is in the cotton trade. I will tell you all, but let me hear what Sattar has to tell me."

The rector looked immediately conscious. "Yes, forgive me. I am as anxious as you for good news."

Sattar shook his head, setting his long hair looping into his lean cheeks. He wore it tied back, lacking his turban, but it must have loosened as he rode. "That I cannot give, for the news I have is bad."

Giff's muscles tensed. "Say it!"

"You remember, sahib, it was my design to follow these rogues?"

"When you came to me last, yes. Was it the fellow Sam hanging about here?"

"I know not the man's name, but I knew him for the same with the evil eye. The other with him was of the village, I think. Him I did not recognise."

"But you followed Sam? I take it he left here?"

Sattar nodded. "Within a day. He remained one night, watching."

"The rectory?" His great-uncle's tone was both sharp and apprehensive.

"It is so, reverend sir. How he knew my master was here, I know not, but this house he watched."

Impatience gnawed at Giff. "And then?"

"He broke his fast and then rode away. I followed. He met with the other at a village perhaps five miles distant. I could not get close enough to hear them, but together they rode again."

"Did you find where they live or lodge?"

"No, sahib, for they rode to this place near to the sea. I have learned the name. Weymouth, it is called."

Ice slid down Giff's back. "Weymouth? The deuce! Delia is there!"

"That whom you brought here, sahib. It is so."

His uncle was looking perfectly horrified. "But what could they want with Delia? What should take them there?"

Giff's mind was already streaking ahead. "The fellow Barney must have followed you, sir. They know I had Delia up before me and that she rode here with me. I see it all, damn their eyes! They are not such fools as I took them for. Sam stayed here to keep an eye on me and sent the other to see where you took her."

"But, gracious heaven, why, Giffard? How can it possibly serve them to —? Lord above, will they seek to harm her?"

"I think not." Grimness entered Giff's tone. "They suppose, and rightly, that I will follow her there."

"You had that intention?"

Giff bridled. "Did you suppose I should not seek to thank her? She saved my life!"

Sattar's hand was on his arm. "Sahib, wait! You have not heard all."

Giff turned his eyes on his henchman, his insides roiling. Whether fear for Delia or anger was uppermost he could not have said. A curse on the rogues! Was it not enough he had put the wench in danger of her life once already?

"You do not attend to me, sahib!"

Giff drew a hard breath and let it out, striving for calm. "Go on."

"Believing you tied here by your wound, sahib, I took opportunity to remain and to watch. Enough taverns are there, and I found one out of the way near where these men took lodging."

"Well?"

"I think they seek only to keep watch on the woman. They know where she lodges with the old one. One watches there and follows. Then he gives way to the other, turn and turnabout."

"They spy on her all the time?"

"It is so. They cannot enter where she goes, for she moves with those of station, like the white sahibs and their womenfolk at home. But they wait and follow."

"Waiting for me to show up."

The rector exclaimed, but Giff hardly heard him. He burned with rage and remorse both. Was this his cousin's doing? On the thought, he turned back to Sattar, interrupting his great-uncle's flow.

"Have they met with my cousin? Is he in Weymouth too?"

The old man's eyes raked him. "Not so. I saw him not. Nor did these meet with him in my sight."

"Could you have missed it?"

"It is possible, sahib. But also is it possible the first man met with this cousin before he met with the fellow Sam."

"Yes, for Piers may have instructed them to use Delia for a decoy."

The rector leaned across the table between them. "What do you intend, Giffard?"

A snort came from Sattar. "He will go chasing the tiger, reverend sir, as he always does. No matter that you and I may warn of danger. Even Master Favell could not curb his reckless ways, foolish boy."

Giff ignored him, but he reckoned without his great-uncle.

"Giffard, I beg you to think well before you run your head into a noose."

"Do you expect me to let it go? They are menacing Delia!"

"No, they are awaiting your coming. You said so yourself. Will you oblige them? And Piers, if indeed this is his doing?"

Giff smiled and his uncle recoiled.

"Good God, boy, you look a very devil!"

"That he is, reverend sir. Sahib, this is no time to have the devil in you!"

Determination hardened in Giff's heart. "It's the very time. Don't fret, Uncle. I have a trick or two up my sleeve yet."

The expression in Captain Rhoades's face was sceptical, and Delia could not blame him.

"You've seen those fellows here, ma'am?"

"No, as I told you, I cannot say I recognised either. But the suspicion crossed my mind with this incident of the rowboat. And since you were called in, I felt I should mention it."

"But do you have any grounds to suppose these same fellows were in the boat?"

Delia began to wish she had not requested a moment of his time. She would sound decidedly foolish speaking of intuitions and the horrid feeling of being watched she'd experienced several times now.

It had been not she, but Miss Watkinson who chose to report the incident to the militia captain. A redoubtable creature of mature years, she'd been prominent among the bathers the other morning, notwithstanding her well-padded and bosomy figure which she shrouded in a billowy garment. Delia rather admired her for stoutly continuing to do as she chose despite the unkind ridicule she attracted. She was voluble in her complaints and led a coterie of ladies in the initial protest to Mr Rodber, the Master of Ceremonies.

He had expressed great concern, bringing the matter up with the town's justices, but Miss Watkinson was not satisfied.

"We need these miscreants laid by the heels. I refuse to have my morning bathe curtailed in this fashion. It is too bad. Why, the season has barely begun."

On the warpath, to the general entertainment of the company gathered in Weymouth for the summer, she sent for the militia. Lady Matterson seized the opportunity to beard the captain.

"Never mind all this nonsensical lamentation, sir. A piece of work about nothing! What news have you of those fellows who waylaid us on the highway?"

None, was the answer, much to her chagrin. But Delia, on sudden impulse, waited for her aunt's attention to be distracted and begged the captain to go apart with her for a moment. But the business was proving difficult.

Delia changed tack. "You will think me fanciful, I dare say, but I have once or twice felt here as if I was under scrutiny."

The captain's features relaxed into a near grin. "I dare say, ma'am. You are, if I may say so, youthful and pretty enough to draw such looks."

Flushing a little, Delia waved a dismissive hand. "I don't mean in that way. I meant in the way of being spied upon."

His brows rose. "Why should you think anyone might wish to spy on you, Miss Burloyne? And common footpads? Such men don't commonly come after the people they've sought to rob. What possible reason could they have?"

A cogent reason indeed, but Delia could not speak of it. It was obvious the captain thought her foolish beyond permission. Irritation claimed her. "They were not robbers, sir. You know very well they were chasing one of their own, or so we supposed."

"Then they've no reason to be hanging around in Weymouth."

They had if they thought Giff might seek her out. But she could hardly say so. It was the only logical explanation for their presence in the town, if Sam and Barney were indeed here. The advent of the captain had seemed an ideal opportunity to be rid of the whole suspicion. Only Delia could not tell him the truth. She tried one more throw.

"Will you at least search the place, sir? After all, you've not found any trace of them elsewhere."

He reddened. "Not for want of looking, Miss Burloyne. It's my belief they are long gone." He glanced away and stiffened. "As must I be too."

Delia followed where he'd looked and saw her aunt approaching. Heavens, she'd want to know what they were talking of!

Captain Rhoades executed a small bow. "Your servant, ma'am."

He made good his escape, marching off towards the door that led to the vestibule of the Assembly Rooms where the exchange was taking place.

Delia watched him go and turned to face Lady Matterson, thinking fast. "I was giving him a more accurate description of those men, Aunt Gertrude."

Her aunt snorted. "The man's an incompetent fool. If I don't miss my guess, he'll do nothing to settle Miss Watkinson's mind either. Not that I hold with this rebellion of hers, idiotic woman."

But in the late afternoon, when they left the Rooms to return to Mrs Tuckett's house for dinner, Delia was gratified to catch sight of two militiamen clearly engaged in scouting the area. As she crossed the street, supporting her aunt, she saw one uniformed individual accost a rough-looking fellow heading towards the beach from the Esplanade.

"It looks as if the captain is making an effort after all," she observed, drawing her aunt's attention with a pointing finger.

Lady Matterson huffed a little. "Much good may it do him. Does he suppose they are waiting about to be discovered?"

Delia could have said much, but she held her peace. If she had not been able to see the owners of the eyes she was convinced were watching her, how would the captain's men find them?

As they dined on a roasted fowl accompanied by stewed cucumbers and pickled French beans, she toyed with the notion of sending to St Michael's in Stepleton, begging the rector to warn Giff to stay away from this place. But if his enemies were indeed watching her, she dreaded giving any sign that she might be in contact with him. She could send Sally to the post office with a letter. But who was to say they were not also watching her maid?

The best she could hope for was that Giff would not think of coming anywhere near Weymouth. Indeed, when she thought about it, there was no reason for him to do so. If those ruffians supposed there was more to their relationship than a casual encounter, they would very soon learn their mistake.

Delia had reason to be glad of the presence of the militia over the next couple of days. She was conscious of no eyes and her nerves settled. On the second day, Miss Watkinson declared her intention of resuming her morning bathe and her acolytes clustered around, exclaiming and debating until Lady Matterson loudly reminded the company that tomorrow was Sunday.

"Then we will swim again on Monday," declared Miss Watkinson. "Will you join us, Miss Burloyne?"

Delia, in attendance at her great-aunt's side while that lady played at casino with two of her cronies, had taken no part in the discussion. "I shall be glad to, ma'am, if my aunt permits." She turned to Lady Matterson, half expecting a veto.

"Certainly, child. I always thought it a piece of nonsense to be making such a fuss all for a mere rowboat."

Miss Watkinson bridled, but chose not to lock horns on this occasion, instead turning back to her herd of sheep. "Then I think that settles it, ladies. We bathe on Monday, come what may." She nodded to Aunt Gertrude. "We will meet in church, Lady Matterson."

It had not taken long for Delia to discover the rivalry existing between her aunt and the maiden battle-axe who clearly fancied herself a social leader in Weymouth. Miss Watkinson was apt to instigate pleasurable outings and harry those attending.

missed her maid, who went off with alacrity, and was
to enter the church when a rough-looking fellow
nearby caught her attention. Something about the set
ce looked familiar, although he was slouching against
the corner, a wide-brimmed hat pulled down over
that she could not see his face. It might be either
se ruffians, for all she knew.

e feeling she'd not had for a while overcame her
the wretch watching her? A shaft of sheer fury went
. This was not to be borne!

thinking of the wisdom of what she did, Delia
ftly towards him and halted a couple of feet away.
llowing me again? How dare you! If you think to
d by it, you may think again. Your quarry is not
ll never come. You may tell your master I said so
is disgraceful persecution!"

had stiffened at her approach. As she ended her
sed his head and one hand reached to push up the
at.

t through Delia, and her limbs turned to water.

"As if she seeks to supersede Mr Rodber," scoffed Lady Matterson.

"But why, Aunt, does it trouble you? It's not as if you attend such excursions."

"I'd rather sit on a cactus! But I've no doubt she will inveigle you into going, dratted woman." She pointed her fork at Delia across the table. "If you fail to find a husband, Delia, I hope you will not emulate Miss Watkinson."

"In what way, Aunt? Not that I've any intention of so doing." The reflection that since meeting Giff she'd not thought of matrimony passed through her mind, but she banished it.

"Oh, she makes a fetish of her spinsterhood. Extolling her freedom, if you please. As if we had not all seen how she tried for years to ingratiate herself with every bachelor who came near the place."

Delia could have blushed for her former self. Until the vicar's niece, Edith, had advised her to do otherwise when she was staying with her friend Jocasta last year, she'd done exactly that. Inwardly cringing, she could not help a flash of relief she'd been cured of such conduct before she ran into her adventuresome prince. Not that she was foolish enough to hope for anything in that direction. But at least she'd not disgraced herself.

"I can safely promise you that I won't emulate Miss Watkinson in any way at all, Aunt."

"No, and she wouldn't dare to try and draw you into her circle, thank the Lord. Though I would be loath to stop you from enjoying any excursions she may arrange. Galling she might be, but she is indefatigable in that line and I most certainly won't allow my prejudice to curtail your pleasures."

Disclaiming any desire to go on excursions proved fruitless.

"Nonsense, child. You must at least cross to the Isle of Portland. And you will like to visit the castle, I dare say. You young females are always enchanted by ancient ruins. Though why a pile of broken stones and half fallen walls should be romantic I have never understood."

Nor Delia, if it came to that. Nothing could be romantic to her now, if the truth be told. All pretensions to romance had been superseded by a single day of breathless excitement in her humdrum life.

Sunday dawned overcast and chilly, threatening rain. Lady Matterson took one look out of the window and declared her intention of remaining in bed for the morning.

"Her ladyship can't abide a dull day at the seaside," said Miss Pegler upon giving Delia the news.

"I expect she feels cheated by nature." Amused, Delia asked if she might pop in to see her great-aunt when she'd finished breakfasting. "I must ask her permission to go to church without her. Are you taking her in a tray, Peggy?"

"I've already done so, miss. In truth, I suspect my lady is a little worn down. She won't admit it, but she finds the daily round here a trifle tiring these days."

"I'm not surprised, Peggy. I'm half exhausted myself already."

It was evident, when Delia presently went into her aunt's bedchamber, that the elderly maid had gauged the matter correctly. Lady Matterson, who was partaking of rolls and tea, looked worn, her face a trifle grey. The weather clearly provided a convenient excuse for a rest.

Concerned, Delia could not refrain from enquiry. "You look peaky, Aunt Gertrude. Are you sure you are not still suffering from that knock on the head?"

A languid hand dismissed the lacked its usual bite. "Nothing enough." A small sigh was a "Well, perhaps a little under signify."

"I'm minded to call in Doct

"Don't you dare! I won't prescribing one of his foul tas rest won't cure, Delia, don't f

Perching on the edge of th back of her hand to her aunt at least."

"Of course I've no fever.

"A couple of rolls? Tha There was no fish, but Mr could you fancy a slice of k

Lady Matterson rolled l fuming, girl? Pegler will m I shall do very well. Fe yourself!"

"What, at St Mary's? hope the sermon is shor

"Dreadful child! Mak you dare tell anyone it me from venturing fort

Thus adjured, Delia went out with Sally t door. Once the comp escorts enough. She v Matterson, and a few she got there.

She dis just abou loitering of his star the wall a his eyes s one of tho

The eeri again. Was through he

Without crossed swi "Are you f get any go here and wi and cease th

The figure tirade, he rai brim of his h

Shock swe "Giff!"

CHAPTER SEVEN

Lifting a finger to his lips, Giff glanced swiftly about. They were temporarily alone. He seized Delia's arm. "Come out of sight!"

She did not resist, but a frantic whisper reached him. "What are you doing here? You shouldn't have come! Those men are looking for you!"

"I know it," he returned, hustling her around the side of the church and out of sight. He drew her into the shadows between two windows. He'd experienced the oddest leap of pleasure in his chest when his flower girl finally appeared, but he came under fire before he could open his mouth.

"Giff, are you mad coming here? If you knew Sam and Barney were in the area — though how you should I can't fathom! — what possessed you to set foot in the place? I had almost written, but I was too afraid they would take note of it."

He could not suppress a grin. "Is this all you have to say to me? I wasn't sure of my welcome, but I didn't expect to have a peal rung over me the instant you saw me."

Consternation flooded Delia's face and she reached out both hands, which he took without hesitation, holding them hard. "Oh, I am glad to see you indeed! Can you doubt it? But you shocked me, you wretch!"

"No avoiding that. I meant to accost you, and it was bound to come as a surprise."

"Surprise? You're lucky I didn't swoon!"

He released her, laughing. "My plucky flower girl? No chance of that."

Her gaze flicked over him, dropping to his leg. A frown came. "Your wound! Is it mended? Did you ride? Oh, how could you be so reckless?"

He threw up his eyes. "Don't you start! I've heard enough of my recklessness from Sattar. Not to mention my great-uncle."

"Sattar?"

"My Indian servant. You've not met him yet, but he's seen you."

Delia's eyes widened. "What, you mean he's the one who was watching me?"

"He was watching the men who were watching you."

To his surprise, Delia let out a breath of sheer and obvious relief. "Then I wasn't imagining it. Thank goodness! I'd begun to think I was being fanciful, and Captain Rhoades clearly thought so, though he did have his men search the town. I saw them questioning a rough-looking fellow the other day."

"Who the devil is Captain Rhoades?"

"He's the militia captain here, but why are you growling at me?"

Giff had not realised how his voice had changed, though he was conscious of a burn in his chest. "I don't know. Didn't realise I was growling. What does this militia captain have to do with you, I'd like to know?"

Delia eyed him in frowning puzzlement. "Did your uncle not mention him?"

"When?"

"Well, he must have told you what happened when we were on our way back to Weymouth."

Giff regarded her in frowning silence, thinking back. A vague memory surfaced. "I do recall his speaking of it, but my head was none too clear."

e went, but with lagging steps, and glanced back. He threw
fterthought at her before he could think what he was
g.

d don't go hobnobbing with that damned militia captain,
know what's good for you!"

nses in total disarray, Delia slipped into the church and
o the nearest pew, only half aware of faces glancing her
e pastor did not pause in his oratory, which rang loudly
through the vaulted and pillared interior to drown out
ounding murmurs and her own thudding heart.

sudden presence and the brief exchange felt even
e a dream than their forest encounter. To see him here!
uch a guise. To think he was at this moment slipping
he streets of Weymouth. To where?

ad he said? An Indian servant had told him she was
He came for her! A bubble of elation set her
all over.

to recall what they'd spoken of in those brief stolen
Heavens, she'd said nothing she'd have wished to
ad complained of her ringing a peal over him and
. Instead, she could have told him how she'd missed
adfully. How he'd spoiled her for any other man.
she'd met here could in any way oust him from her

vens, what was she thinking? Of course she could
him any of that. Where had it all come from? She
him, and yet his abrupt eruption back into her life
er to overset her completely. Oh, but how crazy
me at all! He *was* reckless. And what in the world
aying he would confront Piers? Where and how?

"They were searching for me, Giff. My aunt's maid sent for
the militia once she had ascertained that my aunt was not
severely hurt."

The burn died down. "Oh, and this captain was in charge?"

"Yes. And the other day they sent for him here because two
men in a rowboat came close where we ladies were bathing."

An image of her slithering through the waves unclothed leapt
into his head and became riveted there. With difficulty he
forced his attention on to what Delia was saying.

"I wondered at the time if it was Sam and Barney, but I don't
think it could have been. Only I seized the chance to try and
persuade Captain Rhoades at least to search the town. And it
worked, Giff, for I haven't felt them watching me now for two
or three days."

He snapped back to the danger still confronting him.
"They're not gone."

Apprehension flickered in her gaze. "How do you know?"

"Sattar has them under observation. They're hiding out in
their lodging."

She seized his arm in a painful grip. "They could have seen
you! Oh, Giff, I wish you had not come!"

He set his hand on hers. "And I hoped you'd be pleased to
see me."

"Of course I'm pleased." She released her grip, snatching her
hand away. "But I'm scared too. I can't bear the thought of
them succeeding."

"Devil a bit. Even if they saw me, they'd not recognise me.
You didn't."

She gave an odd sort of laugh. "No. I thought you a very
ruffian."

He bared his teeth at her. "Perhaps I am."

She made no answer, surveying his unshaven cheeks and the spotted neckerchief as if she sought to memorise his features anew. "You haven't answered me about your wound."

A husky note in her voice caught at his senses. A strong desire to caress her surprised him. He suppressed it, forcing his concentration back. "It's healing well. I hardly feel it."

Her brows drew together. "You were limping. I saw it."

"No, you didn't. You were too dazed to notice anything when I brought you round here."

"Well, I've remembered now, so I must have noticed."

"Delia, my leg is perfectly fine," he said with finality.

She gave a little sigh. "I must accept that, I suppose. But you haven't explained why you ventured here, especially knowing the enemy was in the area."

A perfectly ridiculous feeling of chagrin entered in. Giff tried to ignore it, but it would not be contained. "Why do you think I came, foolish wench? To make sure those fellows did not menace you, of course."

"They didn't menace me, you idiot man! They're waiting for you. And you have to do exactly what they hoped for. You really are the limit, Giff! Why could you not stay away?"

Her indignation warmed him. He grinned. "I wanted to thank you for saving my life."

Delia rolled her eyes. "By putting your life back in danger?" Her voice became urgent. "You must go away again at once!"

Giff drew himself up. "I've no intention of going away. I'm going to confront Piers."

"Well, you won't because he's not here."

"He's staying in a village close by."

She gasped, looking horrified. "No, Giff! You've got to hide!"

"I can't keep on hiding. I have to end this."

"Yes, by getting yourself killed! Oh, pr[a] Giff!"

He was gratified by her vehemence a[n] not hesitate to throw it back at her. suggested it, or so my uncle said."

"What are you talking about? I sugg danger?"

He relented. "Not precisely. You'll [

She seized both arms this time. "I you to be safe."

"Oh, there's no danger, Delia, do[

"No danger? He wants you dead,

"He'll not get his wish. It was that day. And Piers must know Time I changed my tactics."

Delia let go, eyeing him in peculiarly gratifying. "What do [

He could not resist teasing. over-anxious flower girl." H[briefly to his lips. "I must appearance in church."

"Are you going back to St[

"No, I told you. I'm stayi took her by the shoulder["Go, Delia!"

She hesitated, looking b eyes he knew an impulse would not do at all.

"Are you real?"

He was surprised int[I'm real, you daft wenc[

Did he mean at gunpoint? Was he thinking to fight the man? *Oh, Giff, what are you about?*

Her mind threw images across her inner eye: of his unshaven and mobile countenance, his snarl of bared teeth, his smile, his lifted eyebrow, his laughter and the growling tone in which he'd asked about Captain Rhoades.

The last sent a flitter down her already unruly veins. She heard again his parting words. She must not hobnob with the captain? But she'd no intention of it, what in the world was he at? Did he suppose she might make a slip and give away his presence in the town? Wild horses would not drag it from her!

No, of course Giff must know that. Then, why had he thrown that warning? If she knew what was good for her, he'd said. No, growled. Just as he'd growled the captain's name when she mentioned it.

Heat flooded her as the truth dawned. Giff was jealous! His attitude was possessive. *My* flower girl, he'd called her. As if he owned her.

He does own you.

That voice again! Delia banished it. Such nonsense. Giff was a fugitive. And if she was not careful, he'd be a dead fugitive.

She reviewed the thought. She? No, she'd meant he — Giff. He must be careful. Except that he was anything but. She drew an unsteady breath. The truth now, Delia. She'd meant exactly that. *She* must take care of him, for the wretch would not take care of himself.

But how? What could she do? She must save him. *She must.*

Feeling feverish, she strove to calm her mind. Her attention focused on the parson and she realised she'd been looking directly at the pulpit without seeing the man. He was droning on still and his words came through.

"Be strong and courageous. Do not be afraid or terrified because of them, for the Lord your God goes with you; he will never leave you nor forsake you."

Strong and courageous? Yes, and calm. Be calm, Delia. She listened to the preacher, trying to keep her mind from flitting back to Giff. Her breathing eased in a moment, and she was able to think a little more clearly. She reviewed what Giff had said. He meant to confront Piers, but he had preparations to make. What these might be, Delia had no notion. But it did not matter. It gave her a little time.

He must not be seen in Weymouth by those horrid creatures. They'd been kept at bay by the presence of the militia, but these were gone now.

Then her first task must be to get them back. Which meant sending for Captain Rhoades. A sliver of apprehensive excitement shot through her at the thought of going against Giff's express prohibition. But she must not waste time wondering how he would react. She was doing it for him, after all.

Next, she must find out all she could about this wretched Piers. How could she have neglected to do so before? She'd meant to question Aunt Gertrude, had she not? Had she done so? No, she'd wasted her energies worrying about being spied upon, about whether to send to Stepleton, and dreaming of Giff when she ought to have been working on his behalf. Really, she was as careless as he. Well, not quite that, because no one could be as reckless and stupid as Giff when it came to doing what any fool could see must put him in danger of his life. Well, she was not going to emulate him. She would act with caution and purpose.

Thus determined, she fended off Miss Watkinson's enquiry about her tardy arrival once the sermon was finally over. She had no time to waste on that nonsense.

"My aunt did not care to venture forth in this weather, and I had to see her settled before I left."

"She is not indisposed, I trust?"

The eager note did not escape Delia and she recalled Lady Matterson's instructions, though they seemed far from important now. "Not at all. She can't abide the rain, you must know."

Miss Watkinson seemed intent upon accompanying her as they turned towards the Assembly Rooms. "Oh, I understand how she feels. Though I think the sun is peeping through, do not you?"

Delia gave a cursory glance at the overcast sky. "It will have to clear fully before my aunt will venture out today, I fear."

It occurred to her that she might with advantage use Miss Watkinson's besetting sin. She considered herself an authority, did she not? Then let her prove herself.

"You must know the area round about very well, Miss Watkinson?"

The woman simpered. "Indeed, Miss Burloyne. I flatter myself I have few rivals in an intimate knowledge of the environs of Weymouth."

"And its inhabitants too, I imagine," pursued Delia, adopting the sycophantic note that used to be her stock in trade with gentlemen before she learned better.

"Oh, my dear, there is scarcely anyone I don't know in these parts." Miss Watkinson's round cheeks coloured a little as she dropped her voice. "I don't like to boast of it, but even His Majesty has given me a nod once or twice when walking upon the Esplanade. I've seen it from the corner of my eye, for naturally I would not dream of the presumption of looking at him directly."

Amused, despite her avowed mission, Delia made sure to look impressed. "You are honoured indeed, Miss Watkinson." But she must deflect the creature's attention. "I suppose the gentry living in the vicinity don't come to stay here, or do they?"

"Not if they are close enough to make a daily excursion of it, but indeed it would be difficult to make the most of the amenities if one did not stay in the town. An early morning swim, for example."

"Of course, yes. I had not thought. Then I dare say we may expect Lord Baunton to arrive at any moment," Delia ventured, holding her breath.

Miss Watkinson's steps slowed as she turned to gaze into Delia's face.

"Lord Baunton? If you mean Piers Gaunt, he is not Lord Baunton, for all he has possession of Waldiche Keep."

A pitter-patter started up in Delia's bosom and she hoped she was not blushing. "Is that his home? Is it far? I'd heard him mentioned as living close by."

"Close by? No, indeed. Waldiche village is some way to the west along the coast, you must know." The creature's avid eyes raked Delia's face. "Have you an interest there, Miss Burloyne?"

"Good heavens, no! The name came into my head, that is all. In what connection I heard it I cannot remember."

The woman's curious gaze intensified and Delia could only be glad they had almost reached the Assembly Rooms. As she stepped up to the door, however, Miss Watkinson slipped a hand through her arm and leaned in close, whispering. "Do not take it amiss if I give you a hint, Miss Burloyne."

Pausing in the vestibule, Delia looked round at Miss Watkinson's enlarged features all too close to her own, the eyes full of meaning. "Hint?" Her heart was behaving like a wayward clock. "What do you mean?"

Miss Watkinson cast a quick glance at the stream of gentry coming through, chattering in their twos and threes. "Let us slip into the ladies' retiring room, my dear Miss Burloyne."

Delia was urged willy-nilly up the stairs and into the room set aside for the ladies, with its bench of conveniences, a long mirror and a dressing table. Miss Watkinson lifted her skirts and sat herself down on the bench over one of the holes containing an inset chamber pot.

Delia remained standing, pretending, for the benefit of the hovering attendant, to prink her hair in the mirror. Miss Watkinson did not hesitate to resume their discourse since they were the only ladies present.

"Do you know anything of Mr Gaunt, Miss Burloyne?"

Delia did not turn, as she could see the woman's reflection perfectly well in the mirror. "Nothing at all, Miss Watkinson. Was there something you wished to tell me about him?"

"Well, I am not one to gossip, as you know, but I feel it my duty to enlighten you, as I would any young lady who might be tempted to — shall we say? — set her cap at the man."

Warmth rose in Delia's cheeks. The impertinence of the creature! She allowed her annoyance to show. "I am not hanging out for a husband, Miss Watkinson, whatever you may think."

"Oh, come now, Miss Burloyne, don't be coy. Every young lady must be desirous of securing her future. I myself, before I recognised how much more freedom I must enjoy by remaining single, had an eye to an eligible gentleman. But Piers Gaunt, I must tell you, cannot be so counted."

115

This was too valuable to be set aside. Delia turned as the woman rose from her seat, adjusting her skirts. "Why so? I understood he's an earl, or as good as."

"Oh, dear me, nothing of the sort, dear Miss Burloyne." Miss Watkinson held her hands over the basin for the attendant to pour water over them from the jug. "The matter was everywhere talked of, you must know."

Gripped, Delia stared at the woman, whose attention held on washing her hands. "What do you mean, Miss Watkinson?"

"I am talking of Piers Gaunt's attempt to accede to the earldom." Miss Watkinson made use of the towel the attendant was holding out. "You see, he was not the heir."

"Then who was?" As if she didn't know!

"A cousin, I believe. An old scandal. I do not know the particulars, but it appears the boy was taken out of the country years ago."

"Then if this Piers was not the heir —?"

"How could he try for the title? That is just my point, Miss Burloyne. Since there appeared to be no trace of the heir, Gaunt hoped he might be presumed dead, but the authorities in these matters would not have it so."

Indignation roiled inside Delia, but she suppressed it, feigning only ordinary interest. "Upon what difficulty?"

Miss Watkinson came to the mirror, but she did not do more than glance at her reflection, turning to Delia with an unmistakeable guise of the avid gossip that dwelled within her. Her voice sank to a near whisper. "There is no proof of the heir's demise. What if he were to return?"

What indeed? Delia pretended ignorance. "Well?"

Miss Watkinson's head went up and she cast her eyes to heaven. "Is it not obvious? Imagine the scandal! The wrangles! Why, a wife would never know from one day to the next whether she had even a roof over her head, let alone losing all hope of any potential entitlement to become Lady Baunton. Such a risk, Miss Burloyne! That is why I felt it my duty to warn you."

"My dear Miss Watkinson, I am scarcely in danger. I don't even know the man." She spoke at random. Anything to deflect attention from the reality of her own knowledge when exactly what the creature prophesied had come to pass.

"Yes, but you may meet him, Miss Burloyne, for he has been known to attend assemblies here, and the theatre too. And Piers Gaunt is an extremely handsome young man. It would not be wonderful if you were to favour him."

Never in this world! Let him be as personable as he wished, Delia already loathed the man. Besides, her loyalties were fixed.

"I thank you for the warning, Miss Watkinson, and I shall be upon my guard. Should Mr Gaunt make an appearance, which of course is not certain."

"Yet it is a fascinating tale, do you not think?"

"Oh, quite. Who is — or rather was — the true heir, do you know?"

Miss Watkinson shook her head so that the ribbons on her bonnet quivered. "I only wish I did. Beyond his having been the late Lord Baunton's son, nothing is known about him at all."

Oh, but she knew. A pity Miss Watkinson had no further information, though. She might have gleaned something useful. But that Piers was known in Weymouth was helpful, if alarming. What should stop him making a public appearance? And he knew her by sight, she must suppose, thanks to his henchmen. If he approached her, how should she behave? Pretend ignorance of the whole affair? He would not believe her. He likely supposed her to be wholly conversant with Giff's history. She only wished she knew more.

"Are you ready, Miss Burloyne?"

Recalling her mission, Delia made haste to follow the stout form as Miss Watkinson exited the retiring room. She lost no time in putting her plan into action. "I must say, ma'am, I am far from satisfied about those wretches who watched us bathing the other day."

Looking gratified, the woman broke at once into belligerent protest. "Heavens, yes, Miss Burloyne! I have a good mind to take Captain Rhoades to task."

"I wish you would! What has he done, after all, to apprehend those men?"

"Just so. Nothing at all useful."

"And he's withdrawn his soldiers from the town, you must know."

"I thought I had not seen them about. It will not do. I shall sit down and write him a note on the instant."

Satisfied, Delia encouraged this scheme. At least she was not obliged to send for the man herself. It was not precisely adhering to Giff's prohibition, because she had every intention of bearding the captain herself once he was here. But it could not be classed as hobnobbing.

Not that Giff had any right to dictate her actions. Besides, she was doing it on his behalf.

The thought was fleeting, her attention returning to the possibility of Piers showing his face. Would he do so? He was staying nearby, Giff had said. If he was going to appear in Weymouth, let him do so before Giff had a chance to confront him. Was there any way she could make sure of his advent?

Cogitating, she joined in a game of speculation got up by the younger element, but she remained abstracted. If only she could lure Piers into town, she might prevent the threatened confrontation.

Instead of joining the bathers on Monday morning, Delia opted to accompany Scoley to the beach again in search of fish. She had no real expectation that either of her quarries would make themselves visible to her, but she could not think of any other way to attract notice. Assuming they had not left Weymouth.

Very different were her feelings on this occasion. Instead of cringing at the sensation of being watched, she sought it, darting glances at every male who came within sight.

She cast special attention into shadowed doorways as she walked beside Scoley, flicking glances along side streets and looking back in case she was being followed. It did not make for a comfortable walk, but that could not be helped.

At last the groom gave her a frowning look. "You're fidgety, miss. Are you afeared?"

Delia opted for frankness. "No, indeed. I'm keeping an eye out for anyone who may be watching me."

"Watching you, miss? Why should they be?"

"Goodness, don't you know the militia were searching the place for those ruffians who set upon her ladyship?"

"Yes, miss, and I spoke with one of them militiamen and he said as how the captain don't believe such felons would dare enter the town."

Much the captain knew! But she could not say so. She prevaricated. "That may be so, but I am not convinced."

"But they'd be sticking their heads in a noose, miss, it don't make sense."

Scoley clearly sought to reassure her. Without giving away the truth, she could say no more. "Perhaps you're right and I am needlessly anxious."

"I wouldn't let nothing happen to you, miss, don't worry."

"Thank you, Scoley."

Though what he supposed he could do against the villainous Sam, who did not scruple to fire pistols at random, Delia could not imagine. She was a little afraid of confronting the beast herself, although it was certain Giff's cousin would not risk his bully boys harming her in full view of everyone in the busy seaside town.

Although at this hour of the morning the place was relatively empty. It was blowy and clouds still hung over a somewhat turbulent sea from Sunday's rough weather. The fishermen had not been deterred, however, for several boats were pulled ashore, each attended by a coterie of servants and the hardier among the gentry. Scoley led the way down the beach towards the nearest vessel and the distinct aroma of fish wafted in the air, vying with the salt and seaweed.

"You'd best keep close, miss, if you're nervous."

"I'm not, but I'll stay within your sight, never fear."

Seeing Scoley's attention concentrated upon the fishermen's catch, Delia resumed a surreptitious inspection of each male within distance of being recognised. After she'd mentally discarded a gentlemen of middle years, a couple of youthful pages, a burly bearded fellow who looked like a coal heaver, and a man wearing a leather apron, it dawned on Delia that she was hunting not for Sam or Barney, but for the rough-looking creature who had yesterday turned out to be Giff.

Chiding herself for an idiot, she was yet unable to help the riffle of anticipation that ran along her veins and prompted a little stamping dance in her heart for a moment. Ridiculous.

The last thing she wanted to see was Giff making a target of himself.

The sound of hawking and spitting close by jerked her attention. Without thinking she turned to look behind and nearly reeled in shock. The ruffian Barney was standing a few feet away, bold as brass. She could not mistake the rough and soiled clothing, the unshaven face with its sharp pointed chin and shifty eyes.

He was looking out to sea, but he glanced back at Delia and touched his hand to his slouch hat.

Gracious heaven, was he saluting her? Acknowledging she knew him and not bothering to conceal himself. What in the world did that signify?

Delia looked to the nearby boat where Scoley was haggling with the fisherman. Should she move nearer? But she did not think Barney represented any danger. And wasn't this exactly what she'd been hoping for?

Pulling her cloak close about her, she edged towards the man. He looked alarmed and backed off a bit. So much the better. He had evidently not expected her to confront him.

Delia lifted her chin and beckoned. "Come here, you!"

Barney hesitated, glanced right and left and then pointed to himself.

"Yes, you! Come here!"

With clear reluctance, he shuffled a few steps in her direction. Close enough, Delia decided.

"You're Barney, aren't you?"

He blinked and his eyes slid from one side to the other. "What if I am?"

"I have a message for your master."

Barney's mouth dropped open. "Eh?"

"You heard me." She kept her tone even, but cold. "Tell him, if you please, that I wish to speak to him."

The jaw dropped further. "What?"

"I wish to speak to him," Delia repeated. "In public. Let him visit the Assembly Rooms and find me there."

Barney scratched his head, dislodging the hat. "I dunno, miss."

"Tell him what I said."

A shrug came. "Dunno what you mean, miss."

Delia eyed him with scepticism. "Yes, you do. You are Piers Gaunt's tool, along with your friend Sam."

Both arms came up and Barney shrank back as if to ward off a blow.

Delia pressed her advantage. "It is of no use to pretend."

"I ain't doing nuffing."

"You're watching me. You've been watching me for days, both of you."

He rallied, straightening up and sniffing. "No, I ain't! Dunno nuffing about it."

"Well, if you've any sense — which clearly you haven't or you wouldn't have got close enough for me to recognise you — you'll make yourself scarce. The militia are coming back."

"What's it to me? Ain't my concern."

"I imagine it's very much your concern. I could have you laid by the heels right now, but I won't do it."

He wiped his sleeve across his nose. "Dang me if I know what your lay is, miss."

"You don't need to know. Just give your master my message."

With which, Delia turned away from him and walked swiftly to where Scoley was holding his stringed fish and handing over the necessary coins.

"Not much of a catch today, miss, but I got a couple of sole for her ladyship's breakfast."

Relieved, she realised he'd seen nothing of the recent exchange with the ruffian. "Excellent. Then let us go back."

She looked for Barney as she turned with the groom to retrace their steps, but the fellow was nowhere to be seen. He'd melted away as easily as he'd popped up behind her. Delia could not help a shiver at the memory of her boldness. What had she let herself in for?

CHAPTER EIGHT

Giff shifted this way and that, trying to see himself in the inadequate mirror. Was the blue frock coat too comfortable a fit? Too bad if so. He hated constraining clothes. Were men still wearing double-breasted waistcoats? And was it too decorative with the broad stripes and silver buttons? At least the buckskin breeches could not be faulted, he hoped.

"What do you think?"

From the bedside where he was engaged in folding clothes and packing them in the portmanteau, Sattar glanced up. "I, Sahib? What know I of English fashion?"

"You've eyes in your head, haven't you? Spent days watching the gentry in Weymouth. Will I pass muster?"

His henchman blew out an exasperated breath and laid the green coat down on the bed. "What matters it if you pass, or you pass not? When you are dead, sahib, no one will care."

Giff's gaze was concentrated on the set of his cravat, beset by a suspicion that its folds, along with his costume, would mark him at once for a foreigner. From the little he'd seen, fashion moved a deal faster in England.

His henchman's sour comment brought his head round. "Are you at that again? Piers won't dare touch me if I'm visible among the fashionable."

"A foolish notion, sahib. Where had you it?"

A reminiscent smile curved Giff's mouth. "From Delia. Or rather, not directly. It's what she said to my great-uncle."

"You take now advice from a woman?"

"Delia is no ordinary woman. Not that she'll be any too pleased to see me flaunting about in Weymouth, even though she did suggest I should make a public figure of myself."

"It is well if the memsahib approves not. She will say, as do I, that a seeming accident may befall you at the hands of these rogues as well if you are visible as not." Sattar resumed his packing, grumbling the while. "It is to the walls I speak. There is no use in talking to as stubborn a boy as ever lived."

Laughing, Giff came to him, giving him a buffet on the shoulder. "Rascally old devil! What should I do without you?"

"Why trouble your head, sahib, when you will neither need me nor anyone in the next world?"

Giff ignored this. "Did you find me a decent lodging?"

"It is fair, sahib," said his faithful retainer, abandoning his scolding. "The town is busy. Sahib Favell would approve it not, but it will serve. Two rooms with meals and I may sleep on a truckle bed at your side."

Giff raised an eyebrow at him. "So you can keep a close eye on me, eh?"

"It is fitting, sahib." He cast an austere look upon his charge. "One servant at the least you must have in your train."

True enough, though Giff was not fooled. No doubt these lodging houses catered for servants. Likely in the attics. But it would serve him better to have Sattar to hand.

"You'd best resume your native guise then, my friend. It will suit my story."

He came under instant suspicion from the old man's hard eyes. "What story is this, sahib?"

Giff grinned. "I've arrived from India and I'm looking about me for a suitable residence. My people came from this area. It's close enough to the truth."

"And what reason have you for this choice of a seaside resort?"

The sceptical note was not lost on Giff. "I have that covered, never fear. I picked up a fever on the ship and I need to recuperate."

Sattar shook his head at him. "None will believe such a tale when they know your name."

"They won't know it. At least, Piers will, but no one else. And he's not going to mention it, is he?"

The dark gaze narrowed. "You do this to lure him to come to you?"

"How else am I to confront him?"

His henchman sighed. "Reckless boy! I am wishing Sahib Favell is here to curb you."

"Devil a bit. Papa Matt would be urging me on. He's the one who started me on this quest, as you well know, Sattar. I'd have been content to remain in India, but Matt wouldn't have it so."

Truth was, he'd come to England to appease his stepfather's guilt. Matthew Favell insisted he'd wronged his stepson in removing him from all claim to his true inheritance. At the time, burning with passion for Giff's mother, he confessed he'd cared for nothing but getting her and the boy away. Later, when the first cotton plantation was established and he was solvent and Giff was growing fast, he'd tried to make amends and written to Lord Baunton. But no reply was forthcoming despite several attempts. The news of his father's death had filtered through at last by way of journals from England. But by that time, as far as Giff could ascertain, Piers had already taken possession of the Keep and was trying to stake a claim to the title too.

If the fellow had been graceful enough to acknowledge the heir's rights when Giff first set foot in Waldiche Keep, he had been of a mind at that time to forgo the earldom. He'd likely have taken the necessary steps to secede, or whatever it was one did in these circumstances. Although whether the title would then pass to Piers he had no notion. He was all too ignorant of the law in this regard.

But when Piers hired men to dispose of him, all that changed. It was war, plain and simple. Besides, a man capable of treachery did not deserve to step into his shoes. And lately, he had an added reason to think of making England his home.

With renewed energy, he turned to Sattar. "Are you done packing?"

The last of the pile of clothes, unearthed from his trunks and picked over to fit his scheme, was fast disappearing. Since it was summer, he had no need to augment his wardrobe as yet, though he'd purchased a warmer greatcoat against the occasional dismal day. He was not yet used to the difference in temperature.

"It is done, sahib. Yet I fear me all will avail you naught."

"Then we'll bid my reverend uncle farewell and take ship back to India. Though I confess it would go against the grain to leave my wicked cousin the victor."

Sattar shot him a look, the dark eyes narrowed again. "And the memsahib? She will sail also?"

An unexpected pang smote Giff. His flower girl would balk at being taken half across the world. Or would she? A plucky wench was Delia. What was that she'd said of their brief adventure? A change in her humdrum life? Would she think of India in the same light?

"You go too fast, sahib."

He had forgotten his henchman. Giff stared at him. Too fast? It had not occurred to him to question his own assumptions about his flower girl. What, had he made up his mind already? Had she?

Mentally, he reviewed his forced encounter with her at Weymouth. It had been as if they continued precisely where they left off. Delia anxious for his safety, he as careless of it as Sattar was apt to complain.

He laughed out. "It's not too fast for Delia, my friend, that much I will swear to."

Sattar shook his head at him, but his mouth twitched at the corners. "Foolish boy you are. Mayhap this memsahib will cure you."

"She may try. I'll give her a run for her money before I knuckle under."

Yet the thought of dancing to Delia's piping was oddly attractive. He enjoyed her railing at him, her utter disregard for anything but his potential danger. By God, but she was his already! Too fast? No such thing.

Her last words slipped into his head. *Are you real?*

Giff laughed aloud, gripped by a violent sensation of possession. He'd show her how real he was! Once this was over. No mercy, flower girl!

The library was by no means as extensive as Hatchard's or Hookham's in London, but certainly adequate to fulfil Delia's excuse to get away from the general company — and her too perspicacious aunt. She was restless, beset by anxiety and a sneaking apprehension.

Had she gone too far? What in the world would she say to this Piers if he obeyed her summons? Every time she reviewed what she'd said to the ruffian Barney the other morning, she was beset by qualms. No response had been forthcoming so far, and she'd resumed what passed for normal life in Weymouth in an abstracted mood that drew Lady Matterson's attention.

"What ails you, child? As jumpy as a cat one moment, head in the clouds the next."

Unprepared, Delia could only blink at her while she mentally passed spurious explanations under review, discarding them as fast as she thought of them.

"Don't stare at me like a moonling, girl! What's to do?"

Goaded, she chose denial. "Nothing, Aunt Gertrude."

The old lady bridled. "D'ye think I'm in my dotage? I know what I'm seeing. I could almost believe you were in love."

Delia's heart sputtered into life and her tongue tied itself in knots. "What? I'm not! Love? What are you —? I've never heard such… Really, Aunt, you do talk utter nonsense!"

Lady Matterson regarded her fixedly for several moments, reducing Delia to a flustered wreck. Oh, help! She knew she was blushing, for heat burned in her neck and face. She wanted to put her hands up to hide it, but that would be fatal. She forced herself to a semblance of calm, staring her aunt out.

The old lady's voice softened. "What aren't you telling me, child? Is he hopelessly ineligible, is that it?"

Delia gathered her forces. "There is no one, Aunt Gertrude. I have no notion of what you are talking."

The attack was taking place at the breakfast table, and Delia found her appetite had deserted her. She laid down the forkful of fish and reached for her cup, feeling a measure of calm return as the hot tea slid down.

A surreptitious glance at her great-aunt showed her the older woman's attention was still on Delia, though she'd resumed eating. Would she leave the subject? Her aunt finished the fish and buttered a roll in silence. Delia watched her take a spoonful of blackberry jam and add a measure of it to the roll, her thoughts wheeling.

Lord, if her aunt knew the truth! Giff ineligible? Impossible more like. He was scarcely a suitor for her hand. She'd never supposed he could be. Dreamed of him, yes. But never in the capacity of a husband. As for love…

Here her thoughts failed her, a squeezing sensation in her bosom making it difficult to breathe. Was it love to be fearful for a man's life? To be trying what she could to avert his falling into his enemy's hands? She'd found him a romantic figure from the first. But there was a difference between fantasy and fact. He was half a phantom, appearing out of the blue, turning her life upside down and vanishing again. No, she could not believe in a future with Giff. Once he was safe, she would slip back into the dull existence that was her lot. Her heart dropped at the thought, but rose again when she reflected that she must first ensure his safety.

Her aunt spoke at last, pulling her out of her thoughts. "Very well, child. I will accept your denials for the moment. But you may confide in me at need, Delia. Who knows but I may be able to help you?"

Delia eyed her, wary and a little tempted. But it would not do. Giff was her secret, and she could share him with no one. She'd been obliged to tell Sally of her adventure, but not a word of Giff's return had passed her lips.

"I thank you, Aunt Gertrude, but truly I have nothing to confide."

A sigh escaped Lady Matterson and her eyes dulled. Guilt rushed through Delia and she almost gave in. But in a moment, her aunt resumed her normal manner.

"If you have finished, my dear, we should start for the Assembly Rooms. I am engaged to play whist with Mrs Poynings and Lord Hadlow. Though if I am again paired with Warbleton, I shall be less than pleased."

She did not revert to the subject of the morning, much to Delia's relief. And once out of doors, they very soon encountered others who had likewise enjoyed their breakfast after an early dip and were ready to embark upon the pastimes of the day.

Delia had deposited her aunt in the card room, where her cronies were gathering, and managed to avoid Miss Watkinson, who was haranguing her acolytes into arrangements for an excursion to the ruined Sandsfoot Castle. Delia would doubtless find herself cornered in due course, but she needed breathing space after the quizzing she'd gone through. Slipping away, she had headed for the circulating library, where she found her mind just as jumpy and distrait as Lady Matterson had described.

She wandered along the shelves, picking out volumes at random and flipping them open. But not a word she read made sense.

Had Barney passed on her message? One would think he would do so immediately. Then why had Piers not made any move? Giff said he was staying nearby. The wretched man had only to ride or drive into the town to find her. Or was she too late? What if Giff had confronted him already? Might they have fought? Was Piers injured perhaps? That would prevent his coming. But then what of Giff's safety? A horrid thought surfaced.

He'd been taken!

Delia's heart began to thump, and she stared at the book open in her hands without seeing it. Yes, that must be it. He was captured. Even dead by now. He'd run his head into danger and the villain's men had murdered him!

"Miss Burloyne?"

Delia's heart jerked with violence. She gave a shriek of fright and the book leapt from her hands.

The voice was male and had spoken low near her ear. As she turned, a gentleman was bending to retrieve the book.

"Good heavens, sir, how you startled me!"

He rose and Delia, still breathless, her pulse racing, found she was gazing at an unknown face. It was alien, yet achingly familiar and she at once knew who had accosted her.

"Mr Gaunt!"

He was engaged in straightening the bent pages of the book she'd dropped, but he looked up at this, surprise in his eyes — so like and yet unlike. "You guess correctly, ma'am."

"It's no guess, sir. I can see the resemblance."

His brows rose and his features creased into a fastidious sneer. The similarity to Giff faded. Giff never sneered. "I cannot say I am flattered. However, I see I was not mistaken. You were in his company that day."

Her pulse was still abnormally fast, but Delia hit back boldly. "I should not otherwise have known how to send to you, should I?"

A thin smile curved his lip, fuller than Giff's she saw now. Piers's features were altogether more rounded, without the lean-toned muscle that characterised her prince. Delia doubted he had the same wiry strength or stamina. "You surprised me, Miss Burloyne, I'll give you that."

"Indeed? Why, I wonder? Did you think me an innocent victim in this farce? Why should you suppose your quarry would try to reach me in that case? That is why you've had me watched, is it not?"

His eyes narrowed. "You do favour a direct approach, ma'am."

Delia eyed him, debating her next move. Her pulse was settling and she could think with more clarity. She opted for duplicity, pinning a smile to her lips. "I could think of no other way to be rid of the horrid sensation of being spied upon."

His brows drew together. She'd puzzled him. Would he admit the truth?

"That's why you sent to me?"

"Why else? It's excessively uncomfortable to feel one is being watched. And those creatures of yours managed to evade Captain Rhoades' men."

His frown persisted. "You bewilder me, Miss Burloyne. How much do you know?"

"About what?"

The sneer returned. "Now you are being disingenuous. I much preferred your frankness. Let us not play games, Miss Burloyne. Have you a message for me from my esteemed cousin?"

So that's what he supposed. Very well, if he wanted candour, he could have it. She looked him in the eye. "The message is from me, sir. If you harm Giff, you had best be rid of me too, for I will bring the full panoply of the law down upon you." She had the satisfaction of seeing him thoroughly taken aback and pressed her advantage. "Think carefully before you attempt to silence me, sir. Unlike Giff, I am not without friends or family."

He was still holding the book and he waved it in an airy manner, smiling again. "My dear Miss Burloyne, acquit me. I have no desire to offer you the slightest harm. Nor, I may add, is it my intention to do violence to my cousin."

"Oh? Then why have you hired bully boys to chase him down? Do they not intend violence? Why then did one of them shoot at him? And with me up before him too!"

"That was a mistake, my dear Miss Burloyne." Evidently unperturbed, he ran an eye across the shelves and found the gap, setting the book back in its place.

"A costly mistake, sir, if the bullet had found its mark in me rather than Giff."

He turned, an expression of regret in his face, in which Delia placed not the slightest belief. "Just so, ma'am. I was excessively angered when I heard of it."

"But that did not stop you setting Sam and Barney to spy upon me."

A muscle twitched in his cheek and the smile did not reach his eyes. "You see, it did strike me that my cousin might follow you here, as you surmised. My only desire, however, was to find an opportunity to discuss our unfortunate situation."

And pigs might fly! But Delia refrained from the snort she wanted to make. Better to play along. "Why should you not send to him in that case?"

"My dear Miss Burloyne, if I had his direction, I might do so. He chose not to divulge it."

"And what of the Reverend Gaunt, sir? Is he not related to you? Why did you not ask him?"

"I did. He denied all knowledge of my cousin."

"So you hired those men to find him? A pair of thieving ruffians? Did it not occur to you Giff would suspect them of an ill intention towards him?"

She could not help the sceptical note and knew, by the rigid set of his mouth, that he was perfectly aware of her true sentiments. He made no reply and Delia lost patience.

"Come, sir. Did you not exhort me to stop playing games? You will not persuade me that your ruffians meant no harm to Giff. That was not the first time he'd been obliged to escape them."

The mask slipped a little. The sneering look had bitterness within it. "Yes, a slippery customer is Giffard Gaunt. Yet I think at last he will see sense and take himself off back to India."

Delia frowned. "That's what you want?"

He laughed mirthlessly. "You suspected a more sinister outcome? My dear Miss Burloyne, there are ways of making someone vanish that need not involve violence, you know."

Delia could barely speak for the rush of fury in her breast. She'd wanted him to admit the truth, but her reaction was unexpected. She forced her voice to calm. "Such as?"

"Why, if Giffard does not choose to take ship from choice, I am prepared to arrange his passage for him."

"Willy-nilly, I dare say."

The smile reappeared, this time in genuine amusement, she judged.

"Astute of you, Miss Burloyne. That is the matter in a nutshell."

Could it be so? The reprieve from the threat of Giff's death was balm. Yet Delia found it impossible to believe in this man's sincerity.

"What should stop him returning, even if you did force him aboard a ship?"

"Stowaways, Miss Burloyne, do not in general fare well. I do not think Giffard, without means or assistance, would easily make his way to England from America."

She could not prevent a gasp of shock. He smiled, and Delia almost recoiled. There was true evil in his eyes.

"You could not suppose I would make it easy for him by shipping him back to India? That would indeed be a fool's game."

For a moment, Delia did not answer. Her mind was buzzing and she began to think she'd made an error of judgement. The words flew from her mouth as they entered her mind. "You're telling me this because you want me to warn him off. You think I may have influence with him."

The sneer returned. "Such an impulsive fellow, Giffard. Chivalrous too. I feel sure he will choose an honourable path."

She could not stop the protest. "Honourable? Where is your honour, sir? You are a usurper!"

"Nothing of the kind, ma'am." His voice became a purr. "I have carefully avoided any such accusation, despite the report of my cousin's demise. Do you suppose I will let myself be ousted by this pretender?"

"He's not a pretender! Giff is the heir."

"Or some bastard who thinks to take what is not rightfully his. Which is how Society will see it, should he be so foolish as to make a public outcry."

"Yes, because you'd make it appear so."

"You may count on it. I'll not relinquish what I hold. See that he understands as much."

Unable to think of a suitable retort, Delia could only glare at the man.

His smile mocked her as he executed a graceful bow. "Until we meet again, Miss Burloyne."

Delia watched him walk away towards the library door, beset by a horrid fear her intervention had only made things worse. Piers Gaunt would not easily be bested. He had too much at stake.

CHAPTER NINE

Delia would have welcomed a period of quiet reflection before facing her great-aunt, but the moment she set foot in the Assembly Rooms she was pounced on by Miss Watkinson.

"Miss Burloyne! Just the person I wanted to see. You must promise to go with us to Sandsfoot Castle. One cannot be in Weymouth without seeing the ruins, and I have set up an expedition for tomorrow. If the weather should be inclement, we will postpone it until the day after, but Mr Rodber is confident the weather-wise have it right for sunshine on the morrow. Do say you will come, Miss Burloyne, for we are to be quite a party. We will go in carriages, for there will be enough walking when we get there."

Far too preoccupied to make any objection, Delia found herself committed and at once regretted it. Not that she minded the trip. It would serve for a useful distraction, except for taking her out of Weymouth. Suppose Giff made another of his flying visits and she missed him? Unthinkable. Somehow she must get word to him of his cousin's schemes. If only she knew how.

What if she were to write to the rector? Had he any notion of Giff's present whereabouts?

Her thoughts were interrupted as Miss Leigh accosted her, agog with excitement.

"Is it not romantic, Miss Burloyne, to be visiting the ruins at last? Mrs Dicker has given permission for me to go and I can hardly wait. You are coming, are you not?"

Tugging her attention to the girl, Delia agreed to it. She could not but pity Tabitha Leigh, obliged to fetch and carry for her invalidish relative. She'd seen how Mrs Dicker's complaint made her crotchety and apt to snap.

"I am glad she can manage without you for a while."

The girl blushed. "Oh, she is too amiable to prevent me enjoying myself. She says her maid may replace me for the time."

Did she indeed? Then why was her maid not in evidence more often? But Delia refrained from saying this aloud. "I have yet to gain my aunt's permission," she said instead, "but I'm sure it will be freely given."

A faint hope that Lady Matterson might object died at birth. She was more likely to encourage Delia to go, especially after the breakfast table inquisition. Indeed, it would be fatal to make the slightest suggestion of missing it. Aunt Gertrude would infallibly jump on it as proof of her assertions.

Accordingly, Delia made an effort to appear delighted with the prospect when at last the game of whist came to an end and the plan for the expedition was broached as they crossed the street towards their lodging.

"Oh, I know all about it, my dear. That wretched woman has been buzzing about all day like a raving hornet. No one could fail to have heard her haranguing everyone to join her scheme."

The irascible note was pronounced, and Delia eyed her aunt closely. "Did you lose at whist, aunt?"

"Nothing of the sort. I was partnered with John and we won several rubbers."

"Then what troubles you?"

A piercing eye was trained upon her. "I don't see why I should confide in you, girl, when you won't accord me the same courtesy."

Warmth rose in Delia's cheeks, and she could not prevent the snap in her voice. "I'm sorry you feel that way, Aunt Gertrude."

Lady Matterson's brows shot up. "Hoity-toity! Take that tone with me and I shall know what to do about it, young madam!"

Delia knew she ought to apologise, but her bosom was too full of conflicting emotion to be able to utter the necessary words. In silence, she made to knock on the door, but was forestalled by its opening before she could do so. Miss Pegler waved them in.

"I saw your ladyship from the window. Dinner will be served within the hour, I hear from Mrs Tuckett, my lady, so you may take a rest upon your bed first."

"I have no intention of taking a rest. Bring wine to the parlour, Pegler. Delia, you will accompany me."

Having delivered her orders, Lady Matterson climbed the stairs and swept into the small parlour provided for their use, taking possession of the chaise longue. Once settled, she pointed to the nearest chair. "Sit!"

Sighing, Delia complied. Her rebellious mood was fading. How was she to evade the inevitable questions? If she'd been accused of distraction at breakfast, she was now ten times as assailed by horrid thoughts. Giff's danger lurked in her bosom like a malignant parasite, but how to get word to him was paramount. She could think of little else.

"We will settle this once and for all," Lady Matterson began.

Delia gathered herself. "I apologise, Aunt Gertrude. I should not have spoken so rudely."

Her hope of diverting the old lady was thwarted at once. "Never mind that. You would not have done so had I not hit a nerve. Come, Delia. It is plain to me you are labouring under considerable stress. If you are constrained by secrecy, tell me so. But don't pretend there is nothing on your mind. I was not born yesterday."

A crack of somewhat hysterical laughter escaped Delia. "Far from it, Aunt!"

"Well then?"

She was cornered. Drawing a breath for courage, she looked her aunt in the eye. "I am indeed pledged to secrecy, ma'am."

Lady Matterson at once looked perturbed. She hesitated, fidgeted restless fingers and then blew out a concentrated breath. "Fiddle-de-dee! Hoist on my own petard!"

Delia had to laugh. "I didn't mean it so, ma'am."

Her aunt's lips twitched and there was a gleam in her eye, but she held her countenance. "Well, at least you admit there is something."

Miss Pegler came in with a tray at this point, rather to Delia's relief. Lady Matterson was far too correct to continue the discussion within her maid's hearing. She sipped at the glass of claret while Peggy turned to Delia.

"And for you, miss?"

"I'll take half a glass, if you please. My head is not nearly as hard as my aunt's."

That did draw a crack of laughter from the old lady. "Namby-pamby creatures, you young gels today. We learned how to take our wine in my day."

"Yes, and a good deal more besides, I don't doubt," Delia retorted, glad of the excuse to change the subject.

"I grew up in a robust age, child. A trifle rough and ready perhaps, but we knew how to live."

Though she'd heard ad nauseam of the courtly world, the flirtatious and rollicking pastimes and the alleged derring-do of her great-aunt's early life in the previous century, Delia was only too eager to encourage her in reminiscence of the past if it would keep her off the present.

"Yes, you have said I don't know how many times, Aunt, that we are all tame by comparison and I fear you are right. If I am to judge by my dull life at least."

At once she realised she'd erred. Peggy had left the room and Lady Matterson pounced.

"Not so dull on our journey here, was it?"

"True."

"And you've been peculiar ever since, Delia."

Her cheeks warmed, but she rallied. "In what way peculiar?"

"Behaving like a cat on a hot bakestone half the time and dreaming away the other half."

Delia took a fortifying sip of wine and did not answer, avoiding her aunt's too knowing eye.

"It's not that wretch of a captain, is it? The militia fellow?"

Delia almost spat out the wine. "Good heavens, no!"

"Thank the Lord for that! What your mother would say to such a union I dread to think." A frown drew her brows together, and her tone became accusing. "Is it the truth? You went apart with the man."

"To discover if he'd had any news of those men," Delia said, glad to be able to deflect that ridiculous notion.

Lady Matterson eyed her over the rim of her glass as she drank. "What made you suppose they might be in Weymouth itself?"

Oh, help! Must her aunt be so observant? She would have to let slip a tithe of the truth. "I thought I caught a glimpse of one of them, that's all. No doubt I was mistaken."

"A glimpse? Where? Why did you not tell me?"

"On the beach, when I went with Scoley to buy fish. I didn't want to worry you, Aunt."

"Commendable, but mistaken, girl. Did you suppose I would shake in my shoes?"

Delia smiled. "I know you are a deal more robust than that, to use your own word. But I saw no reason to spoil your enjoyment of the season."

Lady Matterson bridled. "And you think it's not spoiled by you going about with a face like a thwarted moonling?"

Gurgling helplessly, Delia had to put her glass down. Her aunt's face did not crack a smile. "Is colourful language another attribute of your generation, ma'am?"

"Don't try to put me off, girl!"

Delia sighed. "You are altogether too fly, Aunt."

"At my age I ought to be."

"Not necessarily. One cannot say the same of some of your companions."

Lady Matterson tapped the arm of the chaise longue. "You won't deflect me into discussing the shortcomings of my cronies, child."

"I know, ma'am. You are nothing if not tenacious."

"And you are admirably close-mouthed, Delia, and if I was not devilish anxious about you, I would leave you be. But I am and I can't."

Touched, Delia rose and crossed to sink down beside her on the chaise longue, taking her aunt's free hand. "It's a poor return for your attentions, Aunt Gertrude, but the story is not my own. At least, not entirely. And…" Hesitant, she began playing with the fingers she held, looking at them rather than the too knowing eyes.

"And?"

It was gently said and Delia looked up, startled to see affection in her aunt's softened features. An unprecedented rush of tenderness affected her not a little.

"I will tell you, but not yet, dear Aunt Gertrude. There is — there is danger for — for the person involved, you see, and I must protect him."

Her aunt's gaze did not stray from her face. She seemed to consider Delia for a moment before she spoke. "Tell me this, child. Are you in danger too?"

"Oh, no. He — *they* mean no harm to me. I am perfectly safe, Aunt."

"But this he is not?"

Delia shook her head, struggling not to blurt everything out. But she could not betray Giff. "Far from it. I know — I have reason to know, more so today, that his danger is acute."

Again her aunt hesitated, clearly reluctant to leave the subject. "Can I help in any way, Delia? I have influence in certain quarters."

"Not for this, Aunt. There is nothing you could do. There is little I can do, if truth be told. But I can't sit idle and not…" She faded out, aware she was saying too much. Any more and she would end by telling Aunt Gertrude the whole story.

"Have I met this he of yours?"

"No! Of course not."

"Then it is plain you've not told me all that happened to you that day. I've suspected it all along. It did not occur to me until later, but you were far too dishevelled and dirty for the story you told. And I could swear I saw blood on your gown."

Dismayed, Delia stared at her. For a moment the stern look held. Then Lady Matterson broke into an unaccustomed tearful smile. She set an arm about Delia and pulled her into a hug.

"Keep your counsel, child. In your place, I should do the same." Releasing her, she added, "But call on me if you need help. I am not made of china and I will not easily break."

143

Grateful and moved, Delia thanked her. But she was glad Peggy chose this moment to announce dinner, for she could not take much more without ending by confessing all. Aunt Gertrude chose to speak of other matters while they ate, although it was evident from the narrow looks she cast at Delia that the discussion was not out of mind.

Since the theatre company were performing that evening there was no further opportunity for debate. Delia was glad of the distraction, though the worry of how to get word to Giff niggled at the back of her mind. By morning, she'd decided to write to the rector and the new problem arose of how to find the time and an excuse to absent herself for the purpose. If she avoided bathing, she would still have to wait with Aunt Gertrude for her turn to be dipped. She could not, dressed so informally, pretend to go to the beach and instead slip off to the library where there was provision for letter writing. Nor was there opportunity afterwards, what with the business of dressing and partaking of breakfast.

At least Lady Matterson could not quiz her again since Mrs Poynings, who was not feeling up to being dipped, was invited to join them for the meal. Mrs Tuckett served her with coffee while she waited for her hostess and Delia to finish dressing, and then Delia was obliged to listen to an account of her present ailment as the stout dame tucked into fried fish and several slices of a fresh baked loaf lavishly spread with butter.

Impatience gnawed at Delia, but at length the two elder ladies were ready and the whole party set out for the Assembly Rooms where Miss Watkinson was holding sway.

She leapt on Delia the moment she caught sight of her. "It is of no use, my dear Miss Burloyne. The whole scheme has come to naught. Would you believe it? Just when the weather is perfect for our expedition."

A little fillip of hope thrust up in Delia's breast. In her anxiety and preoccupation with sending to Stepleton, she'd left the wretched proposal to visit the ruins of Sandsfoot Castle out of her calculations.

"Why, what has happened, Miss Watkinson?"

"Quite a chapter of difficulties indeed. It is too bad! Two of the carriages are unfit — one with a broken trace, I believe, and Lord knows what with the other. Lady Tarporley fears she has taken a chill after her dip, and of course neither Caroline nor her devoted son will leave her. And to cap it all, Miss Leigh has turned her ankle!"

Delia with difficulty suppressed a flutter of amusement, not unmixed with a whoosh of relief. "Gracious, what a catalogue! Could we not rearrange it for another day?"

"Without doubt," came acidly from Lady Matterson, who had listened to the complaint with growing irritation in her face. "Fuss about nothing! What matters it if the outing must be postponed?"

"But I had it all arranged," mourned Miss Watkinson. "Who was to travel with whom and in which carriage. And the picnic hamper ready prepared. I don't know what we are to do!"

"Deuce take it, woman, it's only a minor setback! When you've had as many disappointments as I, Miss Watkinson, you may learn to take them in your stride." With which Lady Matterson turned in the direction of the card room, exhorting Mrs Poynings to follow.

Feeling for Miss Watkinson, whose cheeks assumed a somewhat ruddy hue while her eyes snapped dangerously, Delia lowered her voice. "My aunt is a trifle twitty at present, ma'am, which at her age is not to be wondered at."

The other's high colour began to fade and she wafted a hand. "I have known Lady Matterson too long to be troubled, my dear Miss Burloyne." Her tone became petulant nevertheless. "However, it is extremely frustrating when I had everything settled and it is all to do again."

"It must be so indeed, ma'am. But perhaps you may produce the hamper here later? We might picnic on the grass outside, perhaps."

Miss Watkinson brightened. "An excellent notion, Miss Burloyne! I will go at once and discover who would enjoy the treat."

She marched off and was very soon to be seen trotting from one group to another, making notes in the little book she carried in her reticule.

Delia followed her aunt to the card room and found her already settling to her usual game of whist with Mrs Poynings, Lord Hadlow and Mr Warbleton. Satisfied she would be happily occupied for some time, Delia made to leave the card room and almost ran into Mr Rodber coming in, accompanied by a gentleman.

"Ah, Miss Burloyne, well met. I have the pleasant task of making our newest arrival known to our company here, so this is most opportune."

With an inward sigh, Delia resigned herself to a further delay. "Certainly, Mr Rodber. How do you do, sir?"

She transferred her attention to the gentleman standing a little behind him and suffered a rude shock. Attired in clothes of as much quality as any other in the room, his hair neatly tied in a queue, stood a man with a clean-shaven face Delia could not mistake.

"Miss Burloyne, allow me to present to you Mr Giffard, lately of the Indian continent."

With unholy triumph, Giff took in the effect of his sudden advent upon his flower girl. He'd hoped to surprise her, but this was beyond anything.

Her eyes flew wide, her freckles were drowned with colour and she appeared incapable of coherent speech. "*What*? I mean, who —? Giffard, did you say? Good heavens! How — how do you do? Or rather, welcome, sir. I'm — I'm very p-pleased to meet you."

Unable to prevent the quirk at his lips, Giff bowed, taking the hand she had extended, clearly without intent. "Delighted to make your acquaintance, Miss Burloyne. You render Weymouth brighter than I had expected."

Her flush deepened and she flashed him an indignant look. "Thank you! I mean — you exaggerate, sir." She visibly pulled herself together and dropped a curtsey. "How very gallant of you, Mr Giffard." A narrow look came as she rose again. "Do you make a long stay?"

He held her eyes. "My plans are uncertain, ma'am."

"No doubt! I mean, are they?"

"Until I have had leisure to look about me, yes." Aware that a number of eyes were on them, he bowed again. "I will hope for an opportunity to better our acquaintance, ma'am."

"Yes, indeed. Sooner rather than later."

There was a snap in her voice, but her colour returned again as she glanced at the Master of Ceremonies, who was looking a good deal surprised. As well he might. Giff had accosted the fellow on Sattar's advice, learning that his good offices were apparently essential to introduce him into the society of Weymouth. His henchman had thankfully not wasted his time in the town while keeping an eye on Piers's men.

"I must beg you to excuse us, Miss Burloyne," said this worthy, waving an expansive hand. "Mr Giffard has a number of people to meet."

"Yes, of course." Delia cast him a meaningful look. "I was on my way to the library."

"You are a great reader, ma'am?"

"No! Yes! I have a letter to write. Or, no, I don't any longer." She gave a little shudder, closing her eyes briefly. "Your pardon, sir. Excuse me, if you please."

Delia bobbed a curtsey and slipped past, head down as she exited the card room. Amused, and a little guilty at having caused her so much discomfiture, Giff watched her leave, finding the sway of her hips under the muslin gown unexpectedly enticing. How soon could he end this farcical spate of introductions and find the library?

"Come, Mr Giffard, I must present you to some of our oldest and most faithful summer visitors."

Turning his attention to the indicated table where a quartet of elderly persons were engaged at cards, Giff discovered he was under the scrutiny of a pair of sharp eyes belonging to a formidable dame of advanced years. A riffle of familiarity went through him. Could he know her? Surely not.

"Allow me to present…"

Mr Rodber went into his litany and Giff strove to pay attention as he indicated that very female.

"Lady Matterson, who is responsible for bringing our young Miss Burloyne with her this season."

So this was Delia's aunt? She looked to be little the worse for wear after her ordeal at the hands of Piers's tools, he decided, as he murmured a greeting and made his bow. On the other hand, she was regarding him with a gimlet eye that he would have found intimidating if he was not as interested in her as she appeared to be in him. That eye continued to appraise him as the other members of the four were introduced, Giff surreptitiously noted. Had she seen his exchange with Delia? Disapproval, then? She could not suspect, could she? His flower girl would never betray him, that he would swear to.

The introductions done, Mr Rodber took it upon himself to present Giff's credentials. "Mr Giffard has lately returned from India. I have no doubt he will have many interesting tales to impart."

"India?" Lady Matterson's brows were climbing her forehead. "How long were you in residence there, sir?"

"All my life, ma'am, bar my first few years."

"Then you are English?"

"Indeed. My people were from these parts."

"Your people? I don't recall any of the name of Giffard."

The accusatory note was pronounced. Did she suppose him to be some upstart mushroom trying for a rise in the world? He kept his tone bland.

"The Giffards were never of note, ma'am. I doubt your ladyship will have encountered them." Bowing, he looked enquiringly at the Master of Ceremonies and glanced at the next table whose occupants had paused in their game to watch.

"Indeed, we must move along. My lady, my lord."

With a bow, Mr Rodber extracted them and moved away. Giff followed with alacrity, conscious of the eyes boring into his back. Lady Matterson promised to be as acute as her niece, which did not augur well for his scheme to find an opportunity to be private with Delia.

Once all the occupants of the card room had been introduced, any hope Giff had of escaping was thwarted as Mr Rodber led him into the principal room where he was immediately waylaid by a stout woman of middle years with a masterful air.

"Mr Rodber, there you are! I am determined to reorganise the expedition to Sandsfoot Castle for tomorrow, provided you can assure me of the weather's continuing clement." She cast a cursory glance at Giff and her eyes widened. "Why, who is this? Do I detect a fresh arrival come amongst us?"

The master of ceremonies appeared a little flustered. "Yes, yes, Miss Watkinson. I would have presented you at once, only you were elsewhere at the time." He altered his tone to one of urbanity, which Giff suspected was habitual. "Yet no time like the present. Allow me to introduce Mr Giffard, who is, as you surmised, newly arrived." He turned to Giff and wafted a hand towards the woman. "Our most assiduous visitor, Mr Giffard. We are indebted to Miss Watkinson for a great many enhancements to our sojourns in this place. Indeed, I don't know what we should do without her."

This was uttered with an unctuous inflexion and a sycophantic bow towards the creature. She looked to Giff like one of these pushy battle-axes who constituted themselves, for no good reason, the leader of any society in which they found themselves. He'd known one or two in Kolkata. Intimidating females, every one of them. At least this one did not appear to have a henpecked husband in tow.

Miss Watkinson was smiling graciously upon him, preening at the flattering words, which she clearly felt as her due. "Delighted, Mr Giffard, and you must come to Sandsfoot Castle with us tomorrow, if the weather holds. We had arranged all for today but were prevented by several unavoidable circumstances."

Giff was not about to commit himself to anything. "Indeed, ma'am? What is Sandsfoot Castle?"

"A ruin, sir, and one of the unmissable sights of Weymouth. You must come, I insist upon it." Turning back to the other fellow, she put up a finger. "But the weather, Mr Rodber? What have your sources to say?"

"As far as I have been able to ascertain, dear lady, we are to expect sunshine for the next several days."

"Excellent. Then I may enjoin our friends to regroup tomorrow. We must hope Lady Tarporley is sufficiently recovered to release her son and daughter for the event. And Mrs Dicker must manage without poor Miss Leigh. That girl is very much in need of a treat. Miss Burloyne is already promised, for I caught her before she left the Rooms and secured her at once. I trust you will join us, Mr Giffard?" She tittered in a manner both irritating and familiar. "I warn you I shall not take no for an answer."

But the moment he heard Delia was going on this infernal expedition, Giff had made up his mind. Exploring ruins? What better opportunity to get her alone? "I shall be delighted, ma'am, and must thank you for including me on so short an acquaintance."

"Gracious, my dear sir, we stand on no ceremony here, do we, Mr Rodber?"

The man bowed but his lips compressed. Likely as the accredited leader of Weymouth society he stood on a good deal of ceremony, if the fellow who did such honours back home was anything to go by. But Miss Watkinson was again regarding him, with an intent look and a crease between her brows.

"Giffard? No, the name is unknown to me. But you look familiar, sir."

"Impossible, dear lady," cut in Mr Rodber, speaking in a lofty fashion. "Mr Giffard is but lately returned from India.

None of us may claim prior acquaintance. Besides, he informs us his people were not wont to move in fashionable circles."

This was not precisely what Giff had said, but he hoped it would serve to put the woman off. She might well have acquaintance with the Gaunts, for all he knew. His great-uncle claimed he had a look of his mother. The last thing he wanted was to have her name dragged up, along with the ancient scandal. His stepfather had ever supposed there must have been a deal of talk after their flight.

But Miss Watkinson appeared less than satisfied. "Still, I do believe you look like someone I have met, Mr Giffard, though I cannot think who at this moment."

"One of these inexplicable resemblances, perhaps," suggested Mr Rodber. "I must say it did not strike me, and I venture to think I am acquainted with everyone who matters in these parts."

Miss Watkinson visibly bridled. "Well, and so am I, sir." She cast a patronising smile upon Giff. "It will come to me, I dare say."

Heaven forbid! Though if the confrontation he sought came about in this town, there was no saying what might come out.

"And now we must move along, ma'am, if you will forgive us. I venture to think Mr Giffard will like to be shown our further amenities, will you not, sir?"

Yes, the library! And immediately. But Giff refrained from saying so. "Your good offices are very much appreciated, sir."

The battle-axe, bestowing a gracious nod upon Giff and a stinging look upon his host, passed on. It was plain she resented the dismissal. No doubt she locked horns with anyone who dared to cross her.

The Master of Ceremonies did not appear ruffled by the woman as he led Giff towards the vestibule. He tittered, lowering his voice. "If only females were permitted the task, I am persuaded Miss Watkinson would prove a rival to my position here."

"You've been reigning for some years, I take it?"

Mr Rodber coughed. "I can hardly claim to reign, sir. Certainly not when His Majesty is apt to honour us with his presence. He has visited the Rooms and he enjoys the theatre. Not that his privacy is to be disturbed, you understand, especially when he takes his dip from his bathing machine. But he is perfectly affable if you should happen to meet him on his walk."

It was news to Giff that the King frequented Weymouth. "Is he in residence?"

"We believe he is expected in a matter of days. He stays at the Duke of Gloucester's house. His brother, you must know. He acquired the Lodge in the '80s. We have thus had the inestimable privilege of His Majesty's visits ever since."

"That must have done much to render the place fashionable, I imagine."

"Just so, sir. Where the highest in the land goes, Society inevitably follows." A sour note entered his voice. "Though His Highness the Prince of Wales has rendered Brighton something of a rival resort."

Fast overtaking Weymouth in popularity with the cognoscenti, according to Giff's great-uncle. The rector had entertained his days of recovery with many a tale, bringing him to some degree up to date. Although he'd naturally followed events at a distance, and a good deal past their occurrence, from the journals from England that Matt eagerly perused. Giff had a sneaking suspicion his stepfather still missed his homeland, despite his success in India and the long and happy

153

marriage he'd enjoyed once the scandalous divorce had set Giff's mother free.

If he succeeded in securing his rightful inheritance, Giff planned to invite Matt to return. At least for a prolonged visit. His half-brother Charles was just about old enough to run the plantations in Matt's absence.

But that was for the future. He brought his attention to bear on Mr Rodber's explanatory footnotes about the buildings they passed as they traversed the Esplanade. Impatient to chase down Delia in the library, Giff sought his mind for some plausible excuse. He found one, interrupting without ceremony.

"I wonder, sir, if there are historic documents in the library here? The lady — Miss Watkinson? — interested me about this castle. It is a hobby of mine, you must know, to delve into such things."

In fact he had little interest in ancient monuments, although he'd enjoyed playing as a boy around the terracotta temples at Bishnupur. But it served to divert Mr Rodber.

"Indeed, yes, sir. You will find a number of histories of one sort and another, and a good many maps too."

"Would you object to showing me where to find the place? If we are to visit this castle tomorrow, I should like to find out what I may at once."

"Certainly, sir. Follow me."

A very few minutes brought them within sight of the library, but Giff balked when the fellow showed signs of guiding him inside. He didn't need the man digging around to find tomes and maps he had no desire to see.

"I should not dream of troubling you, Mr Rodber. I have taken up quite enough of your time as it is." He then held out his hand in a determined way. "I must thank you for the kindly welcome and for smoothing my path."

"Not at all, Mr Giffard. I am only too happy to be of service." He took the hand, shook it with formal grace, gave a flourishing old-fashioned bow, and at last departed.

Letting out a whoosh of relief, Giff dived into the building and lost no time in hunting the place for Delia.

Perched on a window seat, her nose firmly buried in a book to which she paid not the slightest heed, Delia was barely able to contain her soul in patience. Giff's sudden appearance had thoroughly discomposed her, and she was torn between delight at seeing him and fury at being taken off guard.

Why could he not have found means to warn her? Mr Rodber must have taken her for a ninny. Or, more likely, thought she'd been bowled over by a handsome face. Well, that she could not deny. He looked even more like a deity dressed smartly than he had in the rough gear of their first encounter. The shock of seeing him pop up perfectly turned out in the Assembly Rooms was severe. Her heart had first tried to leap into her throat, and then bounded around in her chest like an excitable frog. She'd never been so disconcerted in her life. If only he would come, she had a good deal to say to him on the subject of giving her a fright. Along with the news of Piers which she now might give in person. Which made her need for the library redundant since she no longer had to write a letter to the rector. Except that she'd indicated this was where she would be. There was nothing for it but to kick her heels in hopes of his finding her here.

Typical of Giff to come upon her without warning. Just as he had the other day outside St Mary's. But at least she'd been able to express herself then. On this occasion she'd behaved like a perfect fool, and if Aunt Gertrude was watching there was scant hope she would not have observed it.

What was he doing here dressed like that? Mr Giffard indeed! What had he said the last time? He had a plan of some kind and this was it, no doubt. She recalled his mysterious air then and the spurious front of urbanity now. The wretch had meant to take her by storm. She could see amusement in his eyes, now she thought about it. Oh, only wait until he caught up with her!

But it seemed an age that she waited, cursing Mr Rodber who doubtless found it necessary to tour Giff around the plethora of visitors. Oh, help! He would introduce him to her aunt. Inevitable her suspicions would be aroused. How in the world was she to deflect Aunt Gertrude now?

She kept a surreptitious eye out for entrants to the library, casting a sneaky glance towards the door each time she heard footsteps. She'd positioned herself suitably to be able to see the doorway and chafed as first one of the older resident gentlemen entered and sat down to read the daily journals at the table where two others were already ensconced. He was followed by a clerkly fellow Delia did not know, who went directly to the shelves, hunting them with evident purpose. In dread that someone she knew would come in and accost her, Delia regarded her book with assiduity, turning the page from time to time though the printed words held no meaning for her.

At length a quick step sounded and she looked up to find Giff standing in the doorway, glancing around the room. She quickly looked down, not wishing to draw attention to herself, yet willing him to see her. It seemed an age as he strolled casually in her direction, but at last he came to rest a couple of feet away.

"Miss Burloyne, well met." He spoke loud enough to be heard and Delia looked up, throwing him a scorching glance. He grinned down at her, lowering his voice. "Pretend to be surprised."

"I don't have to pretend," she shot back. And loudly, "Why, Mr Giffard, have you come to borrow a book?"

"Just acquainting myself with the amenities, ma'am. Ah, and I had it in mind to find some history of Sandsfoot Castle."

Delia heard this with a leap of satisfaction. "Allow me to direct you, sir, for I know the library well." And under her breath, "Miss Watkinson has collared you already? You are well served, you wretch!"

"On the contrary," he returned in a like manner as she rose and led him away from this exposed position. "Nothing could be more providential."

"Ha! We'll see about that." Delia moved purposefully towards a shadowed a corner where they might, with luck, seize a moment of as much privacy as was obtainable in a public room. "Pretend an interest in the books here, Giff. And keep your back to the room."

"Bossy wench, aren't you?" But there was a laugh in his voice as he obediently extracted a volume and began turning the pages.

"You're lucky I'm not lying on the floor and drumming my heels, horrid creature! How dare you give me such a fright?"

"What a fuss, woman! When it's your own notion I should show myself in society?"

"I didn't mean you to pop up in Weymouth looking like a fashion plate! And you could not have chosen a worse time, for your horrid cousin was here yesterday."

Giff's eyes lifted from the book, the blue as keen as steel. "Was he so? Now why, I wonder?"

"Because I sent for him, if you must know."

His brows flew up and the narrow look vanished. "Have you run mad, Delia?"

Her cheeks warmed, though she abated not one jot of her belligerent tone. "Very likely. I expect I took leave of my senses the moment I met you, *Mister* Giffard."

His grin was positively gleeful and the insouciant and reckless manner she knew well came back. "My influence, is it?"

"Yes, it is!"

"Excellent. Then you won't object to sneaking off at this expedition tomorrow so we can talk."

"We're talking now."

"Not for long. Too risky. Quick, tell me why you sent for Piers? How did you do so?"

Delia cast a glance towards the end of the library where the gentlemen present were situated. None were paying them the least attention. There was time yet. "I accosted the fellow Barney."

"Deuce take it! They're still watching you?"

"I believe so. And I've not seen Captain Rhoades or his men about."

Giff's gaze narrowed once more. "Him again? Just as well."

An exasperated sigh escaped Delia. "Will you stop being nonsensical, Giff?"

"I'll not have him sniffing around you, so don't think it!"

She could not withstand the thrill that shot through her at hearing the possessive note, but she spoke in a repressive fashion nevertheless. "Shall we keep to the point?"

Giff grinned again. "If you insist, Miss Prunes and Prisms."

She flashed him a look. "It's no jesting matter, Giff. Piers is perfectly determined on keeping you out. His attitude chilled me, I don't mind telling you."

"How so?"

She gave him a ready account of her exchange with his cousin, not omitting her disbelief in his talk of a more merciful end than his victim suspected.

"He might say he only thinks to send you to America, Giff, but I'm so afraid his purpose is more sinister. I'm terrified that if chance offers, he will kill you."

Giff had listened to her story with a more serious mien than she'd seen since the day they met, but at this he laughed. "He may try! I've a trick or two up my sleeve yet, Delia, never fear."

"Yes, but I do fear! I can't help it."

His features softened and those intense eyes roved her face. "My plucky flower girl. You won't buckle, I know it."

His faith both touched and frightened her. "I will if I can't save you."

"Then you'd best save me."

It was lightly said, but his smile embraced her. Delia's heart melted and she smiled back.

Giff drew in a sharp breath, his eyes holding hers. "If we weren't in a public place…"

Warmth flooded Delia as the conviction seized her that he wanted to kiss her. She'd never truly supposed he might find her desirable. For a breathless moment her surroundings vanished. She felt as if she and Giff were the only two people in the world.

And then he spoke in his natural voice. "I came to Weymouth with intent, Delia. I want to draw Piers out. I hope he comes again in no time. I'll be ready for him."

The strange sensation disintegrated and Delia was back in the library with her heart horridly exposed. She set her eyes on the shelves so she need not look at him. "You think he will come the moment he hears of your being here?"

"I'm hoping so. I aim to force a confrontation."

Feeling as if she spoke from somewhere outside herself, Delia tried to ignore the disappointed creature within who felt just as dull as ever. "He's not going to hail you as his cousin, is he, when you are claiming to be Mr Giffard?"

"Not in front of people, I suppose. But I'm hoping he'll find a way to challenge me."

"Challenge you how?" She scarcely knew what she was saying for the acute sense of being two people, one of whom wanted to believe what had just happened while the other pooh-poohed it as an impossibility.

"To a duel."

Delia came to herself with a bang. She turned on him. "A duel? No, Giff!"

His brows were lowering, and there was a smoulder in his eyes. "I prefer a fair fight. This underhand dealing chafes me. I'd have dealt fairly with him, but Piers chose stealth and treachery and he's going to pay."

She'd not seen this side of him before. He was as changeable as quicksilver. And, truth to tell, even more alluring with this dangerous edge to him. But it would not do. "What if he wins? In a duel, I mean."

A perfectly saturnine smile curled his lip. "He won't."

His confidence both alarmed and impressed her. "You can't know that, Giff."

"I know my own strengths." He seemed to shake off the unusual mood. "Never mind that. I'd best leave you. That aunt of yours looks as sharp as a knife. If she gets wind of this havey-cavey conduct she'll have my guts for garters, I'll be bound."

"She's more likely to demand the story from me," said Delia on a rueful note. "She's already suspicious, and I had to admit there was more to that day than the story your uncle concocted for me. I said I was sworn to secrecy."

"Curse the creature! Well, it can't be helped. But I'd best be off. We're strangers, remember."

"Then see you behave like one to me." The beginnings of amusement lightened his face, and she sharpened her tone. "Don't dare tease me with your eyes, you wretch, or I'll…"

"You'll what?"

She ignored the dance in those infuriating orbs. "I'll have thought of something by the time it's necessary, I assure you."

He grinned. "I believe you. Never fear, I'll behave."

"Well, see you do, or it will be the worse for you."

He cast up his eyes. "I've landed myself with a shrew! Go away, you scolding wench, and leave me to regain my manly dignity."

Delia laughed and left him, albeit with reluctance.

Much to Delia's astonishment, Lady Matterson made no attempt to prise her story out of her, though she made reference to the new arrival.

"Mr Giffard? Oh, yes, Mr Rodber introduced him to me."

Aware of her aunt's narrow gaze as she broached the subject, she kept her eyes on the shoreline where a party of children were playing at chasing the waves.

At the behest of Miss Watkinson, a number of Weymouth gentry were sitting on the grassy bank below the Esplanade, or on the larger rocks at the edge of the sand, picnicking on the viands that had been prepared for the aborted expedition. Some preferred their customary luncheon elsewhere, but Lady Matterson and her cronies, none of whom had the least intention of visiting Sandsfoot Castle, which they declared they had seen far too many times already, had taken advantage of the offerings and, ensconced on a bench brought out for the older residents, were tucking into the chicken and savoury patties with gusto, following these up with apricot tartlets and large slices of plum cake. Miss Watkinson harried the waiters and darted from group to group, ensuring everyone received their share and soliciting compliments upon her choice of fare.

There was no sign of Giff, but that did not prevent his name from coming up on several lips.

"A most personable young man, I thought," said Mrs Poynings, "and not at all rag-mannered."

Mr Warbleton, who had spent some years in the Orient, bridled. "What, because he's from India, ma'am? D'ye suppose there ain't Society enough for a young feller to learn how to behave?"

"Not if we're to go by your conduct, Warbleton," put in Lord Hadlow with a hearty laugh.

Lady Matterson intervened. "Don't set him off, John, you know what he is."

Indeed, Mr Warbleton's already high colour deepened and he was clearly ready to take umbrage. Bouts of bickering between the two elderly gentlemen were apt to break out often, though Aunt Gertrude assured Delia they were the best of friends.

"Did you not think him handsome, Miss Burloyne?"

Delia turned to Mrs Poynings. "I hardly had a chance to observe him, ma'am. I was in a hurry to get to the library."

The widow's gaze became sly. "You had time enough to blush, my dear, for I saw it."

"That will do, Emily. You are putting her to the blush now. I've no doubt all the young ladies reacted in similar fashion."

Grateful for her aunt's intervention, Delia managed a light tone. "Oh, well, he seemed gallant enough. Miss Watkinson says she secured him for tomorrow, so perhaps I will have a chance to observe him more closely."

Mrs Poynings tittered. "Not if Miss Tarporley and Miss Leigh have anything to say to it."

Since both Caroline Tarporley and Tabitha Leigh were a deal younger and prettier than she, this jibe would have found its mark if Delia had not a clandestine rendezvous in prospect on the morrow. Even so, she was conscious of a tiny sting. Giff might be her secret, but she had no claim upon him.

Lady Matterson, casting her friend a scorching glance, stood up. "Come, Delia. I am tired and need my rest." A nod to her friends. "We will see you all after dinner."

Rising with alacrity, Delia offered her arm. They were scarcely out of earshot before Lady Matterson spoke her mind.

"Silly woman! Pay no heed to her, Delia. She has never got over how long it took to get her fubsy-faced daughter off." She gave a tiny sigh. "Emily does not mean to be spiteful. She will be sorry presently, and I shall have to endure a barrage of apology and justification for her having spoken so meanly to you."

"It is nothing to me, Aunt. I am not jealous of either female."

Her aunt cast her one of her sapient looks as they walked away along the Esplanade. "Didn't seem to me you'd any reason to worry over that young man casting his eyes elsewhere."

"Why should I? I scarcely know him." Her pulse flittered uncomfortably and she kept her eyes on the cobbles, as if she was minding their steps.

"Yet he clearly had some effect on you."

"I was taken by surprise, Aunt." Which was the absolute truth. "I very nearly ran into Mr Rodber as he came in."

"Ah, that is what discomposed you, is it?"

The sceptical note was pronounced. Delia took refuge in silence, looking towards their lodging to see if Miss Pegler had come down to open the door. "It looks as if Peggy has not seen us."

"She's not there. Gone on an errand for me."

Delia looked round. "What errand?"

"Something I needed, that's all. Your Sally is deputising."

This was so unprecedented, Delia could not help feeling suspicious. Why should not Aunt Gertrude reveal where Peggy had gone? And what could she be doing that must take half the day to accomplish?

The question did not occupy her mind for long. As Sally appeared to answer the doorbell, it occurred to Delia that it might be useful to take her into her confidence. If she needed to send to Giff, who better than Sally to take a message? Except she had no notion where he was lodging. She must ask him tomorrow.

By the time the morrow dawned, however, Delia was so out of charity with her erstwhile prince she was almost ready to murder him herself. Reappearing in the principal Assembly Room during the evening entertainment, which consisted of a quartet of musicians playing on a dais while the company chattered amongst themselves paying scant attention, Giff appeared to be bent upon making himself the life and soul of the party.

Since he held off from Delia beyond what might be regarded as acceptable politeness, she was unable to take him to task for exposing himself in such a way. Seething, and deeply mortified, she watched as he charmed first one group and then another. Even Miss Watkinson came in for a share of his attentions. Preening, she stopped by Lady Matterson's chair where Delia was in attendance.

"Such an amusing creature, Mr Giffard! Fascinating tales of India he has to tell. Wild tigers and a haunted temple! A ruin now, he says, expressing the hope he might discover a ghost at Sandsfoot Castle tomorrow."

He would discover a ghost all right. A phantom from a forest ride. And be lucky if it did not slap his silly face for him. Haunted temples!

Next came Mr Warbleton, who hobbled over all smiles for having enjoyed a half hour of reminiscence. He interrupted Lady Matterson's conversation with Lord Hadlow without ceremony. "Sound young feller, that. Knows his cotton inside and out."

"Cotton?" Lord Hadlow's bushy grey brows wiggled alarmingly. "What's cotton to do with being sound?"

"Everything to do with it. Feller has a plantation over there. Highly lucrative, the cotton trade. Won't be short of a penny or two, which means you young ladies will all be on the catch for him." With a nod to Delia, who had nothing to say.

Unlike Lady Matterson, who was crushing. "I dare say. But without family, he may whistle for a suitable bride."

She cast a glance at her great-niece as she spoke, and Delia cursed the warmth rising in her cheeks. Did Aunt Gertrude suspect she already had a tendre for Giff? Was it meant for a warning?

The evening began to seem interminable. Delia's only solace lay in treasuring up what she planned to say to Giff the moment they managed to steal a moment alone at the ruins. If they so managed. Just as Mrs Poynings predicted, Caroline Tarporley, putting in an appearance escorted by her brother, lost no time in gaining an introduction and remained talking to Giff for several nerve-wracking minutes. Delia's surreptitious observation put her in a ferment of jealousy as Caroline laughed and blushed, with Giff leaning towards her more than once. Hateful creature! He was nothing but an atrocious flirt. And he'd had the temerity to take exception to her speaking to Captain Rhoades.

Well, if he dared to refer to her as his flower girl after this, she would have something to say to him. What he hoped to gain by making himself the talk of Weymouth, she could not fathom. Did he suppose it must get back to Piers? But his cousin had no spies within the Assembly Rooms. Or had he?

A chill entered her breast. Her aunt once more thoroughly engaged with Lord Hadlow, she took the opportunity to eye the resident visitors in turn. No, this was silly. Ridiculous to suppose Piers had an ally in any of these. But what of the servants? Several waiters passed to and fro through the evening, bearing trays as they supplied thirsty gentry with suitable refreshment.

166

It was conceivable that Giff's cousin had bribed one of these to report on his movements. But would he already know of Giff's advent? Yes, there had been time enough for either Sam or Barney, presumably still on the watch, to report back. He'd come soon enough when she'd sent her message. But Giff was bent upon luring him into appearing in person.

Her petty jealousies forgotten, Delia watched Giff's antics with different eyes. Yes, he was making himself agreeable to everyone. Making himself as visible as he could.

All at once, she noticed Giff looking towards the entrance. He gave a nod and turned away. Delia's gaze followed where his eyes had led and discovered an oddity. A man in foreign clothes and wearing a turban? She was close enough to see that he was elderly. An Indian? This must be the fellow he said was watching Sam and Barney as they watched her. He'd planted his own spy in the town!

Within a very few minutes, Giff was seen to be making his farewells. He passed by where Delia and her aunt were situated, bowing. "I must say goodnight, ma'am. My servant awaits to see me to my lodging."

Lady Matterson looked towards the Indian, whom she'd evidently also seen, and inclined her head. She gave him one of her sceptical looks. "Very wise, sir. The Weymouth streets are notoriously dangerous."

Giff laughed. "Hardly, ma'am. But Sattar knows the way and I do not. I gather we were too late to find a more central establishment."

"Then the matter becomes comprehensible."

But her aunt's tone remained all too knowing, and Delia winced inwardly. She must somehow have given herself away.

"Miss Burloyne, your servant." A brief and conspiratorial wink was cast upon her. "Until the morrow."

Delia felt the warmth rise into her cheeks and could willingly have hit him. She spoke as repressively as she could. "We must hope the weather holds. Until tomorrow, sir."

Next moment he was gone. Only then did it strike Delia that her aunt had spoken nothing but the truth, albeit with sarcasm. Giff's Indian servant, who looked to be sturdily strong despite his years, was with him for protection. A stab in the dark was all it might take.

CHAPTER TEN

Finding means to slip away from the party at Sandsfoot Castle proved easier than Giff had anticipated. The flip side of the coin to flaunting his presence last evening was the difficulty of finding himself too much surrounded. He was glad he'd had the forethought to ride Tiger instead of allowing himself to be inconveniently placed by the battle-axe who ushered the party into the carriages in divisions of her own making.

Young Lord Tarporley, a pleasant fellow if a trifle raw, had also elected to ride. Giff thus had an excellent excuse to converse with him as they ambled along behind the carriages rather than singling out his flower girl too soon.

Delia was situated alongside some chit who was recovering from a sprained ankle. An excellent turn since she was unlikely to do much walking and could not delay a bid to escape.

"I did not think to bring my groom," commented Tarporley.

Giff looked back at Sattar's tall figure riding at a discreet distance in the rear. He maintained a non-committal tone. "No?"

The young man coloured. "I mean no offence, sir."

"None taken."

"It's just that I supposed there are grooms enough with the carriages to take care of the horses while we explore."

"True. Sattar is more henchman than groom, however, and will have it I am not fit to be allowed out on my own."

It was merely an excuse, but Tarporley chose to take it up. "He's been with you a long time?"

"All my life."

"Ah, that type of retainer, eh?" Tarporley gave a despairing sigh. "I have a nurse of that cut. She cannot be persuaded I am a man grown and insists upon treating me as if I were two instead of twenty."

Giff eyed him. "You've inherited your title young, I take it?"

"My father died when I was a boy. But I've more or less taken over from my trustees, thank the lord! My uncles are quite as bad as my nurse, I may say."

Giff laughed. "I'm sorry for you, then. Do they scold and prophesy disaster if you are left to your own devices?"

"Not quite. But everything I suggest is subject to a catechism as if I must pass a test before I may make a decision."

"Good God! You'd best tell your uncles to go hang themselves!"

"I wish I might! Only I can't deny they have kept my estates in excellent heart. And prevented that fellow Gaunt from encroaching upon my lands."

His tone was disgruntled, but the name was enough to send the blood rushing through Giff's veins. It was out before he could prevent the words. "Do you mean Piers Gaunt? Of Waldiche Keep?"

Tarporley looked round, frowning. "Yes, he's my neighbour. Do you know him?"

The deuce! Now what was he to say? He prevaricated. "I've heard the name." The boy's frowning puzzlement showed this to be an inadequate answer. "My great-uncle mentioned him. He's a rector and lives not far from Dorchester. He was obliging enough to enlighten me as to the gentry living round about." It was largely true, and he hoped it would pass muster.

Tarporley gave a discontented grunt. "Well, if you take my advice, you will avoid the man."

This was too valuable to miss. "May I ask why? Did you say he was trying to encroach on your lands?"

"The fellow does not seem to know his own boundaries. Mind you, he was not brought up to understand his lands, as I was. If they are his. Caused the deuce of a stir when he took over the property. Apparently there's a son of old Lord Baunton, though the word is he's dead. But Gaunt can't prove it, so he hasn't been able to establish a claim to the title. I don't know the ins and outs of it, for I was still a minor at the time, but my uncles followed the entire procedure since it nearly concerned my interests."

What an extraordinary piece of luck! But could he question the man more without revealing his true identity? He would have to find an opportunity another time, however, for the carriages were slowing.

"Ah, we've arrived, sir."

"You've been here before?"

"Upon several occasions. Weymouth is a favourite haunt of my mother's. We come here whenever she is in poor health." He touched his hat. "Forgive me. I must see to my sister's comfort."

The young man rode on and Giff slowed, signing to Sattar to catch up with him. He lost no time in passing on what he had heard.

"This fellow's uncles must know a great deal about the business. I'll have to cultivate his acquaintance."

"You will tell him your real name, sahib?"

"I may have to."

"Is that not foolhardy?"

"Possibly. But it's the first hint of a potential ally. The boy can't stand Piers, and his uncles may have vital information."

He dismounted and his henchman followed suit. Giff gave Tiger's reins into Sattar's keeping. "Stay close and keep your ears open. I'll whistle if I need you."

"You think I am not watching your back, sahib? If any come, I will see them before you."

Giff grinned. "Then you whistle, old sobersides. I've got to find means to confer with Delia."

The mêlée caused by the battle-axe attempting to herd everyone into a group afforded Giff his chance. Passing close to Delia, he affected to gaze up at the ruined edifice with admiration.

"Here is history indeed, do you not think, Miss Burloyne? I must immediately make a circuit."

She was quick to follow his lead. "Oh, yes, Mr Giffard. I would be interested to see it from the ocean side."

"Would you indeed? Take my arm, if you will, ma'am." She did so with alacrity and Giff began to lead her away, lowering his voice. "Quick, before that battle-axe notices our departure."

A gurgle reached him. "She's too busy rounding them all up."

Locating the nearest corner, Giff strolled casually in that direction, talking of fallen stones, the antiquity of the remains and pointing to gaps in the crumbling masonry. Miss Watkinson's voice was heard just as they began to round the corner.

"Miss Burloyne! Come back! Mr Giffard! It is dangerous!"

"Pretend not to hear!" He continued on his way, wholly ignoring the shouts. They changed.

"You too, Lord Tarporley? Really, I do not advise it."

"Damnation! The cub is following us."

Delia followed his glance. "He's bringing Tabitha Leigh. It's a good thing, Giff. It won't look so particular for me to be going apart with you."

"We'd best stay ahead, then."

"Miss Leigh's ankle!"

Giff looked round. "What about it?"

"It will slow them down."

A measure of satisfaction entered Giff's breast as this proved true. They gained the lee of the building and were soon walking down the side.

"We must be out of sight now." Delia stopped and took her arm from his, moving as if she would peep around the corner.

Giff seized her hand. "Don't! No need to draw attention to ourselves." He began to pull her onwards, quickening his pace.

She freed her hand. "Giff, wait! We must appear casual."

Accordingly, she adopted a saunter, looking up at the building as she went. Giff followed suit, glancing back. "No sign of the others yet."

She moved closer and a frown creased her brow as she looked at him. "I was going to ring such a peal over you today, but I'm too worried to do it now."

"What, that we might be overtaken?"

"No, that Piers might find means to have you set upon." The frown intensified. "You think it too, or you wouldn't have had your servant escort you back to your lodging last night."

She'd surprised him yet again. Admiration licked within him. "How came you to guess that?"

"It wasn't difficult, Giff. You were so busy making a stir — flirting with every female who came near you as well —"

"Ha! You noticed!"

"I'm not blind! But never mind that. I thought —"

"You do mind it or you wouldn't have mentioned it."

To his intense satisfaction, a flush crept across her cheeks, covering the freckles.

"Be quiet, horrid creature! And pay attention. That's hardly germane."

"It's germane to me."

"Giff, will you behave?"

He grinned wickedly. "I love it when I put you out of countenance."

Her blush deepened and she looked ready to strike him. But her tone was cool. Falsely, he was persuaded.

"We were discussing the prospect of your demise, Mr Giffard."

"If you had a dagger, you'd accomplish it yourself at this moment, wouldn't you, my valiant flower girl?"

She drew in a breath and let it out in a rush. He could hear the tremor in her voice. "No! I want you alive, Giff. Stop teasing me."

Warmth pooled in his chest. He reached out and captured her chin, lifting her face. He dropped his tone to a murmur. "Forgive me?"

Her smile was tremulous and he was touched. "Always."

He hesitated. For two pins he'd kiss her. He wanted to. Only there was that cub Tarporley and his companion, just turning the corner. Too far to hear, but near enough to see. He released Delia's chin. "What were you saying?"

On the words, he turned to resume walking and she followed suit, no longer looking at him.

"I'm not sure." She sounded a trifle breathless. Then her voice became more certain. "Yes, I am though. Giff, do you think there might be a spy in the Assembly Rooms? One of the waiters, perhaps? It would not take much for Piers to bribe one of them."

With a little difficulty, still preoccupied as he was with the effect Delia had on him, Giff brought his attention to bear on his predicament. "Could be. I doubt he's had time to think of engaging someone since he learned of my arrival."

"Then what was your purpose?"

"In making myself talked of? Exactly what you supposed. To make enough stir that I'm certain to be the subject of gossip. Piers will hear of it. He has only to keep his ears open."

"You mean you think he's actually in the town?"

Shock sounded in her voice and he looked round. "Don't you? He hasn't shown himself abroad, but in his shoes, with his hope of luring me to the town by having his men watching you, I'd have secured a suitable lodging and be ready to move in at a moment's notice."

"I hadn't thought of that. Heavens, he might have been staying there when he came to see me!"

"Unlikely. Probably he moved in the moment he heard of my advent. I made sure to show myself when that fellow Rodber took me about."

"And either Sam or Barney saw you and took the word to him where he was previously staying. Then he might be looking for you in Weymouth at this moment!"

"Hardly. He'll have heard of this expedition and will likely bide his time."

Delia was silent for a moment or two. Giff eyed her.

"What are you thinking?"

The frown was back as she looked at him. "How little I really know."

"About this business?"

"About you, Giff. I've had to piece it together from snatches here and there. There's so much I don't understand."

175

It seemed odd to him to think her ignorant, such familiarity as he felt with her. Yet in actual time he supposed their acquaintance was slight. "What don't you understand?"

The frowning look of concentration did not abate. He could not but be gratified by the intensity of her interest in him and his welfare.

"The Reverend Gaunt cannot be your only relative in these parts. Aside from Piers, I mean. What of your mother's family? And your stepfather's too."

The deuce! Must she start on that? He prevaricated. "You mean the Favells?"

"Who are they?"

"Matthew Favell is my stepfather. He doesn't wish me to contact them. There's no point in any event. They don't know me any more than my great-uncle does."

Delia was eyeing him with a look of puzzlement. Giff made no attempt to explain away his sudden surly mood. Her tone became minatory. "Is that all you care for? You have no use for anyone who can't identify you?"

He was nettled. "I didn't say that. And before you suggest I go knocking on Lord Saunderton's door, let me tell you nothing would induce me to do so."

"Who is Lord Saunderton?"

"If he's not dead, my grandfather. He disowned my mother when she ran off with Matt, and I'm having nothing to do with him, or any of that family."

"Then you're a stubborn idiot, Giffard Gaunt!" Exasperation sounded in her voice, but he'd no chance to respond before she was off again. "How do you know your grandfather might not be able to help you? If you insist on being ruled by stupid prejudice, I'm not surprised you have to skulk about like a criminal!"

"Skulk about? Do I look as if I'm skulking about?"

"Where does this Lord Saunderton live?"

"I don't know and I don't care!"

"Yes, you do. At least, you may not care, but you know. I refuse to believe your stepfather did not provide you with all the necessary information."

True enough, but he was too raw with his mother's loss to be remotely willing to proffer an olive branch to her family.

"And if he didn't tell you," pursued Delia in her dogged fashion that now began to irk him, "I'm persuaded your uncle must be acquainted with your mother's family."

He flung a few steps away and discovered they had unknowingly walked past the end of the ruined building. An ocean breeze wafted across the heights where the castle was situated. Giff saw a far edge which must be the start of the cliff, but in his mind's eye spilled images he'd done his best to bury.

His mother had made him promise not to grieve, and it was for her sake he'd come upon this quest, if truth be told. Matt's persuasions would otherwise have fallen upon deaf ears.

"Giff?"

He set his teeth and turned. "Leave this, Delia. I know you mean well, but I don't wish to talk of my family."

Colour flooded her face. "Then I can't think why you wanted me to go apart with you! I thought you wished to discuss what you should do to establish yourself as Lord Baunton, but if you are going to prohibit me from speaking of anything you don't wish to hear, there's no point in my remaining."

With which, she turned away from him and began walking swiftly, not back towards the other couple who were just within sight, but along the ocean side of the building.

Giff called after her. "Why are you heading in that direction?"

"What do you care?" She threw the words over her shoulder, not even troubling to turn.

He cursed and made after her, catching her up in a few swift steps. "Will you stop, foolish wench?" Seizing her shoulder, he brought her to a halt and swung her about to face him.

She showed him a countenance alight with anger. "Go to the devil, Giff! I've had enough of your secrets and you popping up out of the blue and then ignoring me when you choose and refusing to tell me anything. I've wasted quite enough energy worrying about you, and I'm not going to do it any longer." Her eyes were suspiciously bright, and the husky note in her voice gave her away.

Giff's irritation vanished and guilt swamped him. "Don't cry!"

"I'm not!"

"You are, very nearly. I'm a brute and I'm sorry! You deserve better, Delia. Too used to keeping my own counsel, that's the trouble. And I did want to get you alone so we could talk."

She sniffed, the flush beginning to die down so that her freckles reappeared. Giff was conscious of an urge to trace their path with his finger. She'd likely bat his hand away, the mood she was in. Besides, he oughtn't to take liberties with her. Not in view of other members of the party. He looked back as the thought surfaced and found they were a deal too alone.

"The deuce! We're too isolated here. I don't want to bring scandal down on you. Besides, it's windy here. We'd best go back."

Delia glanced behind. "I am sure Lord Tarporley and Tabitha Leigh will come around the corner at any moment." Her gaze swept towards the ocean, but he'd swear the look was cursory. "I'm not cold. Let us go on."

"If you insist. But go slow."

She'd already turned and Giff fell in beside her. Reluctant to upset her further, he waited for what she might say before speaking. Nothing was forthcoming.

"Delia?"

She flicked him a look. "Yes?"

"Aren't you going to talk to me?"

"About what?"

He winced. "Anything you wish."

"You solicited the meeting. What had you in mind?"

She still sounded stiff and he cursed inwardly. He'd blundered badly. Hurt her. Impulse triggered his tongue. "I've to get used to considering your feelings, my flower girl. I'm willing to learn, if you'll trust me to try."

"Then trust *me*, Giff!" She halted again, turning to face him.

"I do trust you. Implicitly. You saved my life."

"Oh, that! No, it's not what I mean."

"What then?"

"Let me in."

Was she insisting on reverting back to talk of his mother's family? How much had he told her before? He could no longer remember. He was silent too long.

"If you don't understand, never mind." She began to walk on again and he followed suit. "What will you do if Piers does not make contact?"

The change of subject threw him, though he'd not wanted to talk of the other. "I don't know. I'm pretty certain he'll show if he can't find means to snatch me away or otherwise dispose of me."

"And you're willing to just wait for any of those things to happen?"

"What else can I do?"

"Try to find someone who can support your claim. And the best place to start is with family, if you weren't so pig-headed about it!"

In a cooler frame of mind, Giff had to concede the point. Whether he could swallow his pride was another matter. He said nothing, reluctant to reopen the argument.

After a moment, Delia spoke again, her tone stiff and constricted. "Very well, I see how it is. I must just steel myself to watching you make a sitting duck of yourself while Piers plans an attack."

Hardly were the words out of her mouth than two men came running from inside the ruins, clubs raised to strike.

CHAPTER ELEVEN

Sheer terror held Delia frozen as she watched the ruffians approach. Then Giff let out a piercing whistle. She cried out and heard his urgent command close to her ear.

"Run! Back towards the others!"

He gave her a push as he spoke. Without will, Delia began to move, then stopped as she saw him start towards the men.

"Giff, no!"

"Get back, Delia!"

Her legs felt like lead and she could barely put one foot in front of the other. Her eyes were on the running men. They were close. Too close.

In seconds they were on Giff. The impact caused all three to stagger. It seemed to Delia a mêlée of grunts and grips that shifted one way and then another. Her gaze found the clubs she'd seen raised, still clutched though neither had found a mark. The scrawny Barney's club hand dropped as a well-aimed kick to the shin caused him to yelp and hop.

The bigger man — Sam, it must be — was grappling to raise his club even as his other hand held fast to Giff's coat. Delia saw him shift back a step. Fear coursed through her as the club went up. It did not fall.

Instead, Giff's fist connected with the man's jaw. His head went back and he released his clutch on the coat.

But Barney, recovering, bored in again. Somehow Giff's leg got behind his and next instant the man was on the ground. Delia could have cheered. Except that Sam, shaking his head as if to clear it, charged in again.

The two grappled. Giff seized Sam's wrist. Was he trying to keep him from using the club?

She could see Barney struggling to his feet. Scrambling for his own club, which he'd dropped. Giff could never hold both! Frantic, she looked back along the building. No one in sight. Where were they all?

Taking in a breath, she yelled for help at the top of her lungs.

Barney, just rising, turned to look at her. Delia backed a few steps, afraid he would come after her. Without thought, she yelled again.

He made a threatening move. She turned and ran, screaming as she went.

An answering shout sounded from a distance. In the background of her mind she heard Sam call out.

"Get over here and help me!"

Delia staggered to a stop, looking back. Barney was turning towards the two men still caught in a staggering bear hug. The other ran at them and the impact threw both to the ground.

To her horror, Delia realised Giff was underneath. All thought of escape left her. She began instead to cast about the ground. She needed something. A weapon! Anything would do.

She could hear more distant shouts and the sound of hoofbeats. Was it rescue? She did not take time to look.

There! A large stone.

Darting to where a white point stuck out of the grass, Delia bent and seized it. It was larger than she'd thought, and heavy. Grunts and curses sounded not far away. Was Giff failing?

She looked up as she managed to lift the stone. The struggle on the ground was violent with protests and groans. Determination and panic drove Delia. Holding her weapon, she hurried towards the group. Her mind concentrated on saving Giff, she vaguely heard the hoofbeats growing louder, but paid scant attention.

Giff was outnumbered. The ruffians would overpower him in seconds.

She quickened her pace. She was within feet of the struggling men. She raised the stone as she reached them and brought it down hard on the nearest back. It made a satisfying crunch.

The man bellowed, arching up. With a soar in her heart, Delia realised she'd got Sam.

But Giff was still beneath him and Barney was pummelling him as he lay, fists protecting his face and head as he kicked out instead and tried to throw off his attackers with his hips.

Delia raised the stone again. At the same instant, a horse thundered into view.

Familiarity kicked in. Tiger!

He reared, whinnying in a fashion as frightening as it was furious. Delia backed off fast as his hooves came down, almost upon the struggling trio. Barney ceased his labours, looking up, face contorted. He gave a strangled cry and rolled away from Giff. Next moment, he was on his feet, belting back towards the ruins.

Sam was frozen, staring up at the great horse. Tiger whinnied again, and pawed the ground, his head coming down almost on a level with the ruffian's shocked face.

Shouts near at hand sounded. Sam took one look back. Then he was up and running, yelling Barney's name on a curse. Tiger wheeled, giving chase.

Delia could hear loud voices, but she had no time to spare to find out what was afoot. She ran to fall on her knees beside Giff's still form. "Giff! Oh, they've mauled you badly!"

He opened his eyes and his face contorted as he winced. His handsome features were marred by red weals, one below his right eye, and another at the corner of his mouth where blood oozed from a wound. "I've had enough of this," he grunted. "Damn Piers!"

He was struggling to sit up. Delia put a hand on his chest. "Stay there! You may be more injured than you know."

"Devil a bit! A few bruises, but I'm not yet dead. Here, give me a hand!"

Without thought, Delia took his hand and helped him into a sitting position. He felt his ribs.

"Ouch! Damn and blast those idiots! They've battered me to pieces!"

"They would've clubbed you to death if Tiger hadn't come."

"Then he'd have trampled them. They'll be lucky if he doesn't do it now."

Delia looked towards the riot going on at the ruin's edge. Someone was struggling with the smaller of the ruffians. "They've got Barney!"

"And the other?"

She lifted a hand to shade her eyes and the scene clarified a little more. "It looks as if he's escaped. Your horse is quiet. I think your servant has Barney."

"Sattar? He's deuced late! What the devil kept him, I'd like to know?"

Delia's gaze came back to him, eyeing his damaged face. "You've every right to be ill-tempered, Giff, but that is for later. What are you going to say? Everyone will want to know why you were set upon."

He looked struck. "Hell and the devil confound it! You're right as usual."

"Well, you'd best think fast."

She glanced back and saw Lord Tarporley heading in their direction. Hurrying figures caught in the periphery of her vision and she looked towards the corner of the building. Several members of the party, including the readily recognisable form of Miss Watkinson, were clearly coming to discover the cause of the fracas.

"We are undone, Giff! If Barney talks…"

He put a finger to his lips. "Leave it to me. Sattar knows better than to let the fellow squeal. And stop calling me Giff, for heaven's sake!"

Abashed, but resentful, Delia went into a spirited defence. "Oh, I do beg your pardon, *Mister* Giffard! Another time I will ignore your need for succour."

He grinned. "You were supposed to be running away."

"Yes, that is my habit, as I'm sure you've noticed."

A laugh escaped him and he winced. "Ouch! Heedless wench, do you want to increase my hurts?"

There was time for no more.

"Oh, Mr Giffard! How dreadful! And Miss Burloyne? Are you injured? I shall never forgive myself if you are! How shall I face dear Lady Matterson?"

Delia got to her feet, leaving Lord Tarporley to assist Giff to rise. "I am unharmed, Miss Watkinson. It is Mr Giffard who took the brunt of the attack."

"Villains! In broad daylight too!"

"Lean on me, Giffard! I have you safe."

"I've never heard of such a thing. In all my years at Weymouth, the Castle has been safe from invasion by footpads."

Footpads? Yes, a worthy excuse.

"Did they get anything from you, Giffard?" Lord Tarporley had an arm about Giff, taking his weight.

"Nothing but my dignity," Giff returned.

He was limping as, with Lord Tarporley's assistance, he began walking back towards the group at the edge of the edifice. Other members of the party were strung out along the side as stragglers came to discover the cause of the commotion. Miss Leigh, likewise limping, called out.

"Oh, are you hurt, Mr Giffard?"

"Hurt? Of course he is!" Miss Watkinson was off again. "What else is one to expect when the place is overrun with ruffians? I shall send for Captain Rhoades on the instant. One of the footmen must ride for him at once."

"No need, ma'am," Giff cut in. "My servant has one of them laid by the heels."

Miss Leigh piped up in a frightened squeak. "One of them? How many were they? Do you mean they are still at large?"

"There were two, but one escaped," Delia said.

"But we must indeed send for the militia, Mr Giffard. We cannot have this sort of thing going on in Weymouth, indeed we can't."

"First things first, Miss Watkinson, don't you think?" Lord Tarporley was diffident. "Should we not get Mr Giffard back to town where he may have his wounds seen to?"

"Yes, indeed we must. Mr Giffard, I beg you will take a seat in one of the carriages."

"Nonsense, ma'am. I'm perfectly capable of riding."

"But you're limping, sir," cried Miss Leigh.

"A little stiff, but nothing to signify."

With which, Giff pushed himself upright and took his own weight, using only a hand on his companion's arm to help him.

Delia's anxious eyes searched his face and found it a trifle pale. He ought not to ride, but it was no use saying so. Besides, she must not appear too familiar. Thank heavens everyone seemed to have forgotten her involvement in the adventure.

Miss Watkinson was still pontificating on the matter of bringing in Captain Rhoades, finding a receptive audience in Tabitha Leigh. Attention soon turned on the tableau ahead, where two horses stood quietly while the Indian servant kept hold of a subdued Barney and members of the pleasure party milled about, talking in low tones.

Miss Watkinson took charge as they neared. "We must return at once, ladies and gentlemen. We cannot remain when there are footpads at large in the area."

Giff halted, waving a hand towards the ruin. "I see no reason to spoil everyone's enjoyment of the day. We have one of them, and the other is no doubt long gone. I shall return with my servant, Miss Watkinson, and we will take the felon. The rest of you must carry on regardless."

But the redoubtable matron would not hear of this. "We could not think of it, Mr Giffard. I for one could take no further enjoyment under such conditions. I am sure I speak for all in this."

Delia had to suppress a desire to burst into laughter as the faces round about showed varying degrees of dismay. It was evident no one had the courage to gainsay their leader.

The matter was settled by Lord Tarporley. "I should not dream of letting you manage alone, sir. And I could not think of allowing my sister to remain without my escort."

"Quite so, sir," said Miss Watkinson. "Let us make our way back to the carriages at once."

She began to herd her reluctant sheep back in the direction from which they had come. Delia hung back, hoping for a word with Giff, deep in conversation with his servant.

Lord Tarporley bowed. "May I suggest you return with the others, Miss Burloyne? I will remain with Mr Giffard and see to his comfort."

There seemed to be nothing else she could do without giving herself away. But at this moment, Barney, who had stood with bowed head throughout, made a bid for freedom. Wrenching his arm from the Indian's grip, he took to his heels. The Indian servant belted after him, but he was a much older man and Barney was running like a hare.

"Hi, you!"

Lord Tarporley started after them, but Giff called him back.

"No need, sir!"

He whistled. Tiger, who'd been standing quietly, instantly took off, cantering after the runners and overtaking the Indian in seconds. He was brought up short by the broken walls of the building as Barney, beating the horse by a hair, slipped through a gap and vanished from sight.

Lord Tarporley had halted, but at this he cursed and rushed towards the building, diving through the gap. The Indian followed suit.

Delia awaited the outcome, moving to join Giff, who was emitting an exasperated curse.

"Too late!"

"You think he'll get away?"

"I hope he does!"

Delia stared. "Are you mad, Giff?"

"No, I was already exercised by the difficulties confronting us if the wretch hadn't escaped."

"What difficulties?"

He eyed her. "Can't you see? You think the fellow would keep his mouth shut? I'm ready to wager he'd not go down alone if he was faced with gaol."

Light dawned. "You mean he'd confess he was hired by Piers?"

"Exactly. That would really put the cat among the pigeons."

"But it would stop Piers surely?"

"And involve me in explanations I have no desire to make. At least not yet. Besides opening the whole affair to scandalous gossip."

"But you'd be safer, wouldn't you?"

"Those two won't dare show themselves again, I'm persuaded."

Torn, Delia watched with anxious eyes for the two hunters to reappear. Tiger was patrolling the edge of the edifice, emitting snorts as he wandered back and forth, poking his head into gaps.

At a whistle from Giff, he desisted and came trotting back to his master, dropping his head into Giff's chest. Delia watched Giff stroke his nose and utter soft words in a language she didn't understand.

He turned his head to look at her. "You ought to go back to the others, Delia."

"Not until I know if they've got Barney." She sighed. "I think it would be better for you if it was all out in the open."

"And I think I'd rather tackle Piers without the world watching."

"If he doesn't get you first. What if he hires more men?"

"He won't get the chance." Giff grinned in the old insouciant way, though it was a trifle lopsided with the injury near his mouth. "I know where he's staying. Sattar didn't waste his time while he had that fellow in his clutches."

Hope burgeoned at last. "He questioned him?"

"To some purpose."

"I'm amazed Barney talked."

"Most men will talk fast enough when pricked by the point of a dagger."

A chill went through Delia. She was almost sorry for Barney and could not help feeling relieved when Lord Tarporley and Sattar emerged from the building empty-handed.

By the time Giff arrived at the Assembly Rooms, accompanied by a dogged Lord Tarporley determined to see him safely bestowed, the battle-axe was already raising hell. The ride into town had been both painful and necessarily slow. He'd been glad of the young man's presence, which at least prevented Sattar from voicing the scold obviously under his tongue.

His henchman, Giff guessed, was mortified at having allowed Barney to escape. But that would not stop him ringing a peal over his master for making a target of himself by going apart and out of his sight.

The opportunity was further delayed when he and Tarporley dismounted outside the Rooms. A groom came running.

"My lord! I've been on the watch for you. Here, give him into my hands."

Tarporley relinquished his reins, turning to Giff. "Let my man assist yours, sir."

"No need. Sattar can manage both horses." With an apologetic look towards his henchman's tight-lipped expression, he added, "See them into the stables."

Sattar switched to his native language. "Are you telling me my business now, sahib? What do you here? Go home where I can see to your hurts."

"Presently," Giff returned in the same tongue. "I must see Delia is none the worse for the adventure." And in English, "Meet me at the lodging."

"I'll see you safely back, Giffard, once I've checked on my sister," said Tarporley.

"Good of you, sir."

"And call for a medical man. I know a good fellow here who serves my mother."

"I don't need the services of a doctor, I thank you. Sattar will see to my hurts."

Lord Tarporley's astonishment was plain. "He must be a boon to you, sir."

"I could not manage without him."

Sattar was still within hearing as he led both Tiger and his own mount away, and turned his head. Giff caught the grim look, but a tell-tale twitch of the lips promised mitigation of the coming scold.

"Take my arm, Giffard."

He did not need it, though his muscles felt stiff, but Giff was loath to offend the lad. And it would present a good appearance. Might be useful to seem worse than he was if Piers had his spies out.

His eyes sought out Delia as he entered the main hall from the vestibule, leaning on Tarporley for effect. The place was crowded, members of the expedition party having evidently joined their respective relatives. But the prominent voice of the battle-axe was to be heard above the general hubbub.

An exclamation came from Tarporley beside him. "Good Lord, she's already summoned that fellow Rhoades!"

The name struck at Giff on the instant. Delia's militia captain! The redcoat caught his eye and he saw Miss Watkinson was busy haranguing the fellow, who looked none too pleased. That would teach him to flirt with other men's petticoats! His satisfaction dissipated at Tarporley's next words.

"I dare say the captain will wish to question you closely, Giffard. If I were you, I'd put him off until you've had your hurts seen to."

191

"No time like the present." As if he had any intention of leaving the field clear while Delia was in the room. "Besides, he can note the damage while it's fresh."

"A good thought, sir. Do you wish to accost him now?"

But Giff's eyes were searching for a particular freckled face. Where the devil was Delia? Then he found her, and suffered a shock. She was sitting with her aunt, who was in company with none other than his great-uncle.

With difficulty, he refrained from exclamation. He was here as Mr Giffard. He could not acknowledge the rector as his relative. Would Uncle George hail him? Or had Delia had the sense to warn him somehow?

He had no chance to discover immediately, for no sooner did Tarporley urge him forward than the battle-axe happened to turn and catch sight of him.

"There he is at last!" She beckoned, raising her voice. "Over here, Mr Giffard!"

Before he could advance more than a couple of feet, the woman was cutting a swathe through the bodies intervening between them, dragging the redcoat along with her, talking all the time.

"See here, Captain? This is the result of your men failing in their duty! If they had captured those felons in the first place, this would not have happened, for I have it from Miss Burloyne that the ruffian who escaped is none other than the creature who has been menacing the town along with his accomplice."

The deuce! What had his flower girl done?

"And she is best placed to know," went on Miss Watkinson, red in the face and clearly on the warpath, "since she believes he may be the very same who attacked poor Lady Matterson on the road."

The captain, Giff was glad to note, was a fellow of somewhat swarthy complexion though of superior height and with a good figure and an unmistakeably soldierly bearing. He looked none too pleased at being told his business, and no wonder. He dipped his head in a slight bow towards the two men.

"I am Captain Rhoades." His eye found Giff's. "You were the victim of this attack, sir?"

"Good heavens, man, you can see he was, can't you? Mr Giffard, your eye is growing dreadfully bruised! I should think it will turn quite black, and who could be astonished at that? What further proof do you need, Captain? How long do you mean to allow this situation to continue? Until one of us is clubbed to death?"

"Give me leave, madam," cut in the captain in a clipped tone. And to Giff, "Sir, you look as if you ought to be sitting. Will you not take a chair?"

"Of course he should be sitting down. Good heavens, Mr Giffard! What are you thinking of to be still on your feet? Lord Tarporley, find him a chair this instant!"

Giff was hard put to it not to laugh as Tarporley began to stutter in response. Clearly he was no match for the battle-axe. But the captain was evidently made of sterner stuff.

He glanced around and pointed to a corner. "Over there, out of the way perhaps? I will be glad to hear your account of the incident at first hand."

"Yes, yes, a good notion," came in hasty accents from Tarporley. "Let me help you, Giffard."

The man began urging him across the room towards the designated corner, which was free of persons. Thankfully, Miss Watkinson remained behind, breaking out in a new direction.

"Gracious, I had forgot the hampers! I must see they are brought in so we may at least eat the delicacies, since that is all the enjoyment left to us of our expedition of pleasure."

With which, she sailed towards the door. To Giff's amusement, the captain gave an audible sigh of relief and began to clear a path before them.

"If you please, ma'am? Pardon me, sir."

The noise in the room had become muted. Devil take it, he'd become the centre of attention! Was every eye in the place upon him? He stole a glance towards Delia and caught his uncle's eye. A faint twitch and a gleam in the old fellow's faded orbs acknowledged him. Giff breathed more easily. Uncle George would not betray him.

He noted a concerned look in Delia's face and stopped by her chair. "I trust you are none the worse for our unfortunate contretemps, Miss Burloyne?"

She threw him an indignant look under her lashes, but inclined her head. "I came off far less badly than did you, Mr Giffard." Her eyes went to the captain in the lead. "You won't keep him too long occupied, I hope?"

"As long as it takes, ma'am."

The repressive note caused Giff to suffer a reversal of feeling. He'd been a trifle in sympathy with the fellow when he was under fire from the battle-axe, but he was damned if he'd have the man to speak to Delia in that tone. On the other hand, it argued a lack of interest in her Giff could not but applaud.

At this point, Lady Matterson intervened. "When you have finished with the captain, young man, I will be obliged if you will give me a moment of your time."

Startled, Giff looked across at the suddenly formidable dame, who was sitting at a slight remove from his uncle and Delia.

"Ma'am?"

She fixed him with a gimlet eye. "You heard me."

"Aunt, please!" Delia's frantic whisper pulled his attention round. She cast him a harassed look and gave an eloquent shrug. What in Hades was in the wind now?

He returned his gaze to the elder lady and gave a bow. "I am at your service, my lady."

Suspicion began to burgeon as he allowed Tarporley to urge him onward at the captain's bidding. The oddity of the rector's presence struck him. What the deuce was Uncle George doing here? He'd met Lady Matterson when he delivered Delia to Weymouth, for he'd told Giff so when he recovered his senses after the shooting. And why now? Was he checking up on his great-nephew? No, he would not blunder in without first discovering how the land lay. Then had he chosen to visit her ladyship? Or was it Delia he had in mind?

His puzzlement increased, but he was obliged to give his attention to Captain Rhoades.

"Sit here, sir. I doubt there is much comfort to be had from any of the chairs in this Godforsak— er … in this place, but there is little choice."

Giff grinned as he took the indicated seat. "That battle-axe driven you to distraction, has she?"

The captain cast up his eyes. "I shall say nothing, Mr Giffard. Silence is always the best defence."

Giff had to laugh. "Very true."

"Are you settled for the present, Giffard?" Lord Tarporley was hovering. "May I leave you? I must see to my sister's comfort."

"Go, by all means. I've kept you long enough."

The young fellow coloured. "By no means. Send to me when you are ready to depart and I will see you to your lodging."

Giff waved him away. "No, no, my dear fellow. I am summoned by Lady Matterson, remember? I shall do well enough, never fear."

"Very well, if you are certain. But do not hesitate to call on me at need, sir."

Giff gave the necessary assurance and watched him hurry away towards his sister, who appeared to be deep in conversation with Miss Leigh. "No doubt rabbiting away about the events of the day," he said aloud.

The captain followed his line of sight. "The ladies? Yet, as I understand it, you were the only one set upon, Mr Giffard?"

Giff snapped his attention back, wary now. "I was."

Captain Rhoades surveyed him with narrowed eyes. "Were you specifically targeted, do you think?"

He was, of course, but he did not wish it known. Not yet. "I have no idea. Miss Burloyne and I had wandered out of sight of the rest of the party, which may well have made us a target."

The narrow look did not abate. "Yet Miss Burloyne recognised the fellow for the same who had been one of the pair who held up her coach on the road. She claims also to have seen him in Weymouth."

"Indeed?" Giff met the questioning look, hoping his expression was sufficiently bland. "I'm afraid I was in no condition at the time to be recognising anyone."

"You did not know the man, then?"

Giff shrugged. "I've never met him before." True enough. He'd seen both Barney and Sam riding at his heels, but never at close quarters until today.

"What about the other? Miss Burloyne tells me he was the more vicious. A burly fellow. Sam, is it?"

"Is it?"

"And the one who escaped was Barney. Is that right?"

"I didn't trouble to ask their names, Captain. I was more interested in stopping them from beating me to a pulp!"

He began to feel there was much to be said for Rhoades' assertion of silence as the best defence. The fellow was astute, he had to give him that. Ought he to cut line and give him the truth?

"I appreciate your preoccupation at the time, sir," came in clipped tones, "but you will allow it is exceptionally unusual for a couple of highway robbers to be skulking in a seaside resort and then to make an apparently deliberate attack upon an innocent bystander."

Giff met the steely look and kept his mouth firmly shut.

Captain Rhoades waited for a moment and then his gaze shifted and held. A quick glance showed Giff he had transferred his attention to Delia.

"The common element in this, Mr Giffard, is Miss Burloyne." His eyes came back to Giff's. "One might be pardoned for supposing the lady to be the intended target, rather than yourself, Mr Giffard. However, I find it hard to discover a single reason why that should be so."

Giff could not withstand a harsh bark of laughter. "You have a point."

"Well then?"

Damnation! He toyed with revealing the truth. Why in the world Delia had said as much as she had he could not imagine. Or, no, perhaps he could. If questioned in this fashion by Rhoades, she might well have thought it more prudent to speak the truth. He refused to believe she would try to force his hand.

"It seems to me, Mr Giffard," pursued the captain, "that there is more than pure chance involved here."

"Does it?"

The fellow was deuced persistent. Lord knew what he really thought was going on!

"Consider the facts, Mr Giffard. Miss Burloyne's aunt is attacked on the road. Miss Burloyne escapes and is obliged to hide in the forest while these men hunt about for her. After the coach has gone, mark you. She is providentially found on the road, and rescued." With question in his eye, he added, "By the Reverend Gaunt."

A nod in the direction of Lady Matterson's party acknowledged the rector's presence. He paused, but Giff refused the invitation, if it was one. The captain resumed.

"Next, Miss Burloyne experiences the feeling she is being watched. Then she perceives two fellows in a boat while she and other ladies are bathing —"

"Does she, though?" This was news to Giff. Delia had not told him that bit. "Bathing where?"

"There is a beach reserved for ladies." The captain's mouth twisted. "Miss Watkinson swims there also."

Giff could not forbear a grin. "Ah. No doubt she was voluble on the subject."

Rhoades winced. "Very much so. But Miss Burloyne took me aside for the purpose of mentioning that she thought these men might be the very same who had committed the highway attack."

A sliver of memory came into Giff's head. When they'd met outside the church, had not Delia said something of this? He'd been too taken up with the notion of her and the captain becoming too well acquainted to give it much attention. Now he wished he'd listened more closely. He tried a nonchalant throw.

"Sounds like the work of an over-active imagination, if you ask me, sir."

"So I thought at the time." The captain's gaze once more became steely. "However, Mr Giffard."

Giff braced. "Yes?"

"It becomes difficult to maintain that stance when this attack occurs within a day of your arrival in the town. Prior to which, it is apparent no attempt had previously been made to do anything but observe Miss Burloyne. And yet this attack is carried out upon your person while you are in company with Miss Burloyne. A lady, mark you, with whom you are barely acquainted. Yet no qualm arises to stop you removing her from the vicinity of any sort of chaperonage. At which point, sir, two men, both known to Miss Burloyne, rush from the ruins with the express intention of clubbing you."

Put like that, Giff found it hard to find an argument in refutation. He raised his brows. "Coincidence?"

A sceptical look came into the captain's features. "I must beg you not to insult my intelligence, Mr Giffard."

"Oh, you're bright enough, Captain Rhoades, I'll grant you that." He eyed the man with a degree of speculation. "Perhaps a little too bright?"

An arrested look came into the other's eyes. "Indeed?"

Giff lowered his voice. "It might be advantageous to meet elsewhere." He glanced across to Delia's party. "I am liable to be occupied for some time, I fear." He touched his fingers to his face and winced. "And I must have my man see to these."

"Tomorrow, Mr Giffard?"

Giff nodded. "My lodging, if you will. It's a little removed from the centre and we may find a nearby tavern."

Captain Rhoades got up. "Will noon suit?"

"Earlier. By noon I'll be expected to make an appearance in this place. Ten o'clock. Or no, come at nine and take breakfast with me. We'll be more private then."

The invitation was graciously accepted. Giff gave the man his direction and the captain bowed and left him.

As he got to his feet, Giff's muscles protested. He paid scant heed, his mind roving over how much to tell Rhoades. He started towards Delia only to find all three of the party standing. An imperious finger commanded him to join them.

"We are retiring for an early dinner, Mr Giffard. You will accompany us."

Giff flashed a look at Delia, who rolled her eyes. Hell and the devil, had his uncle blabbed? Now they were for it.

CHAPTER TWELVE

If she could only sneak a moment with him in private, Delia could warn Giff. He did not look to be best pleased with the turn of events. He was frowning as they left the Assembly Rooms and trooped after Aunt Gertrude, who was escorted by the rector.

Delia hung a little back, casting a significant glance at Giff. He took the hint, throwing a look towards the retreating backs of the elder couple before speaking in a tone loud enough to be heard.

"Will you take my arm, Miss Burloyne?"

"Are you sure you are strong enough, Mr Giffard?"

Lady Matterson's head turned slightly, but she confined her attention to the Reverend Gaunt, speaking in a low tone. Delia immediately followed suit as she set her hand on Giff's arm.

"We are betrayed! My aunt sent her maid with a letter to your uncle yesterday."

"Her maid? Why her maid, for pity's sake?" He was thankfully speaking in a bare murmur, matching her.

"To ensure an early response, she told me. And to insist upon my aunt's being satisfied, if your uncle had proved obdurate."

"Which he clearly did not. Has he told her the truth?"

"I fear so. She's been suspicious for days."

Lady Matterson's arctic tones interrupted them. "You need not attempt to concoct more lies for my benefit, either of you. The cat, in vulgar parlance, is out of the bag."

She had not turned as she spoke, apparently addressing the air. But the Reverend Gaunt threw a quick look over his shoulder, apology in his face.

Delia exchanged an eloquent glance with Giff, who looked rueful. Seeing him about to speak, she lifted a finger to her lips. "Wait! We don't yet know how much your uncle has told her."

"Everything, by the looks of it."

The door of their lodging was within sight, and Peggy was soon seen to be at her usual post. Lady Matterson at once took charge. "We have an extra guest for dinner, Pegler. See to it, will you? And bring wine to the parlour. Follow me, Mr Gaunt."

She went in and mounted the stairs, closely followed by the rector. About to do likewise, Delia found Giff's hand on her arm, and paused.

"Are you ready for this, my flower girl? Shall I slip away?"

Warmth rose up. Ready for what? To face the music? What choice had she? "We may as well get it over with, Giff."

He grimaced. "You may not like the consequences."

What in the world was he at? Her aunt's voice broke into her thoughts.

"Delia! Come up here this instant! You too, Mr Giffard."

"We'd best go up, Giff."

With which, she trod lightly up the stairs, a flurry in her pulse. The moment of reckoning was upon them. And Aunt Gertrude sounded anything but sympathetic. So much for her suggesting she might help!

It did not take long for the party to crowd into the parlour. Lady Matterson held court in her usual fashion on the chaise longue, while Delia obeyed an instant command to sit on the chair next to it. The rector took the seat he'd sat in weeks ago when he'd brought her back, but Giff hovered, eyeing Aunt Gertrude in a speculative way.

She threw out a hand. "Well, sit down, young man, sit down! You look as if you'll fall down if you don't."

He grinned and winced, putting a hand to his damaged mouth. "Bar a few bruises, I'm well enough, ma'am."

"Yes, but to endure such an attack so soon cannot but aggravate your previous injury. A flesh wound from a bullet, I understand?"

Startled, Delia threw a look at her aunt's complacent face and could not refrain from casting another, of reproach, at the Reverend Gaunt.

He put one hand palm up in a gesture of peace, ruefully smiling. "Your pardon, Delia. I could not remain silent when your aunt was in such a worry over you."

"It's not me, sir," she returned, with a pointed look at Giff.

He appeared to be more amused than angry. Or was it a trick of his injured mouth? He was still standing, surveying his uncle through the one good eye. The other was becoming so swollen it took Delia's attention.

"Your eye, Giff! You ought to have raw steak on it or something."

His brows shot up as he turned to her, and Delia gasped. She'd said his name! Nothing could have prevented her from seeking her aunt's reaction.

To her surprise, Lady Matterson looked more smug than angry. She nodded. "Just as I thought." Her gaze returned to Giff. "Do you mean to stand there forever, Giffard Gaunt, or are you going to take a chair?"

Giff laughed, and then hissed in a breath, clenching a fist.

Exasperated, Delia got up, fetched the straight chair from near the door and plonked it down. "Sit!"

He looked rueful, moved the chair nearer to his uncle's, and sat down. "Your niece takes after you, ma'am, does she?"

"Nothing of the sort. Though I'll admit she's a gel after my own heart."

To Delia's relief, Peggy came in with the tray and set it down. "Dinner will be half an hour, my lady."

"Excellent. Delia, you may pour."

Only too glad of an excuse to do something, Delia went directly to the table and lifted the decanter of Madeira.

"You'd best give young Gaunt brandy. He looks as if he needs it."

Delia glanced at Giff and found him evidently enjoying her aunt's acerbic utterances. His eyes danced and he nodded.

"That will be most welcome, ma'am."

She set down the Madeira and picked up the smaller decanter, pouring a measure of the golden liquid into a glass. She took it across and handed it to Giff, who received it with a conspiratorial wink. Warmth rushed into Delia's face and she made haste to cover her consciousness with serving the rector.

Lady Matterson broke out again. "Well, young Gaunt, what have you to say for yourself?"

"Why, nothing, ma'am, until I know what I'm getting myself into."

Bravo, Giff! Delia picked up two glasses, handed one to her aunt, and sat down, raising her own to her lips as the rector took this up.

"I've explained the whole story, Giffard. When I knew Lady Matterson was exercised by a worry that Delia was in trouble, and might be in some kind of danger, I had to speak."

Giff nodded, seemingly unperturbed. "I appreciate the necessity, sir. I'm afraid Captain Rhoades must also learn the facts."

"Rhoades?" Lady Matterson's penetrating gaze reappeared. "What does he have to do with it?"

"He knows too much already. Or suspects there is more to today's attack. He's a more astute fellow than that battle-axe gives him credit for."

Delia saw a spasm cross her aunt's face and knew Lady Matterson found this description both apt and funny.

"Are you referring to Miss Watkinson?"

Giff nodded. "Too busy for her own good, is that one."

"You may say so with confidence. And if you don't wish her to thrust several spokes in your wheel, however unwitting, I suggest you don't give her any reason to suppose you are in fact the long lost Lord Baunton."

Even Giff looked stunned by this.

Delia stared at her aunt. "You know he is?"

"Of course I don't. Never set eyes on the fellow in my life until yesterday." The irascible note was marked, but Aunt Gertrude's implacable gaze remained upon Giff.

His brows drew together. "You believe me then, Lady Matterson?"

"I've no reason not to. And if Piers Gaunt has hired men to silence you, by whatever means, it rather suggests he believes it too."

Here the Reverend Gaunt cut in. "It turns out, my dear boy, that her ladyship knows a great deal about the whole affair. Which, I may say, does not greatly surprise me, since you've told me how many years you've been coming to Weymouth, ma'am." He turned to Lady Matterson as he spoke, bowing his silver head. "The matter caused a deal of talk at the time."

"But I've no proof, sir, as you well know." Impatience sounded in Giff's voice. "It's very well to say Piers knows the truth, ma'am, but without means of proof to oust him, I can't do other than confront the man in person."

A snort escaped Aunt Gertrude. "To what purpose, sir? Are you proposing to settle the matter with a duel?"

Delia could no longer remain silent. "I thought it a ridiculous notion too, Aunt. But there's no doing anything with Giff when he's got a bee in his bonnet."

"You can talk! I never met such a persistent wench. Nor such a bossy one neither."

"Oh, be quiet! If I'd done as you told me, you'd have bled to death!"

"Children, children! Enough bickering, if you please."

Lady Matterson's chiding tones caught Delia in midstride. She'd forgotten where they were. And the trouble they were in. Or were they? So far her aunt had made nothing out of the adventure. Delia had been convinced she would be appalled by its scandalous nature.

All at once it occurred to her that Giff had thought the same. Was that what he'd meant by consequences?

"Your uncle speaks of letters written by, I believe, your stepfather?"

"Matthew Favell, ma'am, yes."

Lady Matterson's gaze remained on Giff's face. "I remember that too. He ran away with Baunton's wife."

"My mother, ma'am."

"What was her name?"

"Flora."

His lips were compressed, and Delia's heart sank as she noted the smoulder in his one good eye.

"I meant her maiden name. Was she not Saunderton's daughter?"

Giff did not answer, and it was left to the rector to respond.

"That is correct, ma'am. Lord Saunderton did not approve Favell's suit and Flora was given in matrimony to my nephew. He was not a forgiving man, I regret to say."

"He knew of the liaison?"

"I imagine so. He was less surprised than angry and humiliated when Flora eloped. What he could not pardon was her taking his heir."

"One can scarcely blame him." A wry look entered Aunt Gertrude's face at Giff's fiery glance. "Yes, I am aware you have no wish to hear that, young man, but it is nevertheless true. A reprehensible act to have removed you. These things matter in our circle. Look how difficult she has made it for you to establish your claim to the earldom."

"My mother is not to blame for that." The snap in Giff's tone was marked. Delia thought she read pain there too. "The earl might have recovered me, had he wished to do so. Instead, he led Piers to believe he might inherit, if he did not precisely groom him to take the reins."

"Impossible! You know nothing of your heritage if you believe that."

Giff's one-eyed gaze became intent. "What precisely does that mean, ma'am?"

Aunt Gertrude's features twitched. "My dear young man, the line must always pass from father to son."

"If possible, Aunt. You know very well there are innumerable cases where it does not."

"Only when there is no direct heir, Delia. The laws of primogeniture are particularly strict. That is why your cousin could not gain his point, Giffard. Indeed, I am surprised no one succeeded in locating you, since you are clearly alive and in excellent health."

"Not for much longer, if Piers has his way," Delia said with a good deal of bitterness, shocking herself with the intensity of her feelings.

"Devil a bit, my flower girl! I'm not yet dead."

"By a miracle, Giff! If Tiger had not come to your rescue —"

He grinned. "Nothing of the kind! I remember you had the matter well in hand. What did you use on Sam? A stone?"

"Yes, and I wish I'd got him on the head!"

A snorting explosion from Lady Matterson made her jump and turn. Oh, help! She'd half-forgotten they were not alone.

"Enterprising of you, my child, if foolhardy."

Giff gave Delia a wink and she felt her cheeks grow warm.

"She's pluck to the backbone, ma'am."

"So it would seem, if all I hear from the rector here is true."

The Reverend Gaunt was smiling across at Delia. "Perfectly true, ma'am, as my great-nephew will confirm, I've no doubt."

Giff's gaze went back to Aunt Gertrude. "I wanted to set her down and let her escape that day. But she insisted on binding up my wound and she took the reins too."

"You'd have fallen off Tiger if I hadn't."

Lady Matterson raised a hand for silence. Her tone changed. "What, may I ask, young Gaunt, is this flower girl business?"

The heat in Delia's cheeks intensified. "It's just his pet name for me, Aunt. It's nothing."

"Nothing? A pet name is nothing?"

Her narrowed gaze was fixed upon Giff as she spoke. He met it with his good eye and did not flinch. "I understand your ladyship, I believe. You need have no apprehension. Once my affairs are settled, I will settle that matter too."

What matter? What was she missing here? Delia was tempted to demand to know what he meant, but a spark of unprecedented hope kept her silent, a thrum in her breast. If she asked, she might discover she was mistaken. Besides, she had no wish to find Giff had intentions towards her based solely on the exigencies of their adventures.

To her relief, Peggy came in to say that dinner awaited them and her aunt let it drop. But once Scoley and Sally had served, Lady Matterson dismissed them.

"Now then, young Gaunt, how do you propose to set about recovering your patrimony? And don't talk nonsense about fighting duels."

Sitting on the bed in his shirtsleeves, his cravat and waistcoat removed, Giff endured while his henchman applied a salve to the bruise around his eye. Sattar had already cleaned and anointed the cut at his mouth, which, he'd discovered on looking in the wall mirror, was also a trifle swollen.

"What is that you are using?" His uncle was watching the operation with interest, perched on the dressing stool. "It has a strong smell of camphor."

Sattar kept at his task as he answered. "Tiger Balm. It is much used in my country."

"Yes, and it stings like the devil," Giff put in, wincing.

"It will heal faster, sahib, as you well know." Sattar glanced towards the rector. "This damage is naught for this boy, reckless as he is. Many times have I mended him."

"You can't blame me this time, old sobersides. And you took your time bringing your ancient bones to the rescue."

His henchman's tone became both stern and resigned. "This I have already spoken, sahib. That place is littered with broken stone, enough to bring the horses to their knees."

Reverend Gaunt intervened. "Shall we stick to the point instead of raking up scores?"

Giff threw a mischievous glance at his great-uncle through his good eye, and slid a look up at his henchman. "Sattar knows my mind, and that I don't mean it. Can't let him ride roughshod over me all the time. I have to maintain my dignity somehow."

A grim smile curled Sattar's lip and Giff was satisfied. He would not escape a scold from his devoted retainer once the rector departed, but it would be a mild one.

"Attend to me, Giffard. What do you mean to do? It did not seem to me that you relished any of the suggestions put forward at the dinner table."

"It's not that, sir. Most of them will take too long. I don't see Piers waiting for me to hunt down whoever may have acted for him in his attempt to gain the title, as Lady Matterson suggested."

"But it's a good thought, Giffard. They, of all people, must be *au fait* with what may be needed to bring the matter to a satisfactory conclusion."

"They, of all people, will require proof, Uncle George. And where am I to find it?"

His great-uncle sighed. "There's the rub, I agree. But at least it will bring the matter into the light."

Impatience rode Giff. "And take years and years to settle while Piers enriches himself at my expense and I grow stale with boredom. Besides, if they acted for Piers, they won't be inclined to pursue my suit. No, sir. I'll do it on my own terms or not at all."

At this point, Sattar requested him to sit still while he removed his shirt. "I must see if you are hurt elsewhere, sahib."

His mind on the difficulties confronting him, Giff allowed his henchman to pull the shirt over his head without protest. An exclamation from his uncle drew his attention.

"Heavens, my dear boy, they have properly mauled you!"

Giff glanced at his torso and found reddened and broken skin down his left side. He touched it and hissed in a breath. "Damnation take that Sam! He must have got me with his club."

"You have taken a bruise to your back also, sahib," said Sattar, peering behind him.

"Probably when they drove me to the ground. Explains why I've been feeling a trifle stiff."

"A trifle! That settles it, my dear Giffard. You are in no condition to be fighting duels. You must find another solution."

"Temporarily, sir. I'll mend fast enough."

Sattar was already smearing his Tiger Balm across these fresh wounds, and to say truth, he was aching all over. Despite his words, he knew there was no confronting Piers across the length of a sword in his present state.

The rector was watching Sattar. "You will have to keep him in check, my friend. Piers is no mean swordsman."

Sattar straightened, giving Reverend Gaunt one of his fiercest looks. "You think he will pay mind to me, sahib? I look every day to be running to Sahib Favell with a corpse instead of a son. If instead I do not jump into the sea for shame."

Giff laughed and gave him a buffet on the arm. "See what I have to put up with, sir? He's been prophesying disaster since we set out from Bishnupur."

"Since I was cursed with a devil boy little more than a babe, sahib. Aged I am by more than my years for having a demon forever at my heels."

Reverend Gaunt smiled at this sally, but the worried look in his eyes did not abate.

Giff leaned across and set a hand on his knee. "Don't trouble your head over me, Uncle George. I've survived worse than anything Piers can do, believe me."

"You may believe, sahib," put in Sattar sourly. "I have said often and often this boy is born under a lucky star."

The rector laughed and rose. "I must go. I trust you are for bed, Giffard? You need to rest."

"Have no fear, sahib. I will tie him in if I must."

Giff had to laugh. "He would too. I'm only glad of my wounds or he'd likely be tempted to use me as he did in my youth."

"I never thrashed you but you deserved it, sahib," said his henchman with dignity.

"I deserved it all too often, you old taskmaster. But I'm glad enough to go to my bed tonight, sir. It's been a trying day."

"To say the least." Reverend Gaunt came across and held out a hand. "I'll say goodnight. I will be here tomorrow, but must return to Stepleton the day following. Know that you may send to me if there is anything I can do, or if you again need a refuge. My house is yours."

Touched, Giff squeezed the hand he held. "I don't know what I'd have done without you, sir. And I'm grateful for your belief in me."

A rueful twinkle came into the elderly rector's eyes. "If you want the truth, Giffard, you are too like my nephew for doubt. In temperament at least. Henry was just such an impetuous fellow. Charging like the bull in the china shop and refusing to count the cost."

Giff said nothing rather than say what was on his mind. He could regard only with odium any comparison to his real father.

The rector's brows drew together. "What puzzles me is why he abandoned the hunt for you. I used to wonder if he knew where you were and chose not to go after you. Why, though?"

Why indeed. The obvious leapt to mind. "If he knew I was in India, it's a fair distance."

"He could have written."

"The lawyers wrote, once he'd been granted his divorce. As far as I know, he never wrote. Certainly not to my mother. And not to me. Matt would have told me if he had."

His uncle's frown did not abate. Giff found it troubling. After all, if anyone knew his father well, it must be George Gaunt. "But Matthew Favell wrote to your father, I think you said? To Henry."

"Yes. My father —" the word felt sour in Giff's mouth — "never replied."

"Those letters must be somewhere."

"Not if Piers destroyed them."

"Which suggests he went through all Henry's papers when he died. He had no right to do so. Only the executors had that right. I do wish you'd speak to Hammersley, Giffard. He must know if there were letters."

Giff grimaced. "When we met at Waldiche Keep that one time which started all this mess, Piers swore Hammersley told him there were no letters from Matthew among Lord Baunton's papers. He said he enquired particularly since it was in his interests to do so."

The rector's features darkened and there was indignation in his gaze. "But you insist your stepfather wrote several times.

Then Piers must be lying. Or he stole them. Who else had a reason to do so? There can be no other explanation."

"Yes, there can." Giff knew his voice had hardened, but it had to be said. "My father destroyed them."

"Henry?"

The shocked tone rankled. "Why not? You've said it yourself, sir. He ceased to look for me. He had no wish to recover me. He may have thought, or hoped, I was dead, or soon would be. Why keep letters to say otherwise?"

"Because you are his heir, Giffard. Henry may have hated or despised your mother, but he had as much regard for his name and the true line as the next man. I refuse to believe he would have acted against his own best interests."

"We differ, sir, as to what he considered his best interests. I can't believe he wished for his son back. Nor to take over after his death. He would have made provision for it. At least to instruct Hammersley to seek me out, which he most certainly did not." Galled beyond bearing, Giff threw up his hands. "Let us leave this, sir. To say truth, if Matt had not persuaded me to try, I should not be here at all. I've no ambition to step into my father's shoes."

"But you are the earl, Giffard, and Waldiche Keep is your seat. There's no getting away from it. Will you permit Piers to keep what is not rightfully his?"

Right at this moment, Giff was half inclined to consign Piers to the devil, and the earldom with him. Why should he care? He had a life in India, one he would willingly resume — with or without his title, in spite of his English roots. And he'd regret none of it.

An image of a freckled face came into his head, and sat there, mocking him.

Yes, there was one regret. If he was obliged to leave his flower girl, that would be a wrench indeed.

He looked into his uncle's anxious eyes. "No, I think not. Or if I can't win, I'll give the fellow a run for his money at least."

Thanks to Sattar, he slept the night through, waking to stiffness and a plethora of aches. Groaning as he sat up, Giff looked with acute suspicion at his henchman, who was opening the drapes at the window.

"Did you put something in that tea you gave me last night?"

"You needed it, sahib." Sattar went to the dresser where he'd laid down a tray. He handed Giff a tall cup. "Drink."

Giff squinted at the dark contents. "What the deuce —! Chocolate? Are you out of your senses?"

"The woman made it. She hears of your injuries and this is her remedy. Drink."

"Am I to be coddled by the landlady now, as well as suffering your rough and ready ministrations?"

His henchman declining to answer such a provocative speech, Giff tasted the brew and found it soothing. "It's good."

A sour smile greeted this admission as Sattar set about preparing his master's clothes. Giff was content to sit back against his pillows and sip, his sore muscles easing a trifle. It hurt to use his mouth, and it struck him that he could see through both eyes again.

"Has the swelling gone down in my face?"

His henchman glanced his way. "Your eye is black, sahib."

"Give me a mirror." He took the silver-backed hand mirror and handed the empty cup to Sattar, inspecting the damage. "Capital! I look like a regular bruiser. I'll be obliged to endure a barrage of comment, I suppose. And that cursed captain is coming for breakfast, did I tell you?"

"No, sahib, but it makes no matter. What time?"

"Can't recall." Giff gave back the mirror. "Take this away, I don't wish to see myself. What's the time now?"

"Near eight, sahib."

"The devil! I remember now. Rhoades is coming at nine. You'd best bustle, man."

Throwing up his eyes, Sattar went off to fetch his hot water and Giff struggled out of bed, groping for the chamber pot. He washed and dressed with the swiftness of long habit, never one to linger over the necessities of life, and was ready in the parlour with a pot of steaming hot coffee and a basket of warm rolls on the table when Captain Rhoades put in an appearance.

"A pity your man let that fellow go," remarked the visitor, casting an eye over his host. "Show that face to the magistrate and the felon would be thrown straight into gaol."

Giff laughed and winced. "Well, I'm glad he escaped, I don't mind telling you. Sit down, man. Coffee?"

The captain accepted a cup and added a small amount of cream, declining the sugar. Giff poured a cup for himself, but left it black.

"I prefer tea myself, but our supplies are low."

The captain had no comment to make on this. "Why are you glad that rascal escaped?"

"Because I don't need the complication. I'm confident he won't be used again. Or either of them."

Rhoades frowned in mute question, but the plump little landlady's entrance with a heavily burdened tray kept Giff from answering.

"There's fresh fish, Mr Giffard, sir. But I've brought beef too, as there weren't a big catch today. But I've took the liberty of doing baked eggs, which I hope will be easier if you find the

216

meat too tough or can't cope with the fish bones with that horrid bruise on you, sir."

Giff responded suitably and the landlady's effusions coming to an end at last, she curtsied her way out and he invited the captain to serve himself, indicating the fish and meat.

"And you, sir?"

Giff grimaced. "I'll stick to the eggs and some rolls. The woman judged aright."

Once he began upon his repast, carefully filleting the flesh from the bones of his fried fish, the captain lost no time in pursuing his reason for being there. "What did you mean by saying those men won't be used again? Who has been using them?"

Giff buttered a roll. "My cousin, Piers Gaunt. You'll likely know him as master of Waldiche Keep."

"Indeed? I don't know him. I've heard of the Keep. Gaunt, you say?" He regarded Giff as he chewed, not with suspicion, though his eyes were keen.

"Gaunt, yes. It's my name too."

Rhoades showed no surprise. "I see. Not Giffard?"

"My Christian name."

The captain nodded, his mouth full. When he'd cleared the obstruction, he took a draught of coffee and set the cup down with a determined air. "I hope you mean to enlighten me, sir."

Giff gave him a wry look. "I didn't invite you here for nothing, Rhoades. I'll tell you the whole story. But I must first request your promise to honour my confidence, especially as it concerns Miss Burloyne."

"You begin to interest me extraordinarily, Mr Giffard. Or rather, Mr Gaunt. You have my word."

"Stick to Giffard, if you will. And thank you. Miss Burloyne's entrance into the whole affair was purely accidental."

"But not her remaining in it, I take it?"

Giff was betrayed into a snorting laugh, which caused a sharp pain. He winced and set down a forkful of egg. "Miss Burloyne, my dear fellow, is a woman of decided opinions. And a great deal of determination. She wouldn't back off if the whole world ordered it."

Warmth grew in his breast as he recalled Delia's assault on Sam and her anxious efforts to warn him all was revealed. No, she would never willingly desist in her efforts to keep him alive.

The captain picked up the coffee pot, poured himself a refill and set the spout over Giff's cup. "More coffee? I gather this recital may take some time."

"I'll be as brief as I can."

Giff nodded for the refill and embarked on as succinct an explanation of his circumstances as was feasible while the captain, having demolished his fish, began upon the beef.

"I've no proof, of course, which is why my cousin has taken an underhand route."

The captain finished off the last of his portion of beef and shifted the plate aside. "You think he wishes to dispose of you? What, murder?"

"Not outright. He was open enough when he spoke to Delia — Miss Burloyne. Apparently he thinks to ship me off to the Americas. How I don't know, but that's what he said."

Rhoades ruminated for a moment, frowning. Giff eyed him. He'd told his story only because the fellow was so suspicious. He'd not supposed he might assist in any way, but a thread of expectation grew in his breast.

At last the captain looked up. "He'd have to bribe the skipper of a ship to take you, since one presumes you'd be a tied-up unconscious bundle. You'd not walk willingly up a gangway."

Giff was startled into a snorting laugh. "Hardly."

"At gunpoint? Knife point? Sword point?"

"I've enough science to prevent any man enforcing me under such conditions."

A grim smile curved the captain's mouth. "Yes, I imagine you have. You've soldiered?"

"No, but I've been trained in Indian ways. My servant Sattar, in his youth, was lethal."

"Interesting."

Giff returned to the point. "Piers has to catch me before he can bribe anyone to remove me, permanently or otherwise. And I doubt he'll use the same rascals again."

"What do you mean to do to establish this claim of yours?"

"To tell the truth, I don't yet know. I meant to force my cousin into fighting me face to face, but that must wait now."

"Because of your present injuries."

"Just so."

Rhoades drummed his fingers on the table, the frown still on his brow. "I'll have my men patrol the town. It will be expected in any event after this attack. That will at least keep your cousin's ruffians from showing themselves."

Giff thanked him. "Though as I said, I imagine they have rendered themselves useless by their bungling yesterday."

"Yes, it was foolish to try for you in broad daylight with any number of persons in the vicinity. This cousin of yours must be growing desperate."

This was a new idea. "I'd not thought, but you're right. Delia too. It was her notion that I should parade in public. She thinks being visible ought to protect me, but so far Piers has lain low."

"Because you are parading, as you call it, under a false name?"

"I didn't want an open scandal."

"That I can understand. I doubt you'll avoid one in the end, however."

Which was all too true. Had he been unnecessarily cautious? No, because revealing his true identity might give rise to the truth of his adventure with Delia, and he could not endanger her reputation.

Rhoades got up. "If I can be of assistance, call on me." He grinned. "I'll do a little flaunting of my own, Mr Giffard. It can't hurt for your cousin to see you've a redcoat among your acquaintance."

Giff returned the smile. "Good of you, Captain. Who knows? Your presence might even induce Piers to come into the open."

"Because he can't get at you secretly. You know, it occurs to me that his scheme to make you disappear becomes less viable the more you are seen to be surrounded by people who know you."

"That is just what Delia said. It would make a deal of noise."

"Yes, I think we must alert Mr Piers Gaunt to the fact you are not without friends and well-wishers who, should you inexplicably vanish, might be inclined to ask questions."

Waking betimes after a restless night, Delia was conscious mainly of a desire to see Giff at the earliest possible moment. She wanted to know how he did, of course, but his health was not the most urgent of her preoccupations. She must make it clear to him that he was under no obligation to make her an offer, though the necessity was galling.

It was all Aunt Gertrude's fault. She might have known the worst would be saved for the gentlemen's departure last night. No sooner had the parlour door closed behind them, with Miss Pegler to lead the way downstairs, than Lady Matterson fixed Delia with that gimlet eye.

"You will oblige me at once, Delia, with the answer to one question."

Unsuspecting but wary, she'd set down her empty teacup. "Yes, Aunt?"

"Have you taken leave of your senses?"

Delia blinked. "I beg your pardon?"

"We will set aside the saving of lives and escaping from the coach —"

"You told me to escape from the coach!"

"— which appears to have been unavoidable, but what in heaven's name possessed you to become embroiled in that young man's struggle to regain his title?"

"It was not by choice!"

"Not by choice that he came to Weymouth, of all places? Not by choice that you went apart with him at Sandsfoot Castle? Not by choice that —"

"No, I don't mean that!" Delia defended herself with vehemence. "I didn't ask those ruffians to come here, did I? I had no thought of seeing Giff again once the rector brought me here, only those men were watching me. And though indeed I didn't know it, Giff's servant was here too because he was watching them. It was not by my design, Aunt, and I won't be blamed!"

Which did not appease Lady Matterson in the least. "Don't tell me, girl! You are in a fair way to doting on that boy and he on you, if I don't miss my guess."

Heat flooded Delia from head to foot as embarrassment warred with resentment. She hit back strongly. "My feelings are irrelevant, ma'am, and so are his."

"Not to my way of thinking, miss. I don't deny he's a handsome creature, but what if he can't regain his patrimony? Have you thought of that?"

She'd thought of little else for the past weeks, but it would not do to say so.

"Then he'll go back to India and I'll never see him again," she snapped. And found herself weeping like an overflowing river. Shocked, and struggling to stop, Delia turned away from her aunt's too knowing eyes and hunted her pockets for a handkerchief.

"Here, take mine." Aunt Gertrude's hand appeared, a folded white square in her fingers. "Just as I thought. You're in love with the wretch, aren't you?"

Delia snatched the handkerchief and wiped her eyes, blowing her nose with defiance. "It's b-been a t-trying d-day, that's all."

She choked a little over the words as the tears kept coming. Her aunt said no more, for which she was grateful as it enabled her to resume control and swallow down the urge to cry until she could cry no more.

She heard Lady Matterson moving about and presently a silver flask appeared in front of her face. "Medicinal brandy, my child. I keep it handy for emergencies."

It was so typical Delia hiccupped on a laugh as she took the open flask. "You are perfectly dreadful, Aunt Gertrude. Brandy flasks and pistols! I don't know how you have the gall to ring a peal over me."

"Drink, girl! At my age I'm entitled to ring all the peals I want."

Delia gave a watery chuckle and capitulated, sipping a little of the fiery liquid. It put heart into her and she took a couple more sips and then handed it back. She watched Lady Matterson screw the lid back on and move to the mantel, slipping the flask behind the clock.

"That's where you keep it?"

"I have to hide it from Pegler. She doesn't approve." Resuming her seat, she patted the cushions next to her. "Come here to me."

With reluctance Delia obeyed. She sat at a slight remove, but Aunt Gertrude grasped her hand and held it in her papery clasp.

"Now, my child, let us cease this pretence and discuss the matter sensibly."

A sigh escaped Delia. "I find it hard to think sensibly about Giff, Aunt. He takes too many risks and I can't help worrying."

"The only risk worth thinking about is the one to your reputation, Delia. If your conduct becomes known —"

"It won't become known, why should it? None who know the truth will betray me. And I'm careful to behave circumspectly in public."

"You call it circumspect to go apart with the man?"

"It was perfectly legitimate at Sandsfoot Castle. We were exploring."

"Fiddlesticks!"

"Well, at any rate, we looked as if we were."

"And what in fact were you doing, if I may make so bold?"

Delia pulled her hand away. "Talking! Giff did not make love to me, if that is what you think."

"But he could have done. That's the point."

Delia's pulse skipped a beat and a warning of disaster loomed in her head. "What are you getting at, Aunt Gertrude? Be plain with me, if you please."

Lady Matterson's chin went up. "Hoity-toity! As if it wasn't plain enough. There's been sufficient to compromise you ten times over."

"Compromise me?"

"And if you don't know it, I'm certain young Giffard does."

Delia's heart was behaving in a manner as uncomfortable as it was distressing. The last thing she wanted was to have Giff thinking he was obligated to marry her. All at once she recalled his cryptic comment to her aunt. What had he said? Something about having the matter in hand once his affairs were settled. She'd been puzzled by it at the time.

"He — he's said nothing about it to me," she ventured.

"Naturally not. He's in no position to do so at present. A pretty sort of fellow he would be to be offering in his current nameless state."

"He's not nameless," Delia retorted, stung. "And I wouldn't accept him if he did offer!"

"Then you ought to be in Bedlam, foolish child! I admit it's not the match I would choose for you, but it's too late to be repining."

Thoroughly agitated, Delia lost no time in refuting this. "It's no match at all if it's done merely to satisfy convention. I won't have Giff forced into it. For such a reason? Besides, it's unnecessary. Nothing happened between us, and —"

"Don't you want to marry the creature? It's clear you care for him, after all."

"That's scarcely the point, is it?"

"Ha! Then you admit it?"

Her discomposure complete, Delia knew not what to say. She took refuge in the lateness of the hour, rising sharply. "I'm tired, Aunt. I'm going to bed."

"Very well, but don't think we're done with this, Delia, because I have a deal more to say to you on this subject."

Delia groaned and dropped a curtsey. "Goodnight, Aunt Gertrude."

She retreated in disorder and found Sally waiting to put her to bed.

"Dearie me, Miss Delia, you look worn to a frazzle and cross as crabs!"

"I'm both, and I don't want to talk about it!"

Sally fussed and soothed as she divested her mistress of her garments and bundled her into her nightgown. "Shall I fetch you up a cup of warm milk, Miss Delia?"

Knowing she was unlikely to sleep, Delia thanked her and climbed into bed, there to give herself over to incessant and useless fretting which culminated in a single determination. If Giff truly believed, as Aunt Gertrude seemed to think, that he had to marry her to save her reputation, she must disabuse him of the notion at once. She could not endure to marry him for such a reason as that. It would be too humiliating. Inexpressibly painful too.

Until she'd been accused, she had not examined her true feelings. She'd been dazzled by Giff's first appearance. And subsequently both amused and infuriated by him as well. The thought of his danger had occupied her mind to the exclusion of all else. But now she was forced to think about it, she could not help recognising the force of her emotions. She couldn't bear the idea of his dying because it would be torture to lose him.

Not that she held him, nor expected to. But to know he was alive somewhere in the world would, she'd thought, have been her comfort. Only now did it occur to her that she did not want to lose Giff at any price. Except the price of the anguish it would cause if he married her because he must and not because he loved her.

It became imperative to ensure he made no such offer, if it could not come from his heart. And Delia had no reason to suppose that it could. Once or twice he'd looked as if he might take the liberty of kissing her. A guilty thought when she recalled Aunt Gertrude's suspicions. He'd been possessive when she'd mentioned Captain Rhoades that first time. But she dare not take either of these things for proof of his affections being engaged.

Men, after all, were possessive by nature. And they made no qualms about taking liberties with girls, if she was to judge by the conduct of her brothers. Felix had kissed one of her school friends, but was not in the least in love with her.

No, and merely because Giff called her his flower girl, she could not suppose he meant anything more by it than a careless endearment. She dared not suppose it. Better to believe him indifferent. Or not quite that. He valued her friendship and her loyalty, that much was true. But if there was more, Delia had not seen it.

She slept only fitfully, beset by nebulous dreams she could not remember on waking. Except that Giff figured in them and her cheeks were damp with seeping tears. The morning could not come soon enough.

Yet no sooner did sleep leave her completely than her heart misgave her with the necessity to broach the whole affair with Giff. How in the world did you tell a man you had no intention of marrying him if he offered without love? Especially when he had not brought the subject up.

Feeling worn, her nerves shredding, Delia got out of bed and rang for Sally. She must get out. The sun was up and the day looked fine. She would dress quickly and go with Scoley to see if there was any fish to be had.

Sally arrived with her morning chocolate, which she drank while the maid went for hot water and passed a message to Scoley to wait. Delia endured Sally's clucking as she dressed, but refused her offer to accompany her mistress to the beach.

A brisk breeze was blowing as she went down the Esplanade with the groom, but several boats drawn up the sand indicated that the fishermen's catch had been successful.

"Looks like we'll get some today, miss."

"Let us hope so."

It always put her aunt in a better frame of mind when she was served freshly caught fish. Mrs Tuckett, knowing Lady Matterson's preferences, always removed all the bones and presented the fillets lightly fried in butter with a parsley and cream garnish. Delia might hope to escape further discussion of the business now preying on her mind.

She did not accompany Scoley to the boats, choosing instead to stroll down near to the edge of the surf where the salty wind on her cheeks blew off a little of her agitation.

Delia breathed in, watching the glint of golden light upon the blue deeps. She shifted her gaze to the far horizon, her mind trying for an image of a foreign shore. India. Such an enormous distance! It took months to travel the seas between, so she had heard. If Giff should fail! If he should sail away…

A sharp pang seized her. She could not do it! She could not speak to him of obligation, of offers, or even the very idea of marriage. She might as well cut her own throat!

"Well met, Miss Burloyne!"

The familiar voice shattered her thoughts and she spun, blinking into the sneering features of Piers Gaunt.

CHAPTER THIRTEEN

The usurper had come up all too close, crowding Delia even on the vast expanse of beach. She could see the mockery in his eyes. He had meant to astonish her.

"Sir?" She stepped back a pace, trying to gather her scattered wits.

He was as well turned out as he had been upon the last occasion, sporting a maroon frock-coat and tight breeches, both much more stylish than Giff's. But Delia had no attention to spare for anything but the fact of his accosting her in this manner.

"What do you want with me, sir?"

His lip curved into the sneer he'd shown her last time. "Can't you guess, ma'am? You are my conduit to Giffard, since he will not face me in person."

"Nothing of the sort! It's you who is the coward, sir."

The sneer did not abate. "Prudence, Miss Burloyne, not cowardice."

Thoroughly incensed, Delia lost all caution. "Yes, for you know well Giff will challenge you if you show your face."

His brows rose. "He's a fool if he supposes I will meet him."

"No, you wouldn't dare!"

A gentle laugh came. "My dear Miss Burloyne, there is no question of daring. I have no mind to risk public exposure of this battle of wills."

Then he did not wish the world to know of it. "Because it will harm you more, I don't doubt."

"Not at all. The tale of the lost heir is a fiction, my dear Miss Burloyne, fit only for novels. In real life, these things are decided by the Crown."

"Which won't be in your favour."

"Oh, I think it will."

"Because you are attempting to be rid of Giff by foul means?"

"Because he has no proof or he would have produced it. Also because a prolonged wrangle on the matter is likely to prove both expensive and tedious. I may say Giffard is at one with me on this."

"How do you know?"

"He said as much when he so foolishly presented himself at Waldiche Keep in the first place."

Nonplussed, Delia could not think how to proceed. Then she recalled that it was Piers who had approached her. "You want me to take a message to him?"

He inclined his head. "Just this. I am open to negotiation."

Delia could not prevent the words from leaving her lips. "You are at a stand! Sam and Barney have made a mess of things, have they not?"

His lips tightened and a steely look entered his eyes, but he spoke with all his usual urbanity, if a trifle clipped. "If Giffard is of a mind to pay a visit to the Keep —"

"Ha! So you can have him overpowered there instead? Do you take him for an idiot?"

"Let him bring protection if he doubts me. Tell him I have a proposition to put to him."

A proposition? Deeply suspicious, Delia eyed the man. She did not trust him an inch. He was brewing mischief, she was sure of it. "What proposition?"

"That, Miss Burloyne, is between Giffard and myself. I will be awaiting him at the Keep." He executed a bow and turned to go.

Urgency engulfed Delia. "Wait!"

Pausing, Piers looked back. "Yes?"

"Why Waldiche Keep? Why can't you meet him here? At his lodging. Or yours."

"Because I choose to meet him on my own ground."

"It's not your ground!"

The sneer reappeared. "Possession is nine points of the law, Miss Burloyne."

With which, he left her standing, striding away across the sand towards the Esplanade.

Delia looked to the boat where Scoley had gone to buy fish. She was sorely tempted to go after Piers, to see where he was lodging. Then she remembered his mention of Giff's servant Sattar, who must already know. She uttered a low curse. She ought to have discovered if Piers meant to return to the Keep immediately. Or no, he'd said Giff should send him word.

Why should Giff waste time on that? Why wait? He could just go to the man's lodging at once and force the issue. Ask him what he meant by this.

Negotiation? What negotiation was possible? Giff was the earl. She did not for a moment believe Piers meant to relinquish what he held. Did he propose to offer him money? Some kind of share?

Impatience claimed her. She looked to the boat and was relieved to see Scoley returning.

He held up a couple of small fish as he neared. "A meagre catch, miss. This was all I could get."

"It doesn't matter. We must hurry back."

The groom's face took on concern. "Trouble, miss?"

"No, no. It is only — I have remembered something and I must speak to her ladyship."

In fact she was desperately trying to recall whether Giff had told her the address of his lodging. If he had, she could not remember it. Even if she knew it, she could not go there. Aunt Gertrude would have a fit! It was bad enough she already thought Delia compromised. If she was to go visiting Giff at his lodging, she might as well throw her cap over the windmill this minute.

Gnawed now by apprehension and impatience rather than her earlier heart-sore agitation, she could not refrain from hurrying Scoley back to Mrs Tuckett's apartment house.

She would have to wait until Giff made an appearance in the Assembly Rooms. But what if he was too stiff and sore to make the effort? No, she could not wait. She would have to write. But then who would know where to take the note?

Arrived at the lodging, she hurried up the stairs and went to her room to remove her light cloak. Her hair had become a trifle wild in the wind and she sat down to make a repair, brushing it back and putting in a couple of pins.

Her mind continued to turn over Piers's words, but for the life of her she could think of no sort of negotiation either possible for him to make, or that could be acceptable to Giff.

By hedge or by stile she must get word to him. She would counsel him to confront Piers in Weymouth and demand to know what he had in his head.

Now that Lady Matterson was *au fait* with the truth, Delia did not hesitate to acquaint her with this latest development. As she'd hoped, it served to turn her aunt's attention away from further discussion of her prospects vis-à-vis Giff and a marriage to save her face.

Anxious to get to the Assembly Rooms at an early hour in hopes of his making an appearance, she went to her aunt's room as soon as she'd finished prinking her hair. Scratching on the door, she opened it and poked her head into the room.

"Are you still abed, Aunt Gertrude?"

Lady Matterson was sitting up against her pillows, sipping from a tall cup, from which wafted the unmistakeable aroma of hot chocolate. "Come in, child." She added, as Delia slid into the room and crossed to the bed, "What's to do? You look to be more agitated than you were last night."

"I am, and with reason," Delia returned, perching on the edge of the bed. "That wretched Piers accosted me!"

The old lady's brows rose. "You've been out?"

"I went to the beach with Scoley to buy fish." She threw up a hand. "For heaven's sake, don't scold, Aunt! You know I often do so."

Lady Matterson disregarded this. "Why did this Piers accost you?"

"He wants me to give a message to Giff."

"Does he know then of your liaison?"

"There isn't any liaison! How can you talk so?"

"Well, I don't know what else you call it. Secret trysts and clandestine goings on!"

With difficulty, Delia controlled an urge to argue. "Piers sought me out once before, in the library." Remembering the circumstances of that meeting, she amended this. "At least, he came to find me because I sent to him through the man Barney."

Lady Matterson's gaze narrowed alarmingly. "It seems to me, young madam, that your conduct has been a good deal more reprehensible than I supposed."

"Yes, never mind that now, Aunt," Delia said hastily, nevertheless feeling her cheeks grow warm. "What is of importance now is that Piers is up to something."

"Such as?"

Glad to have deflected her, Delia gave her a rapid account of what had passed between herself and Piers Gaunt.

"To my mind he is planning something, for I can't think what possible proposition he could make that might satisfy Giff."

"I wonder." Lady Matterson appeared to give the matter some thought, sipping her chocolate. "A bribe?"

"Hardly, when Giff has his own cotton plantation."

"A division of the spoils?"

"How does one divide up an earldom?"

"Young Giffard retains the title, but leaves Gaunt in possession of the house and lands, perhaps."

"Which would mean Giff returning to India."

Her aunt eyed her. "Is he averse from so doing?"

Delia's heart dropped. "I don't know. The rector told me Giff has said more than once that if he failed he would go back." Aware of her aunt watching her, Delia tried to keep her face from showing the dismay this engendered. She managed a shrug. "It's been more home to him than England. Perhaps he prefers it."

"He has not been in the country long enough to know which he prefers, I surmise."

"But his stepfather is in India. And he refuses to seek out his family here. Apart from the Reverend Gaunt, that is."

"Then it's feasible such an arrangement might suit him."

An image of Giff came into her head, restless and energetic. "He wouldn't agree, even if it did suit him. You've no notion how stubborn he is, and he's furious with Piers besides. He would refuse it on principle."

Lady Matterson set down her empty cup. "I'm glad to know the boy has backbone, if he is as reckless as everyone claims."

"He is shockingly reckless! And proud. And pig-headed to boot. But he's a far better man than Piers will ever be!"

A snort of laughter escaped her aunt. "Bravo, child! There speaks the perfect helpmeet."

Heat flew to Delia's cheeks and she shot up from the bed. "As to that, I have nothing to say, Aunt. But are you determined on bathing today? Or —"

"It's already too late, and I'm not in the vein in any event, what with all the excitement. Ring the bell for Pegler. And send your Sally to ask Mrs Tuckett to bring breakfast forward."

Relieved, Delia did as she asked and hurried away to ring her own bell for her maid. If only Giff was sufficiently recovered to make an appearance, she had hopes of passing the message quickly. And, if possible, finding opportunity to discuss the ramifications.

As it chanced, she was escorting Lady Matterson across to the Assembly Rooms after breakfast when Captain Rhoades hailed her from a little way down the street. Delia stopped and her aunt cast an exasperated look upon the militiaman as he came up.

"Now what's to do? Is there to be no respite from this affair?"

"I beg your ladyship's pardon," bowed the captain. "I only wanted a word with Miss Burloyne."

He cast a questioning look at Delia. Did he fear to speak in front of her aunt? All at once she recalled Giff saying he was going to tell Captain Rhoades the truth.

"You've been with Mr Giffard?"

He nodded, again throwing a dubious glance at Lady Matterson, who snorted.

"Speak your mind, Captain. I've no doubt there are aspects to this business I have yet to learn — and disgraceful ones at that! — but I know at least as much as you clearly do."

"Mr — er — Giffard has been good enough to honour me with his confidence, yes, ma'am."

Impatient, Delia broke in. "Is he coming? How is he? His wounds, I mean. Don't tell me he is too sore and unsightly to walk abroad, for heaven's sake! I've got to speak to him urgently."

"Delia, will you be quiet? We are exposed here. Someone may come out of the Assembly Rooms at any moment."

Disregarding this except to lower her voice a trifle, Delia fixed the man with a compelling eye. "Well, Captain?"

"I understand Mr Giffard plans to make an appearance at noon. He appeared little the worse for the attack, although he is sporting a black eye and a bruised lip."

"Ha! A fitting punishment!"

"Aunt, how can you be so unkind?"

"If your need is urgent," said Captain Rhoades, thankfully cutting in, "may I carry a message for you, Miss Burloyne?"

Delia gave this offer less than a moment's consideration. She must tell Giff about Piers herself, for there was much to discuss. Though how she would manage to be private with him when Aunt Gertrude was choosing to be so difficult, she could not think.

"Thank you, but if he means to come presently, a short delay will not matter."

"I should think not indeed! Do you mean to come in, Captain, or are you off about your duties?"

Captain Rhoades gave another small bow. "I will accompany you, if I may. There are one or two points upon which I hope Miss Burloyne may enlighten me."

Hearing this with dismay, Delia wondered, with some misgiving, how much Giff had told the man. And what he meant to do. Did he hope for her testimony should either Barney or Sam be taken up? Heaven forbid! Aunt Gertrude would be on the rampage if she supposed the true account of that forest adventure might become common knowledge.

A good thing if he did come into the Assembly Rooms with them. She must inform him without loss of time that she could not, under any circumstances, make any such official report.

Once the inevitable greetings were done and her aunt settled into her game of whist with her usual cronies, Delia took a chair by the wall at a slight remove and, with a gesture, invited Captain Rhoades to join her.

"Talk quietly, sir, if you please. My aunt's hearing is acute."

He smiled. "I am well used to Lady Matterson, ma'am. We have clashed swords, as one might say, on several occasions."

Delia had to laugh. "Then you will understand when I beg you not to rely upon me if you are hoping I may supply you with ammunition to lay those rogues by the heels."

A startled frown leapt to his brows. "Is that what you suppose? No, indeed. Besides, I gave my word to Mr Giffard that I would respect his confidence, in particular as to your part in the affair."

Delia could not prevent the warmth from rising in her cheeks. "Yes, well, I hope he made it abundantly clear that my part was purely accidental."

"As concerns the beginning of the adventure? Certainly."

"As concerns all of it, sir. I became drawn in only because Barney and Sam chose to watch me here."

Captain Rhoades pursed his lips. "And that puzzles me a trifle, I confess. What led them to suppose, as I surmise, that Mr Giffard would follow you here?"

"Didn't he tell you? Sam was watching the rectory. Reverend Gaunt thinks he, or perhaps Barney, followed us to Weymouth when he drove me back."

"Yet there was no sign of either when we met on the road."

"Well, you don't suppose they would allow you to see them, do you? At the time, it did not occur to either of us to imagine we were followed, but it must have been so."

"Then how came Giffard's Indian servant into the business?"

"When Sam left Stepleton, I believe he followed him."

"Then had Barney returned in the meanwhile to say where you'd gone?"

Delia thought about this. "I don't know. Perhaps. Certainly one of them must have reported to Piers Gaunt, for Giff's servant found out he was, at that time, staying outside Weymouth. We think he moved in when Giff began to flaunt himself in public as Mr Giffard."

The captain eyed her with an odd look. "Your notion, I understand?"

"Yes, but I had no expectation of his appearing in Weymouth when I suggested it. I tell you, I had not anticipated becoming embroiled to this extent."

"Yet you have no regrets," said the captain with a shrewd look.

Heat crept into her face and she knew she was blushing. "Some, yes, perhaps. But not as it concerns Giff's safety."

An understanding smile came her way. "He is a fortunate man, Miss Burloyne."

Astonished, she stared at him. "Fortunate?"

The smile grew. "To have you in his corner. I know of no other female brave enough to do what you have done."

Furiously blushing, Delia yet stared at him in shock. "I am nothing out of the ordinary, Captain Rhoades."

"On the contrary, Miss Burloyne. Lady Matterson must be inordinately proud of you."

Delia could only blink at him. Then she caught sight of Giff in the doorway, looking like a mutilated thundercloud.

Obliged to endure a barrage of comment and question about his appearance, Giff made slow way as he attempted to get to where Delia was sitting. What the deuce was the perfidious Rhoades saying to her to make her blush so? He had not suspected the fellow would have the gall to try and steal a march on him. After he'd eaten Giff's meat too!

Fortunately, the battle-axe was not in evidence and he managed to avoid Lady Matterson's minatory eye by dint of attending to her colleague who had once been in India himself.

"I'll wager this was nothing to what might have happened in Kolkata. Scimitars and daggers and such. Bandits galore, as I recall."

"True enough, but I had protection in Sattar."

"That the fellow who's with you? Looks to be a fierce guardian, that one."

"None fiercer." Giff made a brief bow. "But I must not interrupt your game, sir."

Skimming past Delia's aunt with a murmured greeting, he reached his quarry only to find Rhoades had upped and left her. He glanced round for a glimpse of the man's scarlet coat and found him missing.

He rolled an eye towards Delia, speaking with menace. "Did that treacherous hound come here only to monopolise you? Where the deuce has he gone?"

She gave him an exasperated look. "And good morning to you too, Mr Giffard!"

He dropped into the captain's vacated seat. "Don't you good morning me! What do you mean by encouraging that blasted redcoat to hang about you?"

"What do you mean by growling at me, horrid creature? I've a good mind to wash my hands of you!"

This was said in a rebellious mutter, though Giff noted Delia's lips still curved in a spurious smile. Remembering where they were, he cursed under his breath.

"Can't we get out of here?"

"Not without attracting attention. Besides, I've no wish to go apart with you if you're going to be ridiculous about Captain Rhoades."

She cast a wary eye towards Lady Matterson as she spoke and Giff's irritation was superseded by panic.

"Damn it, we must go elsewhere! Can't talk under the eye of that aunt of yours."

He was treated to a speculative look, and then Delia spoke in a languid tone to be readily heard by those nearby. "It is inordinately stuffy in here, Mr Giffard, don't you think?" She lifted her fan and plied it vigorously, briefly concealing her face as she signalled with her eyes in a frantic manner. She got up. "I think I will take a turn outside."

He rose with alacrity and offered his arm, trying for a similar note. "Allow me to escort you, Miss Burloyne."

Casting a glance at Lady Matterson, he saw at once that she'd seen through this piece of by-play. A minatory look came his way, but she confined her remarks to Delia.

"Don't stay out in the sun too long, child."

"No, ma'am. I am only going to enjoy the sea breeze for a little."

Was this permission for a tête-à-tête? Then Lady Matterson knew something he did not, did she? It struck Giff all at once that Delia was labouring under suppressed anxiety. He'd been coxcomb enough to suppose her to be concerned at being caught with Rhoades, but that couldn't be it. Not if her aunt was ready to allow them time alone.

He leaned close enough to murmur as he began to lead a path through the room. "What's to do?"

"Not here!"

He could only just hear the whisper, and then young Tarporley, damn the fellow, was in the way.

"I trust you are a little less stiff and sore today, sir? I see that eye has blackened."

"It looks worse than it is." Aware of Delia eyeing him, Giff moderated the curt tone. "I'm well enough, I thank you."

"I've just had a word with Captain Rhoades. He says he intends to have his men patrol the town and environs."

Capital! Just who he wanted to talk about. Couldn't the dratted fellow see he was trying to get to hell out of this damned place? "Good notion. Though I doubt the rogues will dare show themselves again."

"I wish that fellow of yours and I might have caught the rascal!"

Yes, and subjected Giff to all the scandal he wished to avoid. Impatient, he pinched Delia's finger and heard her hiss in a breath. But it had the desired effect.

"If you will excuse me, my lord, I'm feeling decidedly warm and Mr Giffard is kind enough to escort me to walk on the grass verge."

Tarporley flushed and stood aside in haste. "I beg your pardon, Miss Burloyne. I'm sorry to have delayed you."

She gave him a smile. Too sunny for Giff's taste. Did she mean to flirt with every eligible male in the place?

"It makes no matter, sir. I'm sure Mr Giffard must be gratified by your kind enquiry."

Oh, must he? Infuriated more like. Why the deuce couldn't people mind their own business?

They managed to reach the vestibule without further delay, and Delia released his arm as she stepped through. There were two elderly ladies seated on one of the benches still set below the Esplanade, chatting idly as they enjoyed the prospect of the ocean with its usual quota of boats tacking across the bay, but the grassy bank was otherwise free of an infestation of nosy persons, to Giff's relief.

Delia led the way to a place on the grass far enough removed from the couple to afford privacy and sat on a convenient boulder, setting her face towards the shore as if she sought to catch the salt breeze on her cheeks.

Giff was momentarily diverted by a sudden realisation that his flower girl was a good deal more attractive than he had supposed. No wonder Rhoades was buzzing round her like a bee at a honeypot!

"How in Hades did you manage to grow so pretty since I last saw you?"

She looked up, her freckled features breaking into laughter. "Are you out of your mind, Giff? First you behave like a bear with a sore head because I was talking to the captain. Then you start showering me with compliments? I make every allowance for your injuries, but that is the outside of enough."

"It's scarcely a shower to notice how pretty you've grown, is it?"

"Since last night? I think you must have a concussion or some such thing."

He plonked down on the boulder, holding her gaze. "Why did your aunt let me bring you out here? And don't fob me off with nonsense about concussions."

"You can talk! After your nonsensical behaviour? Aunt Gertrude knows I must talk to you urgently, that's why. Though you made me so cross, I'm not sure I have any desire to help you."

He captured her hand and brought it to his lips. "Forgive me! I thought Rhoades was making up to you, the fiend!"

Her cheeks grew pink and she withdrew her hand. "Nothing of the sort. He had questions for me. He wanted me to clarify a couple of points in your story, that's all."

"Oh."

Feeling nonplussed, Giff eyed her for a moment. She did not meet his gaze, turning her eyes towards the sea again.

"You don't fancy Tarporley either, then?"

To his satisfaction, that made her turn, though there was a spark in her eye. "Will you stop behaving in this fashion, Giff?"

"I'm just trying to make sure of you!"

Colour flew in her cheeks. "Well, you need not. And if you are thinking of — of what my aunt may have implied last night, then I wish you to know…"

She faded out, looking away. What in Hades was she at now?

"Wish me to know what?"

She turned back and it came out in a rush, her voice a little squeaky. "That you have no need to think me compromised, or that you are obliged to — to make me any sort of — of reparation. There, I've said it."

Her meaning penetrated. Did she suppose he wanted her because he felt obliged? Utterly ridiculous. But before he could think how to refute the notion, Delia spoke again.

"We would be better employed talking of Piers. I've been anxious to tell you. He gave me a message for you."

His attention snapped in. "Piers? A message? How, pray? How did he give you a message?"

"He caught me on the beach this morning. He suddenly came up behind me. It gave me a horrid shock, I don't mind telling you."

He wanted the substance of the message, but his attention became diverted. "What were you doing on the beach? Don't say he invaded the ladies' swimming area?"

"Of course not. How should he? I went with the footman to buy fish. I have no idea if he saw me by accident or followed me, but there he was all of a sudden."

Giff's senses were by now on full alert. "What's the message?"

"He wants to meet you. He says he has a proposition to make to you."

"A proposition? What the devil does that mean?"

"You may well ask. I wish you won't trust him, Giff. I believe he means mischief. He wants you to go to Waldiche Keep."

"The devil he does!"

"Exactly so." Delia was back to her usual animated self, he noted in passing, all her consciousness vanished. "Aunt Gertrude suggested he might offer to split the prize."

"How?"

"I could not see it either, but she thought he might say you could claim the title while he kept the house and lands. And he might well think he could do that, for he reminded me possession is nine points of the law."

Giff turned the notion over. "Well, it's better than shipping me off to the Americas, I suppose."

Delia showed him a shocked face. "Giff, you're not going to let him get away with it, are you?"

"Devil a bit!" He recalled his first intention at the outset of handing over the lot, if only Piers had proved worthy. Odd to think he'd ever considered it. "He's getting away with nothing of mine, I've said it before. But we don't know what this proposition is, do we?"

"No, and I don't believe he has any proposition at all, if you want the truth. It must be a ruse to get you into his power."

Giff nodded, but absently. If he could get into the Keep, he might find opportunity to search the place. Though whether there was anything useful to find remained a question.

"I asked him why he could not just meet you here. At your lodging or his. But he said he prefers to meet you on his own ground."

Giff cursed. "It's not his ground."

"So I told him. That's when he said about possession. Then he walked off before I could ask anything else."

"Damn the man! I'll have to go."

"You can't! No, Giff, it's too dangerous!"

He shrugged. "He doesn't leave me much choice."

Delia leaned a little towards him, eagerness in her tone. "I've been thinking about it. Why don't you pre-empt him? Go to his lodging. Demand to know what he wants."

"If I knew where he's lodging."

"Doesn't Sattar know?"

Giff made a negative gesture. "He moved in while Sattar was with me, I surmise. Canny devil! I suspect he realised he was being watched. I can hardly go knocking on the door of every lodging house in the town."

"No, and if Barney and Sam have made themselves scarce, we have no one to lead us to him."

He quirked an eyebrow. "Us? You're not proposing to come with me to Waldiche Keep, are you?"

Delia gave him a scornful look. "I'd be of little use if it came to a fight."

He grinned. "I take issue with that after yesterday."

She laughed at that. "Yes, but I can't wield a sword or fire a pistol, and I imagine you'd have both on hand. I was thinking you could ask Captain Rhoades to go with you, though."

His mood instantly darkened. "I'll not ask him for any favours if he's going to try and steal yours!"

An explosion of some kind emanated from his flower girl and she glared at him. "Will you stop? Captain Rhoades has no interest in me. And if he did, I wouldn't care. In fact, he said you're a lucky man to have me, if you really wish to know."

His heart lightened. "He did?"

"Yes, but I could have told him how mistaken he is in his ideas, you wretch! I really don't know why I'm bothering with you, Giff."

He gave her a mischievous look. "Yes, you do. And I am a lucky man to have you. I've known it from the first."

To his delight, her freckles vanished as she flushed bright red, and she looked quickly away. Why she was shy of him all of a sudden he could not imagine. Was it this notion she'd taken into her head that he only wanted her because of convention?

He reached to lay his hand over hers where it rested on the rock beneath her. "Delia."

She looked round. "Yes?"

"I'll say it all when I'm in the saddle and can do so with honour. But you've no need to doubt me."

Her lips quivered a trifle and his gaze became riveted. He wanted desperately to kiss them and cursed the confines of their situation.

"Doubt you how?" Her voice was a whisper on her breath, and it shot him through with longing.

"You know what I mean. Don't you?"

"Perhaps. I think. Only…"

"Only?"

She fidgeted, her glance shooting to where his hand still rested on hers. She withdrew it, catching it inside the other as if to cradle it. "Nothing. It doesn't matter."

The forlorn note caught at him. "Yes, it does. It matters to me."

Her gaze met his, a world of question in her eyes. She didn't believe him. For two pins, he'd let the world go hang and show her just how much it mattered. How much she mattered.

"Giffard, there you are!"

Delia turned her head and her face took on a public mask. The moment was at once lost.

Damnation! Must his uncle interrupt them now? Giff rose automatically as the Revered Gaunt came up.

"How are the bruises today, my dear boy? I hardly expected your man Sattar to allow you out of your bed."

Aware of Giff responding to his uncle, Delia scarcely took in what he said. Had he been about to declare himself? Or was it that look again, as if he meant to kiss her?

Her veins thrummed with anticipation and she had all to do to speak with any degree of calm when the rector turned his attention to her.

"Good day to you, my dear Delia. I trust you are none the worse for yesterday's contretemps?"

"Not from that, sir, no." She glanced at Giff. "Should we not confide this latest business to the Reverend Gaunt?"

"What, about Piers?"

"Yes, of course. He may have good advice for you."

The reverend was glancing from one to the other. "What's this? Has my other nephew surfaced again?"

Giff let out a grunt and proceeded to relate the circumstances of Delia's morning meeting on the beach. He was looking decidedly sulky. Really, he was so boyish. Merely because he did not get his own way. Which, if her suspicions were correct, was probably just as well. The whole matter of their relationship was too distressing to endure discussion. Especially when he would not say anything until he had gained his earldom. But what if he never did? She thrust this thought to the back of her mind and tried to concentrate on the discussion going forward.

"I am with Delia on this, my dear boy. I find it suspicious that Piers should invite you to the Keep."

"Yes, but if I can't find him here, I will have to go, sir."

"Why not have Sattar hunt him down in Weymouth? He seems to be eminently capable."

"He is, but if Piers does not show his face in town, how should he find him? Besides, he may already have left for Waldiche."

"Then you must go armed. And accompanied."

Delia chimed in at this point. "Will you go with him, sir?"

The Reverend Gaunt gave a faint grimace. "I fear I will be of scant use. This is young men's work."

"Well, I said he should take Captain Rhoades, only he is so stubborn and stupid —" casting a vengeful look at Giff "— he won't do it."

"I didn't say I won't. I just don't want the fellow. And you know why!"

Delia fairly glared at him. Why must he choose this moment to be idiotically possessive? As if she had the slightest interest in the captain! Or indeed vice versa. Why must he obstinately continue to believe otherwise? After her assurances too.

"It seems to me an eminently sensible notion, Giffard. Indeed, you might go accompanied by a whole platoon of militia, if the captain is willing."

At that Giff let out a rather wild laugh. "I hardly think I'll need an army to subdue Piers. I can manage him. As long as I have Sattar."

The rector seemed less than satisfied. "That is all very well, my boy, but the fellow must have a plethora of servants at the Keep. Not to mention these creatures of his who have been plaguing you. They may not choose to show their faces in Weymouth, but —"

"The deuce! I had not thought of that!"

Delia watched Giff fretting in silence for a space. His uncle waited, clearly anxious. As was she, if truth be told. How was she to contain herself in patience, obliged to sit about doing nothing while Giff took himself off to Waldiche Keep and the Lord knew what fate? When he was too pig-headed to take sensible reinforcements too.

He snapped his fingers suddenly. "Young Tarporley! He's a neighbour after all and knows the place. I'll take him."

The rector's brows rose. "You will trust an untried youngster instead of a seasoned soldier? Come, Giffard, this is foolish beyond permission!"

The stubborn tilt to Giff's chin did not drop. "Or I could ignore Piers and refuse to co-operate." A look of satisfaction crossed his face. "That's it. I won't go at all and be damned to him!"

"Quite improvident, my dear boy. Not that I believe for a moment you will be able to resist."

Giff at once took issue with this dictum, but Delia paid no heed to the ensuing argument. As little as his uncle did she place any reliance on Giff having the patience to refrain from finding out what Piers wanted. But a notion was filtering into her head.

Need she stand idle after all? Perhaps there was something she could do. Preferably without Giff's knowledge. He had flown up into the boughs when she'd raised the matter of approaching his family yesterday. But need he know anything of it?

She regarded the rector in a speculative fashion. He would know where to find them. Might she suborn him into helping her?

The first necessity was to engineer an opportunity to talk to him alone. To this end, she waited for a break in the discussion which came sooner than she might have hoped.

"Oh, for pity's sake, sir, very well!" The exclamation was accompanied by Giff throwing up his hands and rolling his eyes. "I'd best go and track the blasted man down now."

Her attention caught, Delia quickly rose from the boulder. "If you are talking of the captain, Giff, you must promise me you will not accuse him or — or even mention this idiotic notion you have in your head."

He turned a fiery look upon her. "Why shouldn't I? If it will satisfy —"

"Because it's embarrassing, you stupid creature!" Realising the rector was looking both amused and puzzled, she turned to him with a deprecating look, lowering her voice. "Pay no heed, sir. I'm sorry to embroil you in this, but Giff's conduct —"

"My conduct? What of your conduct, pray?"

She turned on him. "But I haven't done anything! Nor has he. Really, you are perfectly nonsensical about this, Giff. And for nothing." She met his smouldering gaze and the fire slowly died out of it.

A self-conscious laugh escaped him. "I'm sorry, Delia. Can't help it. Every time I think of you and him with your heads together…"

"If we had our heads together, which I strongly dispute, it was only so that we might not be overheard. For all you know, the man is married. Have you thought of that?"

"Ha! You think that would stop him flirting with you?"

"Oh, be quiet!" Exasperated, Delia turned to the Reverend Gaunt. "I am going inside, sir. Have you spoken to my aunt this morning?"

Throwing an amused look upon his nephew, the rector offered his arm. "Allow me to take you in. If I were you, my boy, I would waste less time on fripperies and concentrate on securing your inheritance."

Giff let out a resigned breath. "Yes. Fine. I am clearly outnumbered here. I'm off!"

With which, he strode away to the door into the Rooms. Delia, seizing the moment, hung back when the rector would have urged her to follow.

"Wait! I must speak to you, sir! I have an idea and I think you may be able to help me."

He frowned but allowed her to lead the way back to the boulder and sat down as she did. "I presume whatever it is has the purpose of furthering Giffard's aims?"

"Yes, but you must say nothing of it to him, sir."

"Why? Surely he ought to know of any plan concerning him?"

"Not this one. He would utterly condemn it and I'd find myself unable to carry it out."

The rector looked amused. "I hardly know whether to be entertained or alarmed, Delia."

She laughed. "It's nothing dangerous, I assure you. Only Giff refuses to have anything to do with his family, and I am determined to go and beard his grandfather."

"Lord Saunderton? Flora's father? Good heavens!"

"Why, is there some difficulty?"

The Reverend Gaunt grimaced. "None beyond the fellow's being quite as pig-headed as Giffard, and a good deal worse-tempered."

CHAPTER FOURTEEN

Within moments of being shown into an upstairs saloon in Saunderton House, it was plain to Delia that the Reverend Gaunt's assessment of Giff's grandfather was, if anything, understated.

The room itself was depressing enough, with its dark-panelled walls and the curtains half-drawn against the sunlight. Enthroned on a huge, leather-upholstered winged chair, one gouty bandaged foot raised up on a stool before him, sat the most crusty-looking old gentleman Delia had ever seen. His countenance must once have been comely, but was now marred by broken veins, pinched, thin lips, a long beak-like nose and grotesque overgrown eyebrows. He peered at the visitors through an eye horribly magnified by a quizzing glass.

"Gaunt? That you? What in hell's quivering teeth brings you into my lair? Must know I ain't receiving."

The rector, with more courage than Delia could summon up, approached the man, holding out a hand. "So your butler informed me, my dear Saunderton. I overbore him, however, on the score of long acquaintance."

Lord Saunderton gave him his hand but released it immediately, snorting in a fashion reminiscent of Aunt Gertrude. "Pah! Ain't seen you for years! Not that I've any wish to see you now either!"

"But I have a strong desire to see you. I've brought someone to meet you, my friend."

Delia, who had kept well behind, drew a tight breath as Lord Saunderton's inimical gaze found her.

"Eh? Who's this? What d'ye mean by trotting stray females into my house, Gaunt? Ain't it enough I'm plagued with that niminy-piminy girl of mine?"

By this appellation Delia presumed he referred to the unfortunate and faded lady who had first received them. In order to gain entry to the establishment, the Reverend Gaunt had asked not for the master of the house, but for Miss Saunderton. The plan was formulated upon the journey, which was made, at Lady Matterson's insistence, by coach.

"You can't go all that way in a gig, my dear man. And I'd prefer you had Scoley and Vowles with you in case of mishaps."

"Nothing is going to happen to us, Aunt Gertrude. We were only waylaid the last time because those men were after Giff."

"Nevertheless. You had best take a change of linen with you. Indeed, I am of a mind to send your Sally along too."

But in this she was dissuaded by the rector, who assured her the journey there and back to Saunderton House, which was situated near Little Bredy, could be accomplished comfortably within the day.

"It is highly unlikely that Saunderton will invite us to remain for any length of time. Indeed, if he offers us so much as a glass of wine I should be astonished."

"True. He's a shocking old boor!"

"He was not as bad until Flora's defection."

"Poppycock! I knew him as a young man and he was perfectly rag-mannered then. Thought himself a touch above his fellows. It does not in the least surprise me to hear that he thrust his daughter into marriage with your nephew instead of allowing her to marry Favell. If you ask me, he came by his deserts."

It was news to Delia that her aunt knew all about the scandal involving Giff's mother. She might have questioned her about it before. There was no time now, with Giff already on his way to Waldiche Keep, having secured the assistance of Captain Rhoades and Lord Tarporley both, with the latter's groom tagging along to take care of the horses while the business of the day was accomplished. Giff's henchman Sattar made up a force of four, all armed and ready for any trickery.

The entire plan had been held up for several days, Giff having been persuaded by his uncle to allow his present wounds to heal a little before flinging himself into further danger. The respite had been welcome to Delia. Giff established his position in the social scene of the town, and if she was irked by the necessity to share him with the rest of the world, at least she had the satisfaction of seeing his facial bruises fading.

His decision to delay no longer coincided with the arrival of the King in Weymouth. A convenience that allowed Delia's plans to go forward without drawing attention, since the world and his wife could talk of nothing else. A glimpse of His Majesty was the sole ambition of all. Delia sent Scoley to Stepleton to summon the rector, who arrived the night before Giff's proposed expedition.

Within half an hour of Giff's cavalcade riding out of Weymouth, Delia and the Reverend Gaunt set off on their own mission, sped on their way by an admonition from Lady Matterson.

"You take care of my great-niece, Gaunt, do you hear? You'll find me as fierce as Saunderton if anything happens to her this time!"

Her head full of possibilities, Delia had no fears at all beyond the certainty Giff was going to be furious. Not that she cared for that. It was for his own good, after all. Though whether the mission would be fruitful seemed doubtful.

"If Lord Saunderton is so boorish and horrid, sir, do you suppose he will let us in at all?"

The Reverend Gaunt, relaxed in his corner of the coach, turned his head. "We will not take that risk, Delia. I should have had little to do with the family were it not that my own daughter has been a lifelong friend of Miss Saunderton. I do not mean Flora, but her sister Dowsabel, poor woman."

"Why poor woman?"

"She suffered for her sister's sin. As one tainted by the scandal, Saunderton would not permit her to marry at all, and when their mother died, Dowsabel was obliged to take charge of the household. A thankless task, according to my daughter, which I have no difficulty in believing. However, we may at least get into the place by enquiring for her rather than for his lordship."

Giff's aunt, as Delia realised this Dowsabel must be, proved a colourless, timid creature, dressed in an old-fashioned striped gown with a cap over her soft brown curls. She had a tendency to speak in hurried whispers, casting scared glances towards the door from time to time. She was mystified and troubled by the rector's request.

"But why do you wish to see him, dear Reverend? He never sees a soul, you must know."

When she heard the reason, Miss Saunderton paled and sank into the nearest chair, gazing at the rector with brimming eyes. "Flora's son? Alive? And in England?"

"Indeed he is, my dear. There can be no doubt."

Miss Saunderton shed tears, much to Delia's embarrassment. She was glad the Reverend Gaunt chose to sit by the woman and pat her shoulder, murmuring comfort. But the first words out of her mouth as she recovered filled Delia with indignation.

"But this is terrible! Papa will be furious! Oh, dear, Reverend, you cannot tell him, really you cannot."

"I must, Dowsabel. Giffard is in considerable difficulty, and we are in hopes that your father may be able to help."

"Help? Papa? You must be mad! He will never do so. Why, he refuses even to allow Flora's name to be spoken in this house."

"Well, it's going to be spoken," Delia broke in with some heat, "whether he likes it or not!"

Miss Saunderton's pale eyes turned upon her, in some astonishment. She had been largely ignored up until this moment, beyond an odd glance when she was presented to the creature.

"Hush, Delia!" The rector took Miss Saunderton's hand. "Miss Burloyne is by way of being Giffard's champion, my dear Dowsabel. It is too long a story to tell you now, but we are trying to establish Giffard's claim to the Baunton earldom and Waldiche Keep."

Miss Saunderton's look turned to dismay. "You cannot suppose Papa will help you, surely? He will be as mad as fire! I dread to think what he will say if you tell him the boy is coming here."

This was too much for Delia. "Let me tell you, ma'am, that Giff is quite as adamant as your father. Nothing would induce him to come. Which is why we are here in his stead."

Miss Saunderton put a hand to her bosom, her face filled with sudden misery. "I wish he might. I should dearly love to see Flora's son. He was a very babe the last time I set eyes on him. A bonny little boy he was too."

"Well, you may meet him at my house in Stepleton, my dear Dowsabel. But at present, pray bring us to your father."

Miss Saunderton looked at once fearful. "Oh, no, I dare not! He will roar at me, sir, and very likely throw his stick or snuffbox at me."

"Then show us to his room and we will go in alone. Be assured I shall not tell him your part in allowing us into his sanctum."

Now that she was confronted by Giff's appalling grandfather, Delia could not blame his remaining daughter for being terrified. She came forward in obedience to the rector's beckoning finger, but found it hard indeed not to crumble when that hostile gaze looked her up and down as the rector stepped aside for her.

"This is Miss Burloyne, who has a request to make of you."

"Request? Request? Damned impertinence! Burloyne? Never heard of you."

Delia drew a breath. "But you know my great-aunt, Lady Matterson, sir."

The ferocious old eyes raked her. "What if I do? No reason why I should do anything for every stray relative she cares to throw in my way. Ye'll get nothing out of me, girl!"

Daunted, Delia threw a glance at the rector, who urged her on with an encouraging jerk of his head. Her stomach felt tight, but an image of Giff's features flitted through her brain and she stiffened her resolve. Lord Saunderton could do nothing to her after all. And she'd endured Aunt Gertrude's scolding without flinching.

"I don't want you to do anything for me."

The old man snorted. "Then what do ye mean by disturbing my peace, wench? Go away!"

To be addressed by the same term Giff used towards her, but with far less warmth, had an oddly strengthening effect. She straightened and looked the old misery in the eye. "It's not for me, sir, but for your grandson, Giffard Gaunt."

To her astonishment, the old man flinched as though she'd struck him, throwing up a hand as if to ward her off. Delia thought she saw an expression of agony in his eyes, but it was swiftly superseded by one of violent fury. He fairly spat his words, leaning towards Delia, his features suffusing with colour. "How d'ye dare come to me? Who d'you think y'are, forcing your way into my house?"

"She did nothing of the kind, Saunderton," snapped the rector, in a tone Delia had never heard from him. "If you wish to blame anyone, blame me. This girl means nothing but good and I won't have her abused, do you understand?"

The militant eyes turned on him. "Then ye should've kept her out of my house! Good? It's doing me no good, I'll have you know. Likely send me off in an apoplexy!"

"Then control your temper, my friend."

His lordship fairly sputtered, but Delia took instant advantage of his being temporarily lost for words, speaking with as much vehemence as she could command.

"Sir, I don't care whether you want to hear it or not, but you must understand your grandson's life is in danger. Piers Gaunt hired bullies to try to kidnap him, and very likely murder him into the bargain. I am persuaded you cannot wish for his death, however little you may care that he has come home."

Lord Saunderton, who had been muttering throughout, now burst into speech again, still looking and sounding savage. "Thought the cub *was* dead. Had no word of the boy since Henry sent me those letters."

Delia's heart began to thud and the Reverend Gaunt became suddenly intent.

"What letters, Saunderton?"

"From Favell! Feller had the infernal impudence to write to the man from whom he'd stolen both wife and son. Henry thought I'd wish to know that abandoned female had died. Pah! Dead to me from the day she took off!"

The bitterness came through beneath the biting tone, but Delia was too wound up to care. "Did you keep the letters?"

Violence returned to both face and voice. "Keep 'em? Of course I didn't keep 'em! Threw them on the fire!"

A mewl of despair escaped Delia's lips. "Oh, how could you be so cruel? It's not Giff's fault that his mother took him away! He's your grandson, sir!"

Lord Saunderton raised clenched fists. "He's no grandson of mine! For all I know, he's Favell's whelp! Even Henry couldn't be certain of that."

"Oh, yes, he could. And he was." The rector's tone was clipped. "You impugn Flora's honour beyond what she deserves, sir. I can assure you my nephew had no doubt whatsoever that Giffard is his son."

The old man banged his clenched fists on the arms of his chair. "Then why did he not send for the lad, eh? Why be content to leave the boy in India, if he believed him to be his true heir?"

"It makes no odds what he believed, Saunderton, as well you know. Giffard was born in wedlock and he is the legal heir to the earldom."

"Yes, and all he is lacking is proof of his identity, sir," chimed in Delia. "Even if you've destroyed those letters, I am convinced you could help him if you chose."

"I don't choose, wench! I want nothing to do with the cub. Let him go back where he came from, for he ain't welcome here."

Beginning to despair of making any impression on him, Delia hunted her mind for an argument to use and recalled what he'd said earlier. "Why did you think he was dead?"

"A good point, Delia. Favell wrote only of Flora's death, but I know for a fact he wrote to Henry more than once."

Excitement rose in Delia. "You said letters, in the plural, did you not? What was in the others?"

"How the devil should I know? D'ye think I memorised every word?"

"But did Giff's father tell you he was dead?"

"Don't be a ninny, why should he?"

"Then why did you think so?"

The old man's face worked for a moment. Then it burst from him as if torn out of his heart. "Because Piers told me so!" He breathed deeply, recovering a measure of control. "Damned young scoundrel! Took him to task when I heard what he was up to, horning in on my grandson's rights. Said he'd done his damnedest to locate the boy. Said his contact in India had written to say Giffard had perished of one of the fevers they have there, soon after his mother's demise."

The Reverend Gaunt was aghast. "But he did not produce such a letter! Nor was Hammersley privy to anything of the kind. And he'd set his own enquiries in train. He had no address, for Henry kept silent on that score. Yet he passed the letters to you, Saunderton."

"You should have kept them," Delia cried. "You had no right to destroy them!"

Lord Saunderton flew into another passion. "No right? Who are you to tell me my rights? Ah, enough! I've had enough of

261

this! Out! Get out, both of you! Never let me see your face again, wench!"

Delia backed away as the old man groped for the stick leaning against the fireplace surround. But the rector held his ground.

"Very well, we'll go, Saunderton. But know this. You do yourself harm by your obstinacy, no one else."

"D'ye think I care? All I want is to be left alone!"

Goaded, Delia could not refrain from retort. "You will be, sir! Giff will never seek you out, be sure. If you ever wish to see him, you will have to buckle!"

Grabbing his stick, the old man brandished it. "I buckle? I'll see him in hell first! Out, I say! Get out of my house!"

The Reverend Gaunt urged her towards the door. "Come, Delia. There is no point in remaining."

"But we've failed, sir! I can't bear it!"

"It was a long shot at best, my dear," said the rector, low-toned. At the door, he turned, raising his voice. "We'll bid you farewell, Saunderton."

The old man roared and the stick flew across the room. "Get out! Out, I say!"

In haste, Delia seized the door handle and scrambled through ahead of the rector. He shut the door behind them, letting out a resigned sigh.

"Devilish fellow!"

"I think he is half mad, sir!"

"A trifle senile, I fear." He patted Delia in a consoling manner. "You did your best, my dear Delia."

"I feel a good deal frustrated, sir, I must say. I had high hopes we might persuade him to help Giff."

"Yes, I know you had. However, our efforts are not entirely wasted. We have at least proof of Piers's perfidy. If he could lie to Saunderton, his whole conduct becomes suspect."

As if it had ever been anything else! But Delia refrained from saying it. She was too disappointed by the failure of her mission to pursue the subject. And Lord knew what scheme the fiend had cooked up to confound Giff at Waldiche Keep. Thank heaven he'd been persuaded to take Captain Rhoades.

"Come, let us leave this place, my dear. We will find a decent inn and —"

"Reverend Gaunt!"

The whispered interruption caught them as Delia was about to set her foot on the stair. Turning, she beheld Miss Saunderton tiptoeing towards them, a finger at her mouth.

"What is it, Dowsabel?"

"Hush! Come away, if you please! And step softly."

The rector cast Delia a mystified look, but followed as the lady glided on tiptoe back the way she had come. Delia trod as silently as she could, a faint thread of hope creeping through her dejection.

Miss Saunderton led them along a gallery, down a narrow corridor and opened the door to what proved to be a small parlour at the back of the house. It was altogether lighter and more cosy than her father's domain, with a pretty chintz pattern to the cushioned seats of two gilded armchairs, a sideboard loaded with books and knick-knacks and a little sewing table.

"This is my retreat. He does not even know I have appropriated it."

Sympathy for the creature overlaid Delia's anxiety about Giff. "How have you managed to keep it secret from your papa?"

"For years now, he has been unable to walk without the assistance of his valet, thank goodness." She threw a hand to her mouth as if she would stuff the words back in. "Oh, dear, I should not —! You see, his gout pains him so and it makes him peevish. But sit, sit!"

Delia stood her ground, exchanging a glance with the rector, who shrugged and indicated she should take it up.

"We do not mean to stay, Miss Saunderton. Had you something you wished to say?"

"To show you, rather. Forgive me, but I was listening to your interview with Papa, and —"

"What, did you have your ear to the door, Dowsabel?"

Amusement sounded in the rector's voice, but Delia was at once intrigued. "What is it, Miss Saunderton? May it help Giff?"

She waved agitated hands, gliding towards a neat little bureau placed under the window. "I do not know, but perhaps it may. I was not outside the hall door, Reverend. There is a servant's door in the panelling. I always hide there if I wish to spy upon my father's sanctum."

For such a timid creature she sounded quite unabashed. As she spoke, she was sliding out two stands either side of the desk and pulling down a panel that rested on them to form a table for writing.

"Then you heard everything?"

"Yes, Miss Burloyne, and it was just as I feared. I knew he would fly into a pelter. Only I had forgot those letters, you see."

"You knew of them, Dowsabel?"

"Oh, yes, though I was not able to save them all."

A pulse began to thrum in Delia's veins as Dowsabel Saunderton slipped a hand into her bosom and lifted out a small key on a ribbon. She cast an apologetic glance at the rector.

"I keep this always on my person, Reverend, for there is no saying with Papa, even though I am persuaded he cannot know I use this room."

So saying, she fitted the key into a long narrow drawer in the interior of the desk and turned it. Delia watched with burgeoning excitement as she lifted out a batch of papers tied with a ribbon.

"I keep all my private letters here, you see."

"Do you tell us you have the letters your father said he burnt, Dowsabel?"

She was carefully untying the ribbon, handling the package with care bordering on reverence. But she looked up at this. "I have what I managed to salvage. I knew they were important, for I heard Papa roaring and cursing when he took them into his sanctum to read. I slipped in the instant he left and snatched them from the flames."

"Good heavens!"

"How brave of you, Miss Saunderton!"

She was separating the pile of papers, setting some aside on the narrow top of the desk. "Oh, no. The edges were badly singed and much of the lettering is too burned to be legible. But I kept them in tissue in hopes it might preserve them."

"You are a heroine, Miss Saunderton," declared Delia, her heart soaring with hope as she moved to join her at the bureau.

"There, you see."

With care, Giff's aunt laid a folded package of tissue on the writing surface and gently opened it. A couple of sheets of badly scorched parchment lay revealed, such writing as was unmarked clearly fading. Delia put out a hand, but Miss Saunderton grabbed it.

"Take care! The sheets are so dry they may crumble at a touch."

"Best to try to read them where they are, Delia." The rector was at her shoulder. "Pardon me, Dowsabel." He put the woman gently aside and took her place, leaning over the parchment.

"Can you read anything on it, sir?"

"Give me a moment, Delia. The lines are close. Thank the lord we have sunshine today!"

Delia glanced at the window, from where a good deal of light threw onto the writing surface, illuminating the letters. She would dearly love to try to decipher them herself, but it made more sense for the Reverend Gaunt to do so, since he knew so much more about the family.

"Is it from Mr Favell, sir?"

"This is Henry's hand."

"Your nephew?"

"Yes, and it seems to bear out what Saunderton told us. *I thought it only right to…* Then it is unreadable, but it goes on, *Flora's death…* and again, *the boy is…* then *health*."

"Then he is saying Giff is alive and in health, though his mother is dead?"

"So it would seem." He turned his head. "Dowsabel, you don't object if I move this one to see the rest?"

"Do as you must, Reverend. If young Giffard may benefit, I am only too glad for you to read them all."

Read them only? Would she let them out of her hands? They must be given to Giff! But she held her tongue on the urgent words as the Reverend Gaunt carefully prised the top sheet away.

"It is extremely dry," he commented as the sheet crackled upon being moved. He set it down on the other half of the tissue and peered at the parchment below. "Ah, this is not as badly damaged. A trifle browned, but I can still see the letters even where it is darkly burned."

Eager now, Delia bent to peer at the writing. "Is it from his stepfather?"

"I don't know the hand, so we may assume it is Favell. If I turn it … yes, there is Matthew's signature."

"Oh, thank heavens! Read it, sir!"

"There is a deal of preliminary explanation about writing at all, but here he says, *I could not think it right to leave you ignorant of my beloved Flora's demise. A virulent fever took her, along with our only daughter. She has left me two fine sons, one only born of my loins. The other is your own Giffard, sir, and I am of a mind to send him home. He has grown into an excellent young man and while it will distress me to lose him, I consider it my clear duty to restore him to his rightful patrimony. I cannot find it in my heart to withhold him from the destiny that is his by right of birth. He is your heir, sir, and I await only your request for his return to Waldiche Keep, upon receipt of which I will despatch Giffard forthwith, despite the pain his parting from me may inflict. I have loved him as my own but never concealed the truth of his origins from him. He stands ready to come to you that he may learn to know and understand his duties before he must take them up.* And he ends with the hope of hearing by return and the usual salutations."

Delia could not contain her elation. "This is fantastic, sir! We have the very thing needed to prove Giff's claim."

"It may not be enough." The Reverend Gaunt looked grave. "This proves only that he was alive at the date of this letter."

"Well, and it tells us Mr Favell had the intention to send him back."

"Yes, but it is evident Henry did not send the required confirmation." He bent to the letter again. "What is the date here?"

Miss Saunderton intervened. "I fear the date has been burnt off, Reverend. But I can tell you when it came. It was six years ago — no, seven, I think."

"Two years before Henry died! And Giffard had received no summons from him, that I know for a fact."

Appalled, Delia gazed at him. "Do you think he did not mean for Giff to inherit? Was it indeed his doing that Piers should step into his shoes?"

The rector considered this. "He made no mention of it to Hammersley, so far as I know. But nor did he inform the lawyer of this letter. He knew the boy was alive, and he did not destroy the letter. He may have dithered, his pride preventing him from doing what was right. His death was sudden and unexpected, so it may be he meant to send for Giffard in the end."

"He should have done so at once! And why isn't it enough, sir? What more does Giff need?"

"Proof of identity. Who is to say he is Giffard Gaunt when all is said?"

"Well, you, sir. And Miss Saunderton here."

The rector looked dubious. "We have neither of us seen him since before he was breeched. It is true he has a look of Flora, but I can see no trace of Henry in his features."

Delia's stomach felt hollow all at once. "But you don't doubt he is Giffard Gaunt, do you?"

The rector's grave countenance relaxed into a grin. "Not in the least. He is too like Henry in temperament for doubt. But it is not for me to offer proof, Delia."

"Yet these letters must count for something, surely?"

"Indeed. We will take them to Hammersley."

"The lawyer? Should we not take them directly to Giff? I was thinking we ought to make for Waldiche Keep on the instant."

"Dorchester is at much the same distance, and the sooner Hammersley sees these the better. Besides, there is no point in chasing after Giffard. The last thing he would want is for you to become embroiled in the brawl that is no doubt brewing at the Keep."

CHAPTER FIFTEEN

The ride to Waldiche Keep was accomplished in some three hours on the road, with a halt at an inn for refreshment and to rest the horses. Giff was conscious of a thread of disquiet and some degree of frustration.

If he was honest, he'd enjoyed the intervening days of inaction. It made a pleasant change to pass a few days without going in fear of attack. His distrust of Rhoades as concerned Delia notwithstanding, the man had kept his word to have his men patrol the town with the result Giff felt safe for the first time in what seemed an age. Besides which, the opportunity to spend at least some part of the time in company with his flower girl was a considerable advantage.

But the inevitable could not be long put off. He hardly felt his bruises and he was looking more himself. His strength was back and the confrontation with his cousin must be faced.

Tiger was itching to gallop, but out of consideration for his companions, Giff took the ride at an easy pace. No point in tiring the horses. Besides, he was in no frame of mind to do Piers any favours. The man could wait upon his convenience.

The nag of what his cousin had in mind, however, did not abate. Delia would have it the fellow meant mischief. She might well be right. On the other hand, if Piers was at an impasse, he might be willing to think in terms of compromise. Though Giff was disinclined to comply with anything less than utter capitulation.

The approach to Waldiche Keep ran through a wooded valley before the road began to rise. Giff called out a warning. "Keep an eye out! This place is ripe for ambush."

Captain Rhoades brought his mount up alongside. "But the fellow does not know you are coming. How should he set up an ambush?"

"For all I know, he's had men on the watch for days."

"In that case, we must hope the sight of so many will deter them from acting. And if it is the two men who have been on your tail, I believe you said they were poor shots?"

Giff snorted. "Good enough to graze my thigh."

"Then let us quicken our pace. A moving target will be more difficult to hit."

"Possibly, but the rise to the Keep is steep. We need to preserve the horses."

The captain nodded and began instead to train a hunting gaze on the surrounding trees. No sudden attack occurred, but Giff was relieved when they rode out of the woods and began the climb towards the old Keep, its remaining ruined turret now visible at the top of the incline. The sight struck a chord of memory in Giff, as it had the first time he approached. He had no real recollection of his old home, but he had been surprised to note a feeling of recognition as he entered the building.

It was not, as might have been expected, a castle. Little remained of the original structure beyond part of the crumbling outer wall. The present house, built on the flat land to the rear and added to over the centuries, had a higgledy-piggledy aspect, with one wing in the style of Queen Anne and a later façade to its pillared frontage. The cavalcade entered via an old stone archway that let onto a drive, culminating in a wide sweep of gravel in front of the building. Giff dismounted and handed his reins to Sattar.

"You and Lord Tarporley's groom had best find the stables and see the horses rubbed down and fed." He lowered his

271

voice and switched to Hindi. "Leave them in this other fellow's charge, Sattar, and get yourself into the house. If we need you, I'll whistle."

Tarporley and Rhoades were on the ground, both shaking the stiffness from their joints. Giff jerked his head towards the entrance.

"Looks quiet enough, gentlemen. But I'm ready to wager we were observed as we rode in."

"Undoubtedly, I should think."

Tarporley hung back. "Do you wish us to come in with you, Giffard? Or shall we wait as back-up?"

"Good God, no! If I go in alone, I might as well not have brought you. A show of strength may deter my cousin at the outset."

He had of necessity taken Tarporley into his confidence as well as the captain. The boy was very much shocked and had been more than willing to do what he might to assist Giff to establish himself.

"I'd be only too glad to have you for my neighbour in place of your cousin, Gaunt."

"Until I'm in the saddle, stick with Giffard, if you would."

Striding up to the porch, he seized the iron bell and pulled. A clamour sounded within the building. Giff slid his sword part way from its scabbard and hammered the hilt on the door for good measure. As it slipped back into place, he heard footsteps within and the door opened.

The elderly butler Giff saw on his previous visit stood in the aperture. He was a portly fellow with a lugubrious mien and bald dome. His gaze took in Giff and widened as he noted his companions.

"We're here to see my cousin, Piers Gaunt."

"You mean the master, sir?"

Giff set his teeth. The master forsooth! "He's expecting me."

The man bowed and set the door wide. Giff walked into the wide hall, reflecting that it looked gloomy even on this sunny day, with its dark wood-panelled walls and a mere splash of light casting shadows on the flagged floor.

On impulse, Giff accosted the butler as he turned from shutting the front door. "Have you been in service here for many years?"

The fellow inclined his head. "Around twenty, sir. I began as a footman."

"Ah, then you won't have known Lady Baunton."

An odd look passed over the man's face. "No, sir. Mrs Joyce, however, was here in her ladyship's day. The housekeeper, sir."

"Was she? Fetch her, will you?"

The man looked taken aback, but he bowed and moved in the direction of a door to one side. "If you will wait in the Red Saloon, sir, I will inform the master of your arrival."

It was the same room into which Giff had been ushered before and he liked it even less upon a second showing. The upper part of the walls were papered in a dull pinkish shade with a rich red pattern, the lower half covered in the ubiquitous dark panelling, which matched the heavy old-fashioned chairs and sofas ranged around the walls. If the rest of Waldiche Keep was done out in much the same fashion, he would have a hell of a task on his hands to change it to suit his personal tastes. Or Delia's, if it came to that.

"Our houses in India are a deal more bright and airy," he remarked, when the butler had departed.

"It is a trifle on the gloomy side." Tarporley was looking about with interest. "Gaunt must use this room rarely. The upper floor rooms are a little more inviting."

"You've been here often?"

273

"Occasionally. Gaunt does not entertain a great deal. Nor did his father. I beg pardon, I mean your father."

Giff refrained from snapping back that old Lord Baunton was no father of his. Of course he was, or why in the world was he here? Despite all, he began to wish he had remained in India. What had he to do with all this pompous grandeur?

"Do you remember it at all, Giffard?"

Giff looked across to where Captain Rhoades was inspecting a painting of a hunting scene that hung over the fireplace. "Not in the least. I was but three when my mother left." Impatience claimed him. "What the deuce does Piers mean by keeping me waiting? And where's this wretched housekeeper?"

Rhoades was eyeing him. "Do you suppose she might recognise you?"

"Only if she sees my mother in me. My uncle says I have a look of her."

"Will it help if she does?"

"I have no notion what will help. I'm ready to grasp at any straw, to be frank."

At this point, the door opened and Piers walked in. He cast an eye across Giff's retinue and a sneer curved his mouth. "You brought reinforcements then? I thought you would."

Seething, Giff glared. "What else did you expect? This is Captain Rhoades of the militia and this —"

"Yes, I know Tarporley well." Piers nodded towards the captain. "I've seen you about in Weymouth."

"Indeed? I've not seen you, sir."

The sneer became more marked. "I dare say. I am disinclined to flaunt myself abroad at this present. No doubt the reason leaps to the eye."

Rhoades glanced at Giff as if for guidance, and Tarporley was looking baffled.

"Yes, they are both familiar with the situation. Rhoades had to know when your hirelings attempted to club me the other day. And Tarporley, as your neighbour, offered his services. He told me of your encroachment on his lands."

"Did he?" A mocking glance went Tarporley's way. "Or should we say his encroachment on *my* lands?"

"But it appears they are not your lands, Gaunt," the young man snapped, his eyes smouldering.

Giff put up a hand. "Peace! Let us hear what my cousin has to offer by way of compromise — if it is that. A proposition, you said, Piers?"

His head went up, the eyes keen. "Shall we discuss that in private?"

"Not if you mean to try a fall with me."

"In my book room? With witnesses on the premises? I am not such a fool, Giffard. Come!"

With which, he turned for the door. Giff threw a warning look at the other two men and signalled with his eyes and a jerk of his head. Rhoades nodded. Satisfied they would follow discreetly and remain within range, Giff left the room and found Piers waiting in the hall.

"The book room is at the end of this wing. Follow me."

Giff trailed behind him through the hall and along corridors, his eye drawn to the panelling that prevailed throughout. Hideous. It made the place both bleak and discomforting. He could not blame his mother for leaving, even had Matt not been in question. The prospect of living in it filled him with revulsion, comparing poorly against the airy comfort of his home in Bishnupur. Positively palatial when set against this monstrosity.

The library proved a large apartment, a degree more welcoming, with wide windows letting onto a view of rolling hills beyond. Yet it too was dulled by the dark wood of shelving all around the walls, the leather spines of the tomes within, and the huge desk dominating the open space. The only touch of lightness and colour came in the red-patterned carpet and the stark contrast of white marble in the mantelpiece and surround to the fireplace.

Piers took up a stance before this, leaning his elbow on the mantel and cocking his head on one side as he looked at Giff. "You are wondering what I could possibly offer to satisfy you."

Giff threw up his eyes. "Cut line, Piers. I'm in no mood for your false poses. What do you want? Tell me in plain words."

The thin mouth curved in that mocking look. "In plain words then, cousin, I am prepared to forgo attempting to appropriate the title if you will return to India and leave me in possession of the estate."

A short laugh escaped Giff. "Just like that? What, are you proposing to act as my steward? Agent?"

"Call it what you will. I care nothing for such terms. But I don't propose to run the place for your benefit. I will continue as I have done. If you choose to let the world believe I do so on your behalf, so be it. In reality, however, you will cede all rights in the property to me."

"Will I, by God?"

"If you are wise."

"And if I'm not?"

"Then the battle continues, cousin. You have no proof, or you would have presented it by this time. You may choose the long game and waste your substance — which I understand to be considerable — fattening the pockets of dilatory lawyers while we wrangle. These things go on for years."

Giff eyed him, a rise of contempt in his breast. "So I'm to overlook all these attempts on my life and your avowed purpose of having me kidnapped and shipped off to the Americas?"

Piers did not look in the least disconcerted. He smiled, unpleasantly. "Again, you have no proof, Giffard. You cannot say any of these attacks were by my instigation."

"Oh? I collect you did not then speak frankly of your schemes to Miss Burloyne when you met first in Weymouth?"

"Her word against mine."

"But if we capture your felons, they can be made to talk."

The sneer came. "I know nothing of any felons, my dear cousin."

"That won't fadge. My man saw you in conversation with Sam and Barney."

"Indeed? And do you think a ragtag Indian servant will be believed over a gentlemen in good standing, with a viable claim to become a peer of the realm?"

Giff's rising temper got the better of him. "Damn you to hell! You will never be a peer of the realm!"

"Yet I am here in Waldiche Keep, Giffard, the master of all, while you must prove your identity before you can hope even to begin to oust me."

His poise and certainty infuriated Giff, but he mastered it. He would get nowhere by losing control. The worst of it was the villain was right on all counts. For two pins he'd walk away from the whole mess and go home. He didn't even like the place.

Yet a devil rode him and he would not allow this hypocritical fiend to best him. He threw his head back and looked his cousin in the eye.

"You made a fatal error at the outset, Piers."

The other's brows rose. "How so?"

Giff smiled, but he spoke in a grim tone. "When I first came here, I had some such notion in my head. If you'd granted my coming the observance of civility and trust, I had in mind some such arrangement as you've outlined."

For the first time, Piers's air of assurance wavered. His brows came together. "I don't believe you."

"You wouldn't. It's true for all that. I'd no real wish to exchange India for England, and my purpose was to see how the land lay and act accordingly. But you, my friend, chose to demonstrate how unfitted you are to be entrusted with what is, after all, my inheritance."

There was no smile now, no mockery. But the man's eyes flashed at the last. "So you will choose a paltry revenge? I might have guessed it."

"Paltry? After the way you've acted towards me? Whatever I may choose to do, you've brought on yourself."

"Very pretty talking. In fact there is nothing you can do."

"Isn't there?" Giff withdrew the hilt of his sword. "How if I kill you now?"

Piers actually laughed. "In cold blood? I hardly think that is your style, Giffard."

"Not in cold blood. But we'll fight it out, Piers. Here and now."

"What, in the book room?"

"Don't be ridiculous! We'll go outside. I presume you have a sword?"

"You can't make me, you fool!"

"Can't I? You forget I've got back-up. Isn't it fortunate both are gentlemen? Two of them to see fair play, Piers."

The sneer was back in force. "When both are on your side?"

278

"You may have Rhoades to serve you. He's militia and no doubt scrupulous to a fault." Giff headed for the door. "Come, Piers. I'll call them in."

"Wait!"

Halting, Giff turned. "Yes?"

"This is folly!"

"Because you know I'll win?"

Piers took a hasty step forward. "It's your challenge, so I have the choice."

"I'm not fighting you with pistols, if that's your hope. I've already sustained a wound from one of your hired ruffians, I thank you." He stared the man down. "Besides, if you hope to be rid of me in this way instead, are you sure you're the better shot?"

Piers hesitated. "You've already stated you intend to make this a killing matter."

"Perhaps. I might let you live."

"Oh, don't be a fool, man! This is nonsense and you know it."

"I don't know it. I've been itching to fight you for days. I prefer an open contest. If you manage to pink me, I'll fall in with your proposition. If you lose, we go forward on my terms. Agreed?"

There was fear in his cousin's face now. "You've not stated your terms. How do I know you won't take it to the death?"

It was Giff's turn for mockery. "If you were dead at my hands, I'd have to leave the country, wouldn't I? How would that serve me?"

Piers appeared to breathe more easily. "Very well, if you insist on this course."

"It's quick and decisive. Let's go!"

Reaching the door, Giff tugged it open and found both Tarporley and Rhoades on the other side. He grinned. "Did you hear?"

Rhoades nodded, speaking low. "You really want me to act for him?"

"One of you must, and he won't trust Tarporley."

"That's true enough," the young man conceded, "considering the quarrel between us. I certainly would not trust him."

By this time, Piers was at the door. He seemed a little more himself, though his voice was a trifle shaky. "I'll need to fetch my sword."

"Go with him, Rhoades!"

Piers cast Giff a glance of dislike. "Do you suppose I'll make my escape?"

"I don't know what you'll do. One thing I do know. You can't be trusted."

Captain Rhoades stepped up. "I'll accompany you, sir. Which way?"

Piers shrugged and headed down the corridor towards the hall, the captain on his heels. Tarporley gazed after them.

"Do you really mean to fight him?"

"Yes."

"But what will you gain by it?"

"The upper hand, my friend. He's badly frightened. I think he suspects I may kill him after all. I threatened to."

"You won't, though?"

Giff let out a short laugh as he started off along the corridor. "Hardly."

"You won't lose your temper?"

"I never lose my temper in a fight."

"What if he's a good swordsman?"

280

"I don't fear his skill. I doubt he's had as much practice, for a start."

Arriving in the hall, Giff found a rather stout, elderly dame hovering near the stairs, the butler in attendance. Her dress proclaimed the housekeeper, and he did not need the man's introduction to tell him this was the female who had been here in his mother's day.

"This is Mrs Joyce, sir."

The woman bobbed a curtsey, peering up at him as Giff neared. Her eyes widened. "Mercy me! You do have a look of her, sir, that's certain. Are you Master Giffard indeed?"

CHAPTER SIXTEEN

A pulse leapt in Giff's chest. "You know me?"

Mrs Joyce's startled eyes appeared to devour his face. "I think I must say I do, sir, for the resemblance is uncanny."

"I had not thought I looked so like my mother."

"Oh, her features were more delicate, as I remember, Master Giffard, but so were yours when last I saw you. Gracious heaven, it is you!"

Giff seized the woman's plump hands and held them fast. "Can you swear to it, Mrs Joyce? Dare you say for certain I am the same you knew as a child?"

The woman's hands returned the pressure of his. "I am as certain as I stand here, sir." She freed one hand and reached up in a tentative fashion. "May I, sir?"

Giff, his breast a tumult, nodded. "Go ahead."

He felt her fingers on his face, trembling as they touched the fading wounds.

"How did you come by these, Master Giffard?"

He grimaced. "It's a long story, Mrs Joyce. But, come, tell me how it is you know me for my mother's son?"

She stood back a little, her gaze still riveted. "Now that I look at you more closely, sir, I cannot quite tell. It is not so much your individual features, except for the eyes. Indeed, I think you have more of his late lordship in the nose and jaw. It is perhaps the way your hair grows and the shape of your face, I think." Her expression changed, became shadowed. "I beg your pardon, sir, if I am speaking too free."

"The devil you are! Your words are gold to me, Mrs Joyce. Say on!"

She looked hesitant. "Might I instead show you, Master Giffard?"

"Show me what?"

The housekeeper threw an apprehensive glance towards the upper regions where Piers had gone with Rhoades. She dropped into a near whisper. "If you don't object to coming to my room, sir…"

Giff turned to Tarporley, who had witnessed all with evident astonishment, and noted the butler still present at a slight distance and looking bemused. He addressed himself to Tarporley.

"Tell Piers I will meet him in the old ruins of the ancient keep, will you?"

"Certainly." The young man came close enough to murmur. "But need you still fight?"

"I don't yet know." Giff turned to the butler. "You'd best come with us. I don't want you alerting your master."

"He won't do that, sir," said the housekeeper, but she beckoned the man as she led the way towards a door leading to the back premises.

Aware of an unruly pulse, Giff followed her through the door and found himself in the area devoted to domestic offices. The clatter of pots and pans penetrated the corridor they were traversing, but Mrs Joyce stopped before they reached the kitchen, entering a neat little apartment which was clearly her housekeeper's room. She closed and locked the door behind the three of them, casting an admonishing glance towards the butler.

"You must never speak of this to Master Piers, Adam." And to Giff, "Dunford and I are to be married, sir, when we both retire. He will not betray you."

283

Giff nodded towards the man, but his attention was concentrated on the housekeeper. "What did you want to show me?"

She selected a key from the bunch hanging from the chatelaine at her waist and, moving to the smaller of two cupboards, bent to insert it into the lock of the lower section. Giff waited in some degree of anxious impatience as her arm and head disappeared inside the aperture, with a degree of huffing and puffing as she set up a search. Her voice came muffled.

"Here it is!"

She emerged and, with a trifle of difficulty, extracted a small framed picture and held it up. Giff took it from her as Dunford sprang forward to help the woman to her feet.

Turning the frame, Giff regarded the portrait it contained in stunned silence. The image depicted was of a young woman holding an infant, rather in the manner of the virgin and child. The two faces were practically identical, both wearing lush locks of golden brown, the babe's a shade or two lighter than those of the mother. His mother. There was no mistaking Flora Gaunt's familiar features, though they were a good deal more plumply youthful than he remembered. His hair had darkened with the years and he knew his eyes were a trifle more deep-set, his brows more prominent.

"You've kept this all these years?"

Mrs Joyce's eyes were rimmed with wet. "His lordship ordered all her portraits to be burnt, but I could not bear to obliterate all trace of her. I was very fond of her ladyship. As sweet and gentle a mistress as you could wish for."

"Yes, she was always good with servants. But she was not as biddable as you might think, Mrs Joyce."

"So we discovered, Master Giffard, when she went off so sudden. None of us had the least notion she was planning to escape."

"Escape? You call it that?"

Mrs Joyce sniffed and hunted in her pockets, pulling out a square of linen handkerchief and dabbing at her eyes. "It was not a happy marriage, sir, that I would swear to. Neither she nor he were at all fond. They barely spoke. And I know for a fact his lordship had a —" She broke off, consternation leaping to her eyes.

The inference did not escape Giff. "He had another interest? A mistress?"

"Oh, I beg your pardon, Master Giffard! I had no right to — "

"I prefer the plain truth, Mrs Joyce. Who was she?" A disturbing notion leapt in his head and he gave it immediate voice. "You are not going to tell me he was in a liaison with Piers's mother, are you? Is he my father's bastard, Mrs Joyce?"

Having collected both Tarporley and Sattar, Giff made for the ruin of the original keep, passing back through the archway and setting a path across overgrown terrain towards the scattered blocks of old stone and the partially standing wall. Whether the place was suitable for a swordfight remained to be seen. He'd chosen it at random, thinking only it was sufficiently removed from the house to provide a modicum of privacy. The last thing they needed was servants gathering to watch.

Tarporley pointed. "I can see Rhoades."

Giff caught a flash of the captain's red coat up ahead, between the trees. "Looks as if he's found a clearing of sorts. Good man."

A mutter of Hindi came from behind. "Foolish boy! Why must you fight?"

"Piers needs a lesson," Giff returned in the same language. "I'm in two minds and the fight may settle it."

Tarporley glanced from one to the other. "What is it, Giffard? You've not said if that woman confirmed your identity."

No, he'd kept silent on that head, merely enquiring if Piers had come down. Upon learning Tarporley had delivered the message and Rhoades had escorted his cousin to the ground, Giff lost no time in following.

He switched back to English. "She showed me a portrait of my mother dandling an infant."

"That would be you?"

"Without doubt. But it is scarcely adequate proof."

"Her testimony then?"

"Perhaps."

Truth was, he was less concerned with proving himself than with the implications concerning Piers's origins. But he must have the mastery over the man before anything else.

Captain Rhoades had evidently seen them as the party approached the ruin, for he waved and called out a greeting.

Close up, the wall was much higher than Giff had at first supposed. Its curve provided a convenient protected space, but pitted with fallen blocks, worn by time. Where the wall had come down altogether, evidence of its considerable width was visible in the foundation as Giff crossed to where Rhoades and his cousin were standing.

Piers was looking grim, a trifle pale, his arrogant stance somewhat reduced. He was in possession of a sword, already unsheathed, its point resting on the ground. He waved a hand to encompass the space. "You appointed an impossible rendezvous, cousin. We can't fight here."

Giff had to agree. There were too many obstacles to trap unwary feet. Neither man would be able to concentrate. Rhoades spoke before he could say as much.

"I've had a look around. If we move some fifty yards in that direction, there is a clearing. It should prove adequate, I think."

Piers cast him a glance of dislike. "You can't know there are not stones hidden in the grass."

"Tarporley and I will walk it first."

So saying, he beckoned to the younger man and together they went off towards a belt of trees further into the wooded area that had grown up beyond the ruin.

Piers lifted his eyes to Giff, an echo of his usual mockery within them. "You are determined on this foolery?"

"What do you think?"

Giff remained at a little distance, studying the man with revived interest. He had to concede the fellow was personable. How to descry any particular resemblance? Apart from their great-uncle, Giff knew none of the Gaunt males. Nor had he seen any portrait of his father. Piers's father had been the younger of two brothers, which was all Giff knew of him. If there was more to it, would Piers know? It might explain his obsessive determination to hold on to what he had gained. Did he believe himself entitled? Had Henry Gaunt encouraged him to think it? Such questions might never be answered. Oddly, though, despite every wish to ignore it, the possibility Piers might be his half-brother must inevitably change the game.

The man was clearly nervous. Giff doubted he'd had occasion to duel before. Was he even in the habit of keeping in practice with a fencing master? All gentlemen learned the art as a matter of course, so Papa Matt had told him when he began such instruction while Giff was yet a boy. Matt had been assiduous in ensuring he was properly educated for his true sphere, and what he had omitted in other forms of combat, Sattar had supplied.

A hail from Rhoades drew his attention back to the matter at hand. He nodded at Piers.

"It seems we are in luck. Shall we proceed?"

Piers hesitated, eyeing him askance. "I wish you will tell me what you intend."

Giff raised his brows. "But I've told you. We're going for first blood, Piers." He looked the man up and down. "Are you afraid? You need not be. Sattar here is expert at dealing with wounds."

The sneer appeared briefly. "Afraid? I? By no means. Let us go."

He turned, striding off in the direction the two seconds had taken.

Satisfied, Giff followed, Sattar on his heels.

"He fears you, sahib. Dare I trust your anger will not lead you into taking his life?"

"Devil a bit, old sobersides. I'm not as reckless as that. Besides, it won't suit me to make this a killing matter."

"Ha! You like it not, this England. I thought it was so, sahib."

"I could learn to like it, I think."

Sattar gave him a sidelong look. "It is the memsahib, yes?"

The image of his flower girl leapt into Giff's head. There was a question indeed. He was no longer willing to consult only his own preferences. And if it came to remaining, what the deuce was he to do with Piers?

It did not take long to reach the clear space Rhoades had located. Tarporley came up at once, while the captain relieved Piers of his sword.

"The ground is safe enough, Giffard. Let me take your sword while you remove what clothing will hamper you."

"Right. Let's get this over with."

Giff unbuckled his sword belt. Sattar was waiting to take it, but he waved him away, giving his instructions in Hindi. "Move off to a little distance. I want you to be seen to be impartial. Don't interfere unless my cousin proves treacherous."

His henchman nodded and made his way to a position out of the immediate environment set for the fight. Giff removed his coat and flexed his arms.

"Your boots, Giffard? The grass may be slippery."

"I'll keep them on. They are well worn and I'm wary of unseen stones."

Tarporley looked worried. Giff glanced across at his opponent. Piers had taken off his coat, but had likewise left on his boots.

"My sword, man!"

He took the rapier in hand, waited while Piers did the same and then moved in, feeling the familiar rush of power pour into his breast at the proximity of danger.

A brief salute and Giff dropped into the *en garde* position. It felt good to be facing his cousin across three feet of steel instead of wondering where the next attack was coming from. Like this he was in command, knew his own strength and the outcome rested on his skill and stamina. All at once, remembrance of what Piers's scheming had put him through swept in, leaving him hard, cold and vengeful. Now the fellow would pay.

Wasting no time, Giff opened with an attack direct, aiming high. He saw the startled look in Piers's eyes as he brought up his weapon to parry. He'd not expected so swift a beginning. So much the better.

Giff leapt back briefly and again lunged, took the parry, slipped his rapier under his opponent's and lunged again. Piers gasped out as he just managed to catch the blade. Then he jumped back out of range, gazing at Giff out of wide, scared eyes, his wrist shaking as he brought his arm back to keep the sword in guard.

"Not so amusing when it's your life on the line, is it, my friend?"

Piers bared his teeth. "Damn you!"

He lunged in *quarte*. Giff parried, dropped back, took a second violent swing with a wild aim on his sword and beat it off with a strength that near tripped his opponent as he fell back. From the corner of his eye Giff saw Rhoades step in from his position on the side lines, sword at the ready. Did he mean to intervene?

Piers cursed, regained his balance and his guard both, his wary gaze on the point of the sword Giff was holding steady.

"Had enough, Piers?"

For answer, his cousin lunged again, his aim uncertain. Giff parried, retired, and parried again as his cousin kept up a frenzied attack. Trying for confusion? It would not work. Giff saw how he lunged without bothering to try for a proper opening, without knowing which part of his opponent he meant to wound. The man had been angered by Giff's taunt, just as he'd hoped. Foolish when facing a naked sword. A cool head was essential.

Giff parried mechanically, looking for the sign that Piers's wrist was tiring. As his cousin retired, ready for another lunge, he saw the point waver. It was time.

He went into the attack, feinted as Piers sought to parry, and threw his strength into the lunge, his point aimed high for Piers's sword shoulder. Just in time the man managed to deflect the intended target, but uttered a cry as the point sliced across his upper arm instead. A red stain sprang up.

Next instant, Rhoades leapt in. "Put up!"

His sword clashed with Giff's just as he pulled back. Giff cursed.

"Leave be, man! Did you think I meant to do more damage?"

The captain did not answer, but sheathed his own sword and turned instead to his principal. Piers was clutching his injury with his free hand, staring blindly at the welling blood, his sword still held at the ready. Rhoades seized Piers's sword at the hilt.

"Enough! You're bleeding, sir. Let go!"

Piers's nerveless fingers opened and the captain took the sword and tossed it aside, out of the way.

"At least you did not strike some vital part, Giffard."

This was Tarporley, coming up to relieve Giff of his sword. He gave it up to his second, but his eyes remained on Piers, who had gone deathly pale and was swaying alarmingly.

"I think he's going to swoon. Sattar!"

The shout brought his henchman at a run, but the captain was already at Piers's back, lowering him to the ground where he sat in a dazed stupor. Sattar was unwinding the cravat from about his own throat. He dropped to his haunches next to the injured man, addressing the captain.

"Give me leave, sahib. I will arrange."

"I'll hold him. He's losing consciousness."

Giff eyed his cousin's pallid features. He was lying heavily against Rhoades with his eyes closed. "Have I damaged him badly, then?"

Sattar was engaged in slicing off Piers's shirtsleeve with his dagger. "It is the bleeding, sahib. Some men it shocks."

He ripped the sleeve down and laid bare a gash, seeping red. Tarporley handed down a pocket handkerchief and Sattar used it to staunch the blood. He looked up at Giff.

"Give me yours too, sahib, to make a pad."

Giff dug his handkerchief out of his breeches pocket, studying the wound as he did so. It looked to be more long than deep. He handed over the square of linen. "A flesh wound. Tit for tat, then."

"What do you mean?"

"His men gave me one when they shot at me," Giff told Tarporley.

"They also gave you a black eye and a split lip. Or had you forgotten?"

"Devil a bit. But the other kept me down for days. This evens the score a little. He'll be out of action for a while."

Piers's lids lifted and he managed a hoarse mutter. "Not for long. Should've killed me while you had the chance."

"Be quiet, man," snapped the captain. "Will you not own yourself bested even now?"

But Piers made no answer. A sighing breath escaped him and he sank a little more sluggishly into Rhoades's hold.

"He's out." Giff curled his lip. "He's game enough, I have to give him that."

"But little skill," returned the captain. "His aim was all to pieces."

"He's likely out of practice." Tarporley gave Giff a rueful smile. "I'd not meet you for a fortune, Giffard. Have you fought often?"

Giff was watching Sattar wind his improvised bandage tightly around his cousin's injury, halting the blood, but he looked round at this. "I've had occasion to do my share. There are plagues of bandits in certain areas back home. And Sattar keeps me in practice."

Rhoades looked up at him with a frown. "You consider India your home, then?"

A pang smote Giff. "It's all I've known. I remember little to naught of this place."

No one spoke for a moment, and Giff found himself again wondering what he was going to do. He shook off an unaccustomed feeling of despondency. First things first.

"Are you done, Sattar?"

"Almost, sahib." He tucked the end of the now stained cravat into itself. He looked from one to the other of the three men. "To get him up is now the trick, sahibs all."

Tarporley looked dubious. "Should we not carry him?"

"Better he walks, sahib. A man is stronger for moving. If he lies still, he becomes weaker."

Giff nodded. He needed Piers as alert as they could make him, and Sattar knew what he was talking about. "Can you wake him, Rhoades?"

"I can try." Rhoades peered down to the body he held. "Gaunt! Can you hear me?" A groan rewarded him. "We're going to get you up, man. Come, try to stand."

Between them, Rhoades and Sattar managed to lift Piers. He cried out, his eyes flying open as the Indian slipped under his injured shoulder.

"I must support you, sahib. The captain will take your other side."

Willy-nilly, Piers began to walk as the two bore him slowly towards the ruins again.

Tarporley was wiping Giff's sword with his already bloodied handkerchief. "Sheathe this, Giffard. I'll take your cousin's sword."

Giff inspected his blade and saw it was wiped nearly clean. He dropped it back in its scabbard and joined the young man as he set off after the others.

"What do you mean to do, Giffard?"

"That remains to be seen. I've questions for Piers, and my decision may be based on his answers."

Tarporley eyed him with unconcealed dismay. "You don't mean to leave him the field, do you?"

"It may come to that."

"After all you've gone through at his hands?"

"I've repaid him for some of it."

"But he's usurped your seat, man! Surely you mean to take it back?"

Giff eyed him with some degree of amusement. "You'd rather have me for your neighbour, I take it?"

"Infinitely! And I believe you are mad even to think of letting him hold what is yours."

"Oh, I won't do that."

"Well, thank God for it! You had me worried there for a moment."

Giff refrained from speaking of what was in his mind. Until he knew for certain whether his suspicions had foundation, nothing could be decided. Indeed, no decision could be made until he'd spoken to Delia, if it came to that. And to say true, he still had no valid proof, either of identity or ownership.

Whether a portrait of a mother and infant would do was doubtful. Not to mention the testimony of a woman who had not seen him for more than twenty years, and then as little more than an infant.

In fact, unless Piers could furnish a different tale, he was no nearer his goal, despite having bested the man in a fight.

CHAPTER SEVENTEEN

The uproar following upon the party's return from the ruins prevented Giff from having speech with his cousin for some time. Her partiality notwithstanding, the housekeeper was horrified at the fight.

"How could you, Master Giffard? Why, you might have killed him!"

"I never intended to go that far, Mrs Joyce."

"Far enough, sir!" And, turning to the butler, "Dunford, send at once to Dr Egerton!"

Wholly ignoring the gentlemen, she was off in a whirlwind of directions, bustling the servants gathered in the hall where Piers had been deposited in a convenient chair.

"You there! Help Bines to carry the master up to his room. Bines, you must put him to bed and see to his comfort. I will set Cook to make a tisane and brew a posset against the doctor's arrival. Until then, give him water only."

Giff saw Sattar nod approval at this and was not surprised when he entered into low-voiced conversation with the fellow Bines, presumably Piers's valet.

Rhoades left the man in the care of members of his household and came to Giff's side. "We appear to be *de trop*. Is this a convenient time to make our departure?"

"By no means. At least, you may go if you wish. Tarporley too. But I must have words with my cousin before I can leave."

"We won't desert you, Giffard," said Tarporley from behind him. "Unless you have duties, Rhoades?"

The captain shrugged, his eye on the cavalcade now beginning to make their slow way up the stairs, Piers chaired between two stout footmen, Sattar following in colloquy with the fellow Bines. "Nothing that cannot wait. But I confess to feeling a trifle sharp set. Is there a decent inn hereabouts?"

The reference to food resonated with Giff. "A good point, my friend. However, I'm reluctant to remove from here. Who knows but this crew may refuse to let me re-enter after this?"

"My home is within reach, Rhoades. You and I may go there, perhaps. My people will feed us. Indeed, it might suit to remain overnight if the business cannot be settled soon."

But at this point, the housekeeper came up. Having despatched various people on errands, she evidently had time to see to the invaders. She was looking harassed, but the belligerence had lessened. "Now then, Master Giffard, I suppose I must see to your comfort as well, little though you deserve it."

Giff hid a smile at the severity coming from a creature quite a foot shorter than he and as plump as a goose besides. "A repast of some kind would not go amiss, Mrs Joyce, if it is not too much trouble. These gentlemen, however, are happy to repair to Lord Tarporley's establishment to find sustenance there."

The housekeeper bridled. "Nothing of the sort, sir! Do you suppose I keep so mean a table that we cannot feed you all?"

"We thought only to spare you the pain," said Tarporley.

She turned on him. "As if you had not taken your mutton in this house time and again, my lord! Yes, I well know who you are and that you've not been a friend to the master since the old lord went to his maker, but I won't have it spread about the county that we are inhospitable in Waldiche Keep."

Which silenced Tarporley, who reddened and retired from the lists. Satisfied, Mrs Joyce looked all three up and down.

"Well! You've dirt and blood all over, the lot of you! You will please to clean up before sitting down to table in this house."

With which, she turned to two hovering maids and beckoned. "Ellie, show these gentlemen to the blue bedchamber. And you, Grisel, fetch up a large jug of hot water to that room straight. Now, I've to see Cook."

One scorching glance over the men and she sailed off towards the nether regions, presumably to put all her arrangements in hand.

The captain leaned in with lowered voice as they began to follow Ellie the maid, who was leading the way upstairs. "I feel as if I've been reduced to the status of a scrubby schoolboy."

Giff laughed. "Yes, I might as well have been listening to Sattar. He's just such a tartar."

"Like my uncles," sighed Tarporley. "They talk to me as if I'm a nincompoop."

"I didn't expect it from Mrs Joyce, I have to say. Not after the way she was damn near in tears when she showed me that portrait."

The captain paused on the stairs. "What portrait?"

Giff explained on the way, but the subject was dropped when they entered a large bedchamber. The maid held the door as they trooped in and Giff was agreeably surprised to find it a deal less gloomy than the downstairs rooms. Light splayed from two wide windows onto a blue patterned carpet, which was matched with blue curtains tied at the posts of the bed. But best were the walls, papered throughout in a pattern of birds and flowers in blue on a cream ground.

Tarporley sank down onto the bed. "What a day! I could use a tot of brandy."

Giff had just shrugged off his coat for the second time. "An excellent thought." He dug into the pocket of his coat and brought out his flask, handing it across. "Here, my friend. Well-deserved too."

The young man took it, but hesitated. "What about you?"

"You first."

Rhoades, who had also removed his coat, came up to them, grinning, a similar silver receptacle in his hand. "Great minds, Giffard." He unscrewed the cap and raised the flask. "To a happy outcome!"

Giff watched him drink, his mind returning to his besetting problem. Happy? If truth be told, neither one nor the other of the two possibilities could be said to be entirely happy.

Rhoades smacked his lips with satisfaction. "That's better. A wash and a meal and I'll be as good as new."

He offered the flask to Giff, who held up a hand. "Keep it. I'll take a sip of my own when Tarporley is done. Besides, I dare say the butler — Dunford? Yes, Dunford — will supply us with suitable wine."

Tarporley handed over the flask with a word of thanks. "What do you mean to say to your cousin, Giffard?"

"I'm in two minds. I can't decide if I want to remain in the country or not."

"But you intend to establish your rightful claim, I hope?"

"That might take years of wrangling." He gave a rueful laugh. "I'm not a patient man, I'm afraid."

Rhoades laughed out, stripping the cravat from his neck. "I think we've both understood that." He unbuttoned his waistcoat, an odd look in his eye as he flicked a glance at Giff. "Mayhap Miss Burloyne may teach you to be a little less ready to leap before you look."

Warmth crept into Giff's cheeks, and he eyed the man with a resurgence of suspicion. "You can say that? You've an interest there yourself!"

The captain threw aside his waistcoat and looked up, astonishment in his face. "I? Have you run mad, Giffard?"

"I've seen you seizing chances, hobnobbing with the wench."

"Yes, when I had to question her. For the lord's sake, man! What are you, an Othello? Besides, anyone can see she's head over heels for you."

A cascade of warmth swept through Giff. Hope soared. "You think so?"

"I had the same notion," came from Tarporley, now also divesting himself of some of his clothes.

There was time for no more, for a knock at the chamber door produced the second maid, armed with a jug, and a footman, bearing another along with towels and other personal accoutrements.

"I'll fetch another basin, sirs," said the maid, setting down her jug and bobbing a curtsey.

"Mrs Joyce said as I'd to stay and help, sirs." The footman brandished a clothes brush and a couple of combs.

Rhoades waved the footman towards the bed. "Put them down. Is there a slop bucket?"

The man indicated the deep bucket under the washstand and set down his burdens on the bed, holding a towel ready for Rhoades who was already splashing water into the basin set into the wash stand.

"When you're ready, sirs, I've to show you to the breakfast parlour."

The presence of the footman precluded any conversation beyond that pertinent to washing of hands and faces, brushing of coats and hair and retying of cravats.

Giff found his thoughts returning to Piers and the revolving questions in his head. A nuisance the discussion with his cousin must be postponed. Presumably he would find it near impossible to accost him again until the doctor had been.

The meal, of roast beef and ham pie, accompanied by buttered artichokes and French beans, followed by a bath pudding, a plate of fresh fruits and another of gingerbread, raised Giff's spirits a trifle, but he found it hard to join in with Rhoades and Tarporley, who had fallen into jocular mood and were exchanging the kind of stories confined within a male arena as they passed around the wine bottle.

By the time he was at last able to secure an opportunity to go to Piers's chamber, the hour was advanced and it began to look as if a return to Weymouth would be out of count. Anxious to talk to Delia, Giff cursed at the delay. But at last, Mrs Joyce pronounced the master enough rested to be able to have a visitor.

In yet another panelled apartment, Piers was sitting in state in a massive four-poster, propped against pillows, his injured arm reposing in a sling.

Giff cast a distasteful glance around the room. Yet another instance of the dismal style that characterised the Keep, though its accoutrements were rich. Maroon velvet curtains adorned the ornate bed, the dresser was of mahogany inlaid with a Chinese design and the chairs were upholstered in heavy brocade. Only the late summer light coming through the windows relieved the sombre atmosphere.

Piers had evidently just finished partaking of some kind of broth, or perhaps the threatened posset. He handed the empty bowl to his valet and scrunched up a napkin lying on his lap.

"Take this, Bines, it's a mess." He waved Giff forward with his free left hand as the valet relieved him of the offending napkin. "Thanks to you, cousin."

"Because you are obliged to use the wrong hand? Not for long, more's the pity."

A grim smile crossed the man's face, but he turned to the valet first. "Leave us, Bines. Stay! Send Dunford up with wine."

The man hesitated. "Dr Egerton did not advise it, sir."

"To hell with Dr Egerton! What do you think I care if it sends me into a fever? Fetch it!"

Bines bowed and removed himself. Giff took his place by the bedside, eyeing Piers, who was already flushed.

"Going as fast as you can to the devil, Piers?"

"What do you care? It would suit you down to the ground if the wound festers and I die of it."

Giff grunted an oath. "Well, if you're determined to go to perdition, we'd best talk while you're still able." He looked about, spied a straight chair set against one wall and went to fetch it. Plonking it down by the bed, he sat, stretching out his legs and shoving his hands into his breeches pockets. He read dislike in his cousin's face as he watched these manoeuvres. The sneer was back in place.

"Well, cousin. You've taken the point. What is your will?"

Giff raised his brows. "So easy, Piers?"

The other shrugged unwarily and winced, hissing in a breath. "Damn you!"

"Are you damning me for the suffering my handiwork is causing you, or for winning?"

"Both. And for existing."

To his own surprise, Giff was conscious of a sliver of hurt. He crushed it, snapping back. "I regret incommoding you by living, Piers, but my doing so does not lessen your crimes. You tried to be rid of me, but still I'm here."

"Yes, I can see you clear, I thank you. May I know what you propose to do with me?"

The mocking tone irritated Giff, but he held back the urge to respond in kind. Bickering would get them no further forward, and he had urgent questions.

"That must depend."

"On what? If it's promises you want, I'm in no position to refuse to make them. But I tell you now I've no intention of running in your harness."

"In other words, you'd revert to your own interests the minute my back is turned."

Piers's lips curved in the sneering look he'd clearly perfected. "I'm relieved you understand me so well."

Giff hardened his tone. "I understand this too. You've coveted what is mine from the start. And I've a pretty good notion why."

A wary look came into Piers's eyes. He seemed to study Giff before answering. Weighing his response? "It's true I've long been fond of the place. Unlike you, I grew up knowing it."

"You lived at the Keep?"

Piers looked away. "No. Like Uncle George, my father took orders. He had the vicarage in Uncle Henry's gift. We lived not a stone's throw from the estate."

"My father let you run tame here, I surmise."

Piers's head whipped round, his eyes fierce. "Why not? When his own son had been taken? We became close. He taught me as he would have taught you, had your mother not stolen you from him."

The words were roughly said, but Giff detected an edge of pain under them. Had Piers grown up resenting his inferior position? Chafing at the thought he could never own what he so freely enjoyed? Giff could well imagine it and felt reluctant sympathy. While he had flourished under Papa Matt's benevolent rule and his mother's unstinting affection, his inheritance left behind but secure — or so Matt had thought — Piers had been encouraged to think himself hard done by because he could not partake of it.

"It seems my father did you a disservice, Piers."

His cousin did not answer. He turned away, a brooding look in his face.

Giff hesitated. Was it time? Should he speak now? Or was it better to leave it? If he brought the subject into the open, it could never be closed again. Yet if he did not, he was limiting his choices. Piers had clearly stated he should not be trusted. But might this change things? He changed his position, pulling his feet back and sitting up straighter. "Piers."

The man's head turned, all trace of mockery gone. There was a dull acceptance in his face. His voice came low. "Well?"

Giff took on air, steeling himself. "Tell me true. Are you my half-brother?"

Shock flashed in his cousin's eyes. Then his chin went up and he sat forward in a bang. "How in hell's name did you come to that conclusion?"

"Never mind. Is it true?"

"You impugn my mother's memory!"

"And my father's too. Is it true?"

"How in the name of all the devils of hell should I know? He didn't tell me so, if that's what you think."

Giff held to his own stiffness. "But you suspected it."

Piers threw his head back. "Damn you to hell!"

"If you wish, but I will be satisfied on this point, Piers."

"Go to the devil! Do you think it gives me any pleasure to think we are more nearly related than as cousins?"

"It might make a difference to me, however."

Piers's gaze narrowed. He fell back against his pillows, surveying Giff. "How so?"

"I don't yet know. But I'd have more consideration for a half-brother than a mere cousin. It would also provide a motive for conduct that by rights ought to land you in gaol."

"Gaol? You can prove nothing, Giffard. I've told you that already."

"And I told you not to be so cocksure! I may still choose to charge you by way of the law."

"I'd be acquitted."

"Are you certain of that? And what of the scandal?"

Piers cast him a glance of acute dislike. "Why should I care? You'll ruin me in any event."

Giff let out an exasperated snort. "Let us be clear about this, my friend. Wherever you end up, your actions have taken you there. It's not what I have done, nor what I may do."

The sneer returned to his mouth. "I collect I applied the sword to my own arm?"

"Oh, don't be such a confounded fool, man! I gave you your own again, that's all."

"You left me no choice but to fight. I'd no wish for it. And you brought your so-called friends to aid and abet you. You are the aggressor, Giffard, not I, and so I shall tell the world."

Giff leapt up. "There is no talking to you! I'm wasting my time." He thrust the chair away and strode to the door, the determination forming in his head to be done with the wretch for once and for all.

"Wait!"

Turning at the door, Giff threw the man an impatient look. "What now?"

Piers was frowning. "You've not told me what you intend?"

"I've not decided yet. But be sure it will include your removal from Waldiche Keep!"

With which, Giff flung open the door and slammed it behind him. He stood fulminating for a moment, fury and disappointment vying for supremacy. Why could the wretch not at least have tried for a compromise? Was he so sunk in considering himself a victim of fate he could not even take an olive branch offered in good faith?

Beginning to walk along the gallery, but slowly, Giff's mind churned along with his gut. This was not how he'd hoped to end it. Whether or not Piers was his father's bastard seemed now to be irrelevant. He'd half hoped to find Piers reclaimable if he'd been able to hail him for his brother. Could he ever truly have left the fellow in charge of his estates? When Piers had himself avowed he would not keep any promise he might make?

Disappointment was winning. This effectively cut his choices. India had never felt so far away. And Waldiche Keep was becoming a prison to him.

Reaching the stairs, Giff began to descend, his mind still back in the chamber, the image of Piers's recalcitrant features imprinted there.

"Giff! Thank goodness! I was afraid you'd be up there for an age!"

His attention snapped in, and he halted on the stairs, seeking the source of the most unexpected voice in the world. "Delia! What are you doing here?"

CHAPTER EIGHTEEN

Barely able to speak for the thumping in her chest, Delia beckoned Giff down. "We had to come! We went first to Mr Hammersley, and he is with us."

"You mean the lawyer Hammersley? Who is we?" Giff reached her and grasped her fingers, making them tingle.

Delia clung to his hand, though his face was shadowed in the gloom of the wide hall, lit only by a single candelabrum. "Your uncle escorted me. I have so much to tell you, but what of Piers? Captain Rhoades says you fought." She passed a frantic glance over his person. "You are not hurt, are you?"

He grinned. "Devil a bit. It's Piers who is injured this time."

"He deserves it, the wicked villain!"

"Yes, there was some satisfaction in drawing his blood, I'll admit."

The anxiety that had been riding Delia for hours began to subside, and she sighed out a relieved breath. "Thank goodness you are all right! I've been on the fidgets ever since we left your grandfather's house."

Giff's face changed in an instant and he released her, stepping back. "My grandfather? What the deuce!"

"For heaven's sake, don't get upon your high ropes, Giff! I had to go, and it's a good thing I did, let me tell you. Though he's the most horrid old man, and quite mad."

Giff made an impatient gesture. "I told you I wouldn't sue to him at any price, didn't I?"

"Yes, which is exactly why I said nothing to you about my intention."

"So you went behind my back! Delia, how could you?"

Bitter disappointment made fury bubble up. "Very easily, you pig-headed horrible creature! And when I think of what I've been through at his hands, and all on your behalf, I could readily hit you, Giff!"

She turned on the words and headed back towards the open door of the hideous downstairs saloon into which the party had been shown on arrival a short time before. They had found both the captain and Lord Tarporley in possession, and Delia had swiftly learned of the fight and that Giff had gone up to confer with Piers.

A hasty footstep sounded behind her and Giff seized her arm, swung her around and caught her into a strong embrace. His voice came muffled and low. "Forgive me, my darling flower girl! I'm an ungrateful brute!"

Delia's fury melted into astonishment, and then, as the import of this address sank in, elation soared. He did care! She struggled to free herself and his hold loosened, but he kept his arms about her. She looked up into his face and found him rueful.

"I'd been wishing for you, Delia, for I don't know what to do and I wanted to consult you."

She caught her breath. "Never mind that. What did you call me?"

Perplexity showed in his eyes. "When?"

"Just now."

"Flower girl?"

"More than that!"

His arms fell away. "Delia, is this a moment to be talking in riddles? We've much to discuss. Where's my uncle?"

Delia blew out a frustrated breath. "You will drive me demented, Giff! I must be out of my mind even to think of —" She broke off in haste. If he was not going to speak of what lay between them, then she could not either. She pointed. "He's in there, with Mr Hammersley and the others."

She moved on the words, walking into the saloon where the light was brighter. In addition to the wall-sconces, several candelabra had been brought in and placed, one on the mantel, two others on convenient tables.

The rector hailed Giff as he came in behind her. "There you are, my boy! What have you done with Piers? These fellows tell me you pinked him."

"In the shoulder, yes. He's languishing in his bed, still determined to see me damned if he can."

Delia waved the lawyer forward. He was a portly gentleman with a measured air and a habit of speech to match. "Mr Hammersley, here is Giffard Gaunt. Will you please tell him what you've said to us?"

"Ah, is it you indeed, sir?" He bowed with punctilio. "I am relieved to see you sound in body, my lord."

Giff's astonishment was plain. "My lord? You acknowledge my claim?"

Hammersley bowed again. "We have still to pass the matter through the proper authorities, my lord, but this I believe will prove to be, ah, a mere formality."

Much to Delia's confusion, Giff said not a word. He stood staring at the lawyer as if he could not believe his ears. She wanted to reassure him, to hug him in triumph, but the presence of so many gentlemen stopped her from doing either. She was glad when the Reverend Gaunt stepped in.

"It's true, Giffard. We discovered letters from your stepfather at Saunderton's house. Henry sent them to him some six years ago."

"Letters?" Giff's voice was hoarse. "The one Matt wrote to my father? To tell him he would send me home at a word?"

Delia could not keep silent. "Yes, that letter, Giff. Your father sent it to your grandfather to let him know your mother had died."

"However, it was not that letter which convinced Hammersley," the rector broke in, "but Henry's letter to Saunderton."

"Yes, and we had no suspicion of it," Delia said, eager now, all her former excitement remounting. "We thought only of Mr Favell's letter, and feared it might not be enough, for all it proved is that you were alive at the time, and that was six or seven years ago. But as it turned out, Mr Hammersley was more interested in your father's note."

Giff still appeared dazed. "How so?"

"Ah, my lord, if you will allow me to explain."

"I wish you would."

The interjection came from Captain Rhoades and Delia looked quickly round, as did the others. She'd half-forgotten the presence of he and Lord Tarporley.

The captain flushed. "I beg your pardon! It is none of my affair, of course, but Tarporley and I have become so involved, we are as curious as Giffard here, I believe."

Giff let out a laugh. "You've earned it, both of you."

He sounded much more himself, to Delia's relief and delight. And his features had lightened considerably, she discovered, turning back to look at him again.

The lawyer cleared his throat. "If I may, sirs?"

The Reverend Gaunt waved them all to silence. "Let the man speak without interruption, or we will never get to the point."

Giff nodded, his gaze turning once more upon Hammersley, who coughed again.

"Indeed. Ah, the fact of the matter is, my lord, that his late lordship's acknowledgement in this letter chimes with his words to me when I was called to his deathbed. Lord Baunton was sinking fast, I fear, but he said — and I recall his words verbatim — he said, 'The cub was alive. If he comes, let him inherit. If not, the boy can have it all.'"

The storm came back into Giff's face and Delia's heart sank. She'd been afraid of this. She threw a frantic look towards his uncle, dropping her voice to a whisper.

"Reverend Gaunt! Did I not say so?"

He moved to pat her shoulder, and smiled his reassurance. "Give him time, Delia. We cannot expect Giffard to be other than dismayed by such a legacy."

"Dismayed? That's what you call it, Uncle?"

"Disappointed? Angered? I do understand, my dear boy, how dismissive it sounds."

Rather to Delia's surprise, Giff did not take this up. She saw his chest rise and fall and his jaw tightened. But the expected explosion did not come. He addressed Hammersley instead.

"Yet, as you are no doubt aware, my father did not send for me as my stepfather, Matthew Favell, expected he would. Now it appears he knew from the letter I might come anyway. Yet you made no attempt to locate me, Hammersley."

"On the contrary, my lord, I made every attempt. And, ah, failed miserably. I had no knowledge of your whereabouts. If his late lordship, or, ah, even Lord Saunderton, had seen fit to open their lips upon the matter, I should never have supported the attempt of Mr Piers Gaunt to try for the title."

"Except that you knew my father wished him to take it all, if I could not be found. The 'boy' you speak of in his last words to you is Piers, I take it?"

"That is so, my lord."

"While I was 'the cub'."

"Indeed. I, ah, took it in that light, my lord, knowing of the bond his late lordship had formed with Mr Piers Gaunt."

"Bond! Yes, I know all about that, I thank you. He admits he ran tame here and says my father taught him as he would have taught me had I been present."

Indignation overtook Delia. "How horrid of him! When he could easily have sent for you. Do you suppose he wanted Piers to inherit?"

Giff's lips compressed and he did not answer. Was there something more he did not wish to divulge? She recalled him saying he wanted to consult her. Was it about this?

Before she could think of it further, the rector moved to Giff, setting a hand to his shoulder. "What is in your mind, Giffard? Tarporley here says you have not determined what you wish to do. But surely this must change things?"

Giff seemed to drop a little of his guarded abstraction. "Yes, I dare say. But whatever I decide, I am still left with the problem of my — cousin."

Catching the hesitation, Delia wondered at it. But her indignation at Piers overtook the thought. "Do with him? By rights, he should be in prison instead of lying in state in your house. You don't know the worst of what the wretched creature did, Giff."

His brows drew together in a troubled look that increased the niggle engendered by his previous utterance. "Trying to have me removed is not enough?"

"Nothing is enough for him, Giff. When your grandfather took him to task for taking your place here, Piers told him you were dead. He said he'd heard it for a fact from a contact in India."

"But Hammersley here claims not to know where I was."

"Piers knew." The rector's tone was grim. "I imagine he'd seen the letters Favell sent to Henry, whether by design or no. He must also have known they were in Saunderton's possession, so he had to fashion a lie to silence your grandfather's objections."

"You see, Giff? He's ruthless and deserves no clemency whatsoever."

But to her consternation, Giff's brooding look persisted. She longed to demand enlightenment, yet hesitated since he said nothing himself.

"This is a day of triumphs, Giffard," came from Lord Tarporley, who moved in to clap Giff on the back. "What with the portrait the housekeeper showed you, and now this, there can be no doubt of your rights to be master here."

"Portrait?" Delia's glance went back to Giff. "What portrait?"

"Of my mother holding me as a babe. Mrs Joyce kept it when my father ordered all her portraits burnt."

"Burnt? Oh, he must have been as crazy as that dreadful Lord Saunderton!"

"Crazy with rage, Delia, my dear, but Henry sobered soon enough," soothed the Reverend Gaunt. "I should like to see it, Giffard, if I may. Of all people, I must recognise both faces."

Giff seemed to shake off his abstraction. "Rhoades, you are nearest the bell-pull. Will you ring?"

The captain moved to comply, but his gaze went to Lord Tarporley. "Do you suppose you and I should repair to your house while it is still light?" He threw a glance at the window. "I confess I've no mind to ride back to Weymouth through the night hours."

"Indeed, yes. We cannot expect Mrs Joyce to accommodate so many. Perhaps you would partake of my hospitality, Hammersley?"

The lawyer accepted Lord Tarporley's offer with alacrity. "I thank you, my lord. I must have speech with both gentlemen, but since Mr Piers Gaunt is indisposed, I dare say the interview had best be postponed until tomorrow."

Delia withdrew her attention from the ensuing discussion of who would go or stay and how they would get to the neighbouring estate as the exigencies of her position leapt to mind. She sank into a chair, recalling her great-aunt's dictum that she take a change of linen with her. Delia could only be glad she had complied, but the fact remained she was in a house of males without the vestige of a chaperon.

She might with propriety have stayed in an inn if the rector had also put up there. But to be accommodated at Waldiche Keep, with both Giff and Piers on the premises, was another matter altogether. The Reverend Gaunt's presence must help, but an older lady ought to be in residence to lend her countenance or she would be quite undone.

With the departure of the three gentlemen least connected with the events of the day, Delia was conscious of relief. Moreover, no sooner did the housekeeper grasp the situation than she took immediate steps in several directions.

"I will fetch the portrait in good time, Reverend, but I must first see to the lady's comfort. I can't have you remain here, miss. We have a cosier parlour upstairs, and the gentlemen may join you there. Besides, you will wish to refresh yourself, and I dare say a light supper will not go amiss?"

Shown into a pleasant bedchamber, Delia was glad to put off her bonnet and wash away the travel stains. She had just combed her hair and was pinning it into place when a maidservant entered the room, a white nightgown over her arm which she laid upon the bed.

"Mrs Joyce said to bring you this, miss. And I've to put up a truckle bed and sleep alongside you, miss, for Mrs Joyce says as how it ain't fitting otherwise."

Warmth crept into Delia's cheeks as a disreputable thought snaked into her mind — of a certain gentleman perhaps seeking entry to her chamber. She quashed it and smiled at the girl. "Thank you. What is your name?"

"It's Ellie, miss."

"Is it your nightgown, Ellie?"

"Oh, no, miss. It's one from the linen closet."

A pulse thrummed in Delia's bosom. Might it have belonged to Giff's mother? Or, no. For all she knew, there had been other ladies living in the house in past times. She was grateful to have her needs met, however, and must be glad of the plan to have Ellie sleeping in her room, which would satisfy Lady Matterson. She hoped.

When she was ready, Ellie led her to the upstairs parlour where she found both Giff and the Reverend Gaunt, partaking of wine. It was not cold, but a fire had been lit in the grate and Giff was propping up the mantel while his uncle was seated in an easy chair to one side.

He looked up as she entered and smiled. "You look a degree more relaxed, my dear Delia." He set down his glass and lifted a flat square resting on his knees. "Come and look at this, my dear."

She crossed to him, at once caught by the picture he was holding up, of a woman dandling a child. "Gracious, is this your mother, Giff?" She took the picture and held it to the light falling from a wall-sconce behind the rector's chair. Her mind threw at her a vivid remembrance of Giff's face at the very first instant of their meeting when he'd captured her behind the tree.

"Do you think we are alike?"

She glanced at Giff. "Yes, indeed. In this, you are the image of your mother."

A laugh came from the Reverend Gaunt. "Hardly. He's only a babe."

"I don't mean that. I mean you look like her now. At least," she amended, gazing more closely at his mother's pictured features, "you did at the instant I looked at this. Now I can descry differences. Her lines are softer, more round, and I think your nose is more prominent. But the general look is unmistakeable."

"People were used to say as much when I was growing up, it's true."

The rector took a sip of his wine. "Well, we must show it to Hammersley in the morning. Though I doubt he will find it as convincing as the letters." He looked at Delia. "I've been telling Giff here of our adventures."

"What, with Lord Saunderton?" A riffle disturbed Delia's pulses as she lowered the portrait and looked at Giff. Had it revived his anger?

"Exactly so. And he is conscious of his debt to his Aunt Dowsabel."

Delia set the portrait down on a convenient side table and moved back to the centre of the room. "You told him how she saved the letters?"

Giff's expression was enigmatic, to say the least, but a muscle twitched in his cheek. His eyes caught and held Delia's. "He told me everything. I'm sorry you were obliged to endure my grandfather's bad temper. He can go hang, for I won't go near the man."

"I told him you wouldn't. He's even more stubborn than you, Giff." She eyed him warily. "I hope you don't mean to take after him. He's perfectly vile."

Giff broke into a grin and his features lightened. "If I do, you have leave to throw things at me instead."

She had to laugh. "Don't worry, I'll soon tell you if you start behaving in that obnoxious fashion."

"I'll warrant you will, shrewish wench that you are!"

"Shrewish? Thank you very much, Giffard Gaunt!"

Mischief crossed his face and the light in his eyes made her heart sing. "My pleasure, flower girl of mine."

"Oh, be quiet!" She turned to the Reverend Gaunt. "I wish you will tell your nephew to stop teasing me, sir."

"You seem to me eminently capable of telling him yourself, my dear Delia. I hardly think you need my intervention."

"No, she doesn't, sir. She's more than capable of keeping me in my place. Which is why —"

He broke off as the door opened, and Delia was left wondering, in some agitation, what he had been about to say.

The elderly butler who had let them into the house entered the room. "Supper is served in the breakfast parlour, sir."

He was looking at Giff as he spoke, and Delia could not help wondering how soon the servants might transfer allegiance. He was evidently not yet 'my lord' in their eyes.

"Thank you, Dunford. Shall we?"

The room designated, with a cold supper of a number of dishes and delicacies laid out on the cloth of a round table, was an apartment about the size of the cosy parlour. Candelabra on the sideboard and mantel provided light enough to see what was on offer. Delia accepted a helping of cold roast beef and a portion of sliced pie, but was too much on tenterhooks to eat a great deal. In the presence of the servants, conversation was stilted and confined to generalities.

Her surreptitious attention held on Giff while she toyed with a tartlet. Was he merely thoughtful? Was it fanciful of her to think him subdued? There could be no doubt something was preying on his mind. Several times he cast a distasteful glance at the panelled walls, adorned only with a couple of paintings depicting rural scenes.

Delia was grateful to the Reverend Gaunt, who kept up a more or less one-sided conversation, dredging up a story of one of his parishioners to which Delia paid little heed. She was pretty sure Giff heard nothing of it.

The repast at an end, she was glad to rise, and relieved when neither gentleman tarried.

"Let us accompany Delia, my dear Giffard. There can be no occasion to sit over wine at this juncture."

Giff blinked and seemed to shake himself out of abstraction. "No. I mean, yes, I am with you."

Delia had taken the rector's proffered arm and was aware of Giff following as the butler led them back to the cosy parlour. The Reverend Gaunt settled her on a small sofa at a little remove from the fire and himself took the chair he'd previously occupied.

Giff hovered for a moment, his gaze on the butler. The man was pouring from a decanter into one of two glasses brought on a tray by the footman who had assisted him to serve supper. Evidently, Dunford's punctiliousness did not allow him to omit the port.

The filled glasses were presented on a silver tray, and Giff's impatience was clear in the way he swiped the glass off it.

"If you will ring when miss requires tea, sir, it will be brought directly."

"Yes, very well," Giff snapped. "That will be all."

As the butler, looking offended, bowed and withdrew with his acolyte, Delia glanced up and caught Giff's eye. He gave her a swift smile and took the seat beside her. The rhythm of her pulse at once became uneven.

"Thank the Lord we have a moment to ourselves at last," he said, as soon as the door was closed. "I've got to talk to the both of you, for I'm in a hellish quandary."

The rector paused with his glass halfway to his mouth. "About Piers?"

"Mainly about Piers. But also about what I'm going to do. I can't decide that, however, until I've settled what to do with Piers."

Delia, turning to sit sideways, regarded him in some confusion. "But why should you do anything with him? Once he is ousted for good, he will cease to be your concern, Giff."

To her dismay, his face took on a look of utter distress. "It is my concern, and I can't ignore it." He glanced from her to his uncle. "This is for your ears only, both of you. It's to go no further."

"What can you mean, Giff? Is this something horrid?"

"Horrid enough to change everything. Piers is my half-brother."

Too stunned to reply, Delia merely stared at him. The image of Piers's face leapt into her head and the notion at once made sense. Before she could say as much, the rector spoke.

"Do you know this for a fact, Giffard? Or is it another ploy by Piers?"

"By no means. He took umbrage when I taxed him with it, blustering about his mother's honour. But he didn't deny it."

"And you take that for proof? When you know the man has always an eye to the main chance?"

"It's not as simple as that, sir. Look at the way my father used him, as if he was indeed his son. And Hammersley supplied the clincher, if I needed convincing."

Delia found her voice. "Also he looks like you, Giff."

"But Giffard looks like Flora," objected the rector. "You said as much yourself."

Giff took this up before she could answer, rolling his glass between restless fingers. "Only in a general way, according to Mrs Joyce. She spoke of seeing my father's individual features in me. She said the resemblance to my mother is in the shape of my face and something to do with hair and eyes, as I remember."

"I can't be as specific as that," said Delia, "and I have no notion what your father looked like, but the first time I met Piers, it struck me that he looked like a more rounded version of Giff."

Giff looked both dismayed and eager as he turned to her. "Then you believe it?"

"I do, yes. Moreover, it explains his obsession with taking your place."

"That's what I thought."

Delia set a hand on his arm. "Does it make it less hurtful to you, Giff?"

He grimaced, but did not react to her touch. Conscious, Delia withdrew her hand.

"It complicates things. I can't serve my brother as I might serve a mere cousin."

The Reverend Gaunt had taken a sip of his port, but his frown did not abate. "I no longer wonder at your expression of difficulty, my dear boy. What will you do?"

"That's just what I'm asking you both. What should I do? Instinct urges me to be rid of him, for he has said in so many words he will never cease to plague me."

A feeling of panic crept into Delia's breast. "You must be rid of him, Giff. You'll have no peace otherwise."

"Yes, but in what manner?" Giff's voice became intense. "I won't give him up to the law. I can't let him languish in gaol."

The rector gave a mirthless laugh. "Not to mention the scandal that must ensue. And if it is true that Henry played his own brother false and subsequently did his best to instil into the boy a sense of deserving what he could not have, then there is some excuse for Piers."

A silence fell. Delia, aware of Giff's tension, found she was gripping her fingers together. Her thoughts were in turmoil. On the one hand, she ached for his distress, but on the other, she was cruelly exercised by the notion of Piers continuing to be a threat to him.

A wild idea entered her head and she said it before she could think of its implications. "You could send him to India, could you not?"

"What, and inflict him on Matt? Have you run mad, Delia?"

"But, Giff, he can't remain in England, a constant danger to you." Anxiety riding her, she gripped his arm again. "He has not your honour, Giff. He knows he is your half-brother, you say, yet he could still plot your death."

His hand covered hers and his eyes burned. "Do you suggest I descend to his level? I will not. Nor would I dream of despatching him where he might do harm."

Delia let go, wrenching her fingers out from under his. "But you'd let him remain where he may at any moment make a treacherous and fatal attempt upon your life? Oh, you are reckless indeed!"

322

Giff was on his feet. "Why in Hades do you think I'm asking you and my uncle to help me? Do you think I'm stupid enough to trust him?"

"I don't think you stupid. I think you pig-headed and obstinate and altogether too forgiving. It's not as if you knew he was your half-brother before today. What would you have done if you had not found that out?"

Giff paced across the room and then back to the fireplace. He set his glass down on the mantel, the liquid in it barely touched, and looked at his uncle, who had so far refrained from cutting into the argument. "What would you do, Uncle George?"

The Reverend Gaunt was regarding him with a look Delia found enigmatic. What in the world was in his mind? Intrigued, she was about to ask when he spoke at last.

"Is it only Piers that troubles you, Giffard? It hardly seems as difficult a problem as you make out. If you don't wish to send him to India, my dear boy, for which I admit I have some sympathy, you may choose to despatch him instead to America."

Delia's mind jumped. "The very thing! It's what he planned for you, Giff. That would be sweet revenge indeed!"

"Yes, my dear Delia, but if I read Giffard aright, what to do with Piers is only part of the problem. Is it not, dear boy?"

He did not answer, but the discontent in his face deepened. A riffle of alarm went through Delia. The rector was right. He had seen beyond the surface.

She broke into speech. "What is the matter, Giff? Why aren't you happy? Events are moving so fast, much more rapidly than we expected, and your goal is within sight. It's what you wanted, to oust Piers. You will be master of Waldiche Keep and recover your title."

He curled his fists and hammered at his temples. "I know, I know. It's what I've strived for."

His distraught aspect worked upon Delia's heartstrings. Before she knew it, she was up, catching at those unquiet fists. "Giff, tell me!"

He did not attempt to release himself, but let out an overwrought breath. "I hate this place! I don't want to live here. I don't even want to live in England. At least, I don't think so."

Shock made her release him and step back. Her heart plummeted. Her voice came out an anguished whisper. "You want to go back!"

He did not meet her eyes, his gaze swinging to his uncle, who put out a hand towards him. "My poor boy. You are missing India, is that it?"

A sound as agonized as Delia felt escaped Giff. "It's my home." He wafted a hand to encompass the room. "This isn't. It's dark and gloomy. It's not what I'm used to."

Delia sank onto the sofa, the desperate hope she'd cherished, which had fluctuated crazily, rapidly dropping. In the background of her despair, she heard the Reverend Gaunt, speaking in a bracing fashion.

"Not now, perhaps. It is not to be expected, my dear boy. You don't know the place. But you will grow accustomed. And you may change what you don't like. Besides, once you have established an agent to take care of the estates, you may take time to visit India and perhaps spend a couple of years with your stepfather."

Giff drew in another heavy breath, but did not look to be encouraged. His glance travelled from his uncle's face to the walls and thence to Delia. His expression changed. It came to her she'd been staring at him. Had she allowed her feelings to sit naked in her face?

"What do you think?"

There was vibrancy in his tone, but she was hard put to it to answer with any degree of calm. "It's — it's not my decision, Giff."

"It might be." Harsh and urgent.

Her heart jerked and began a heavy tattoo in her breast. His eyes holding hers, he came to sit beside her, catching one of her hands. "Delia, could you live here? Would you wish to? If I asked you to come with me to India, would you do it?"

She trembled, hardly able to believe the words were coming out of his mouth. Such words as she'd never thought to hear. Somewhere in the back of her buzzing mind, she heard the rector speak.

"Dear me. I fear I am somewhat *de trop*."

Delia hardly noticed him rising. Nor did Giff, it seemed. A soft click signalled the closing of the door.

Giff's voice was softer, almost a murmur. "Well, my flower girl?"

She could not speak, mesmerised by the look in his eyes. Then all ability to think left her as Giff's arm came about her and he drew her close. So close, she could see the faded bruise at the corner of his lip before it met hers and she had to close her eyes.

An eon later, Delia came to herself as from a dream. Her pulse was in disarray, her mind chaos and her body thrummed with an unaccustomed heat. She became conscious of a fierce embrace and Giff's voice came guttural in her ear.

"Do you care enough, my precious flower girl? Are you mine?"

Her heart's answer came without will. "Yes. Oh, yes, Giff, always!"

He drew away, looking down into her face, urgency in the beloved features. "Will you be with me? Will you go where I go?"

A thread of panic snaked into her bosom. "To India, you mean?"

"To the ends of the earth, if need be. You never balk, my plucky wench, at anything. I want you with me, don't you understand?"

There was fire in his eyes, passion in his voice, such demand as she'd never hoped to inspire. Bemused and enchanted both, Delia uttered the first thing that came to mind. "You want me with you? *Me?*"

A sudden grin dispelled the unusual intensity. "Who else, silly wench? Do you see another female in the room?" He had his hands on her shoulders and Delia thrust them off, agitation claiming her.

"But you haven't even said you love me!"

He groaned. "Must I? Can't you tell?"

"No, I can't, horrid creature! At least…" She eyed him in sudden doubt. "Oh, help! This is not because of Aunt Gertrude, is it?"

Giff reared back. "Who the devil is Aunt Gertrude?"

"Lady Matterson, I mean. This is her influence, isn't it? She made you think you had compromised me."

"Devil a bit. Nothing of the kind."

"She did, Giff!" Delia thrust away from him, dismay increasing. "I'd almost forgotten it. That night when she summoned us both because the rector told her the truth. And you made some kind of pledge."

"Delia —"

"No, let me say it, Giff! I've tried several times, but somehow never managed to get it out. I can't bear it if you are forced to this by — by convention and what people may say."

"You know me better than that, Delia. When have I ever done anything for the sake of convention?"

Her perturbation did not abate. "Don't pretend, Giff, please! You made Aunt Gertrude believe you would make all right once you had achieved your aim, and now you have, or nearly so, and here you are asking me … asking me…" Her voice failed and she stared at him, aghast. His words replayed in her head and she found no mention of any offer. It burst out of her. "But you haven't!"

Giff's brows flew up. "Haven't what?"

"Asked me!"

"Delia, are you trying to drive me out of my mind? What the deuce are you talking about?"

She drew a shuddering breath. "You've not said it, Giff. Are you — are you asking me to marry you?"

He cast up his eyes. "No, I'm asking you to run off with me like my mother ran off with Matt. Idiotic wench! Of course I'm asking you to marry me."

"Well, you never said so."

"I should have thought you had sense enough to realise it."

Delia's throat tightened and her eyes pricked. Her voice came out a croak. "I haven't. I've no sense at all where you're concerned. Oh, Giff!"

Consternation warred with amusement in his face and he attempted to gather her into his arms.

Delia held him off, her hands at his chest. "And it's not because of Lady Matterson?"

"Why? Won't you marry me if it is?"

"No! Well, yes, I suppose."

"You suppose?"

"You need not bite my nose off!"

"Then stop being ridiculous!"

"It's not ridiculous, Giff." Of a sudden, her eyes filled and her voice turned husky. "I didn't do what I did to entrap you or be rewarded or force you into being obliged to offer for me."

"Don't you think I know that?" His tone had gentled and he captured her hands in his. "You can't think I'd have said as much to your aunt if I hadn't made up my mind to have my flower girl at any price days before."

"Had you? Truly?"

"I can't imagine how you don't know it, my darling girl, when you took me to task for telling you not to flirt with Rhoades almost at the outset."

Her heart squeezed in her chest. "You were jealous?"

"Furiously so."

She drew a shaky breath and sighed it out. "Yes, you were perfectly idiotic about it."

"Well, take heed, wench of mine, because I'll be even more idiotic if I catch you so much as looking at another man!"

Disregarding this, Delia eyed him, sniffing back the tears. "What would you have done if you had failed to oust Piers?"

"Persuaded you to marry me and come back with me to India," he said, without an instant's hesitation.

Delia's tears spilled over and she could not speak. Giff released her hands and took her into his arms. With gentleness this time, cradling her against him. Delia melted into the warm embrace. And then his lips were gentling hers, murmuring between kisses words she'd longed to hear.

"I do love my flower girl… I can't live without her…"

Sighing in contentment, her tears arrested, Delia responded with fervour. "And I love my reckless prince…"

Giff broke away, laughing. "Prince? What nonsense is this?"

Delia's cheeks warmed. "It's nothing. A silly dream of mine, that's all."

A frown came into his eyes. "I'm no prince, Delia, if that's what you mean. I'm not even a fit earl, if you want the truth. I don't know if I can play the role."

She gripped one of his hands. "You don't have to. Just be yourself. If it comes to that, I'm no fit countess. We'll muddle through together, Giff."

"But if I can't bear it? If I want to go home?"

She smiled from the heart. "Then we'll go together."

He drew in a breath and sighed it out in a bang. "I knew it wouldn't scare you."

"It does scare me. But it scares me more to think of letting you out of my sight to do whatever reckless thing you get into your head to do next."

Giff laughed, catching her back into his arms. "I must be mad, saddling myself with a wench who won't hesitate to nag me any time she doesn't approve of my conduct."

"No, and you've only yourself to blame, Giffard Gaunt. You have been amply warned."

He kissed her again. "I'll take my chances. The rewards will be worth it."

Which, Delia decided, precisely mirrored her own sentiments. Giff was no fairy-tale prince, but life at his side promised such a whirlwind she might welcome the odd moment of dullness.

A NOTE TO THE READER

Dear Reader,

Delia had made an appearance in several stories before this one and she hadn't fared very well. I thought she deserved an adventure and to find her "prince" at last. Mind you, when I put her in this story I had no idea she would turn out to be such a "plucky wench" as Giff is wont to say.

The funny thing about characters is that they don't reveal themselves except as shadowy figures when they first appear in the writer's head. But once they get onto the page, they seem to spring to life and show unexpected facets that surprise their creator quite as much as themselves.

I never know how a scene is going to go when I start writing it. The basic idea is there, but the action runs away from me, seemingly by itself, and characters say things I have never consciously imagined. The truth is, I believe, that writing comes from a place a little below conscious thought and once you tap into that you no longer operate in a mechanical way, thinking things out.

But when it comes to editing and research, it's a very different matter. Places spring into life just as much as characters, but at some point one has to look at the realities of existing in that specific space. Hence Weymouth.

This was one of the more popular seaside resorts and became so for one simple reason. King George III chose it for his sea-bathing excursions. One of his brothers had bought a house there and the King went to stay with him to recuperate when he had been unwell. He liked it so, he kept coming.

Needless to say, the fashionable world followed him there and Weymouth only lost its attraction when the King's heir, George, Prince of Wales (later the Prince Regent) chose Brighton for his summer excursions and built the Pavilion. The Prince brought the younger set with him, leaving Weymouth at last to the elderly and those with less pretension to follow fashion.

Today, you can still see the colourful statue of George III, erected in his honour in Weymouth "on his entering the 50th year of his reign", which Delia would not have seen in this story as it was not built until a few years after the date of her sojourn in the resort. I dare say, though, that when it was being put up, she was in India, visiting her husband's relatives!

If you would consider leaving a review, it would be much appreciated and very helpful. Do feel free to contact me on **elizabeth@elizabethbailey.co.uk** or find me on **Facebook**, **Twitter**, **Goodreads** or my website **www.elizabethbailey.co.uk**.

Elizabeth Bailey

Sapere Books is an exciting new publisher of brilliant fiction and popular history.

To find out more about our latest releases and our monthly bargain books visit our website:
saperebooks.com

Printed in Great Britain
by Amazon